RUTHLESS

Mickey Hadick

PARKSIDE bks

PARKSIDE BOOKS
HOLT, MICHIGAN

Print ISBN-13: 978-1-956533-05-7
ePub ISBN-13: 978-1-956533-06-4
Date of publication: December, 2021
Edition revision: January 8, 2022

Cover graphics by 100Covers.com

Print cover design by Mickey Hadick
Interior design by Mickey Hadick

Published by Parkside Books
Holt, Michigan
ParksideBooks.net

That which is crooked cannot be made straight, and that which is wanting cannot be numbered.

Ecclesiastes 1, Verse 15

Other books by Mickey Hadick:

Fiction:

Ten Stories
Sally and Billy in Babyland
The Forgettable Marriage of Lina and Joe
Welcome to Willieville
HIVE

Nonfiction:

Boss Lessons

Sign up for updates at:

MickeyHadick.com

RUTHLESS

Mickey Hadick

1

1979 A.D.
Northern Ohio

Samantha sat alone in the front room, staring at the television on a Friday night. She looked at the phone on the wall. No one had called her in two days. Her friends had gone somewhere without her, again.

The TV show was about a family with growing pains, relationships and teen rebellion—normal problems, like her own family. But the television mom hadn't run away. The television dad came home every night. The television siblings got along.

Sure, the youngest child of the television family died before the time of the show, and everyone in the family carried a sadness with them, like a medallion on a ribbon around their neck. The shared sadness drew them together. They were sad, but there was love.

Sitting alone was her own fault for saying no to her friends so many times before.

This was her senior year and graduation was only six weeks away. In the fall, she'd go somewhere to college—the pile of college catalogs and application forms on the floor next to the television nagged her—and then she'd get a fresh start with new friends.

Or so she hoped.

Lori, her older sister, walked in the front door. "Is Dad here?" she asked as she slipped off her Converse oxford sneakers. She wore them untied, more like clogs than sneakers, with the laces knotted at the end so they wouldn't slip through the grommet.

"Nope," Samantha said, pleased that Lori was there but avoiding eye contact.

Lori moved far enough into the room to look at the television. Then, distracted, she took down her own graduation photo from the shelf on the wall and examined it, chuckling at the three-year-old portrait.

Samantha gazed at her sister, hopeful they'd have some time together. That would make staying home worth it, or so she hoped. When Lori looked, she seemed impatient and annoyed.

"Is Dad here?" Lori asked.

"No. Geez, I already told you."

Lori glanced at the television again as she went into the kitchen. "Where's he at?"

"The tavern. What do you think?"

Lori returned with a Tab and shoved Samantha's legs out of the way to sit down.

"That was rude." Samantha scooched to the other end of the sofa.

"Sorry. What are we watching?"

"Family."

Lori got up. "You mind if I change it?"

"I mind. I'm watching this."

Lori flipped the channel and sat back down. "I'll only be here a couple of minutes. I need to ask Dad something and then go see Rebecca."

It was a cop show. Their father was a cop, and he hated the show because it was unrealistic. Samantha hated it because it was stupid. "This show sucks," she said.

"Yeah, that's the point. You don't have to even think about it."

Samantha glared, hoping Lori would notice how bothered

she was. Lori hadn't spoken to her in months, busy with college or whatever, and now she just barged in.

Bored with the show, Lori looked around the room, searching for something. "Rebecca's all upset about wanting to break up with this guy she's screwing. She wanted me there for, you know, support."

"Can't Rebecca just get high, flip her hair and get whatever she wants?"

Lori turned her head. "What are you talking about?"

"They're rich. Things *always* work out for her."

"Wow, you little bitch."

"Don't they though?"

"You know nothing about Rebecca."

Samantha stared at the television, but a mild regret was taking the place of her annoyance. "So what happened?"

"The guy showed up, and she screwed him anyway, even though she had a date with her actual boyfriend tonight. She called me in hysterics, and I talked her down. She's afraid the creep will show up again later tonight, so I'm going to stay at her house with her tonight. If he shows up, it'll embarrass the crap out of him."

"Gross. Is it another married business partner of her father?"

"Worse. It's going to be super weird."

"Who is it?"

"You don't want to know." Lori got up and turned off the television.

"Hey what the hell?"

"You said it was crappy. I have to go pretty soon, anyway."

"I'm so sick of you just acting like you're in charge."

Samantha walked out of the room.

"Hey, come on. Just sit for—"

"Screw yourself."

As Samantha walked up the stairs to her bedroom, Lori called after her, "I love you."

Samantha said nothing in reply.

Samantha's bedroom was the converted attic of the bungalow. She shared it with Lori, but her sister hadn't slept there since the previous summer.

The walls angled in so they could stand only in the middle, below the peak of the roof. The beds touched the sloping ceiling. Students' desks—surplus from the school—tucked into the dormer left space enough for two chairs, but nothing else.

They each had a dresser and a chest for their clothes, and they shared a rack for dresses, which separated their beds in a weak illusion of privacy.

Samantha grabbed a book and sat on her bed to read. She didn't care that Lori changed the channel any more than she cared about her friends going to a party without her.

If she had known this evening would be so boring, she might have called Blaine earlier, and watched television with him. Blaine didn't care what they watched, as long as he could get high.

Lori left a few minutes later.

Samantha considered running after her and asking if she'd stop by the next day to see her, but she lingered too long before the car started and drove away.

Samantha awoke to the sound of the front door.

"Everything okay?" her father called from the foot of the stairs.

Samantha needed a minute to remember. The book had fallen to the floor. Lori's bed was empty.

"Yeah. Did Lori talk to you?"

"No. She was here?"

"Yeah."

"Did you tell her I was at the bar?"

"Yeah."

"Okay. Must not have been that important."

"I guess not."

There was a brief pause. "You want the light out?"

"Yes, please."

"Goodnight, Sam."

"Goodnight, Dad."

The knock on the front door woke her up. There was enough light from the windows to see Lori's undisturbed bed. That was no surprise. Samantha had indulged a hope that Lori might return to sleep here, rather than her apartment on campus on the other side of Cleveland.

They knocked on the door again. Didn't whoever it was at the door know it was too early to wake up on a Saturday?

She heard her father's bedroom door open. "Hang on," he said.

"Dad?" she heard her father say, meaning that her grandfather was at the door.

She sat up in bed. Her grandfather hadn't visited their house since her mother left four years ago.

"Do you want coffee?" her father asked.

"No thank you, David," her grandfather said. "I have bad news."

"Dad?" Samantha said, loud enough for him to hear. "What's wrong?"

Samantha jumped out of bed. "Dad?" She was still wearing the jeans and T-shirt from the day before and scrambled down the stairs.

Her grandfather, standing just inside the front door, wore a jacket and tie. "Let's sit down," he said.

Samantha moved to the sofa and waited for her father to join her before sitting down.

"What's going on?" her father asked.

"There was an accident."

Samantha glanced at her father. His jaw muscles clenched, and he swallowed.

"Out on the lake," her grandfather continued. "She and some boy were on a boat. How all this happened is unclear..."

"How bad is it?" her father asked.

Her grandfather cleared his throat. "Lori is dead."

Samantha found herself on the floor, sobbing, thinking she was still asleep and having a nightmare, and then coughing until she was on the verge of vomiting.

They pulled her back to the sofa and her father tried to hold her, but her arms and legs kept thrashing and she pushed him away.

Her father wrapped her in a blanket and that helped her calm down. Then he wrapped his arms around her, and his weight on top of her felt okay, and she could breathe.

"No," she said. "No, no, no..."

After a while she realized her father was crying, and she worked her arms free to hug him, back.

"But why," he sobbed. "Why were they boating at night?"

"We don't know," Grandfather said. "The Coast Guard found them."

"I don't understand."

Aunt Jan came in the front door and leaned over them on the sofa, holding Samantha's hand and consoling them. "You poor dears," she said.

Then Aunt Jan left them to make coffee.

Her father and Grandfather talked, but Samantha couldn't understand what they discussed. She could only think of how Lori had said, "I love you," but she hadn't said it back to her.

At some point, Aunt Jan sat on the edge of the sofa next to Samantha. "Let's have you lie down."

Aunt Jan helped her up and took her to the sewing room. She had to clear some things off of the small bed and shook the dust off of the pillow.

"I hadn't realized this room was like this," she said.

Samantha didn't like Aunt Jan's tone. Aunt Jan had never liked her mother, and they never talked unless it was at a family party. After her mother left them, Aunt Jan's contempt flowed. Only when Lori had yelled at her did the insults end.

"This room will be good enough for now, honey," Aunt Jan

said. "I'll check on you in a little while."

The room had been her mother's place to sew, make things, or just read. She admitted it was messy, but didn't worry about it. Samantha loved to be in there with her mother, doing her homework while her mother made a dress or a skirt.

Samantha wanted to cry again, but she thought she must be out of tears. Or maybe she was just too exhausted to cry.

She fell asleep.

When she woke up, the house was quiet. She found her Aunt Jan alone in the kitchen, cooking eggs. "Where's my Dad?"

Aunt Jan turned towards Samantha, her head tilted to one side. "He and your grandfather told you they had to go somewhere."

"What? No, they didn't."

Aunt Jan returned to the eggs on the stove. "I was here when they said it. You didn't hear them. It's okay. You're still upset."

"Of course I'm upset. Shouldn't I be?"

"Oh sweetie, yes." Aunt Jan turned off the gas and took Samantha in her arms. "This is the most upsetting thing in the world, and I didn't mean to make it worse."

"Where did they go? Why couldn't he stay with me?"

"They had to go to the Medical Examiner's office, in Cleveland, to identify your sister."

Samantha groaned. "Why did this have to happen?"

"I don't know, Sweetie. We may never know."

Samantha made her way to the front room and collapsed on the couch. She rolled to her side and opened her eyes. Staring back at her from atop the television was Lori's senior picture. It was the prettiest Lori had ever looked in her life, with the curls of her blonde hair surrounding her face, her skin a light shade of gold from the sun, and her opal-blue eyes sparkling. It captured all the best features of Lori's beauty, but also the spirit of adventure she never seemed to lose, and how the only thing that made her sad was losing at basketball or softball, because she loved to compete more than anything.

"Sam?" Aunt Jan called from the kitchen. "Come and eat."

"Who put this picture here?"

"What picture?"

"Lori," Samantha said. "Who else?"

"Oh," Aunt Jan said. "I did."

Of course she did. Samantha's senior picture remained on the shelf in the corner. It was a picture Samantha didn't hate. Her red hair flowed past her shoulders. Her pale skin glowed with a touch of warmth, something the photographer did with lighting. Too much light emphasized her freckles, which she hated. Her green eyes sparkled—her best feature—thanks to Lori's help with makeup before the photo shoot. She'd never bothered with makeup again.

"Your food's getting cold."

Samantha ignored her. She didn't care about food. What was the point?

Aunt Jan came into the room. "Sweetie? It's important to eat. You need your strength."

Samantha realized Lori had said she was going to see Rebecca, who had some dumb problem. What happened over there that Lori ended up on a boat?

Samantha got up and walked past her Aunt Jan to the phone on the wall just inside the kitchen.

"Who are you calling?"

Samantha scanned the wall surrounding the phone for the phone number. "Rebecca," she said. "Cherry-one, two-nine-three-three."

"Rebecca Marko? Why in the world are you calling her?" Aunt Jan lowered the cradle, ending the call before Samantha finished dialing.

"Hey. Do you mind?"

Aunt Jan shook her head. "I think you should wait until your grandfather talks to Rebecca's father."

"What? What do you mean?"

"Mr. Marko is President of the City Council. I think it's important that he hear the news from your grandfather."

"She and Lori were best friends, so she needs to know."

"Fine, but it's not your place to tell her."

Samantha dialed the number again. Aunt Jan was wrong about this. "Lori said she was going to talk to Rebecca," she said. "I'm going to ask her what the hell happened over there."

Jan took the phone from Samantha and hung it up. "Oh, no. That is not appropriate."

"What?"

"Your Uncle Tom is Chief of Police. If there are questions to be asked, he'll ask them. I mean, I don't even think your father would do such a thing, and he's a police officer."

"Are you serious?"

"Yes, I am. I know you're upset, but there are procedures for such things. We have to allow the police to do their duty."

"It's just a simple question. Rebecca was her friend. I think she'd want to talk about it."

"Your sister's tragic death was an accident, so it makes little sense to ask questions."

"You're not going to let me make a phone call?"

"No, I'm not. Now please eat your eggs."

Samantha turned and walked out the front door.

2

Blaine lived alone five houses down the street. He was two years older and had been her friend since she was four, when she was first allowed to play on her own with other kids.

As she turned up his driveway, she realized Blaine may not have heard. He'd had a crush on Lori forever, same as almost every boy in the city. This was going to devastate him.

Blaine's mother died when he was just ten, and then his father died four years ago, around the time Samantha's mother left. Now this.

Samantha was crying by the time she reached the front door, both for herself and Blaine.

As she raised her hand to knock, Blaine opened the door. He was crying, his soft face mottled with pink, his dark hair matted on one side where he'd slept on it.

They stood in the open doorway, hugging as they cried.

"How did you know?" she asked.

"Your Aunt Jan just called," he said.

They staggered to the sofa and sat at opposite ends, staring out the window. Samantha pulled her legs up under her, aware that she was barefoot and still wearing the T-shirt and jeans she'd slept in.

"This is so weird," Blaine said. "What was she doing out there?"

"We don't know."

"And who was she with?"

"We don't know."

"It's crazy."

Samantha wiped her nose with her sleeve. "I'm was going to call Rebecca, but my Aunt Jan stopped me."

"Why?"

"Jan can be that way."

"I would think Rebecca would want to know."

"Yeah, so I'll just call her."

Samantha hugged her legs in for a moment, less certain now about talking to Rebecca as she was just ten seconds before. "Now I'm afraid. What do I say?"

"You want me to call her?"

"You could tell her, and then I'll ask her, you know, after you break the news, if she knew why Lori went on a boat ride."

Blaine nodded. He got the white pages from his kitchen counter and looked up the number. "I don't think the Markos are listed."

"Sorry, it's Cherry-one, two-nine, three-three."

Samantha listened to him dialing, confused by how none of this seemed real except her insides ached. She wanted to go back to sleep and wake up and have everything back to the way it was.

"Hello?" Blaine said.

Samantha realized what he would say next and her throat tightened and she felt nauseous. She hurried to the bathroom and turned on the faucet, covering her ears with her hands and groaning to drown the noise.

She sat on the edge of the bath tub and rocked back and forth, noticing the hairs and dirt on the floor along the wall. The garbage can was overflowing with empty toilet paper rolls. There were yellow stains on the floor beside the toilet.

There was a gentle knock on the door. "I guess I'm done," Blaine said.

Samantha opened the door and avoided Blaine's look as she passed him and went into the front room. "What'd she say?"

"She said she knew about it."

"She did?"

"Your Aunt Jan called her."

"What? Okay, did you ask her if she knows who Lori went out on the boat with?"

Blaine shook his head. "She hung up. She said she didn't want to talk about it and hung up."

Samantha made her way to the sofa and sat down. "Maybe she didn't want to talk to you about it."

"That could be," Blaine said. He was on the recliner, rocking himself. "That was the most I'd ever said to her before. She didn't even know who I was, even though she would have flunked Algebra if I hadn't done her homework for her. And I wasn't even in Algebra that year."

Samantha curled up on the sofa. "This is so insane. It can't be true. It has to be a dream."

Blaine lifted a plastic bag of weed onto his lap and rolled a joint. "That's how it was with my mom," he said. "I still don't believe it."

"I know."

"With my dad, I believed it, which felt a lot worse." He lit the joint and held in the smoke before blowing it towards the ceiling.

He offered it to Samantha, but she shook her head.

"Rebecca didn't want to talk to me?"

"I didn't have time to ask. She hung up."

Samantha took several deep breaths and then stood up. She went to the phone and dialed, turning the rotor.

It rang ten times and then Samantha hung up.

"Maybe she doesn't want to talk about it," Blaine said.

"I'll call back later."

Samantha called back a few minutes later and returned to the couch when Rebecca didn't answer. She called several more times over the next two hours.

Blaine offered to make her breakfast, but she wasn't hungry. She felt sick.

At some point, her father knocked on the front door and let himself in. "There you are," he said. He seemed about to say something else, but then he noticed the smell of pot and looked around.

Blaine's bag of weed was on the table next to the recliner.

"Have you been calling Rebecca this morning?" he asked.

"Yeah," Samantha said. "I wanted to ask her—"

"Well, stop it. She's very bothered. She called the police about it."

"I just want to ask her where Lori went?"

"How the hell would she know?"

"Lori was going to see Rebecca when she left the house last night. Maybe Lori said something."

Her father took a breath and rubbed his eyes. "Okay, fine. But we don't have to worry about that. Let the Coast Guard look into the accident, and if the police need to investigate, they will."

"I can't ask a simple question of Lori's best friend?"

"No. Your Uncle Tom has assured her the phone calls will stop."

Blaine had come in and sat on the recliner, and moved the bag of weed onto the floor.

"Let's go," her father said. He turned to Blaine and said, "You should know better. Your father was a cop. I ought to run you in. Is that what you want?"

"Leave him alone," Samantha said.

"Are you coming home or are you going to spend the day, this day of all days, sitting around getting high with a loser?"

"He's not a loser." Samantha said it with anger, wanted to yell, but she cried instead. "His heart is broken too."

"That doesn't give any of us an excuse to break the law. Now are you coming home?"

"Fine," Samantha said. "Just leave Blaine alone."

She got up from the couch. When her father reached for her arm, she moved out of his reach and went around him.

"Bye, Blaine," she said. "Thanks for letting me stay here."

"No problem," he said.

"I love you."

Samantha looked back at Blaine, but her father got in the way, blocking her view.

# # # #

The houses in the neighborhood were all two-bedroom bunga-lows. Samantha liked the sound of it: two-bedroom bungalow. It had both rhythm and the alliteration. Bungalow was a funny name, anyway, like a mistake you make, but then you live in it for the rest of your life.

The bungalows stood side-by-side on forty-foot lots, set back a dozen steps from the sidewalk. Walking past you could hear televisions, radios and conversations inside each house, and kids playing out back. Built in the 1940s, the tiny houses at-tracted white people from Cleveland afraid of black people, or so it seemed to Samantha.

She'd read articles about "white flight," but discussing it with her family had only drawn their ire.

Almost everybody was white in the neighborhood, except the Osmans, who were Lebanese. The funny thing was, theirs was the only house that wasn't a bungalow. It was a two-story because the Osmans had enough money to be different.

The bungalows were not identical. Some had awnings or porches. Some were brick, others painted wood. Most had dormers in the roof, but a few did not.

Their house was in the middle of the street, and Samantha looked at each of the houses as she followed her father along the sidewalk from Blaine's house back to their own.

The lawns were turning green, and some wives had dug up the front flower gardens.

"You okay?" her father asked, glancing over his shoulder.

Samantha didn't respond. She wasn't sure she recognized the houses, even though she'd seen them all her life. Everything was different now.

"Your grandparents and cousins came over. It's a time for family."

"Blaine is family."

"You know what I mean."

Walking across their lawn, Samantha could hear her grandfather and Aunt Jan talking inside the house. Those two always talked the most. But when she and her father walked in the front door, the conversation ended. Grandpa Pete sat on the recliner; Aunt Jan and Grandma sat on the sofa. Her cousins, Derek and Ana, sat on the floor. Uncle Wally stood in the hallway, just outside the room, looking lost.

They all hugged her, saying how sorry they were, and crying.

Samantha didn't want to deal with this. She wanted to go to her room and sleep. If it was just her Grandma, she could handle it. Grandma rarely spoke.

Once all the hugging was over, Aunt Jan headed for the kitchen. "I've got my Hungarian goulash ready. And we picked up some bread, so let's eat."

The adults ate at the kitchen table, with Uncle Wally standing at the sink because there weren't enough chairs. Samantha and her cousins ate in the front room.

Samantha refused the goulash on principle and ate two packages of Pop Tarts followed by a bowl of Sugar Pops.

Derrek, who was a year older, wouldn't make eye contact, but he said, "Bummer. This sucks."

"Tell me about it."

They turned on the television and turned the dial back and forth, deciding which of the old movies to leave on.

Samantha listened to the adults in the kitchen. Jan and Grampa Peter assured her father he'd done nothing wrong. That young people have choices to make. He couldn't live Lori's life.

"I don't know," her father said.

They repeated their arguments, propping him up, forgiving

him, assuring him there was nothing he could do.

"You shouldn't talk about her," Samantha said. She went to the kitchen doorway and said it again, louder, "You shouldn't talk about her."

"Sam, honey—"

"You shouldn't talk about Lori like it was her own fault. It's not fair."

"We don't mean it like that, Sweetie."

Samantha cried. She didn't want to, but she couldn't help it. "Then you shouldn't say it like that."

"You know how kids are these days," Aunt Jan said.

"Excuse me?" Samantha said, wiping her nose on her sleeve. "Do you know what Lori was doing last night?"

Aunt Jan looked at Samantha but said nothing.

"Do we know how she died?" When no one responded she said, "Well, do we?"

"No, we don't," her father said.

"Then don't talk about her like you know what happened."

Samantha returned to the front room and sat on the floor next to her cousins.

When the television was quiet, she heard her Aunt Jan say, "She needs to learn that life isn't fair."

3

Francine Tennyson liked these days best of all, up early on the first warm day of Spring and alone in her second-story flat. The only things on her agenda were to shop for food at the West Side Market, and to maybe stop in for the music portion of the festival she'd listed in the newspaper. It depended on whether Robaroni, her boyfriend, worked overtime.

A reporter covering the communities in and around Cleveland, she was a reporter in title only, as her beat comprised answering calls about upcoming civic events, and finding a place for them in the newspaper. When she started the job, she had been diligent about verifying the authenticity of the request. Now she had gotten to know the festivals and was on a first-name basis with several of the organizers. When she visited an event, it was to sample the pastry or hear a band because the reporting was done before it started.

Still, it was a good job. She had every intention of moving up in the newsroom, delivering feature stories with a byline and getting her own column.

For now, she was on the tiny balcony overlooking the garbage cans in the alley, and the sun warmed her shoulders. She had coffee and toast and the Saturday Press. It didn't hurt that the breeze pushed the stench of the garbage cans away.

The phone rang before she turned the first page. She had dragged the phone to the kitchen table, just inside the door, anticipating a call from her mother in Florida. "Hello?"

"Hey, it's me," Robaroni said. "Just wanted to make sure you were awake."

"Yes, I am. Why do you—"

"Did you hear about the boating accident?"

"No."

"I don't think anyone has. It's kind of weird."

"Are you at the station?"

"Pay phone. My partner had to use a toilet. I heard over the horn that they sent a black and white to stand guard at the Coast Guard station."

"Doesn't the Coast Guard have their own guards?"

"Yeah. That's weird."

"Okay, I'm intrigued."

"I also called a friend who's in the Coast Guard, stationed there. He was on the cutter when they picked up the wreckage."

"Drowning?"

"Yeah, but the boat was on fire. A fisherman called it in."

"Who died?"

"A black guy from the Village."

"Wait. Are you saying a black family lived in the Village?"

"He had his driver's license, so yeah," Robaroni said.

"How old?"

"Early twenties, I think."

Even with no racial tension, it would be an interesting angle because of the flaming boat, and a tear-jerker with his life cut short. Although a cautionary tale might be the angle Hal, her editor, wanted to use. "What a shame to go out like that. You think he was an avid boater?"

"They think he stole the boat."

"They think that because he was black?"

"No, because the boat belongs to the Marko family."

"Prominent lawyer and President of the Village Council?"

"Yeah. Him."

"Oh shit."

"Yeah, but that ain't the half of it. The other one that died was a woman, Lori Sykora."

"Those Sykoras?"

"Yes. Peter is the mayor. Tom is the police chief. Son-in-law is the fire chief."

"Aren't there TV news crews down there?"

"Nope."

"That's weird."

# # # #

Francine dressed and grabbed her Folio. She called the number that Robaroni gave her.

"United States Coast Guard," a man's voice said. "Lieutenant Second Grade Bryer Brown speaking."

"Wow," Francine said. "Do you always answer like that?"

"Who's this?"

"Francine Tennyson," she said. "Rob Maroni told me a little about what happened, and that you might tell me more?"

"Sure," Bryer said. "It seems like there's a story here if you can put it together."

Putting the story together was not the hard part. Francine thought about how unlikely it was that Hal would assign this story to her. "I don't know that I'll get to write this story, but if I get a picture of the wreckage, it might convince my editor."

"Can you get here soon? The Cleveland Police might move the wreckage for forensics."

"I'm leaving as soon as we hang up."

"If you get here before two, you can also get a picture of the Morro Bay."

"Morro Bay?"

"That's the cutter that recovered the wreckage and the deceased."

"A cutter?"

"It's a big boat."

# # # #

There was wrought iron fencing on the landward side of the Coast Guard station. The gate at the driveway was open and un-guarded. The parking lot was almost empty. But because of the police cruiser in front of the gate, she parked on the road.

"Sorry lady," the tall cop said. "Only Coast Guard personnel past this point."

"My name's Francine Tennyson," she said, and offered her business card. "I'm with State Farm Insurance. If you would just notify Lieutenant Brown..." It was a gambit she'd learned from Murray, one of the older reporters.

The cop shook his head. "What's with the camera?"

Francine had a Canon F-1 hanging from her neck. "I'm a claims adjuster. This will only take a few minutes..."

The cop looked again at the business card, flashed it to his partner, who shrugged. The cop looked back at the station. There was a guard house, but it was unmanned.

An officer in a white uniform emerged from the building. He used the clipboard in his hand to wave at them.

"That must be Lieutenant Bryer," Francine said. "May I?"

The cop nodded.

As Francine walked past, she said, "If either of you need any insurance, be sure to call me."

The building was a low, squat, ugly thing made of cinder blocks. There were three boat slips—each about the size of a basketball court next to the building with a wide channel out to Lake Erie along a stone break wall.

"Ms. Tennyson?" the officer said. "I'm Lieutenant Brown."

"Call me Francine," she said.

"I thought I'd have to come up with some story for the cops, but here you are."

"If anyone asks, I'm with State Farm."

"Aye-aye."

He was tall, around six feet, and moved like a soldier: straight posture, firm handshake, plenty of eye contact.

"Is that it?" she asked, pointing at the tarp covering something bulky next to the water.

"Yes. Oh, and the story I told is that you're from Bayliner, and you're just verifying the model of the boat for me."

"Aye-aye."

Bryer raised the edge of the tarp, revealing a section of the wreckage. It looked nothing like a boat.

"How do you even know it's a Bayliner?"

"The registration number on the hull was intact. We have access to the registration database, and we know who owned it. I called the yacht club and confirmed the missing boat."

"This is awful," Francine said. "Why didn't it just sink?"

"It was a fiberglass boat lined with a foam. They build them like that to reduce noise and help with flotation."

"I still can't picture it as a boat." There were markings that resembled a boat on one side of what must have been the hull. The warped edge was black from the fire.

"How does a boat burn on the water? Wouldn't the water put out the fire? Or am I being stupid."

"Not at all. Fire is a chemical reaction. Fiberglass is a flammable epoxy. Once it catches fire, it burns like oil. Very hard to put out, even in the water."

"Okay."

"If it had been an aluminum boat, the flammable materials inside the hull would have burned, and maybe melted and warped the hull. If the hull was breached, the engine would have dragged it to the bottom."

"But not this one."

Bryer returned to a section of the tarp and lifted it. "This had one or more outboard motors, and the eyewitnesses reported it was going at full throttle. My guess is that it flipped over and the part of the hull with the engine and the fuel tanks broke off. Those motors are at the bottom of the lake."

"And this part floated because of the foam?"

"Yes. The hull was on its way to burning right down to the water line. Then it flipped, spilling gasoline and catching the underside of the hull on fire." He crouched down and pointed at the singed areas resting on the cement.

"And you helped recover the deceased?"

"I'm afraid I did." Bryer looked around. "There were burns on both bodies. We found them floating nearby, within half a mile of the wreckage."

"They drowned?"

Bryer shook his head. "They were floating because of air in their lungs. They didn't drown."

"The flames killed them?" Francine caught herself. "No, you'd jump first, right, if you're on a burning boat?"

"If I couldn't douse the flames, I'd abandon ship. Maybe a couple of burns on the hands or feet, but not like these bodies got burned."

Francine took a breath. "I'm not sure if that's good news for them or not."

"It seems to me they were dead already when the flames reached them."

"Ugh. Grim. Was it murder-suicide?"

"The only thing I'm sure about is that if you drown, you sink, at least for a few days."

"How do you know they didn't sink and bob back up?" Francine cringed, remembering that two people were dead.

"It takes a couple of days for the body to bloat with gas. The lake is still pretty cold, so it might have taken a week. At least that's what the scuttlebutt is on the ship."

"So they were both dead before the boat crashed?"

"If I was a betting man," Bryer said, "I'd say they were dead before the boat caught fire."

"Holy heck."

"But you didn't hear that from me."

A truck approached the police detail at the gate. It was a dump truck, the thing crews used to patch potholes in the road. The cab was blue and there was a logo on the door. The passenger leaned out the window to chat with the cops on guard, and then a cop moved the police cruiser out of the way.

"Go around the corner," Bryer said as the truck made its way through the parking lot.

Francine obeyed and waited out of sight, watching seagulls

float in the channel, the water calm behind the break wall. Out on the lake, the wind pushed waves toward shore, with white caps breaking. Not a bad day to be on the water, she thought. This being a chilly day in April, there were no pleasure craft out. Far out across the lake, a cargo ship made its way along the horizon.

Back around the corner, something was happening with the truck. They swung a gate open, the tarp covering the wreckage flapped in the wind. One man chastised the other to show some "fucking strength."

When the truck's gate closed and the cabin doors slammed shut, Francine peeked around the corner. Bryer and another officer had their backs to her. Facing them were two men in work clothes.

The taller of the two men looked like he was in charge of the detail, wearing a wind breaker and a button-down collar shirt. He was older, with white hair in a brush cut, like he hadn't changed it since the 1950s. Thick jaw, wide nose, and gray eyes. He focused on the other officer who explained something to him.

The other man wore grease-stained work clothes, soiled gloves and steel-toe boots. He was bald, unshaven, and squinted at the two officers.

Francine thought that he was the strong back, weak mind type when he looked her way and stared right at her.

She pulled back behind the corner and didn't peek again until she heard both doors open and close and the truck shifted into gear.

As the truck pulled away, a corner of the blue tarp showing above the bed walls.

"That was weird," Bryer said as he came for Francine.

"Are they taking it to forensics?" she asked.

Bryer glanced over his shoulder. "They're from The Village Service Department. My Station Commander was expecting them, like they're old chums or something."

"So no forensics?"

"I don't think so. The guy who owns the boat wants it disposed of."

"But you're still investigating? Like this is your jurisdiction, right?"

"No. If there were smuggling or boating violations, then we'd keep at it. We don't investigate deaths."

"Who does?"

"Cleveland Police have jurisdiction. They'll look into and report on the cause of death."

"That's it?"

Lieutenant Bryer shrugged. "As the Maritime Enforcement Specialist, I fill out accident forms and compile reports. After I reach out to the boat's owner, Marko, about the loss and try to figure out a little more what happened, I'm done."

As Bryer walked her back to her car, Francine asked, "Can you tell me anything more?"

"Listen," he said. "I'm sticking my neck out. The brass can be funny about things," he said. "There's no regulation against showing a civilian a wreckage, but there's no regulation against an annoyed Station Commander ruining my career, either. And people get annoyed over some pretty silly stuff."

"Well, not to worry because I don't have much to go on here."

Bryer handed her a slip of paper. On it were the names of the deceased, Lori Sykora and Michael Keys, and two other names, Fred Bilak and Lou Havel. "Who are these two?"

"Witnesses."

"Witnesses?"

"They saw the boat burning and called it in."

# # # #

Francine returned to her flat and pulled together her notes for the pitch. It was early in the afternoon. Plenty of time to write it and get it to the editor. Best, though, to make him aware, because George, the weekend editor, only knew her as the *girl* who reviewed community events.

This story was nothing like that.

She put herself on a thirty-minute deadline and typed:

> A man and a woman lost their lives on Lake Erie in the early hours of Saturday, April 28, 1979. They were aboard a pleasure cruiser taken from the Cleveland Yacht Club in the dead of night.
>
> Fire broke out aboard the boat as it streaked across the calm waters at full throttle. The Coast Guard was notified around 1:45 a.m., and the cutter Morro Bay rushed to the vicinity and initiated a search.
>
> Fishermen spotted the wreckage shortly after dawn, signaling the Morro Bay with a flare.
>
> Only a small portion of the boat was recovered. The crew of the Morro Bay continued to search from that location and, within a few minutes, recovered both bodies.
>
> The identities of the deceased were not released, as the incident is under investigation by both the Coast Guard and the Cleveland Police Department.
>
> One of the victims was reported to be a black male in his early twenties. The other was a white female, also in her early twenties.
>
> The owner of the boat is Patrick Marko, a prominent business owner and President of the Village City Council. He could not be reached for comment.

The boat was a twenty-eight foot Bayliner with an outboard motor. The hull burned to the waterline, and the engine broke away from the boat and sank.

Neither the Cleveland Police nor the District Attorney responded to requests for comment.

Not her finest work, but no worse than some hacks who'd been writing with bylines for twenty years.

Francine freshened herself up and then placed the call to George.

"Press," he answered.

Francine pitched him the story, closing with, "I have a rough draft. I can have it in your hands in twenty-three minutes."

"Uh, sure," George said.

"See you then."

One thing she'd learned from the older guys was to be specific and sound matter of fact. The hardest part of an editor's job, it seemed, was to get a writer to do something. Tell them it's done, and they say yes.

Francine drove downtown and parked on the side of the building. On weekdays, she had to park below the Terminal Tower and walk for about ten minutes to get to the office. She signed in with security and rode the elevator up to the fifth floor.

The office was busy with the assembly of the Sunday edition. Francine half-expected to run into Hal, the Editor-in-Chief, who showed up in the afternoon most Saturdays to oversee the final story review. George, who worked Wednesday to Sunday to overlap with Hal on Sunday, appeared under siege in his office, as writers and typesetters flowed in and out with the steady stream of questions to answer.

"It's rough," Francine said as she handed George the copy. "Work your magic."

"You don't know who died?"

"Oh, we know. Lori Sykora, age twenty-one, of the Village, granddaughter of Mayor Peter Sykora. Father's a cop."

"Holy mackerel."

"Yeah."

"You're sure about it?"

"I have a reliable source."

"Okay. I'll run it up the flag pole, see if anyone salutes it."

"So what do you think?"

"About what?"

"About my story."

"It's good but, like I said, I gotta' run it up the flagpole."

4

Aaron Key took his coffee out the front door and stood on the top step. He hoped Michael would arrive soon. The boy said he'd stop by, but Aaron needed to make his rounds soon. And Michael wasn't a boy. He was a young man, and Aaron was proud of him.

A crew of little girls, their hair braided, one in a dress, the other two in shorts and a T-shirt, were out playing on this Saturday morning, biking along the sidewalk, squabbling about something, two kids ganging up on the third, then a tantrum, then hollering.

A mom sitting on her front steps across the street shook her head. "You keep making noise and I'll give you something to cry about."

Aaron nodded. You learn that shit early and it sticks.

Louise had done a fine job with both their kids. Alina, married with two kids of her own, had moved to Columbus and into a nice, suburban home. She and her husband were doing all right.

Michael was off to a fine start of his own. Him not showing up was no concern. He was likely at his own apartment in bed with his girlfriend, or at least sprawled on his sofa watching television.

"Something the matter?" Louise asked, leaning her head out the front door.

Aaron couldn't keep from smiling. Louise was lovely, now

in her forties, wearing a dress and makeup on, like she was expecting someone. Her fair, terra-cotta skin always had a warm
glow, quick heat just below the surface. In the morning light,
her cheeks were bright like copper, and Aaron marveled at how
she hadn't changed in all these years...

Especially the part about there being quick heat just below
the surface.

"Nothing's wrong."

"You waiting on Michael?"

"No hurry," Aaron said. "I can get to my route anytime."

"I'll call him."

"That's the problem with him living on the west side. It's a
full forty-five minutes—"

The phone rang.

"Maybe this is him," she said over her shoulder.

Aaron sipped his coffee as he looked around the neighborhood. The houses were small but solid and well-kept. The lawns
mown and tidy, no trash.

"Oh my God," Louise said. "That's not possible."

Her eyes were wide open, and she seemed to be gasping
for breath. "What is it?"

She waved him inside. "I'm going to put his father on the
phone. Please repeat it for him."

Aaron took the phone and held it to his ear. "Who is this?"

"I'm Detective Wagner, with the Cleveland Police. I'm
afraid the Coast Guard recovered a body from Lake Erie this
morning after a boating accident. The name on the deceased's
driver's license was Michael Key."

Aaron looked at Louise. What he heard wasn't possible.
Michael was in the car, driving there now. They were going to
get together this morning.

But Louise was crying.

"I'm afraid your son is dead," the man on the phone said.

She stepped closer, and he wrapped his arms around her.
In that way, they kept each other from falling to the floor.

Aaron drove them to the Medical Examiner's Office. He'd been fine never having to make this trip. Never realized how little he wanted to know it existed. But there it was, set back from Broadview Road, a low building with a tree out front and flowers next to the door.

Inside, there was a lobby and a counter, like a doctor's office waiting room without chairs. "I guess nobody comes here to wait for an appointment."

"Ring the bell," Louise said.

Aaron rang it and then a white woman with glasses and carrying a book came out of a side room.

"Are you here regarding Michael Key?" she asked.

Aaron nodded, and the woman opened a door so they could pass through to the office. It was three desks and a corridor.

Before they started along the corridor, a white man in a sport jacket too small to cover his gut approached.

"I'm Detective Wagner," he said. "Sorry to bring you out like this."

Aaron nodded again. Louise took his arm, and they followed the detective into the building.

At the end of the corridor another white man met them, this one in a lab coat. He was small and avoided eye contact.

He introduced himself, but Aaron couldn't follow what he said, so terrible was the dread he felt about what was in the next room.

"Follow me," the little white man said, and opened a door.

Aaron hesitated. There was nothing good on the inside.

The room was cold and large. There were several tables spaced along the center, with a light above each one. Storage bins along one wall for the deceased. Cabinets along the opposite wall for their instruments.

Aaron avoided looking at the tables in the middle, each one covered by a sheet.

The man in the lab coat led them to the center table and

motioned for them to stand beside him. Without warning, he pulled away the sheet.

There, on the table, was Michael. He looked asleep; his skin was smooth and tan like always, but without the gold tones. His mouth was open, and his left eyelid partially open. He always had that, the partially open eye when he slept, even as a child.

Louise gasped and leaned against Aaron. As she sobbed, he also sobbed, leaning back into her.

"That's Michael," he said. "That's our son."

# # # #

They spent the night in the living room, Aaron dozing in his recliner, Louise napping on the couch. They had insisted that their daughter- and son-in-law take their bed. The babies took Alina's old room.

Even if Alina and Conrad hadn't driven up from Columbus, Aaron and Louise still wouldn't have made it into their bedroom. Nothing seemed right, knowing Michael was dead, and they both seemed trapped when the phone rang and they heard the news.

The afternoon had passed in an interminable daze as waves of sadness, disbelief and second-guessing passed over them.

Why had they ever let him go live in the Village? Sure, this side of town wasn't great, but not that bad, either.

Aaron realized some time during the night that he was hoping against all hope for the phone to ring again, this time with news that it was all a horrible mistake. Their son was alive. Everything would continue as they once had hoped.

He fell asleep and awoke a few minutes later, his heart thrashing, his stomach in knots. Then he'd remember having seen his son in the morgue, and there was no chance it was a mistake.

In the morning, Louise was worse than the night before,

and had trouble answering questions. The lack of sleep and heartbreak weighed on her. How could it not?

Aaron realized he was just as troubled. It crossed his mind that this heartbreak, seeing a son up from childhood only to lose him at the beginning of adulthood, could crush either of them, or both. People died of broken hearts—they'd both seen it happen in every neighborhood they lived. Families devastated by stupid, useless deaths, parents unable to go on. Some turned to drink, or left the marriage, or both.

Aaron was grateful for Alina and Conrad visiting when they emerged from the bedroom holding the babies. Conrad sat in the recliner with the youngest, and Aaron took the toddler, Alicia, with him to the couch, and sat her next to Louise.

"Give your grandmother a hug," he said. "She needs it bad."

Louise cried then and had to apologize to little Alicia, who was also about to cry. "No baby, please. Don't you worry about your Grandma. I want you to be happy. I just need a little time."

Aaron wanted to tell himself he would get past this tragedy and go on living, if only for their grandchildren. He should be the one to show the way, to be strong, but he wasn't sure he knew how.

It had been a day since they got the call. Michael had been dead for more than a day. But they didn't know anything about how it happened. Why was he on a burning boat? Who was the woman who died with him? Who else knew what was happening?

It reeked of trouble, but Michael had not misbehaved since fourth grade when he was sent to the principal's office for laughing at something the teacher said. That seemed to be enough of a scare to set him on a path of learning and self-improvement.

Like his sister, Michael seemed intent on making something of himself. He was going to put his father to shame, and that was just fine with Aaron.

Maybe, once they knew the circumstances of his death, he could think about the future.

Alina took charge of the house as she had learned from the best. She prepared food. She dispatched Conrad with errands and to play with Alicia as needed. The television was on, but the volume kept low. She gave hugs.

Late in the afternoon, the phone rang and Alina answered before Aaron could even think about getting up from his seat.

"She can't come to the phone," Alina said, her voice resolute.

Aaron looked over, feeling the warmth of his daughter's love in her defense of their privacy.

"I don't think so," Alina said. She shook her head, still listening.

"You going to hang up?" Aaron asked, offering his permission in case Alina was not sure.

"No need to be rude," Louise said, directing it at Aaron more than Alina, but loud enough for her daughter to understand.

Alina put her hand over the receiver. "It's a reporter from the Press. She'd like to know more about Michael."

"For what?" Aaron asked for his own benefit. "They're gonna' say whatever they want in the paper, anyway."

Louise sat up and looked at Alina. "What does he sound like? An old white man?"

"It's a woman," Alina whispered. "She sounds young. Very polite."

"Let me talk to her." Louise held out her hand, and Alina stretched the handset to the sofa.

"This is Louise Key," she announced into the phone. "With whom am I speaking?"

Aaron heard the voice, but not the words. She did sound young, whoever she was.

"What is it you hope to learn about my son? What sort of article is it you're writing? What do you know about what happened?"

Louise put her hand over the mouthpiece. "I think we should talk to this woman."

Aaron bit his lip and counted to six. He knew he should count to ten, but that was as far as he could get. "They're going to make him look bad. The less they know, the fewer people will recognize it's our Michael."

"This may be our only chance to share with the world what Michael was like. Let's meet her and get a sense of whether we can trust this woman."

"I'm against it."

"Is that what you want me to tell her? And we gonna' let them print whatever they want without even talking to us?"

Aaron finished counting to ten.

"Okay," he said. "Let's meet her."

"Thank you," Louise said. "You made the right decision."

Aaron nodded. That was what Louise said when she was going to do whatever she wanted. Agreeing with her was a way of showing his love.

5

Francine woke up early on Sunday and had a rare moment of regret that she didn't subscribe to the Press. Living alone the past few years, she went out for the newspaper on the weekends as a ritual to see the neighborhood and inter-act, if only a little, with other people outside of reporting.

This would be the first time she broke a story. It was small, but it promised much more, if only for a profile about the tragic loss of the darling daughter of a prominent family. They almost owed it to the Sykoras to celebrate Lori's life.

There was a Lawson's around the corner where Francine grabbed the newspaper and a package of chocolate-covered donuts—a guilty pleasure.

On days with pleasant weather, she might walk along the road or in and out of the neighborhoods. Today she hurried back, flipping through the sections for a hint of her story, but found none.

Abandoning the coffee and donuts on the kitchen table, she settled into the chair on the rear balcony overlooking the trash cans and opened the front section, scanning the headlines, but saw nothing like her story.

The death notices mentioned neither victim. She didn't ex-pect the family to have called it in yet, but it was common to place news there related to accidental or circumstantial deaths.

Again, no mention of Lori Sykora or the boating incident.

Francine called George. At the sound of her voice, he interrupted. "Hang on."

There was a click on the line, then Hal answered, "Press."

"This is Francine. What happened to my story about the boating accident?"

"We're sitting on it until we know the angle."

"What angle? It was a weird boating incident. That's the angle."

"Yeah, we'll see. Excellent work though."

"But why didn't you run it?"

"Hey, kid, be patient. You'll get your chance."

Francine inhaled, suppressing the urge to scream. It was better to be on the phone, because she might cry if she watched his patronizing smirk. Or she might tell him to go fuck himself. Neither would help her career. "I think this is my chance."

"Hey, did you see it on the news last night?"

"No. I haven't seen it."

"No one knows about it."

Francine took another breath. Only running the story would make it hers. "Okay. I'll keep working it."

"Atta' girl."

# # # #

On Monday morning, as she got ready for work, Francine reminded herself that she was proud to have gotten a job as a reporter at the city's only newspaper. She studied journalism at Cleveland State, landed a job in the clip room, and worked her way up into the newsroom.

But after six years, having learned that none of the men who were reporters started in the clip room, it frustrated her that she hadn't been given a chance to seek and report the news.

Not that she thought the community events were undeserving. In fact, she believed that news of those events would help bridge the gaps in their community.

People who lived on the west side should go to more

events on the east side, and vice versa.

There were fewer differences between the people of greater Cleveland than any of them realized. They clung to a belief of belonging to a tribe, be it ethnic or geographic, and that they had to defend those differences.

Francine believed she could make a difference in the community if she was allowed to tell their stories.

She also believed that politicians took advantage of the ignorance and fear people harbored about different people. The ignorance and fear kept the politicians in power. This was small-potato politics, but her professors had taught her how the same principles worked nationally and across the globe.

A journalist's sacred duty was to bring forth the truth and to share it in a way that all people could understand. There were no minor stories, as her professor used to say; just minor journalists. A one-column description of a church festival could make as big a difference in a community as exposing a corrupt mayor.

And that's how Francine kept herself motivated, relegated to the back corner of the newsroom while the men with bylines and expense accounts enjoyed plum assignments and desks with a view of Public Square.

Today she had a little nugget of truth to share that might give her an edge. Not that she wanted the expense account, but she wanted the chance to use her voice. To remind people they weren't as different than they were being led to believe. The expense account would be nice, though.

As she made her way forward from the back corner to the conference room, she reminded herself that all the desks were messy, piled with papers and folders. Hal Burton, the editor-in-chief, harassed even senior reporters with equal disdain.

There was no reason to think of herself as any less a reporter than the rest.

She had a typewriter on her desk like the others, and she sent her stories to the typesetting team just like the others.

The empty desks in the office told her she was later than she realized for the editorial meeting, and she pressed harder with every stride.

"Everybody know what they're doing?" Hal Burton, the editor, asked as he closed his folder and pushed away from the conference table.

"What about the Sykora death?" Francine asked, drawing stares from the other reporters.

Hal stared from where he was, still seated but not quite at the table.

Murray, one of the older reporters, leaned forward. "What's that? Did the mayor die?"

"His granddaughter."

"He has three. Which one?"

"Lori. The oldest. Boating accident."

Hal took a moment to breathe. "When they call it in, if they want something more than an announcement, I'll give it to you."

"It's a civic event. I'm guessing the funeral will draw hundreds. And it's still possible it wasn't an accident."

Hal folded his hands. "I'm sure the family would prefer to keep it as private as possible. We'll follow their lead."

"But it's still an important accident that the community should know about."

"And I will determine when you write that story. Understood?"

Francine, worried she had over-played her hand, nodded.

# # # #

At around eleven in the morning, as Francine scribbled in her Filofax, Murray sauntered over to her desk in the back corner of the newsroom.

"How's it going?" he asked.

"Fine, thanks."

"You mind?" Murray grabbed a chair and sat next to her desk. Wrinkles and age spots covered his face. His white hair was thinning on top. He shot her a smile, revealing bridge work on the side of his upper teeth. It reminded her of her own father's teeth, and how people of that generation were often missing quite a few because, back then, they didn't fill cavities, but pulled out any problems with pliers and a strong grip.

Francine sat up in her chair and waited. It crossed her mind she should smile, but she didn't feel like it. He was going to ask a favor, like retrieving old articles from the clip files.

"Did Hal say anything else to you about the Sykora death?"

Francine shook her head. Murray was studying her in a way she'd seen no one at the newspaper do before.

"I think you should write it," he said. "Go get the story, at least."

"What if Hal's not interested? Or, worse, angry at me for doing it and then he fires me."

"The hell with Hal. If you have a story, he'll run it. Or at least run it up the flagpole to see if the old man salutes it."

"What the hell does that mean?"

Murray crossed his legs at the knee and folded his hands in his lap. "Hal's the editor, but Crimson is the publisher. You think I'm old? Crimson walked the earth with Noah. And he is particular about what goes into his paper. He doesn't want us to become sensationalist."

Francine shook her head and raised her hands. "Okay, so..."

"So what have you got?" Murray had lowered his voice to a more conspiratorial whisper.

Francine glanced around the newsroom, finding herself playing along. "I have the name of the other victim, and his family will talk to me."

"So there was another victim. I called around, and it wasn't clear."

"Also I have the names of witnesses."

"Witnesses to what?" Murray's voice was just above a whisper.

"They saw the boat burning and called the Coast Guard."

"Sounds to me like you have a story."

"I should write it then?"

"Go get it."

Murray winked and then got up. He sauntered away without another word.

6

That evening, two days after the deaths on the lake, Francine met the fishermen who called the Coast Guard to report the burning boat.

They met after work on Cleveland's south side at a tavern called the Bull Pen. She knew a little about the neighborhood because one of her childhood friends attended Immaculate Heart across the street. Also, she'd reported on the refurbishment of the Cleveland Transit Authority bus depot next door.

The Bull Pen was a throwback neighborhood bar in the lower level of a two-story building with living space on top and a bar on the bottom. It would be anyone's guess what might be in the basement.

Francine paused inside the door to give her eyes a chance to adjust. The tavern's decor looked like they had updated it in the past decade, but the layout had changed little since before Prohibition.

A smattering of patrons hunched over drinks at the bar, their heads cocked upward at the television playing the local news. More men and a couple of women sat at the booths and tables.

"I'm looking for Fred and Lou," she said to the bartender.

He pointed across the bar. "You want a drink?"

She didn't want a drink, but didn't want to disappoint the bartender. "Gin and tonic."

The bartender made the drink faster than Francine could

open her purse.

"It's on the house," he said, waving away her money. "Ladies night."

"Thanks," she said. "What a lucky coincidence."

"Every night is ladies' night."

The fishermen were at a booth in the corner, drinking beer. As they greeted her, Francine made note of the fact that Fred wore a cap with a fish on it, and Lou wore a cap with Chief Wahoo. Otherwise, she wouldn't be able to tell these two overweight men apart. Their mustaches were similar, their jowly cheeks and puffy eyes seemed chosen from the same costume kit, and they both wore a windbreaker over a WMMS T-shirt sporting a buzzard.

"As I said on the phone," Francine began, "I heard from a source that you actually saw the burning boat that Lori Sykora was on the night she died."

"Yeah, we did," Fred said. "Craziest thing ever."

"Is there something going on with that?" Lou asked. "We heard it was an accident, so figured that was that."

Francine took a sip of her drink. "The county Medical Examiner is investigating, along with the Cleveland Police. I'm trying to be ready with a story once they make a determination. It's just such a terrible tragedy."

"That it is," Fred agreed. "Is that what your story's about?"

"My editor wants to respect the family's privacy. But I thought your first-hand account of the burning boat would be an interesting angle."

"You could write it about night fishing, too," Lou said. "We're pretty good at it."

"I bet you are. I mean, why else would you go out on a chilly night?"

"Exactly," Lou said.

Francine shook her head as she sipped her drink. "I grew up there, in the Village, in fact, but we never did much on the lake. I know fishing is big—"

"Huge," Fred said.

"Huge. Yes. But I never heard of night fishing, and there's

probably more like me. So my editor might go for a story about night fishing."

"Some guys swear by it. If you got the boat for it, with gear and everything for the night, it's not all that different from the day. Just drop your line in the water and troll."

"But that ain't us. We need a really calm night because the boat is so small."

"Yeah, so we don't do it that much."

"Before I write that story, though, I'd like to hear about what you saw."

"Well," Fred said, "Lou had a fish on."

"It was a big one," Lou said.

"As I reached for the net, I look up and there's this orange ball of flame heading our way."

"Like a basketball, but on fire," Lou added.

"I thought it was an illusion maybe, because you just don't see such a thing."

"Nope."

"Then I realized it was coming straight for us, like we were going to hit it."

"We'd a been goners," Lou said.

"So what did you do?" Francine asked.

"I tried to get the motor started," Fred said, "but it wouldn't turn over."

"He forgot to choke it," Lou said.

"I didn't forget to choke it. It just didn't start."

"It's an old motor. They do that."

"What I should have done, was just put the trolling motor in reverse. I was so confused, I forgot we even had it."

"Trolling motor?" Francine asked.

"That's a little electric motor," Lou said. "Pushes us along, it's real quiet, and works great if there're no waves or wind."

"Lou leaned over the side and paddled with his hands and turned us out of the boat's path."

"I saved us," Lou said.

"He did," Fred said. "I owe him my life."

"I was saving the boat. Otherwise, I can't fish."

Francine made a few notes, enjoying their delivery. Her father never had a friend like either of these men, and probably would have enjoyed life a little more if he had.

"And then you called the Coast Guard."

Lou nodded. "I was talking over at Don's Bait Shop yesterday, and I heard that a couple of other guys saw the flames across the water. But no one was close like us."

"And we were the only ones to call it in," Fred added.

"How does that work?" Francine asked. "I'm just curious because, you know, I've never fished or even boated. Did you use a radio?"

"No, we don't have a radio. It's just a small fourteen-foot boat. Hardly big enough for the two of us."

"Yeah, so we had to head back in and find a phone."

"I'd never done it before," Lou said, "but I asked the operator to connect us because it was an emergency."

"Saved him a nickel," Fred said.

"So you used a pay phone?"

"There was one at the boat launch, across the parking lot near the road."

"And what time was that?"

"Shit," Lou said, "was it around one-thirty?"

"Yeah, maybe. It took us a bit to get back to shore."

"He ain't got an enormous engine."

"It's big enough."

"Not like on the flaming boat."

"No, them were some big engines: dual 150-horsepower Mercury outboards."

Francine opened her Filofax and noted the time and the engines. "What sort of boat was it?"

"Bayliner, I think," Fred said. "Didn't have time to study it, but that's what the hull looked like as it zipped past."

Francine looked at Lou to give him a chance to comment, and he nodded resolutely.

"Did the police follow-up with you? They assigned it to a Detective Wagner."

Fred shook his head and looked over at Lou, who also

shook his head. "I didn't call the police. Just the Coast Guard."

"I'm just curious," Francine said after draining her glass. "What did you think was going on when you made your way back in?"

"I guess I thought some idiot drunk had really fucked up," Fred said.

Lou nodded in agreement.

"What if the police called? Is that what you would have told them?"

Lou shrugged. "I guess we would have mentioned the guy in the parking lot."

Fred looked at him, and something seemed to pass between them. Lou shrugged again, as if for emphasis.

Fred paused for another swig of beer. "As we docked the boat, there was a guy strapping down his boat out in the parking lot."

"Strapping down?"

"Once you get your boat on the trailer, you pull it all the way out of the water and then you strap the rear end to the trailer so it doesn't bounce off on the way home."

"Was he acting suspicious?"

"Not really," Lou said, eager now to say this part. "His outfit was suspicious."

"How so?"

Fred leaned forward to speak. "He wasn't dressed for fishing. He was dressed for work. Like a mechanic or something."

"A mechanic?"

"Yeah," Lou said. "He wore grease-stained Dickies and steel-toe boots. Like he just got off his shift."

"Bald?" Francine asked. "Kind of shifty-eyed, maybe five-foot-eight?"

"You kidding?" Lou asked. "He *was* bald and shifty-eyed."

"You got a good look at this guy?"

"He was under a light post to strap down his boat," Lou said. "I saw his face clear as day."

"Did he see you?"

"I suppose he did. I walked even closer on my way to the

pay phone."

Francine needed a moment to breathe. "What do you think he was doing?"

"I don't know," Fred said, "but it wasn't fishing. They didn't have any rods or gear. Usually stuff is flopping around the boat, but not them."

"There was another guy?"

"Yeah, a guy sitting in the passenger seat. You wanna' take a shot at him, too?"

"Late fifties, six-foot-one, sturdy-looking with white brush cut."

"I was just kidding because I couldn't really see the other guy. He never got out of the car."

"What was the car?"

Lou thought a moment. "Ford LTD, like a cop car, only if someone painted over the white part with black paint. Kind of sloppy."

Francine took another breath. "Anything else you remember about them?"

"Yeah," Lou said. "He had a seventy-five horsepower Johnson."

"I wish I had a seventy-five horsepower Johnson," Fred said, grinning.

"Me too," Lou said.

Francine stared at them for a moment. "Are you being serious?"

Fred nodded. "That's a lot of motor for a tiny boat like that."

7

Samantha drove to Rebecca's house. It had been three days since Lori died and no one was talking about how it happened, or why. Her father, when asked, shook his head, made a face of sadness and despair, and changed the subject.

She suggested offering condolences to Rebecca—Lori was her best friend, after all—but her father squelched the idea.

The house was far from the other neighborhoods and on a large plot of land with landscaping and a manicured lawn. The house itself was twice as large as anything else in the city. Even the attached garage was bigger than her own house. She felt unwelcome just entering the driveway, passing between the brick walls out by the road.

She'd been to Rebecca's house for a birthday party, which Samantha had hated because she was too young to be hanging around older girls. She went there again as a passenger in her father's car to pick up Lori after a sleepover. Samantha had exchanged only a dozen words with Rebecca, ever.

Samantha felt a tightness in her chest and throat as she approached the front doors. This felt like it was going to be adversarial when all she wanted was to find out about the last moments of her sister's life from someone who loved her as much as she did.

She pressed the doorbell. Inside the house, four notes chimed her arrival.

No one came to the door, and she pressed the button again.

As she peeked through the sidelight, Rebecca's mother appeared at the foot of the stairs across the atrium but, seeing Samantha, turned and went back up the stairs.

Samantha stepped off the front landing. Looking through the large window above the door, there was a movement on the second-floor balcony, but she couldn't quite make out who was going where because of the reflections in the glass.

She heard footsteps approaching across the tiled floor. The door opened and Rebecca's father peered out at her.

"Hello Mr. Marko," Samantha said. "I'd like to speak to Rebecca. If I may, that is."

After a moment, he seemed to understand the question. "I'm afraid she's not feeling well. She's quite distraught, it seems."

"Of course."

"So you understand."

"If I could just ask her one question—"

"No."

He closed the door.

Samantha, surprised, waited a moment. As she turned to leave, the door opened again.

"I'm very sorry for your loss," Mr. Marko said. "Your sister was a lovely girl."

"Thank you."

Samantha walked back to the driveway and paused a moment before getting into her car. She heard music—rock music—from the other side of the house. It hadn't been playing when she first arrived.

She walked around the garage. The side of the house was brick from ground to the roof line, but there were two windows on the second story. One window was open a few inches and there was rock music playing within. As Samantha stood there listening, the song ended and a radio disc jockey—for WMMS—read a promotion for upcoming events that week.

"Rebecca," Samantha called. "Hey Rebecca."

The radio snapped off, and the window shut.

Samantha looked around and noticed a few stones at the

base of the wall. She grabbed a handful and threw them against the window.

"Rebecca!" she shouted.

As she readied another handful, Mr. Marko walked around the side of the house.

"Excuse me. That's quite enough."

"She doesn't sound so distraught up there."

"People grieve in different ways. Apparently, you grieve by bothering your late sister's friends."

Samantha dropped the stones and walked back toward her car. She noticed a white shoe beneath a spreading yew at the corner of the garage and reached in to grab it.

"You've done enough stone throwing for one day, young lady," Mr. Marko said.

Samantha ignored him as she stared at the shoe. It was a white canvas Converse oxford basketball sneaker with laces knotted off—just like Lori would do. It was for the right foot, and Samantha reached back into the shrub, looking for the other sneaker.

"What's that you have there?" Marko asked.

Samantha, convinced the other sneaker was not beneath the yew, held up the Converse for him to see. "This is Lori's shoe."

"I don't see how that's possible."

As Samantha scanned the surrounding area for the other sneaker, Marko snatched it from her hand.

"Hey," Samantha said.

"I'm sure it has no bearing on the incident."

Samantha reached for it, but Marko gripped the shoe with both hands and walked back to the front door of the house.

"Give that back."

"I think you should go home."

"I want Lori's shoe."

Marko faced her before going inside. "If there is any question you need to ask, it's why your sister saw fit to steal the keys for my boat and take a joy ride at midnight on Lake Erie." Then he slammed the door.

Samantha beat on the door and screamed for him to give her back the shoe. "It's not yours, God damn it. It's Lori's, and I want it."

She screamed until she cried, and then she wept and slid to the ground, falling to her knees before landing on her side, sobbing.

Every few minutes, as she caught her breath, she reached out and pounded on the door. "Give me the shoe," she repeated. "Give me Lori's shoe."

"Samantha," her father said, walking up from the driveway. "What the hell is going on?"

"I found Lori's shoe," she whimpered. "Mr. Fucking Marko took it from me and won't give it back."

"What shoe?"

"Lori's shoe. The shoe she had on her foot the night she died."

"You're sure of that?"

"Yes. I swear to God."

"Okay."

He helped her up and walked her back to her car.

"No," she said. "I'm not leaving without the shoe."

"Fine. Just get in the car and I'll go talk to him."

"Get the shoe."

As Samantha slumped behind the wheel of her car, her father went inside the house. When he emerged, he held the shoe in his hand.

"You got the shoe."

"Yes."

"It's a clue."

"What?"

"You're a cop. Take it to the detectives or something, who are looking into Lori's death."

He sighed.

"What? You don't think someone killed her?"

"I don't think this shoe will offer any insight into what happened Friday night."

"But what the hell is it doing here, under that bush? Why

wasn't it on her foot?"

He took a breath and said, "She never tied her shoes. If she wasn't playing softball or basketball, she wouldn't tie her shoes. They were always falling off her feet."

"Yeah, but she always went back for them. It's not like she went around barefoot."

He shrugged. "I'm just not sure—"

"Please take it to Uncle Tom, okay? Have him make a detective look into it. Please."

"Okay," he said. "But we're going to talk more about this. I'm worried about you."

"Fine."

"I think we should start back with the counselor."

"Just give the shoe to Uncle Tom."

# # # #

The next day, they drove to the offices of the Parma Family Counseling Center. Aurelia Delacruz was their counselor, and Samantha hated her.

Samantha thought it pretentious that Aurelia preferred to use the familiarity of first names, but covered her walls with diplomas. Good for you, but the carpeting smells like cat urine and the chairs are uncomfortable.

Samantha hated their sessions, and she hated the awkward feeling afterward of having shared things with a stranger and not accomplishing anything.

But counseling was one of the few times since her mother left that Samantha was in the same room with her father and sister for longer than the duration of a show on television.

This past school year, they'd met there twice: once in October and then in February. Samantha realized the session in February was the last time she saw Lori before the night she died.

As they entered the outer office, Aurelia was waiting for them with hugs.

"I'm very sorry for your loss," she said.

Samantha accepted the hug but wasn't sure what to say. She felt so sad that nothing could sound right.

"Thank you," her father said as he hugged Aurelia. "I'm sorry for your loss, too," he said. "You've been an important part of this family."

Samantha, tired of whatever point her father was trying to make, entered the counseling office and slumped in one of the leather chairs. She stared sideways out the window.

An awkward silence settled on the room. Samantha had braced herself in case Aurelia started the discussion, as she always did, by asking, "How are things going."

This was worse.

Aurelia was looking down at her notes while her father just sat there.

Aurelia began. "This is one of the most troublesome times of your life, I'm sure."

Samantha nodded.

"Funerals often help provide closure and a sense of love, family and community."

"We don't even know if there will be a funeral."

"Of course, there will be," her father said. "Once the Medical Examiner has completed the investigation…"

"Lori's body is in one of those God-awful drawers in some building," Samantha said.

"That's just how these things go," her father said.

"What? You mean I shouldn't talk about it?"

"That's not what I meant."

"Did I speak out of turn in front of the counselor?"

"Of course not," Aurelia said. "This is a safe place for you to say whatever you want. This can be a healing place."

"Samantha, please," her father said. "I don't know what I meant. This is all very confusing for me."

"I'm confused, too, Dad. My heart is broken too. I feel just awful."

Samantha stared at the carpeting, noticing worn spots in front of the seats, like Aurelia hadn't rearranged the furniture in years.

"It's a good thing to acknowledge sadness," Aurelia said. "It's normal for emotions and memories and fear of how to go forward without a loved to confuse us. Lori was special, and your sister, and this is troubling for you."

Samantha nodded.

"She's been staying in bed a lot," her father said.

"So what?" Samantha said.

"That could be a sign of depression," Aurelia said. "Do you feel tired a lot? More than normal?"

"I just don't care. What's the point of getting up, anyway?"

She noticed her father exchange a glance with Aurelia.

"Would you like to come and talk to me without your father?"

"What?"

"It might help you more if it was just the two of us during the sessions."

"This is family counseling," Samantha said.

"Yes, but it's appropriate to adapt to the circumstances. We can also have family sessions, or we can wait until that seems more appropriate."

Samantha looked at her father. He returned the look, but there was nothing showing on his face. He looked like such a cop at that moment, doing his duty, following orders.

"Fine," she said. At least they wouldn't have to exchange awkward glances at whatever the hell it cost per hour to talk to Aurelia.

"We can start next week," Aurelia said.

Silence swallowed the room again. "So, are we done?" Samantha asked.

"If you don't feel like this is a good use of time, yes."

Samantha stood up, but her father didn't.

"I'd like to stay and talk some more, if that's alright."

"Of course," Aurelia said.

"So what am I supposed to do?"

"You can wait out in the outer office," Aurelia said.

Samantha thought of the weird smells out there and hearing their muffled voices through the wall. "I think I'll just walk around outside."

"How will I find you?" her father asked.

"I'll walk over to the mall. I'm going to get an Orange Julius and sit outside."

"Oh," Aurelia said. "You won't go shopping inside?"

"I hate the fucking mall."

Aurelia paused, then said, "Good to know."

A while later, sitting on a bench outside the entrance to the mall and holding the drink she no longer felt like drinking, Samantha cried.

We aren't family anymore, she thought. I'm on my own.

8

Francine found the Key's house but lingered in the car, parked at the curb. This neighborhood reminded her of the Village, with two-bedroom bungalows lined up one after another. Like the Village, these houses were first bought by whites moving farther away from Cleveland's inner-city. But now, after decades of white flight and the riots in the sixties, this neighborhood was ninety percent black.

The neighborhood was quiet, well-groomed and tidy. A few spring flowers had sprouted, reminding her she meant to plant more at her own rental, and should stop at a garden center on the way home this evening.

She realized she was stalling to avoid the unpleasant work of talking to a couple whose son died in Lake Erie. Summoning her resolve, she walked up the front path, ascended the stairs and knocked on the door.

A pretty woman answered the door. She had light-brown skin, glasses perched on her nose, and wore a dress a notch better than what Francine had worn.

"I'm Francine Tennyson," she said. "We spoke on the phone earlier."

"Of course, Miss Tennyson. I'm Louise Key."

"I'm very sorry for your loss."

"Thank you."

Louise showed her in and offered a seat right there in the front room, and sat forward on the sofa to give Francine her attention. They exchanged restrained pleasantries and agreed to a first name basis.

While Louise stepped into the kitchen to get coffee, Francine admired the decorations. On one wall was a series of shelves with family pictures and statuettes. On the other were stunning oil paintings, one of a city street, the other of the shore of a body of water. Not the sort of artwork purchased at a Kmart blue light special.

Without looking, she knew the layout of the house: the ground floor split into the front room, a kitchen, two bedrooms and a bath; the upstairs might be finished space, although her own father had never gotten around to it at their house, and it was just storage space.

"You must forgive us," Louise said as she brought in the coffee. "My husband isn't here yet. He had to take care of his business, which he had neglected the past few days."

"Don't apologize. I'm very grateful you're willing to speak with me at all."

Louise set down her coffee and folded her hands on the table. "I have to admit, I'm a little afraid of what you want to know. This has been terrible, and I worry that they will abuse Michael."

"I promise I'll report the truth. There are a couple of things I don't understand about this accident."

"I understand none of it."

"Have the police talked to you?"

Louise shook her head. "Only to tell us he'd drowned in the lake. I wish I knew why he took a boat out at such an ungodly hour."

"He didn't drown. They were floating, which helped in the recovery."

Louise studied her. "Oh, Lord. What are you saying?"

"They were dead before they went into the water."

"Oh, Lord." Louise lowered her head for a moment. "Would you explain that to my husband when he arrives?"

"Certainly," Francine said. "Had your son ever mentioned the other victim, Lori Sykora?"

"Not a thing. He told me he was seeing someone, but he hadn't brought her here to meet us. I figured..." She shook her head and grabbed her coffee rather than finish the sentence.

"If they meant to go for that boat ride, it seems like it was spur of the moment."

Louise shook her head again. "I didn't raise a fool to go taking what isn't his, let alone go for a boat ride at one in the morning and set the boat on fire."

Francine took out her Filofax and made some notes. "Can you tell me a bit more about him, like was he a student, or was he working?"

"Michael was an A student in high school, got an associate degree at Tri-C, and his bachelor's at Cleveland State. He always worked, starting in high school, paying for his own things, never causing me to worry. Of course, I'm his mother, so I worried, anyway."

Louise cried then and Francine busied herself with her notes, reaching out to pat the broken-hearted mom's arm. Louise took hold of Francine's hand and squeezed it.

"How had he come to live in the Village?"

"I don't know. After he graduated, he got a job at a branch of the bank on west twenty-fifth, so he could have lived here. If I had to guess, it was because of the girl he was seeing."

"And what was her name?"

"Rebecca."

"Just Rebecca?"

"That's all we heard. I just assumed it wasn't serious, yet."

"Is there a picture of Michael I could use? I don't know that we'll use it, but it helps if it's there and ready to go."

Louise took a framed photo off the wall. "This is his high school graduation. I have a copy I'm going to use for the obituary, anyway. So you can take that."

"I will return it to you."

The front door opened. A man silhouetted by the outdoor light stood looking at them.

"That's my husband," Louise said. "Aaron Key."

"Hello," he said.

In the light, his skin was tawny, a yellowish-brown. He kept his hair trimmed short, but he wasn't balding. His eyes were large and his nose Romanesque, and his jaw was strong and distinct. He was fit. Not muscular, but no extra weight, which she noticed because so many of the white men his age around the office carried more than they needed.

"I'm sorry for your loss," Francine said as she offered him her hand.

"Michael was a good boy," Aaron said.

"He sounds like a fine young man," Francine said. "I think the story will be about the tragic loss and the curious nature of the accident. I'm hoping the police will get to the truth."

Aaron nodded. "Can you promise me the story will be true and fair?"

"I promise the story I write will be true and fair."

Aaron laughed. For a moment Francine tried to think of what was so funny. Then it hit her. "Is it because I'm a woman?"

"I'm sorry," Aaron said. "You're fine. It's because my son was black."

"Enough, Aaron," Louise said. "You're frightening this girl."

"It's fine. I'll share the story with you before I submit it to my editor."

"Uh-huh."

Louise rapped her knuckles on the table. "Aaron, why are you suspicious of this young woman's intentions?"

"I apologize," Aaron said, nodding his head. "I believe your intentions are honorable."

Louise folded her arms. "That wasn't much better."

"How confident are you that your editor will print the story you write?"

"Well," Francine said, taking a breath as she selected her words. "I've only had a few regular stories printed, and never with a byline. I do community events."

"When the editor told you to come out here and get this story, what did he say?"

Francine looked Aaron in the eyes. "He didn't send me. I'm hoping this story will be good enough that he'll want to publish it."

"I see."

"There ain't nothing wrong with that," Louise said.

Francine heard the lack of conviction in her voice. "I promise you I will do my best, and that I am, in fact, a very good writer."

"That's nice," Aaron said. "But I'll settle for true and fair."

9

Samantha awoke to the sound of garbage cans being dragged to the curb and raised her head from the pillow to listen. The metal cans scraped across cement, then landed with a thud on the curbstone.

She went to the dormer window. Across the street, workers for the city Service Garage were walking up the driveway to retrieve the next set of cans. It was a service offered to the elderly in the city, or anyone who asked. A few of the men, cops and firemen, were too proud to allow the Service workers to do it for them.

Then she heard the sound behind their house as her father —of course her father wouldn't let someone else take out their garbage—dragged a can past the house and down the driveway, depositing it at the curb. He looked up at the dormer window and waved.

In a few minutes, the trash collectors would appear on the street. That meant it was Friday, trash day.

Samantha sat back down on her bed. She hadn't realized a week had gone by since Lori died. They still knew nothing about her death.

They didn't even have the funeral planned.

A car pulled into the driveway and the door opened and closed. Samantha returned to the window and saw her father talking to her Uncle Tom.

Tom wore his full uniform. He held a large, manila envelope in his hand and, while leaning against his Ford LTD police cruiser, offered the envelope to her father.

By the time Samantha got out the front door, her father had handed the envelope back to Tom, who was getting back in his car. "What's going on?" she asked.

"I'm coming, sweetheart," her father said.

Tom started the police cruiser, nodded to Samantha, and backed out of the driveway.

"What was that about?" Samantha asked as soon as her father stepped inside. "Is there news?"

He nodded. "The coroner ruled it an accident. So we can think about the funeral—"

"No. No, we can't. It's not that simple."

"As much as this pains me, I'm afraid it is."

"Was that the coroner's report? Can I see it?"

Her father sat in the recliner and rocked for a moment. "It's the summary report. Uncle Tom took it with him. There wasn't much detail."

"Then how do you know he's correct?"

"The coroner wrote it. That's his job. We have to trust him to do his job."

She paced from the television to the sofa, both fists gripping her hair. She wanted to scream but knew that would only make her father angry. Then she was mad at herself for worrying about that. Her stomach tightened, and she sobbed.

"Can I read it, please?" she asked, speaking with careful breaths.

"I told you Uncle Tom took it with him."

"Can you go get it and let me read it, please?"

"There's not much with it, Sweetheart. It was just the summary. It's a preliminary determination because they're waiting on the toxicology results, which may take another four or five weeks."

She burst into tears and didn't stop them, staggering to the sofa and sitting down, pounding a pillow with her fist.

Her father sat beside her and wrapped his arms around her. "Sweetheart, I know, I know..."

When she caught her breath, she wiped her nose with the pillow. "Are you saying we can't bury Lori for another month?"

"No," he said. "The examination is over. We can have the funeral and move on."

Samantha shook her head. "What did the police say about the Lori's shoe?"

When he didn't answer right away, Samantha pushed away. "You gave Uncle Tom the shoe, right? Did he give it to whoever is investigating whatever happened?"

"Sweetheart, I don't think it's a clue. I think it's just a shoe."

Samantha came back downstairs in the afternoon to find a breakfast plate and a lunch plate on the kitchen table waiting for her. Her father fried eggs over hard—the only way he made eggs—and a grilled cheese with tomato soup. All of it was cold. She found a Pop-Tart in the cupboard and sat at the table.

Outside, her father was doing something in the garage. She hadn't seen him do that since a brief warm spell during winter, when he spent most of a Saturday organizing his work bench.

One of the chief memories she had of her father was his being out back, either in the garage working on a car, spending hours going back and forth with tools, or practicing sports on the driveway with Lori.

Samantha and her mother would sit at the table, her mother with a book and coffee, she with either a book or some homework, watching as Lori and her father played catch, fine-tuning Lori's swing, or practiced "going to her left." Samantha was never jealous of this time. She had no interest in team sports, and much preferred the quiet time in the kitchen with her mother.

Still hungry, she ate the grilled cheese, doing her best to ignore the surface skin on the soup as she dipped the sandwich.

Her father pulled baseball gloves and bats out of the garage and tossed them on the back lawn. He emptied out a gear bag and slapped a pair of cleats together, knocking off the dried mud.

"You're up," he said as he came in the side door. "You okay? Did you eat?"

Samantha nodded. "Thanks."

"Okay, I think I'm going to go to a softball practice."

He emerged from his bedroom a few minutes later wearing sweats and athletic socks. "What's the matter?" he asked.

"I don't understand what you're doing?"

"I'm just going to spend some time with my friends and doing something I love."

"Okay."

"I think you should do that, too. You should spend the evening with your friends. Go to a movie, maybe. My treat."

"What about Lori?"

"Yeah, right, I should have told you: we'll go to the funeral home tomorrow to make the arrangements."

"When were you going to tell me this?"

"Sorry, but your Aunt Jan made the call to get things—"

Samantha slammed her fists on the table. "I'm sorry too, Dad," she said, catching her breath. "Did you ask Uncle Tom if I could read the coroner's report?"

"No, Sweetheart, I didn't ask but I know he'll be against it. It's an open investigation until the toxicology report is in, and he won't want to share it. I'm not sure how he got a copy, because it's in the jurisdiction of the Cleveland Police. So there's not much your Uncle Tom or I could even do."

She thought of a few things she might say, but she was too familiar with the look on his face. He would not change his mind. "Okay, fine," she said as she stood up to leave the kitchen. "Have fun playing softball."

Samantha went over to Blaine's house around five o'clock once he'd showered after work. She made a double batch of macaroni and cheese, and they ate it in his front room, watching Bugs Bunny cartoons.

Blaine drank a Pabst, and Samantha sipped a Tab. The Gong Show followed the cartoons, and they laughed. Samantha choked up twice, remembering how she and Lori watched the show.

Later, as Samantha scraped out the pot in the kitchen, there was a knock on the door.

"Samantha," Blaine said, "It's for you."

It was her Aunt Jan, standing on the front stoop and looking in. "Samantha, can I speak with you?"

Jan pulled the door closed, so it was just the two of them on the stoop. Samantha folded her arms and leaned against the wrought-iron railing.

"I'd like you to come over to my house," Jan said. "Your father mentioned you were alone, and I thought you could use some family time."

"I'm fine."

"Both your cousins are home, and your Uncle Wally is going to make popcorn..."

"I'm here with Blaine, so thanks anyway."

Jan folder her arms. "But he's not family."

"He is to me."

10

On Saturday, Francine struggled with misgivings about telling this story. She'd heard from Robaroni that the Medical Examiner had made a preliminary determination, and yet, when she mentioned it to her editor, Hal, he shrugged. "Thanks for the heads up," was all that he said.

She hadn't been able to catch up with Murray in the afternoon and wasn't sure what to do about the story. There still wasn't even a death announcement in the Saturday paper.

Robaroni had little to offer, other than it seemed to him there was a story there, but, as a cop, sometimes you can't get to the truth even when you have the evidence in hand.

Feeling the frustration, and asking herself the question of what might have happened, she went to talk to whoever she could. Besides, it was her day off. She could do whatever the hell she wanted.

On the way to her first stop, she drove past her old house. It was a brick, two-bedroom bungalow with awnings and a covered porch. There was no furniture on the porch, as the owners must not have felt it warm enough yet. They had replaced the shrubs in front with azaleas.

Francine saw an older couple down the street working in their front flower bed, but couldn't think of their names. She would have to remember to ask her mother, later on, if they spoke on the phone.

Francine made her way across the Village, drove through

an intersection, found a house number and realized she missed the Marko's house. She turned the car around and looked for an unmarked driveway. Turning in, advancing along the curving driveway, she admired the manicured lawn, the ornamental shrubbery, and the flowering trees.

Emerging from around a bush, she saw the Marko house. In the center of the circular driveway was a statue of a black-faced jockey. She wondered if this property was even within the city limits of the blue-collar, working-class suburb where she and Robaroni had grown up.

Back then, Marko had already been the president of the city council. Growing up, Francine had never wondered where the family lived.

This stretch of road in a distant corner of the city was out of character for the Village. Everywhere else, they packed the streets with two-bedroom bungalows on forty-foot lots, set back thirty feet. Each yard had a driveway. Most driveways led to a detached garage in the back yard; some led to nothing but the back yard.

But the Marko's house was a two-story, brick colonial with an attached, three-car garage. The driveway looped around the front yard. Pillars stood in front of the house, supporting the overhanging roof. A chandelier hung in the alcove, visible through the large window above the front door.

Francine knocked on the door and waited, half-expecting a butler to open the door. After a few minutes, she knocked again. There were no sounds from within. As she pondered knocking again, she wondered if maybe she should have called ahead.

She heard footsteps and a well-dressed, middle-aged woman with a scarf on her head opened the door.

"Mrs. Cherie Marko?"

"Yes," Cherie said, removing her sunglasses.

"My name is Francine Tennyson. Is your husband, Patrick home?"

Cherie folded her arms. "What is this about?"

"A boat owned by Mr. Marko crashed and burned on Lake Erie. I'd like to speak to him about it."

Cherie pointed at Francine with her sunglasses. "Who are you?"

"I'm a reporter and I'm doing a story about the accident on Lake Erie."

"There's no story, so leave us alone."

Cherie slammed the door shut.

# # # #

The neighborhood next to the Village city park, packed with bungalows, was a familiar relief to Francine. An older couple working in their front flower garden just like the Schultzeys— she remembered!—at her old neighborhood.

The Sykora house was in the middle of the street. Approaching the front door, she recalled walking up to Robaroni's house when they were kids and, rather than knocking, shouting at the top of her lungs for him to come out and play.

But here she knocked.

The young woman who answered had to be Samantha, Lori's younger sister.

"Sorry to bother you," Francine said, and introduced herself. "I'm writing a story about Lori Sykora's death, and I'd like to ask you and your parents a few questions about Lori, if that's alright."

Samantha shot a glance over her shoulder. "I don't know if my father would like it."

"What about your mother?"

"She left us a few years back."

"Oh, I'm sorry. I didn't realize."

"Don't apologize. No one talks about it, so, yeah. I don't even know what to say about it anymore myself."

"Would it be alright if I came in to talk? You might be more comfortable."

"Let's just sit here, okay?" Samantha sat on the front steps and so Francine sat next to her.

"I want to do a profile of your sister and Michael Key, who also died on the boat."

"Michael Key?" Samantha put her head down on her folded arms. "I didn't even know who it was. My family hasn't told me anything."

"I'm finding a lot of problems getting to this story."

Samantha raised her head and shrugged. Francine admired her thick, red hair and her distinct features. The nose was large, but it fit her face.

"What was he like?" Samantha asked.

"Oh, I talked to his parents. He'd been a talented student, had a degree in business, and was planning on getting a master's degree. Never any trouble."

"Lori was a little wild, but never any real trouble."

"I found her old clippings for sports and scholastics."

Samantha sniffled and wiped her nose on the sleeve of her T-shirt.

"Do you think your father would talk with me about Lori? I just need a bit of info."

"Maybe. But don't you think the whole thing is a little weird?"

"It's very weird," Francine said. "I know it's ruled an accident, but I think people would like to know how it happened."

"Well then don't ask my family anything like that."

"But would you help me?"

"I would, but—"

"Samantha?" her father said as he walked down the driveway. "Who's this?"

Francine stepped towards him, offering her hand, introducing herself. "I'm very sorry for your loss."

"You're a reporter?"

"Sort of," she said, glancing at Samantha to buy time. "I think it'd be great for the community to hear a bit about what Lori and Michael had accomplished, and maybe—"

"You should leave," he said. "We're not letting our lives get plastered all over the news just because we had some bad luck."

Francine nodded and took a step back. She had a card in the back pocket of her jeans and palmed it while turning back to Samantha.

"I am sorry for your loss." She offered her hand and pressed the card into Samantha's palm. "Call me if you need to talk."

"She won't," her father said.

\# \# \# \#

The Cleveland business district was on the high ground of a raised shelf, bordered on the west by the Cuyahoga River valley, on the north by the drop-off to Lake Erie, and on the east by the slope down to the lake shore, where the Yacht Club nestled under the shadow of the downtown skyline.

Francine took in the view, noting the few low-slung buildings along this stretch of lake shore. Some of those buildings may have had security guards who saw what happened that night. There weren't a lot of skyscrapers, but the skyline impressed from this angle.

There were only five cars in the parking lot. Francine parked as near to the yacht club as she could. At the far end of the parking lot, nearest the road, was an Oldsmobile coupe. It seemed odd, all alone like that.

They fenced the marina off from the parking lot, and the club itself was off to one side.

Francine walked to the far end to confirm that the wrought-iron fence connected to a cement wall which stretched to the water's edge. A motivated person could wade through the water and get to the boats.

Or you could boat into the marina from the lake.

As she walked back toward the club, a man arrived in a Cadillac and, using a key to unlock the gate, made his way into the marina. For a moment, Francine considered following him, but she didn't yet know what she was looking for. The risk of ruining her welcome was not worth it.

Inside the club, there was a lounge, a small shop stocked with boating gear, and a reception desk. The only other person there was a young man behind the counter in the shop.

"Excuse me," Francine asked. "Can you help me?"

"I hope so." The young man, dressed in blue khaki slacks and a collared sport shirt, was in his early twenties.

"It seems pretty quiet in here. That normal?"

"For this time of year, yes," he said, chuckling. "Once it's warm, there's steady traffic in and out of here, and in and out of the marina."

"Just not boating weather, huh?"

"Oh, the sailors take their boats out as soon as the ice thaws and there's a bit of a breeze. But the power boaters like it warm."

"Sure."

"In the summer, it's packed on the weekends until all hours. People just sit on their boats and picnic right here during the day, and party at night."

"Sounds like fun."

"Do you boat?"

"No, just curious. In fact, I wanted to ask about the accident the other night."

He frowned. "Are you a reporter or something?"

"Yes. Just doing basic research."

"Oh, shit, I'm not supposed to talk about it."

"I don't reveal my sources."

"Yeah, but..."

"I'm just curious how they got to the boat. It seems pretty secure out there."

"I can tell you that much," he said. "Whoever took the boat probably had the keys. We keep copies of the keys for the own-ers, if they want us to, like valet parking. But not for that boat."

"So whoever had the boat key had the key to the marina, too."

"Yep. You could say they stole the keys, not the boat."

Francine looked around the shop. "Are there security cameras, or a guard?"

"Nah," he said. "No cameras. We use a security service in the summer, but right now it's just serious boaters going out, and they don't cause trouble."

"So why have a guard in summer?"

"The yacht club folks feel safer if there's a guard. But there's never any real trouble. Sometimes we have to call a cab for someone who has had too much to drink, or someone falls in the water and we get them a change of clothes."

"But if two people show up at one in the morning with the keys to the boat, no one is going to stop them from going out on the lake?"

He shrugged. "My dad keeps his Bow Rider here, and if it's calm, he may take it out at night even if the walleye aren't biting."

"Is that a power boat?"

"The biggest."

Francine turned to leave but remembered another question. "Is it a thing that boats catch on fire?"

"That was a new one for me," he said. "My father had heard of it and said that's why he prefers aluminum boats."

"Do fiberglass boats catch fire often?"

He shook his head. "No. It's pretty tough to get fiberglass burning. Once it starts, you need to sink it to put out the fire."

"So how would you start the fire?"

He cocked his head. "That boat ran on gasoline, and gasoline is very flammable. I would use gasoline."

11

That evening, Fred and Lou were at Benny's Tavern for darts. It was league night, but they were out of contention for the championship, so they were talking more about fishing while tossing darts.

In between sets, as they each downed a shot and a beer, the bartender offered Fred the phone.

"Is it my wife?"

"Does your wife sound like a guy?" the bartender asked.

Fred took the phone. "Hello."

"Fred?"

"Yeah? Who's this?"

"Bill Peleshi. Your house is on fire."

"What?"

"The firemen are on the way, but you might want to get home."

"Where's my wife and kids?"

"Out on the street watching it burn."

Fred dropped the phone and grabbed his jacket. "Come on!"

Lou caught up to him at the car. "What the hell is going on?"

"Just get in."

Fred explained the phone call as they rattled along Jennings, a road so pitted with potholes from the abuses of winter that the traffic lines in the center of the road were only shades of gray.

"That's insane," Lou said.

"No shit."

"You taking the highway?"

"This is shorter."

"Right."

Lou held on to the door handle and the dashboard as best he could, unconcerned even as Fred sped up around slower cars coming upon them in the valley's darkness. The poor roads and lack of street lights were their friend the many times they'd driven home this way, one or two drinks over the limit, avoiding traffic and police cruisers at the expense of a rougher ride.

The route was shorter, but the car's suspension took a beating. Lou braced himself for the looming turn and steep climb up the hill at Old Denison Avenue.

When Fred braked, Lou noticed another car coming up behind them fast, catching up to them.

"Shit," Lou said. "Maybe there's two fires."

Fred punched it up the hill, and the other car followed close behind.

In the first of two hair-pin turns, there was a loud noise and a jolt in their seats as the car behind them ran into the rear quarter-panel.

Lou looked back and saw the dark sky above as the car rolled off the road. It tumbled down the incline, the roof collapsing and the windshield shattering.

Once the engine sputtered, choked and stalled, Lou checked himself for damage. It had bounced him around a bit, but he felt okay.

They landed upright, but with the roof caved in, pinning Fred against the steering wheel, there was little to celebrate. What little Lou could make out from the dashboard light, Fred seemed pretty much dead.

"Fred. Can you hear me? Oh shit. Shit-shit-shit."

Lou was panting, unable to get enough air, and trying to suck in more sent a jolt of pain, like knives cutting him open from the inside out. Then a flash of pain from both legs shot up his spine with every heartbeat. Genuine problems were emerging. He needed help.

He heard a trunk close shut, and Lou thought that whoever hit them must have stopped.

"Oh God. Help. I can't move!"

A bottle crashed and shattered against the hood of the car. Flames erupted and engulfed the car.

"No!" Lou screamed. "Oh shit! Please God—"

Another bottle crashed and shattered against the side door, and flames filled the cabin.

Lou closed his eyes and screamed, his body convulsing but unable to move, his lungs burning when he tried to breathe.

# # # #

Francine closed the book on her finger when the phone rang. She got so few calls it was a novelty during the day. But it was eleven-thirty, a weird time for a call. The story about the boating accident was not going well, and reading was supposed to distract her. Living alone made her jumpy at night. Who the hell could it be?

Part of her wanted to ignore the call, but she took a deep breath and made her way to the kitchen.

"Hello," She said.

"This is Robaroni," Robaroni said. "I'm coming to pick you up, so put some clothes on."

"What? Why?"

"Are you sure it's them?"

Robaroni nodded as he drove. "The cops on scene called in the license plate. The dispatcher recognized one of their names, Fred, because you had me look him up the other day."

"Oh God."

"There's not much left. The heat stripped the paint from

the license plate and damn near melted it. They almost couldn't figure out the numbers."

When they arrived, there was still a police cruiser on the scene. The charred remains of the car sat on a flatbed tow truck as the driver strapped it down.

Francine wrinkled her nose at the smell permeating the car as they slowed to a stop. When she opened the door, she full-on winced at the stench of burned rubber, burned plastic and what she feared to be burned flesh.

Approaching on foot, Robaroni pointed out that firemen cut the car apart to extract the remains of the two passengers. The sides of the car, now just bare metal, were peeled open like a banana.

Rob spoke to the officer who nodded and said, "No souvenirs."

Francine stepped closer and flinched, thinking she'd stepped on an ember. "It's so hot."

"Car fires create an unbelievable amount of heat. The water from the hose boils before hitting the ground. Hell, I've seen cement crack from a car fire."

Rob used his flashlight to show her the singed ground. A fine mist of steam rose from the ground. There was nothing but ash in the middle. The heat charred grass and trees up to ten feet away.

And everywhere the stench.

"Is it being investigated?" she asked.

"Yeah, but there was so little left of Fred and Lou. The only evidence is the car itself."

"That's it then?"

Rob pointed at the houses on top of the hill overlooking the scene. "There are two uniforms going door to door up there, asking if anyone saw what happened. If there's a witness, there's a chance."

Francine looked around, noticing the river making its way to the lake. "I just spoke to them."

"Yeah, about that. Who knows you talked to them?"

"Nobody, I guess. I haven't written that part of the story.

Not that my editor would use it if I did."

"Did you meet them at their house?"

"No. At a bar."

"People saw you talking to them?"

"It was happy hour."

Robaroni nodded. The tow truck started and then made its way up the Old Denison Road hill. The uniforms made one last sweep of the area and headed for their cruiser.

"You need anything?" the cop called to Rob.

"No. We'll head out in a second."

When they were alone, darkness enveloped them.

"This is creeping me out," Francine said. "You think this was on purpose?"

"It's pretty goddam weird that the two viable witnesses to a potential crime would die in another weird accident involving fire."

"What should I do?"

"The notes from your interview with these guys, did you leave them at your apartment?"

Francine tapped her shoulder bag. "I have them here in my notebook."

"I think you should stay at my place tonight."

12

The morning of Lori's memorial, Samantha glanced at herself in the mirror, her one and only black dress held up in front of her robe, unsure if she needed jewelry with the black dress. It's the question she would have asked Lori: How do you dress to honor the person who told you what to wear?

Lori helped her shop for this very dress, purchased for the Honor Society ceremony. Even though Lori cared even less about fashion than Samantha, they'd figured it out together.

Samantha wished the right outfit could fix any problem in the world, but she knew it didn't matter.

Lori had taken a version of her tom-boy youth into jeans and T-shirt teenager. She'd revealed her feminine beauty only for the winter formal and the prom at high school, earning Samantha's respect for fashion sense when it counted most.

Frustrated by the low-ceiling and sloping walls of the converted attic, Samantha also missed how she and Lori would have shared those frustrations with each other as they got dressed for weddings or holiday parties.

"I wish Mom was here," she said as she struggled to see more of herself in the small mirror propped up in the corner.

But of course her mother would be there. No matter what had driven her away, nothing would keep her from her daughter's funeral.

Samantha looked around the room, half-expecting to see

her mother there already, filled with both dread and excitement.

Samantha hated her for leaving, but wouldn't this be the one thing to bring her back? Would losing Lori be a little easier to bear with her mother wrapping her arms around her?

"Dad?" Samantha called as she hurried down the stairs with a dress, skirt and blouse to choose from. "When is Mom going to be here?"

"What?" he called from his bedroom.

Samantha stood in the doorway, holding her robe closed with the same hands grasping her possible wardrobe. "When is Mom coming? I need to ask her something."

Her father was knotting his tie. "She's not coming."

"But she has to. She has to come."

"Honey, I haven't spoken to your mother in years. I don't even know how to get a hold of her."

Samantha threw her dress to the floor. "Find her. You can't bury Lori without Mom even knowing about it."

"Sweetie, I would if I knew where to find her."

He took a step closer, but Samantha backed out of the doorway. "That's bullshit. You chased her away."

"No. No I didn't."

"You had to. She'd want to know if we were alive."

He took another step closer, reaching out with his arms, but Samantha backed into the hallway, turned her back to him.

"You're probably happy that Mom doesn't know. You probably think she doesn't deserve to know."

"I can't do anything about it," he called from inside his bedroom. "It wasn't my fault she left, and I can't tell you why she stayed away."

Samantha waited, expecting him to hug her from behind, and not sure how she should react to that.

"What am I supposed to do?" he asked. "Should I take out an ad in every newspaper in the country? Or call the F.B.I.?"

"Yes!" Samantha screamed. "That's what you should do."

She braced herself for his hug, deciding that she would accept it and, turning, hug him back. When, instead, she heard him close his bedroom door, she cried.

# # # #

The next day, the day men with shovels would bury Lori in the ground, Samantha found herself in the pew, not sure how she got there. Blaine was beside her.

"What time is it?"

"Ten a.m., I think."

"Is it over or just starting?"

"Just starting."

Samantha nodded. That made sense.

"Are you okay?"

Samantha shook her head.

"It's going to be okay."

"No, it's not," she whispered.

Her father sat down beside her, there in the first row. Lori's coffin was just a few feet away in front of the steps up to the sacred area. Behind her was Grampa Peter, Grandma, Aunt Jan, and her family.

Behind them were more people than Samantha ever wanted to deal with for any reason.

The priest was at the lectern and said something. Samantha cared nothing for what he had to say. What was the point? Everybody else stood up, but Samantha stayed seated.

Blaine sat back down, as well. "Do you want get out of here?" he asked.

"Why?"

"You don't seem to want to be here."

"I think I'm supposed to be here."

"Yeah, but... whatever."

Samantha chuckled.

"What's funny?"

She noticed the concern in Blaine's voice.

"Somehow, I still thought my mother would be here. Like

she's out there, somewhere, and doesn't even know that her daughter has died."

"Yeah. That's weird."

Samantha glanced at her father. He was sobbing, wiping his nose with a kerchief, and mumbling along with the service, responding to something the priest said. A prayer. The priest led the congregation in prayer.

"It doesn't matter," she said.

Blaine looked at her, then up at the priest.

At the cemetery, Samantha clung to Blaine's arm as they sat before the grave. Lori's coffin rested on a platform over the hole in the ground.

The tears came in waves, starting low in her stomach as they gathered, then up her chest like a stone, and catching in her throat. She gasped and sputtered, wiping her nose and eyes, then coughing as she struggled to catch her breath.

The priest spoke again, reading from his little book, making the sign of the cross, saying a prayer.

The crowd spread out before them and circled around on all sides. Samantha scanned their faces, hoping somehow that her mother might be there among them, perhaps wearing a scarf and sunglasses, trying to blend in, but doing whatever it took to be at her daughter's funeral.

Maybe revolutionaries abducted her mother some time after she left the family, and that's why the letters stopped arriving. She could be like that rich girl, kidnapped and forced to rob banks. And all the time she was biding her time for her chance to escape.

Then, as her mother prepared coffee and sandwiches for her captors while they made plans to rob a bank in Palm Springs, she somehow heard about the bizarre accident on Lake Erie. With horror, she realized her daughter died.

That very moment, she created a diversion, maybe spilling coffee, and went in search of a mop. But she ran away again—something she knew how to do—and took a cab to the airport.

Using the money she'd secreted away from their bank robberies and hidden in her underpants until she had this chance to escape, she took the next flight east.

She'd arrived at the cemetery just in time, blending in with the crowd, wary of the federal agents looking for her for bank robbery. But nothing would keep her away.

She loved both her daughters more than anything in the world. Now that she'd made her way back, nothing would keep her away from Samantha, her surviving girl. She'd shower Samantha with the love meant for two daughters. Soon, all would be—

"Samantha," her father said. "It's time."

He tugged on one arm while Blaine tugged on the other.

"What's happening?"

"It's over," her father said. "We're going to lunch."

The crowd was breaking up, making their way to cars parked along the asphalt path. She looked back and forth, hoping to see a woman wearing a trench coat, with a scarf covering her hair and dark sunglasses on her face. But there was no one there that fit that description.

# # # #

Samantha sat at the table with Blaine, watching as her family and family friends chatted at the other tables. Dozens of Lori's high school friends and college teammates were there, but also lots of people she'd never seen before.

"Your grandfather knows a bunch of people," Blaine said.

"He's been mayor for ever."

"Fifty years, right?"

"I guess." Samantha shook her head. "They're all talking. Even my dad. It's insane."

"It's just talking."

"But they're always talking. Grampa talks the most. Tom talks the next most. My dad is always talking to Aunt Jan, and then she talks almost as much as Uncle Tom."

Blaine nodded and then scooped potato salad into his mouth like he was over it already.

Grampa stood to one side, surrounded by men in suits, talking, laughing, shaking hands. Tom moved from table to table, sitting down, eating desserts from the plates on each table, sipping his beer before moving on. Her father was near the bar in the corner, shaking hands as people approached. Jan moved from table to buffet, bringing desserts and drinks, always talking, smiling, and waving.

"They could sit with you for a little while," Blaine said.

"I just wish they weren't talking so much."

Julie, Lori's college roommate, made her way to Samantha and offered a hug. "I'm so sorry for your loss."

Julie and Lori shared a dorm room and became friends, bonding over sports, even though Julie was not playing at college. She was tall and fit, a brunette version of Lori, but with a cute button nose. The two of them shared clothes.

She hugged Blaine, surprising him. "Lori talked a lot about you, too, and I'm sorry for your loss."

She sat down, looking a little out of place, and Blaine offered her a Tab.

"Lori loved you both very much. I don't have any siblings, so I hoped to do more with you this summer."

"Well," Samantha said, "Maybe we can do something."

"I'd like that, but I'm moving back to Syracuse."

"What happened that night?" Blaine asked. "Did she say anything before she left?"

"I left for the weekend. I don't have classes on Friday, and my Dad had a thing, so, I didn't even know until I got a call from your Aunt Jan."

Samantha looked at Julie, not sure she understood what she'd just said. "What?"

"Your Aunt Jan called me at my parents' house and told me what happened."

"How did she know your number?" Blaine asked.

Julie shrugged. "The way Lori talked about your family,

they seem pretty resourceful."

"That's so weird," Samantha said.

"Do they have any idea who did this?" Julie asked.

"You don't think it was an accident?"

"No. I mean, she never mentioned dating that guy she was with."

"Maybe he was a secret boyfriend," Blaine said. "She could have secret boyfriends, right?"

Julie shook her head. "She and I talked about all that stuff, and I know for a fact she wasn't dating him."

"You sound pretty sure," Blaine said.

"Yes," Julie said. "I'm sure of it."

"How?" Samantha asked. "How can you be so sure?"

"I'm sorry," Julie said. "I didn't mean to upset you. Listen, my dad is waiting for me. That's the only way he'd let me come, is if he drove me. So I need to go."

Julie got up and hugged Samantha and Blaine.

"Tell your father I'm sorry and give him my love."

She was out the door before Samantha could think of what to say.

13

Samantha wanted to scream. The day had been unbearable. As she craved comfort from her family, they ignored her, and instead worked the funeral crowd like one of Grampa's political fundraisers. Now the adults crowded into the kitchen discussing how their political rivals might exploit Lori's death.

She felt sorry for her father. He'd never seemed to care much for the political discussions. He only wanted to be a cop, and to protect the citizens of the city he loved. Sometimes he seemed sad, sitting at the table with his siblings, father and mother as they murmured about scandals, favors and money.

She felt even worse at the moment for her cousin Anna, pressed into service as a scullery maid by her mother, now scrubbing serving dishes and utensils from the luncheon for the people who brought food to share. Aunt Jan would not return the dishes in anything but clean condition, and Anna was the only suitable candidate to do all the work.

Samantha sat in the front room watching television with Derek, who gently rocked in the recliner, drinking a beer, looking like a trimmer, younger version of his father Wally.

"You going back to school?" he asked.

Samantha shook her head. "I have no interest."

"I wouldn't. Even if they didn't graduate me, I wouldn't go."

"I guess I had enough credits or whatever to graduate last fall."

"Wait, you've been going to school just because?"

Samantha shrugged. "I was taking A.P. classes, so..."

"Screw that," he said. "I would have just sat around drinking."

Samantha felt a tightness in her stomach. She wanted to talk to her father and went into the kitchen for a drink of water, hoping to get his attention. But Anna hadn't washed the cups yet, so she couldn't get a drink.

Back in the front room, Derek was opening another beer. He had changed the channel to the Indians' game while she was away.

"You know what's weird," she asked. "Lori didn't even know the guy."

"What guy?"

"The guy in the boat."

"The black guy?"

"I heard they were dating," Derek said.

"Who?"

"Lori and the black guy."

"What?" Samantha said. "I heard she was not dating anybody."

"Then why were they on the boat together?"

"I don't know, but I wish someone would figure it out."

Derek scoffed. "Maybe she was keeping it a secret, you know, because he was black."

"Her college roommate said that Lori wasn't dating the guy on the boat."

"That proves she was keeping secrets."

"Where did you get this stuff?" Samantha asked.

"Hey, relax. Pretend I said nothing."

Samantha recognized the contempt in his voice. It signaled he was done talking to her about Lori. She'd heard her father, uncles and grandfather end conversations the same way all of her life.

Samantha walked in Blaine's front door without knocking. He

sat in the recliner in the room's corner, just as Derek had been doing, but Blaine was smoking a bowl. He smiled at her and apologized for the smoke.

"It's fine," she said. "You're watching the show I want to watch."

"I figured you'd just go to bed. You looked exhausted to-day."

"I am, but my stupid family is still at my house."

"Tell them to leave."

As she sprawled on the couch, she slipped her hand into her back pocket and found Francine Tennyson's business card.

"Hey," she said. "Did you think it was weird what Julie said today, about the guy in the boat with Lori, that he had been dat-ing Rebecca."

"That was weird," Blaine said. "Also, Rebecca did not come to the luncheon."

"Shit, that is weird. Did her parents?"

"Only the father," Blaine said. "I saw him talking to my boss."

Samantha looked again at the business card. On the back, Francine had written her home phone and a note: "Call any time."

"Can I use your phone?" she asked.

Blaine was cleaning his bowl, scraping the residue into a coffee can. "Yeah. You don't have to ask."

Samantha lifted herself from the sofa and dialed the num-ber on the card.

After the call, Samantha walked to the middle of the room and looked around at the end tables and the floors.

"What's with you?" Blaine asked. "You look like you've seen a ghost."

"You have a newspaper?"

Blaine pointed with his bowl at the tea cart near the door.

Underneath it was a stack of newspapers spilling over against the wall. Samantha crouched down and flipped through them. "Why do you get the paper if you never read it?"

"My father subscribed," Blaine said. "I feel sorry for the delivery boy and keep paying him. So what do you need?"

Samantha found the edition from last week and flipped through the sections as she took it back to the sofa.

Samantha found the article. It was four brief paragraphs about the deaths of two men in an auto accident on Old Denison Avenue. They both had been drinking at the Warsaw Tavern. As they drove home, the car flipped over, caught fire and incinerated them. There were no witnesses, and the medical examiner had ruled their deaths an accident.

Samantha handed the newspaper to Blaine.

"This thing about the Serbian festival?"

"No. The auto accident."

Blaine read the article and looked up at her. "Kind of reminds me of my dad's car accident."

"Those two men were the only witnesses for the boating accident that killed Lori."

"They saw what happened?"

"They saw the boat burning and called the Coast Guard."

"That's weird."

"I just talked to the reporter to tell her I want to help, and she told me to read this first. She thinks it's all related, but she doesn't know how."

"No shit."

"If we help, we could be in danger."

"What do you mean we?"

"Right. You don't have to help."

Blaine rocked in his recliner and dropped the newspaper to the floor. "Are you going to help?"

14

Aaron found himself on the front step again, watching the normalcy unfold around him. People came and went from their homes, driving cars, carrying shopping bags, hustling children back and forth. Kids made their way to school and played after, some hurrying home to drop their bags before coming out to play, others dropping their bags wherever they wanted to play.

Moms yelled from the front door when supper was ready. Dads sat on lawn chairs in their driveway, drinking beer, passing bottles. When people he knew waved, he nodded back to them.

He wanted to feel that normalcy he'd felt before the phone call, before Louise called him to the phone, before they knew Michael had died. But he couldn't find it.

"We have to pick out his clothes," Louise said from inside the screen door. "Should we go together?"

"If you want to, that's fine. But I can check some of my machines over that way and then stop in."

"You're going to go talk to that detective, aren't you?"

Aaron nodded. He'd left several messages for the detective, looking for information on what might have happened. "I still think he should look in Michael's apartment."

"Then I'm going to let you go alone," Louise said. "But you have to promise me you will mind your manners. We do not need more trouble right now. Do you hear me?"

Aaron nodded again, noticed she was crying, and went inside to hold on to her. He knew they would get through this together, but he wasn't sure how.

"I know that look," Louise said. "That detective is going to blame Michael. He's one of those, 'That's what you get for messing around' guys. You remember that principal of the school in Mt. Pleasant? That white man lived for lecturing black boys about what they'd done wrong. No matter who started it. No matter what had happened."

Aaron said nothing to dissuade Louise, but neither did he join in her complaints. He agreed with her, word for word. The principal of the school in Mt. Pleasant had ruined Michael. This Detective Wagner had the same smug, I'm better than you look on his face, the condescending asshole. But to join in her complaints would create a chorus of frustrations neither of them could contain.

They were steeped in more misery than they could handle already.

"If he's going to investigate, I just want to know. That's all. I will not bother trying to convince him what a good young man Michael had become. Someone may know that, but I don't think Detective Wagner will be the one."

Louise held him and rested her head on his shoulder. "We know the truth about Michael. He was a good boy, and a better young man."

"Yes, he was."

This led to tears, and they held each other for a couple of minutes.

Louise patted his back. "Don't do anything foolish. Remember we got two grand babies down in Columbus who will be back here tonight."

Detective Wagner came to the lobby, but he sat in the plastic chair across from Aaron, rather than invite him back to his desk. "Something I can help you with?"

Aaron took a breath. *In time. Not Now.*

This was the first time they'd met since the morgue. Aaron had almost forgotten how tired Wagner looked. His eyes were half-closed, and the skin bagged beneath. The jowls pulled his mouth into a frown. The hair remaining on his head drooped.

"I'm curious about the investigation. Do you have anything you can share?"

"You heard me say the coroner called it an accident, right? I mean, those guys are pretty good at what they do. Way smarter than me."

"But the case is not closed. You're still investigating?"

The detective leaned back in the seat, spreading his legs out before him. "Yeah, I gotta' tell you, in cases like this, with no witnesses, no obvious motive, I just don't see anything coming together."

"There must be something else you can do. You could look at Michael's apartment. Did you talk to the neighbors?"

"Nah. Haven't been over there just yet."

"But you will?" Aaron pulled a key on a fob from his pocket and offered it to the detective.

The detective shook his head. "If I feel the need to go in there, I'll check with the apartment manager."

Aaron wrapped both hands around the key. "You mind if I go in? We'd like to see about Michael's clothes for the funeral." Aaron lowered his head and stared at his clenched fists.

"Shouldn't be a problem," the detective said. "Of course, if you see something out of the ordinary, call me, try not to touch anything. I don't think it'll be an issue."

"You don't?"

"I've been a cop for a while now. You develop a sense in these things, if you see what I'm saying. Call it my instincts."

Aaron pocketed the key. He could tell the detective wanted him to go away, but Aaron wasn't quite ready yet. "The coroner's report."

"What about it?" The detective's voice sharpened.

"I'd like to look at it."

Detective Wagner shook his head. "Mr. Key, there's nothing in there will do you any good, okay? Nothing you want to see, nothing that's going to help you make sense of this tragic accident." He stood up. "Anything changes though, I'll let you know."

Michael's apartment was on the ground floor of a twelve-unit building, set off from the main parking lot on a loop of driveway of its own. An untended stand of trees and brush lined the outer edge of the driveway.

The apartments looked no better, and no worse, than what you'd find on Cleveland's east side. No reason to celebrate it as being better just by looking at it. Of course, most people would tell you it's the lower crime rate that makes it better. What they mean is that the people who live here are better than the people forced to live in a place with a higher crime rate.

They weren't wrong, but it sure wasn't fair.

How his son decided to live in the Village, and remained here for as long as he had, was a mystery. His warm, khaki skin looked olive under a certain light, and that had to help on this side of the river.

His large, brown eyes were speckled with gold, always danced with joy, even when things did not go his way. No one here would think of him as black unless he told them.

Aaron didn't want to think they had killed his son just for living here, but he also didn't know what else to think.

Michael had a job at a bank in Cleveland. He drove a Volkswagen. He golfed and played tennis. It sure seemed he had done everything possible to fit in.

Once inside the apartment, there was a stuffy smell, but nothing out of the ordinary. The place had been closed up for three days.

It was a standard, lousy apartment with a galley kitchen, an eating area, a so-called living room, and a sliding glass door on the opposite end. On the other side of the living room wall was the bedroom, and across from that, next to the kitchen, was the bathroom.

The place looked lived in but not messy. That was one

thing Aaron liked about Michael: he took care of his own stuff. Another thing he liked was that Michael didn't worry about other people's stuff.

Of course, Michael hadn't grown up with fancy things. He and Louise provided more than enough for their children, but they didn't have money for luxuries.

Here in Michael's apartment, there was a pizza box on the floor of the kitchen, upside down. Aaron nudged it open with his foot and it looked to be a full pizza in there, stuck to one side like someone had dropped it. A couple of dirty plates sat dry in the sink, and an empty wine bottle on the counter.

There was a bank statement and junk mail on the dining table. Michael's car keys sat upon them like a paper weight.

In the living area was a stack of Sports Illustrated magazines on the floor.

Next to the television was a stack of pictures. Aaron flipped through these, found what had to be Michael's girlfriend, the girl he'd mentioned but hadn't yet brought around to meet them.

Of course, now he'd never bring that girl around.

Aaron needed to sit down. The thought of his son, the little man he'd played with, raised, and loved so much, was overwhelming.

He flipped through those pictures again. The girl showed up several times. They were at a restaurant, at the zoo, and at a basketball game.

What was the last thing he and Michael had said to each other? It had been a week, at least, when they made plans to shop for new clothes. Michael was going to help him update his wardrobe.

The gaps between phone calls had grown too large, and the calls ended too soon, because he'd worried about the phone charges for calling across the city. Michael had been too busy with Rebecca. All the time he was hurrying to go do something with *Rebecca*.

Damn it. Aaron forced himself up and continued looking around.

The bed was unmade and there were clothes in front of the closet door. The bathroom was cleaner than Louise kept theirs, so the kid had been taking care of things.

Aaron's eyes filled with tears, and he sobbed, leaning against the frame of the bathroom door. The boy had been taking care of things. He didn't want to die. He *liked* it here.

It seemed like Michael walked out of his own apartment and hadn't come back.

So why would he have gone to the marina and stolen a boat with this white girl who wasn't his girlfriend?

The kid was smart. Maybe not Einstein, but who the hell was? Michael had his degree and was working as a teller in a bank. Why would he do something so dumb?

In the closet, the hangers were spaced by an inch, grouped as shirts, pants and jackets. At one end of the rod was a necktie hanger.

Selecting an outfit, Michael wasn't sure if he needed to bring underwear. Was that something you did? Put underwear on the dead before burying them? Of course. He found the dresser drawer and grabbed a T-shirt, underpants and socks.

For a young man just twenty-three years old, Michael had his shit together.

As Aaron approached the door to leave, he noticed a baseball cap on the floor pressed against the wall behind the door. It was sweat-stained and dirty, as if worn in a game. There were initials written in marker on the underside of the bill. Aaron didn't recognize the initials or the team logo on the cap.

He picked it up, though. The hat had to belong to someone other than Michael.

Reaching for his car door, Aaron thought about how he would explain all this to the detective. How could he make him understand that Michael wouldn't do something as foolish as get himself killed on a boat—

"Excuse me," a man said. It was a short guy with a dark complexion, maybe Lebanese or something like that.

"Yeah?"

"You don't live here."

Aaron opened his car door and stowed the clothing in the back seat, tossing the baseball cap and the pictures on the passenger seat. "No, I don't."

"Then what are you doing here?"

Aaron took a breath. "That's my son's apartment."

"And what was his name?"

"Michael Key. I was getting clothes for his funeral. Now tell me who the hell you are?"

"I'm the building manager."

A police cruiser pulled into the parking lot. Then another. Then a third. They all pulled up, boxing Aaron's car in.

"What the hell is your problem?" Aaron asked the man.

The man walked backwards between the police cruisers. "You are."

15

Francine called Robaroni while she ate a hamburger in the McDonald's parking lot just inside the border between Cleveland and The Village.

"Boy, are you lucky," he said. "I got you Michael Key's permanent record."

"Let's hear it."

"Nothing. Clean as a whistle."

"What about school, jobs...anything like that?"

Robaroni laughed. "What, do you think there's an actual permanent record that police have access to? That's just something your fifth-grade teacher told you to make you shut up in school."

"How about his address in the Village?"

"Okay that I have."

"Great," she said. "I never thought I'd do a story about the Village. It seemed so boring growing up there as a kid."

"You should have stuck around a little longer. If I learned one thing in high school, it's that I wanted to be a cop in Cleveland."

"Yikes."

Francine grew up in the far corner of the Village, with only three other kids on her street, and didn't go to school with them. She attended parochial school in Cleveland. She knew little about the Village and had assumed it was a quiet bedroom community.

The apartment complex where Michael lived was a complete surprise. She had no idea it existed.

The apartment building itself was bland. The design seemed to make it easy for residents to park their car near their door, which she appreciated. Toting groceries could be a pain at apartments.

She tried Michael's door but found it locked. A woman in the next-door apartment answered Francine's knocks.

"This is going to sound weird," Francine said, "but I'm a reporter and can you tell me anything about Michael Key, the young man who lived next door."

"Why, is he in trouble or something?" She was in her thirties, a little heavy but pretty, and dressed in slacks and a blouse. She lit a cigarette and offered one to Francine.

"He died last weekend in a boating accident."

"What? You're shitting me."

"I shit you not," Francine said, hoping to connect. "I'm writing a story about him."

The woman nodded as she blew smoke out of the side of her mouth. "I'll be God damned. I guess that explains this morning."

"What happened this morning?"

"The cops came and dragged away some black guy who was in the apartment. I didn't see nothin' until they put him in the car and drove off."

"Do you know what was the problem?"

"Daniel, that's the apartment manager, he said the black guy claimed to be Michael's father."

"That's interesting."

"I'll say. We don't get a lot of police here. It's not like in Cleveland, you know."

"Do you know who called the police?"

"Probably someone across the lawn. With the shades open, everybody can see your business, you know?"

Francine nodded, trying to keep the connection despite the

woman's hostile tone. "How was Michael as a neighbor?"

"Great. I hardly knew he was there. I saw him sometimes coming and going to work. My husband would chat with him and stuff, you know."

"Any problems before today?"

"Nope," the woman said. "I didn't even realize he was black until I saw his father. But then I saw a woman later this morning—I figure it was his mother—when they came back to pick up the black guy's car."

"You think they arrested him?"

"I don't know, and I don't want to know, to be honest."

"And last Friday evening, which is the night he died, anything out of the ordinary?"

"Well, now that you mention it, we heard a scuffle some time last week. It could have been that Friday, because it's been real quiet since then. My husband and I were already in bed."

"A scuffle?"

"Nothing big. It wasn't a fight. Just like someone dropped something and then some talking. They were trying to be quiet, which is nice because it's an apartment and all."

"Did you see anything or anyone?"

"My husband peeked out the peephole. He said it was just some guys going fishing. They had a boat."

"A boat?"

"I guess. You can talk to my husband when he gets home. Seems like that was a boat trip he shouldn't have taken."

"Thanks," Francine said. "This is very helpful."

Francine walked around the building and across the lawn to the apartment opposite Michael's. The lawn was a mere sixty paces. You could watch what happened across the lawn, as the other neighbor said. A voyeur's paradise, if you enjoy that sort of thing.

She knocked on the door. There were footsteps inside and Francine stepped back from the door.

"Who is it," a woman said from within.

Francine identified herself. "I'm working on a story about your neighbor who died last weekend out on the lake."

"Good for you."

"I only have a few questions and no one will even know—"

"Go away."

As Francine walked back across the lawn, a man approaching at a fast pace intercepted her.

"Excuse me," he said. "Who are you?" He was short and out of breath.

"You first," Francine said.

"I'm the apartment manager. I'm asking you to leave our residents alone."

"Oh, well, okay."

"Now who are you?"

Francine identified herself. "Mind if I ask you a few questions about Michael Key?"

"No. I don't want to talk to you about that."

"How about his father, who, I understand, the police arrested him earlier today?"

"You should go talk to the police about him. You want me to call them for you?"

Francine chuckled. "I get the distinct feeling you don't want to talk to me."

"That's right. I don't."

"Maybe I should just go, then."

"Yes. You should go."

# # # #

A few minutes after Francine was back at her desk, the phone rang. Hal, her boss, wanted to see her. She grabbed her Filofax before going to his office.

Hal revealed nothing to her as he sat back in his chair.

"Frannie," he said, using the nickname she hated. "You took a late lunch today, that right?"

"Yes. I had a personal errand."

"I heard there was someone asking around about Michael Key at his apartment today, in the Village. Was that you?"

She nodded.

"Remind me, who was it that told you about the Sykora girl's death?"

"I have my sources."

Hal nodded. "Don't piss off that family. They got connections everywhere around here. People think the sun shines out of the Mayor's ass."

"I think it's a story we should tell."

"You may be right. In fact, I walked the story upstairs and talked to the old man about it."

"What did he say?"

"The old man wants to go slow."

"Go slow? Why?"

"The old man thinks the sun shines out of the Mayor's ass, I guess."

"What about Tom, the chief of police?"

Hal scoffed. "That guy... Listen, that's a guy who doesn't think his own shit stinks. I recommend you don't get close enough to find out for yourself."

"So that's it?"

"That's it, Frannie."

"Thanks, Hal."

Back at her desk in the corner, Francine wanted to make at least one more call about the story, but it worried her who might overhear. Or if maybe they were listening to her calls. Did they do that?

She gathered the phone numbers she needed in her Filofax, prepared her questions, and slipped out of the office without talking to anyone else, and made her way to the Terminal Tower main concourse.

Built in the twenties and completed in the thirties, the Terminal Tower was still the tallest building in Cleveland. The interior reeked of art deco, but it needed a makeover.

What interested her the most were the two banks of old-fashioned phone booths in the concourse leading to the train platforms. The booths were wooden and sound proof with the door closed. Inside, there was a bench to plant your ass and a small writing desk below the phone.

She'd only used them once before, and only as an after thought. But once ensconced inside, she felt safe. She realized this was the place to make calls she didn't dare make at her crappy desk in the reporters' room.

There was a newspaper stand in the main concourse, and she picked up a copy of the Times, bought a few packs of gum, and asked the man at the counter to make change for a few extra dollars.

The onion-faced man, wearing a cap to contain wisps of unruly white hair, handed her the change without comment.

The phone booth smelled of varnish and old shoes. The ceiling light didn't work, but she had enough light through the glass slits in the door to read her notes.

The first number in her Filofax was for the coroner. She didn't expect to get through, but she would try to get close. The secretary put her on hold.

"What is this regarding?" The secretary asked a minute later.

"Lori Sykora."

"We don't comment on current investigations until we determine its status." She hung up.

Robaroni had given her the detective's name. It seemed as if cops were as chatty and catty as anybody else, and Robaroni wanted to be told anything she found out so he could share it around the district.

Calling the main number for District Two of the Cleveland Police, and asking for Detective Wagner, the secretary who answered stumped Francine by asking her name. Francine almost used her own name and stammered until she found the fake one she had concocted and written in her notebook.

"Connie Jones." It seemed clever when she'd picked it, but saying it aloud sounded like a made-up name.

"What's your number?"

She was ready for this and gave the number of the pay phone. With the gum she'd bought, she would wait at least an hour.

She called the Village police next and asked for the Chief of Police, Tom Sykora. "This is Connie Jones from The Press."

"May I ask what this is regarding?" The secretary asked.

"The recent boating accident on the lake involving Lori Sykora."

"Please hold."

Her tone worried Francine. The phone booth didn't feel as safe as it felt before placing the call, and she looked out the window in the door to see if anyone was watching her.

"Mind your own business," the secretary said and hung up.

What worried Francine the most was that this stalling and stone-walling would allow a story to slip away. Regardless of the truth, the story lost relevance quickly. Another story would come along, and no one would care much about what had happened to these two young people on a boat in the middle of the night.

She felt that she owed it to those two young people whom she'd never met to discover their truth and reveal it, whether or not anyone would care.

Her next call would matter the most.

# # # #

Francine inserted a dime into the phone and asked the operator to place a person-to-person call to Julie Lawrence.

Julie's father, Richard Lawrence, answered, and waited while Francine put in three more dimes.

"May I ask what this is regarding?" Richard asked after Francine introduced herself.

"I'm doing a story about your daughter's roommate, Lori Sykora."

"How much do you know about that family," he asked.

"Not a lot," she said. "It seems like it's going to be difficult to learn more. They don't seem to like any publicity unless they deliver it."

"I'll put Julie on the phone. But I'm going to listen in, if that's alright."

"I have a hunch that's my only option."

"It is," he said.

Julie sounded tired and sad, like she was very much at a loss without her friend. "I felt honored that she was my friend and roommate," she said. "She was the nicest person in the world, but she could also be as tough as they come. She was very competitive."

"And she hadn't been dating this Michael Key, as far as you knew."

"Lori never mentioned him."

"Would she have mentioned him, if they were dating?"

"Yes," Julie said. "We talked about that kind of stuff."

"Did she talk about her friend, Rebecca Marko?"

"Yes, a little."

"Was Lori in the habit of taking the Marko's boat?"

Richard spoke up. "That's going to be it, I'm afraid."

"I'm sorry," Francine said. "Was something wrong with that question."

"It seems to me there is something not quite right about the entire matter," he said. "I don't want Julie involved any more than she has to be."

"I only want to get the truth, and I'll keep her name out of it. Not even in my notes."

Richard cleared his throat. "How familiar are you with the history of the Sykoras and their city, the Village, as it's called?"

"Like I said, I don't know a lot. It's embarrassing because I grew up there, at least until I was thirteen."

"I recommend you dig into their past," he said. "I've looked into it deep enough that I don't want Julie too close to them."

"Okay. I guess I'll do that."

"I recommend you don't get too close either."

16

L ater that afternoon, Francine sat at her desk writing up a blurb about a singing competition for high school students, thinking about how to proceed.

Murray was chatting with a sports reporter and glanced over at Francine when he returned to his desk.

She called him. "I need advice," she said.

"What's this regarding?"

"That story we discussed."

"Whose story?"

"My story."

"Okay," Murray said. "Now you're talking. What's going on?"

"Talked to a friend of the deceased, and she implied there's more to know about the Village, that I should look into its history."

"I agree with that. So how can I help?"

"Would you ask Hal to assign me as your research assistant on a story? I need to get into the clip file down in the stacks, but I don't want to use the researchers down there."

"You're thinking they might tell Hal what you're doing?"

"No, but they don't like people messing with stuff. And they talk a lot."

"That's good," Murray said. "Anything else?"

"I may need to track down information at the county for property titles, and more at the library. So the cover story will have to cover that possibility."

The stacks were the rows of shelves, seven feet high, running the length of a room covering most of the third floor. It was a library for the reporters' research needs, covering Ohio and American history.

Almanacs and official government publications, going as far as possible, took up a good amount of shelving. You needed to look up one of the farmer's almanacs from before statehood? There were three to choose from once you found the correct shelf.

There were also state laws, records of the legislature, and The Congressional Record.

Along with all those publications were the collections of newspapers, their own and all their competitors, going back as far as possible.

But the most important space was the clip file collection, which were the articles clipped from old editions and filed under topics.

Of course, the clip file collection was useless without an index. The staff there updated the index each time they made a search, citing the date, topics and the individuals named. They filed duplicate index cards under each of those categories, noting the location of the article and updating cards for retrieved articles.

Francine spent her first eighteen months with the newspaper in the clip file, delivering research for reporters. It wasn't her dream job, and she was the only researcher with a journalism degree. Two of the ladies had degrees in library science, as did her boss, but most of them had backed into the job and stayed for no good reason other than the paycheck.

She'd gotten to know the reporters, though, and developed an affinity for Murray, who treated her as if he had daughters of his own that he cared about.

So the next morning, when she returned, was exciting. She had learned to love the stacks, the smell of paper, and the quiet murmur of voices. It was like moving through past civilization here in northern Ohio.

Also, it was frustrating when things went missing. Some research projects were quick and easy; others, impossible.

Her old boss was still the boss and welcomed her with a smile. "You missed us, didn't you?"

"Of course I did."

"We could pull these for you. We're not that busy."

"Well, it's something I'm helping Murray with. He's kind of mentoring me, so..."

Her boss smiled and nodded. "If you ever need to come back, we'll find a spot for you."

"I appreciate that."

Francine was careful not to overstay her welcome, though. If she lingered, people would grow curious and offer to help.

Murray had come up with a brilliant idea, researching the history of the four large corporations on the edge of the Village, and how it had a positive impact on greater Cleveland. Murry wrote similar puff-pieces in the past, and the multiple subjects to research provided cover.

Francine spent two and half hours researching, and almost an hour catching up with the other ladies. When articles were missing, she didn't even mention it; just made a brief note for herself and kept looking.

In the afternoon, she visited the news stand in the Terminal Tower concourse, and got herself a bunch of quarters. Then, with the clip file tucked in her shoulder bag, she walked the three blocks to the Cleveland Public Library.

It was a sunny afternoon, and the walk was pleasant. Office workers crowded the sidewalks of this part of downtown, from Public Square to the library, coming from and going to taverns, shops and restaurants. She stayed vigilant, though, as Robaroni reminded her almost daily that crimes happened every day close to that area, and to look like a victim was to invite attack.

The library had its own newspaper collection and a clip file in the stacks. She'd gotten researcher access before, and the librarian didn't question her motives or credentials.

This search was far more enjoyable. Without the worry of coworkers wondering if she were alive, she was free to chase a few leads to other stories and related subjects.

The Village, she learned, had been unincorporated land, managed by the county, through World War I. During the twenties, as Cleveland grew in prosperity, the city attempted to annex the nearby area known as the "Village." Inspired or wary, those in the Village voted to organize themselves and applied to the county and the State for recognition as a municipality.

The Village council's president, Yura Bargiel, seemed to focus his attention that first year on a festival celebrating the Village's recognition. The next year, he threw an even bigger festival that coincided with his daughter's marriage to Peter Sykora.

There is no mention of the Village until the following year, 1932, when Yura died of alcohol poisoning. The article suggested that the booze came from an illegal still, but there was no mention of any investigation by the county sheriff.

Peter Sykora took over as president of the Village's council. He was twenty-seven years old.

In 1933, on the eve of the end of prohibition, Peter changed the village into a city, and was elected the first mayor.

Forty-six years later, he was still the mayor.

And Francine now had a manila folder stuffed with Xeroxed copies of clipped articles painting an interesting picture of his leadership and the business owners associated with him and the Village.

17

Aaron lingered in bed on Sunday. From the light pouring in through the windows, he guessed it to be ten o'clock, if not later. On any normal Sunday, Louise would be at the dressing table finishing her makeup for church.

His throat tightened with every breath, as if he might cough or retch. He felt tired but couldn't sleep any longer. He hadn't had a decent night of sleep in three weeks now, dozing for an hour at a time, then lying awake for twenty minutes, forty minutes—who knew—before dozing again.

It was just as bad for Louise, who turned and heaved a sigh as often as not while Aaron stared at the ceiling during the night.

The sound of their grandchildren playing in the front room dragged him from the bed.

While his daughter cleared the breakfast table, and her husband washed dishes, Louise sat at the table reading to the littlest one.

The newspaper was within reach, but he didn't feel like reading. Nothing about the world outside of the people in this house mattered to him at this moment.

"When are you leaving?" he asked.

"Soon," Alina said. "We both work tomorrow and we must take care of things for this week."

"Of course."

"I hope you don't mind," she said. "I can come back again, if it'd help."

"We have to figure this out."

Louise set Alicia down on the blanket as she fussed and went in search of a bottle. "I thought I was doing us all a favor by skipping church today, but that article in the paper about Michael tells me the devil is celebrating today."

Aaron reached for the paper. The article implied that an inner-city black kid from a broken home duped the good white girl from the suburbs and she'd died in a drug-fueled disaster because of Michael.

"That story is a gigantic pile of bullshit, if you'll pardon my French."

Louise sat at the table with Alicia and gave her the bottle. "I'm not defending that woman one bit," she said, "but I noticed the article had no byline."

"Don't that mean she was too ashamed to put her name on it?"

"I don't think so."

Aaron took a deep breath and wound the newspaper in his fist. "I hope I get a chance to ask that woman myself."

"If you do, you'll remember to be kind, and that she may have little control over what happens at that newspaper."

Later that afternoon, after their daughter's family had left, Louise napped in their bedroom while Aaron watched the Indians game. The phone rang and Aaron picked it up on the first ring so as not to wake up his wife.

"Hello?"

"Mr. Key?" a woman's voice said. "This is Francine Tennyson, and I'd like to apologize."

"Oh?"

"Yes sir," she said. "I had no part in that. In fact, my editor knew I was working on an article, but told me nothing of what they published. I don't even know who wrote it."

"Find out who so I can punch that person in the nose. Of course, my wife would't forgive me if I did."

"I would forgive you," Francine said.

"Well then, we'll just leave it in the Lord's hands whether

he brings me in contact with the author."

After a momentary pause, Francine said, "I have one other thing to discuss. Would you meet with me to discuss my investigation?"

The next day, Aaron resumed his rounds but needed to get to his warehouse to resupply his stock on hand. At least a few of his vending machines would be empty by now, and some may be damaged. When a man who needs a smoke can't get cigarettes, he will take it out on the machine that's pissing him off.

Rather than run himself ragged going back and forth to the warehouse, he visited all of his machines first and prioritized the stock. A larger operation would load up a van before making the rounds, but he only had his Coupe DeVille. The trunk was enormous, but he couldn't restock his entire string at once.

He thought of his machines as an empire scattered across the east side of Cleveland, from Murray Hill and University Circle, down to Mt. Pleasant and Corlett, and over into North and South Broadway. It was important to show up and let the proprietors know he had not abandoned his machines. He had learned the hard way that business owners serving the public have little or no loyalty to the vending machine managers renting their space. You let someone else get their foot in the door, and it was nigh upon impossible to get them out of there.

Francine Tennyson had tried to get him to meet during the day downtown, so she could slip out during her lunch hour.

"I have no business in downtown," he said. "I'd love to, but I may never crack that market. You want to talk to me, you'd best come my way. If you dare."

They planned the meeting for four o'clock at the self-storage facility where he rented a full-size unit. There were four people waiting for him outside the gate when he arrived, the reporter being the only person he knew.

"We each brought a friend," Francine said. "This in Rob Maroni. He's a Cleveland Police Officer."

Aaron shook the cop's hand and exchanged nods. It

seemed the reporter and the cop were dating.

The other two people were younger. Kids, in fact.

"This is Samantha Sykora and her friend, Blaine Taylor."

"Lori was my sister," Samantha said. "I'm sorry for your loss."

"I'm sorry for yours, as well."

There was an awkward pause that Aaron was all too familiar with. Dealing with white people over the years, they were often unsure of what to say, or afraid to say the wrong thing, or just plain afraid. The cop was on full cop mode, the reporter seemed interested, and the boy, Plain or whatever his name was, looked scared, like he didn't get out much.

This Samantha was hurting, and the look in her eyes reminded him of the pain he saw in his wife's eyes.

Best to get busy, though, to help the white people through their awkwardness. Aaron unlocked the gate and directed them to follow in their car to his storage unit. He'd said the only way he would meet is if it could be while he re-stocked, but now he felt bad about dragging so many people out to a God-forsaken part of Cuyahoga Heights, just south of Cleveland.

Once he unlocked and lifted the storage unit door, he tore open a box of candy and passed it around. "Anyone wants a pop, help yourself. It's warm, but it's free."

Aaron wished he had chairs to offer them. "Maybe this was a bad idea, dragging you out here."

As Aaron opened the trunk of his car, the visitors leaned against Francine's car, making themselves as comfortable as possible.

"I appreciate you making the time," Francine said. "But I'm curious now what you do."

"I own and operate vending machines," Aaron said. He pointed to the back corner where he had two cigarette machines and a candy machine. "I rent space in businesses, put a machine in there, and keep it stocked."

"That's cool," Blaine said as he helped himself to a warm can of Coke.

"It's like any job. Gets to be a grind." Aaron handed him his pick list. "If you want to make five bucks, go pull all this inventory and load it in my trunk."

Blaine poked around the boxes, looking for items. As he found them, he counted and loaded them into the Cadillac's trunk.

Francine had opened a notebook and stood a little closer. "I've been doing a bit of research, and I thought you all should hear it. But first, Mr. Key, I want to make sure you are aware of what happened last week."

She explained how the witnesses who contacted the Coast Guard about the burning boat were themselves killed in a burning car accident.

"I talked to them before they died. They described a man who was at the boat launch to me, and the man's description matched one man from the Village Service Department who I witnessed picking up the recovered wreckage of the boat from the Coast Guard."

Blaine took a break from digging through the boxes. "You saw a guy from the Service Department?"

She described the man to Blaine. It sounded like every description of every white guy Aaron had ever heard, but Blaine recognized him.

"Sounds like Yakov," Blaine said. "Was there a big guy, white hair, wide jaw, wide nose with him?"

"Yes," Francine said. "He wore a wind breaker."

"That's Milosh. He's the Service Department Director."

"So did they do it?" Aaron asked. "Or are they covering up for someone else?"

"It seems like at least this Yakov had something to do with it."

Aaron scoffed. "It seems like we might get killed for talking to you."

"I don't think so, but I also don't know what we're dealing with. Something very strange happened, and the Cleveland police, the Medical Examiner and the District Attorney are not interested in finding out what."

"Tell them about my family," Samantha said.

"What about your family?" Aaron asked.

"Samantha's grandfather is the mayor of the Village, her uncle is the Chief of Police, and her father is a police officer."

"Family business, huh?"

"Her Aunt Jan is the assistant bank manager," Blaine said.

"What bank?" Aaron asked.

"The city's bank," Francine said. "During the Great Depression, when no one trusted banks, the Village established a municipal bank."

"Does every resident get a toaster?" Aaron asked. "Or just the white folks?"

"I never got a toaster," Blaine said as he carried a box of cigarettes to the car.

Aaron looked at Francine. "All I'm hearing is that things in the Village are like things everywhere, and I shouldn't get too hopeful about getting any answers."

"We may need to find our own answers," Francine said.

Blaine closed the trunk of the Cadillac and offered Aaron the pick list. "All set."

Aaron opened the trunk again. "I appreciate your confidence, but I'm going to check your work before I pay you."

"I guess what I'm saying," Francine said, "is that I'm going to keep digging for answers, but I may need help. I have a lot of information about the history of the Village. Peter Sykora has been the only mayor, going on forty years now, and he's connected throughout Cuyahoga County, the city of Cleveland, and the state of Ohio."

"I know for a fact that his son asked for Detective Wagner to investigate the incident," Rob, the boyfriend said.

The guy had been so quiet that Aaron had forgotten the guy knew how to talk. "Is that because he's such a skilled detective?"

"Nope," Rob said. "He's pretty useless. I don't know how he ever made detective, because I don't think he's ever solved a case."

"Again," Aaron said, "I'm not getting too hopeful here."

"So it may take us quite a while to discover anything about

this case," Francine said. "I wish I could be more confident, but I'm afraid that's the way it is."

After checking the inventory pulled and loaded into the trunk of his car, Aaron gave Blaine five dollars. "I won't mention any of what we just talked about to my wife, because she's worried about things getting worse than they already are."

"I understand," Francine said.

"But I would like to see the coroner's report," Aaron said. "Do you think you could work on that?'

Francine nodded. "I can put in a Freedom of Information Act request."

"You're going to ask the government to send you the information?"

"I am."

"How long will that take?"

"Could be weeks," Francine said.

"The coroner has to send it to you?"

"No," she said. "The Medical Examiner can cite reasons for not sharing it, and they can also redact it."

"I'm going to go out on a limb and just assume you won't get it."

"He might send it."

"Has your research discovered anything about the Medical Examiner?"

"Well..."

"Let's hear it."

"The Medical Examiner is an elected official. Peter Sykora, the mayor of the Village supported him. In fact, when my newspaper's editorial board endorsed him, it was after Mayor Sykora visited the publisher." Francine turned to Samantha and said, "I learned that second-hand so take it with a grain of salt."

Samantha shrugged. "I'm learning a lot about my family."

"Well, this has been interesting," Aaron said, "but I need to go load up my vending machines or I will be in some deep financial shit next week."

"I'll call you when I learn something," Francine said.

"I won't hold my breath."

18

aron waited in his Cadillac parked at the Medical Examiner's office. It was approaching five o'clock, closing time, and he watched the people leaving the building, but not so he drew attention to himself.

The coroner and his secretary walked out and split up as they walked toward their cars. The secretary waved goodbye, and the coroner nodded in reply.

"Excuse me," Aaron said as he got out of his car, parked behind the coroner's. He tried to be as friendly as possible, but the look of terror on the coroner's face was a bad way to start. "Do you remember me? I just need to ask you one thing."

"Ervin?" The secretary called from across the parking lot. "You okay? You want me to call the police?"

Aaron shot her a look but bit his tongue. "My son died. I came here with my wife."

"Oh," the coroner said, breathing at last. "Yes, of course."

"I'm calling the police," the secretary hurried to the front door of the building.

"I will not hurt you," Aaron said. "Okay?"

"If you'd like to talk, it'd be better to stop by tomorrow."

"It's a simple question, doc. I just want to see the report on my son. You said it was an accident, but I just wanted to read about it myself."

"Well, no. That's not how these things work."

Aaron took a step closer. The coroner's eyes widened. But

maybe that would help. "How do these things work?"

"We only share them with the District Attorney or the police, if we feel it warrants an investigation."

"Are they investigating who killed my son?"

"I called the police," the secretary shouted from the door. "You better leave him alone."

"I have little time," Aaron said. "It's in your best interests to let me see it, or get me a copy."

"That can't happen."

Aaron took another step closer, putting the coroner, who leaned against the side of his car, within arm's reach.

"There are rules," the coroner said.

"Someone broke the rules and killed my son. I want to know who, and all you have to do is show me the report."

"Even if I had it, I couldn't show you. I could get in trouble."

"Who has it then?"

"The cops will be here any second," the secretary shouted.

"Just tell me who has it."

"Detective Wagner," the coroner said, his voice shaking. "He has it all."

Aaron recognized the truth in the little man's words. There was desperation and worry in the voice, but not because he was lying. "Sounds like you broke a rule, doc."

"Take it up with Wagner, then. Leave me alone."

"Thanks for your time, doc."

Aaron smiled and waved at the secretary as he got in his car.

# # # #

Aaron knew that he might make a fatal mistake. If any of the options seemed even a little better, he would take that option.

Instead, he was driving into a white neighborhood to drop in unannounced on a cop. What he heard from Francine's cop friend, Rob, was that the guy was a lousy cop. Nothing more dangerous than a lousy cop.

He parked the Cadillac across the street from the cop's house.

The houses were no nicer than where he and Louise lived. Maybe a little worse, as he saw several front yards that needed work, and a few shutters that could use some paint.

Aaron knocked and then moved back down the steps so there'd be no surprises. The drape in the front window shifted, no doubt Wagner taking a peek. An old, single cop like this got few visitors, if any.

The door opened and Wagner stared out at him. One hand was on the door, but the other was inside the house, out of view. "What the fuck do you want?"

Aaron kept both of his hands in front of him. "I want to see the coroner's report on my son, Michael. I want to know what evidence there is."

Wagner glanced up and down the street. They were alone. "There ain't nothin' to see, buddy. Sorry to have to tell you, but it was just a tragic accident. The coroner's report ain't gonna' change that, so—"

"I want to see for myself. He was my son. He was all that I had."

"No hobbies, huh?"

Aaron refused to take the bait. "I'm asking you, man-to-man, to let me see the report. If someone hurt my son, I want to know about it."

"Don't give me this man-to-man bullshit. I'm investigating the case and if I determine something was wrong, I'll let you know. That's it. That's how it works."

"You know what I'm talking about," Aaron said.

The hand Wagner had kept inside the house fell to his side, revealing his 38 Special police revolver. "Unless you back away from my front door, I'm going to drop you where you stand."

"Please," Aaron said. "I'm asking for your help. Are you a father? Do you know what I'm saying?"

"Never had kids, buddy. I was planning on working a few more years, but I'm eligible for retirement, too. So even if the captain ain't happy with me dropping you, I'm pretty sure I'll have enough money to go sit on a fucking beach in motherfucking Florida and watch the young pussy walk by. So get off of my property."

Aaron took a step back. "I'm going to see that report."

"I'm going to make this easy on you," Wagner said. "The report is with the Village police department. They're doing some investigation because, you know, your son and the girl both lived there. We figure they might figure something out."

"So I'll go ask him."

"Don't waste your breath. I looked into it. I did, buddy. There ain't nothing there. It was just a stupid accident. I'm sorry your son died, but you should just let it go."

Wagner stared at Aaron while he backed away and got in the car.

Aaron stayed tense, following traffic signals to a fault, until he was back in his neighborhood.

When he sat down to dinner with Louise, she said, "Are you okay? You don't seem yourself."

"I'm fine," he said. "Just thinking about something."

"Think about it tomorrow. Count your blessings today."

Aaron nodded. "Thank you, sweetheart. That's excellent advice."

19

At the Monday morning editorial meeting, Francine was quiet. Hal didn't talk to her. He didn't even look at her. "Everybody know what they're doing?" Hal asked as he closed his folder and pushed away from the conference table.

"What about the Sykora death?" Francine asked.

Hal froze and closed his eyes for a second. Without looking at her, he said, "Let's talk in my office."

"Fine."

Hal got there first and stood by the door, closing it once she came in. He remained there at the door, one hand gripping the handle, so Francine knew better than to sit down.

"What's going on?" he asked.

"The families buried their children, but there's still no official statement from the police, the Medical Examiner or the District Attorney."

"Maybe because there's no statement."

"My sources tell me the toxicology report is complete, which means the Medical Examiner can complete, and make public his findings."

Hal heaved a sigh and shook his head.

"But I think there's a story there," she said. "An excellent story I want to cover."

"There's no story that this paper wants to cover."

Francine sat at the desk and folded her arms, waiting to speak until Hal sat down.

"There's more to this story than most things we cover," she said. "The dereliction of duty by the Cleveland Police itself is a story. I mean, they haven't done a God damn thing. But I believe the Village Chief of Police knows something about it and is protecting someone involved."

"Your sources again?" Hal shook his head. "Are you sure you want to go there?"

"I want to investigate and find out."

"You're the only person interested in this story. If the Medical Examiner, or the District Attorney, or—"

"That's part of the story," Francine said. "His Honor, Mayor Peter Sykora, everybody's favorite old politician, helped both the District Attorney and the Medical Examiner get elected. That guy is in on every deal in northern Ohio."

"Right there, if that mayor thought this needed more attention, he could muster troops better than the God damn mayor of Cleveland."

"Just let me investigate, on behalf of this newspaper, and use the resources here. I can't do it on my own."

Hal shook his head.

"Will you at least take it upstairs?"

"Are you certain you want me to do that?"

Francine thought for a moment. Hal's voice seemed grave and foreboding, but she was certain that her integrity as a reporter required just one answer. "Yes."

"Okay. I'll let you know."

Back at her desk, staring at the notes in her Filofax, Francine wasn't so sure anymore. Maybe she shouldn't have asked Hal to take the story upstairs.

She should have talked with Murray, first.

Francine made her way over to Murray's desk and explained to him what she'd done. She opened her Filofax on his desk and flipped to her list of participants. "It's gotten big, and I'm not even sure I can handle this."

"Of course you can," he said.

As Murray adjusted his reading glasses to review her notes, Hal walked up to them.

"Can I see you a minute?" Hal asked her and motioned with his head towards his office.

Not feeling confident, Francine left her notebook on Murray's desk.

Back in Hal's office, he wasted no time.

"I'm sorry," he said. "But I've got to let you go. We'll give you two weeks severance pay and..."

She heard little of what he said. When he stopped talking, she noticed him staring. "I can't believe you're doing this."

"I'm sorry. You're a fine reporter and you would have done well, but..."

"But I should have left this story about the Sykora crime family alone?"

"Okay, you see, right there?"

She didn't want to, but she couldn't stop herself from choking up. It was anger more than anything. Of course he wouldn't understand that.

Francine got up and opened the door. There was a security guard waiting for her. He held her jacket and purse in his hand.

"Do you mind if I go back to my desk?" she asked.

"Sorry," Hal said. "Company policy. You can wait downstairs in the lobby, and Security will get whatever you need."

"But it's my desk."

"Everything in the desk that's not a personal belonging is owned by the newspaper, so..."

"Fine."

Francine, burning with humiliation, walked to the elevators, followed by the security guard.

She sat in the phone booth in the Terminal Tower and cried on and off for almost an hour. When that was over, her first call was to Murray, and they met at the tavern across the square.

Murray offered to buy her a drink, but Francine knew that would only make her tired and likely to cry again. That didn't stop Murray. "I'll have a whisky, neat."

He took her notebook out of his briefcase and handed it over. "I didn't look at anything else," he said. "In fact, I buried it as fast as I could, once Hal took you away. I worried this might happen."

"Thanks," Francine said. "Has he done this a lot?"

"Only once before, a long time ago. But I remembered the look in his eyes."

"I think I'm still in shock."

"Take your time with that," he said. "But when you're done, at least you know there's a story here."

"Sure. But I won't have any place to publish it."

"Oh, I think you'll find a place for it. Something like this could go big."

"I guess."

"You know it will, but you have to get the story. Make sure you get it all and don't rush because of a deadline."

"No problem there."

"And for God's sake, be careful. This is one that will stink worse the deeper you dig."

"So what should I do?"

"Learn to dig while holding your nose."

# # # #

Francine felt an overwhelming need to go to the Village for dinner. She and Robaroni ate at the burger joint near the park, leaning on the side of his car, just down the road from city hall.

"It seems so peaceful," she said, pointing with her wrapper at the kids playing in the front yards all along the street.

"It's like quiet guys," Robaroni said. "Those are the ones you have to watch."

"My family never did this when I lived here. Did yours?"

"Not for dinner. But I rode my bike up here for swimming lessons, and I'd eat lunch sitting on the side of the building, right over there, in the shade. Then after swimming I'd come back for ice cream before biking home."

They got ice cream and walked past city hall and into the park. The pool wasn't open yet, but there were children at the playground, on their own, as no adults seemed to watch them.

Drawn like moths to the flame, they continued on past the swimming pool to the softball diamond, where the evening games had started.

They sat in bleachers behind the fence in center field. The stands around the infield were full, and kids surrounded the concession stand behind home plate.

"Isn't this a school night?" she commented, not expecting an answer.

"It's the smell of popcorn," Robaroni said. "No one can stay away from that."

They watched a few innings, and then Francine had seen enough. If anyone in the city cared about the loss of two residents in a bizarre boating accident, you wouldn't know it watching the crowd at the game.

"You want to go?"

Robaroni shook his head. "Do you realize that we're watching the policemen versus the firemen? This is some serious bragging rights being decided early in the season."

"I was unaware."

Rob pointed to the right field bleachers, where several uniformed cops sat, and the left field bleachers, where on-duty firemen sat watching as well.

"I guess this would be a great time to rob the municipal bank," she said.

"And burn it to the ground."

As she was about to suggest they leave one more time, Samantha and Blaine climbed onto the bleachers. They all looked with surprise at each other.

"We should talk," Francine said.

"Okay," Samantha said. "I could use that."

"But not here," Blaine said, and nodded with his head back over at the tennis courts.

The white-haired, thick-necked man she'd seen gathering up the boat wreckage leaned against the fence, and glanced over at them.

"That's Milosh, right?"

Blaine nodded. "My boss."

"What's he going to do?" Samantha asked.

"Nothing, I hope," Francine said. "But let's meet at the Friendly's Restaurant on Middleburg Road."

# # # #

It was after eight o'clock when Samantha and Blaine joined them at the restaurant.

"Did something happen?" Samantha asked.

"They fired me from my job," Francine said.

"Why?"

"Insisting that I work on this story."

"Shit. I'm sorry."

Francine offered a smile. "Now I'll have time to work on the story."

"I still feel guilty."

"It's okay."

"Should I talk to my grandfather or something? Maybe he knows the publisher guy."

"No," Francine said. "Thank you, but no. In fact, don't mention that you talked to me, and don't ask for any favors."

"So what do we do?"

"What do you know about Milosh?" Francine asked.

"He's a dick," Blaine said. "Loves to catch us goofing off on the job. It's like he hates everyone."

"Do you know where he lives?" Francine asked.

"No, but I can find out."

"Don't be obvious," Robaroni said. "We don't know who we can trust."

"I don't trust Milosh," Blaine said.

"What about the other guy," Francine said. "Jakov."

"Everybody knows where he lives," Blaine said. "Above the Kingdom."

"Him?" Robaroni said. "That's Jakov?"

Francine turned to look at him. "Wait, you know about Jakov?"

"I know of the guy who creeped around the Kingdom and cooked corn mash whiskey down there. We used to party down in the Kingdom during high school. Is that shack still there?"

Blaine nodded. "As far as I know, but I never got that close."

"Me neither," Samantha said. "But I think Lori and Rebecca did once."

"When was that?" Francine asked.

Samantha shrugged. "Some stupid party in high school. For all I know, my friends were down there last week. It's a kind of rite of passage for seniors. But not for me."

"Me neither," Blaine said.

"There are stories in the newspaper from the forties and fifties about killings and disappearances around the Kingdom."

"What I heard," Blaine said, "is that Jakov builds a big fire and burns the bodies. Anybody gets too close, they go in the fire."

"I don't believe that," Samantha said.

"Should we go ask Jakov right now?"

"That's not the point."

"The interesting thing," Francine said, "is that the deed of the Kingdom belongs to a corporation in Delaware. It lists the contact as a law firm, also out of Delaware."

"Then it belongs to Samantha's grandfather," Blaine said. "That's another of the rumors."

"He does not," Samantha said. "People think he's rich, but he's not. His house is no bigger than yours or mine."

They were quiet for a few moments, and Francine had an idea. "I think I should go there and have a look around. Anybody want to go along?"

Robaroni nodded. "I'm on swing shift tomorrow."

"Make sure Jakov is not around," Blaine said. "He gets ornery as hell around the garage. I'm sure he's a lunatic down in the Kingdom."

"How will we know whether he's home?"

"Drive past the service garage. If his piece of shit, black Ford LTD is by the gate, then you know he made it to work."

# # # #

Francine and Robaroni prepared for their adventure by having a leisurely breakfast at a diner near her house. As Francine indulged in a second cup of coffee, Robaroni drummed with his fingers on the table.

"Do you mind?"

"I want to get going," he said.

"I was thinking we need a cover story."

"What?"

"In case someone sees us down there, we should have picnic stuff, so we have a reason to be down there."

"Fine."

They picked up a few things at a supermarket. As they dropped them in the trunk of Robaroni's car, Francine said, "Do you have a blanket? If we have a blanket, it'll look more like a picnic."

"Now you're just stalling."

"Am I?"

"Yes. Are you scared?"

"A little."

"Good. A little scared is good. Keeps you on your toes."

"Do you have your gun?"

"We're going to the Metropark, not Glendale."

"Yeah, but do you?"

"Let me worry about that."

"Okay. Fine."

Robaroni slowed down as he passed the Village Municipal

Bank. It was a plain brick building, lacking the columns and gothic elements of banks built before the war. It didn't look like a bank at all.

"How much cash is in there?"

Francine thought for a moment. "They do a weekly payroll, and there are about three-hundred city employees, so we should be able to do the math."

The Service Garage was a mile further along the same road. They built it in the same style as the bank—a large, brick rectangle—but had truck-sized doors along the side.

Robaroni slowed down and pulled onto the driveway's apron.

"Is that the car?" Francine said.

Just inside the gate, parked along the chain-link fence, was a Ford LTD. "Looks like it's a former police interceptor," Robaroni said. "And that he painted it with a brush."

The Metropark entrance was two miles further along after that. The paved driveway turned into gravel as it wound its way down the hill. At the bottom was a circular parking lot. The recreation area was a vast lawn surrounded by trees. A pavilion stood in the middle of the lawn, surrounded by barbecue grills and picnic tables.

"This is lovely." Through a gap in the trees was a stream, and beyond that a thick stand of woods. "Is that the Cuyahoga River?"

"Old Man Creek," Robaroni said. "But don't worry. I have my gun."

"Is no one here?"

"Kids have school, adults have jobs."

They set their lunch on a picnic table and started walking.

Beyond the pavilion was playground equipment, and beyond that a wide lawn with a backstop in one corner.

They came to the spot where the hill pinched in close to the stream, and it seemed this was the end of the park. They made their way along the shore and then the hill angled away.

"This is where the Kingdom begins," Robaroni said.

"You would party out here?"

"More than once. It wasn't easy getting the keg this far, but it also meant cops weren't likely to show up."

They made their way along an overgrown trail through the woods. Thorns caught at Francine's sleeve, and she worried about having to hurry back the other way if they encountered something ahead.

"Wait, why wouldn't the cops show up?"

"The Metropark is in Cleveland, but now we're back in the Village."

"Why wouldn't the Village cops raid the party?"

"You'll see."

At last the thick brush of the woods gave way, and they emerged into a meadow with trees scattered around. The stream was on one side. The steep hill was on the other.

"Right there," Robaroni said, and pointed to the charred remains of a fire. "I'd say there was a party not that long ago."

"What about Jakov?"

"Up ahead."

They crossed the meadow and entered another stand of woods, thicker than the previous one. They emerged into an open area with fewer trees and less fallen limbs and brush.

"It's nice here."

"Jakov gathers up the limbs for his fires, clears stuff out."

Robaroni pointed again. There was a shack at the base of the hill, carved out of the trees. Behind it, trees grew up the slope of the hill. A large fire pit sat in front of the shack, and a pile of limbs and chopped firewood on the side.

"Is it built right into the hill?" she asked.

"Pretty much, but I've never been close enough to inspect it."

"Should we go look now?"

Francine started, but Robaroni stayed put. "I'm good," he said.

"Seriously?"

"Yep."

"We came out here just to look at it."

"Yep."

Francine looked at the shack, looked up the hill and the thick trees towering over it. "How does Jakov get down here?"

"His house is up above. He makes his way down the hill."

Francine considered investigating the hill herself, but then a chill ran up her spine and goose bumps all across her arms and neck.

"Okay," she said. "Let's get out of here."

20

It had been over three weeks since Samantha was last at the Parma Family Counseling Center. She sat across the coffee table from Aurelia.

"This is a transformative time," Aurelia said. "You graduate high school this weekend—"

"I won't graduate," Samantha said.

"Oh? Did something happen with the school?"

"I just mean that I won't go to the graduation ceremony. They gave me my diploma last week."

"Okay. Good."

"They even made me Valedictorian, even though I didn't take any finals."

"Congratulations. I hadn't realized."

"Yeah. Thanks."

"But you don't feel like going to the ceremony?"

Samantha looked up. The tone was scolding, as if Aurelia didn't approve. "What does it matter?"

There was an extended moment of silence. Aurelia seemed to make notes, but Samantha also wondered if she weren't just playing tic-tac-toe against herself, or maybe figuring out what she would buy with the money she was making from this session.

"I mean, that high school graduation alone can be quite traumatic. You've had other disruptive changes in your family, as well. The point being it would be normal to struggle with how you felt about all that change."

"Great. Being crazy is my new normal."

"Is that how you feel? Crazy?"

Samantha shook her head. "I don't know why I said that. I don't feel crazy."

"How do you feel?"

"Sad. I miss my sister. And my mother."

"What about your father? How are things going with him?"

Samantha shrugged. "He's been working the past two weeks. I guess he thinks it's back to the way it was for the past year, except after he leaves to go be a cop, I just stay at home instead of going to school."

Another extended moment of silence.

Then Aurelia said, "It might be useful to find something to do this summer, to help take your mind off of things."

Samantha looked up. "What?"

"Maybe you could enroll in college early, or take a class at the community college. Or maybe find a job. Nothing big, just something to help you move forward."

"I—I don't know." The suggestion didn't confuse Samantha. She'd been considering those things herself. Aurelia's tone confused her. It reminded Samantha of her mother talking to Lori just before her mother took off.

"You're here to learn how to process things in your life. By talking about them, I can help with that."

"I guess I don't know why you're talking like my mother."

Aurelia stared. "That was rude."

"Sorry."

"Perhaps something else is on your mind?"

Of course there was. Her dead sister.

Aurelia studied Samantha with a careful gaze. "Tell me what else is bothering you."

Samantha figured she had to say something and thought a moment. "Everything is so different. The only friend who stops by is Blaine. I freak out my other school friends, I guess."

"You may need to reach out to them once you feel you're ready."

Samantha nodded. She couldn't imagine when that might be.

"Has the newspaper reporter contacted you?"

Samantha looked up again. "Why would you ask that?"

"You mentioned it the last session, after Lori died.

"She called," Samantha said.

Aurelia nodded. "I was just curious if it bothers you."

"I'll let you know."

"How are things with your father?"

"You already asked me that."

"I did?"

After the session, as Samantha drove home, that question about the newspaper reporter lingered in her mind. She didn't remember mentioning the reporter to Aurelia. It was possible she'd done it. There were a few blank periods over the past three weeks.

But it bothered her remembering being asked the question.

# # # #

Samantha was alone at her house, sprawled on the sofa, staring at the television. Going to the counselor didn't make her feel better. If she said this to the counselor, the counselor would blame Samantha's situation. Or her attitude.

She felt the detachment from her school friends. Like those occasions when she came late to lunch and everyone she liked or even just knew had eaten, and she had to find a seat away from everyone else.

Missing the last two weeks of school had killed what little social life she had. Missing graduation and skipping all the parties would be the nail in the coffin.

Now she felt extra guilty for worrying about having friends when her sister had lost her life.

Even Blaine was at work, and wouldn't be home for three

more hours.

The phone rang, and she answered it. Even if it was Aunt Jan, she'd try to talk.

"Hey kid," her father said. "Will you come down to the municipal building? I got something to discuss."

"I don't feel like it."

"It's important."

"I'm sure it isn't."

The municipal building had three sections. One end was the Fire Department, where her Uncle Wally, Jan's husband, was the chief. The other end was the Police Department of Uncle Tom and her father's fame.

In the middle were the administration offices where her grandfather, Peter, presided as Mayor.

Samantha crossed the lobby and entered the administration offices. Her father could wait.

She waved to Gayle, the mayor's secretary, and moved through the hallways avoiding eye contact. She found Blaine on the lower level, filling a bucket with warm water.

"You want to help me mop?" he asked.

"No thanks. Just bored and lonely."

"That's me at night."

"Okay, let's not both start crying."

"You want to go watch softball tonight?"

"Softball is so boring."

"You'll see your classmates. You can hang with them."

"Wow. Are you my mother too?"

"How about you just keep me company while I get high?"

"Sure. Whatever."

As Samantha made her way back to the Police Department, her grandfather intercepted her at the lobby door.

"I need to speak with you, my dear."

Sitting across from him in his office, it reminded Samantha of how much she liked her grandfather. He was old but funny. Everybody in the city liked him, and he liked them all back.

"It's nice to see you, Grampa."

"I have something for you," he said. "A job."

"Oh? Is that why my dad called me?"

"Yes. I discussed it with him, and he thinks it'd be a good idea. You could help my secretary Gayle, or help anyone you want. It'd be a chance to learn how government works."

"Could I work in the Police Department?"

"Yes."

"Where does Aunt Jan work?"

"She's over at the bank. She's manager there now."

"That's the job my mother used to have, right?"

"Yes. Would you like to work there, with Aunt Jan?"

She did not want that, but wouldn't say so. "Maybe here, so I can be near you."

"Wonderful. When do you want to start?"

"I don't know. Monday?"

"Monday it is."

Samantha felt a weight in her stomach and her throat tighten, like those times in school when she was the only person with the correct answer and the teacher heaped praise upon her. "Shouldn't I interview, or at least apply for the job?"

"Why?"

"So people don't think I got the job just because I'm your granddaughter."

Grampa chuckled. "That's why I pay people in cash."

"You mean, like, out of your pocket?"

"It's from the bank, and we put it in envelopes. The envelope is printed with our official Village letterhead."

"Okay."

"When you give someone an envelope full of cash, it makes them much happier than any other way you could pay them."

"So you're saying they won't be mad about me getting a job without applying?"

"Nobody got their job by applying. Only by talking to me."

"Nobody?"

"Nobody. And when you hand them an envelope full of cash, it reminds them how it works."

21

"Do you want breakfast," her father asked in the morning.

"I'll take a Pop-Tart along."

"That's not breakfast."

"Dad, what do you think I've been eating for breakfast the past seven years. You buy them every week."

"I don't know. I guess I didn't realize."

"I'll be fine. Don't worry."

"Do you want me to go in with you?" he asked.

"Why? I've been there a hundred times."

"I don't know."

"I'll be fine, Dad."

Samantha felt sorry for him. He had the day off, and so he seemed at a loss. "If I need something, I'll call you, okay?"

"Alright, I'll be here."

She knew the answer, but she asked anyway. "What are you going to do today?"

"Work on the garage."

He'd been cleaning the garage for years now, tidying up his projects and tools and parts and pieces. It was a place to escape and not think of Lori or Mom, and she had given up asking about the specific projects, as he never completed them.

# # # #

They started at nine o'clock at the municipal building, at least in the City Administration Department. The Police and Fire were on their own schedule.

Without knowing what she was going to do, Samantha went to her grandfather's secretary, Gayle, first.

"I'm here," she said.

Gayle smiled. "We'll get you a desk, first, then we'll figure out what there is to do."

"I get a desk?"

"Of course. What did you think?"

"I don't know. I guess I didn't think about it."

There were departments for Service, Recreation, Taxes and Accounting, Waste and Water, and the Office of the Mayor. There was also the Municipal Bank, but it was located across the parking lot in its own building.

Gayle led her to an area on that floor with several desks. There was an empty one next to her cousin Derek, who worked in the Office of the Mayor since he'd flunked out of Bowling Green that winter.

"Hey," Derek said.

"Would you help her get settled?" Gayle asked. "I'll see about her duties."

Derek showed Samantha where to find pens and paper, and where there was food in the break room. She knew the layout already—like Derek, she'd spent dozens of afternoons wandering the offices to visit her grandfather. No rooms had been off-limits. Being employees, this was more like peeking into closets and cupboards. It was a new level of familiarity.

"Some of these people have been here since we were born," she said.

"Gramps takes care of you if you're loyal. He doesn't care if you make a mistake. Just don't talk bad about him or the city."

"Well, that's good. I guess."

They returned to their office area, but Gayle was not at her desk. "Let's take another walk around," Derek said. "We can kill a little time."

"Okay."

"That's the hardest part. Figuring out how to look busy."

"You have nothing to do?"

"I do," Derek said. "But not a full day's worth. So you have to pace it out so you don't run out."

As they strolled past the Taxes and Accounting department on the lower level, they met Blaine.

"Welcome aboard," he said.

Samantha would have stayed to chat, but Derek pulled her along.

When they were far enough away, Derek said, "I know you like him, but I think it's weird."

"What's weird?"

"That he would take the janitor job and do it."

"What's weird about that?"

"Does he want to be a janitor all his life?"

"I doubt it, but what do you care?"

"I don't care, but I don't want to talk to someone whose life goals are to clean toilets and get high."

Samantha stopped and glared at him. "What are your life goals, then?"

"I plan on being mayor someday. And a millionaire."

"Maybe if both your parents died, you'd have different life goals."

"Okay, fine. Don't get upset."

# # # #

The principal thing to do that morning was to gather the time cards for all the employees and take them to the municipal bank so they could prepare the payroll for the city. Gayle took Samantha along as she made the rounds, stopping down at the Tax and Accounting department first.

There were piles of green cards on the clerk's desk, arranged by department.

"There's a card for everyone," Gayle explained. "Carla, here, compiles them."

Carla offered a type-written report to Gayle. "This is the payroll report," Carla said. "Don't look at it. You can't know what everyone makes."

Gayle held it up for Samantha. The top page was blank except for the words "Payroll Report, June 12, 1979."

"I can look at it though," Gayle said.

"Just don't be shooting your mouth off," Carla said, smiling.

They left Carla's desk and made their way up to the main floor.

"We were just kidding back there," Gayle said. "What other people get paid is none of my business. I don't look."

Samantha felt the tension in Gayle's voice. "Okay. I won't look either."

"Thank you."

Samantha wondered if Gayle wasn't so much warning her as she was asking her not to tattle.

"Where are we going?" Samantha asked with a smile to ease the tension.

"Back to my desk, then you'll run a little errand."

Gayle slipped the report into a large envelope, tied the flap with the attached strings, and wrote "Jan Garczynski" on it and offered it to Samantha. "Take this to your Aunt Jan. She'll know what to do with it."

"Then what?"

"Come on back."

# # # #

The Municipal Bank building was not large in Samantha's estimation. It looked like a large box made of bricks with iron gates over the windows.

The bank was on the other side of the parking lot, set far

enough back from the road that it seemed to be part of the city park, rather than part of the city government.

Inside, it was frigid. She waved to Hank, the security guard, who sat on a chair just inside the door.

"Who you need?" he asked.

"My Aunt Jan."

Hank stood up, his enormous stomach dropping forward over his belt, and he made his way to the counter. The counter stretched to the far wall, and there were four windows. There was only a single teller, a young lady, stationed at the first win-dow.

Hank spoke to her and then waved Samantha over.

"This is the boss's niece, Samantha."

Samantha smiled but couldn't think of anything to say.

The teller was at ease, though. "My little sister is in next year's class. Vickie Fulton."

"Oh, right. We were in band and choir together."

"So what are you up to?"

"I just started at the Mayor's Office." She held up the enve-lope. "Gayle sent me over with the Payroll Report."

"What?" Hank said. "I thought you were just visiting. No-body tells me nothin'."

He led her into the gated area next to the counter and sat her at one of the empty desks.

Meanwhile, the teller poked her head in one office in the gated area and then came to Samantha.

"Jan will be right out."

"Thank you."

"Vickie will intern here starting next week. You two should go to lunch some time."

"Okay, cool." Samantha didn't get along with Vickie, so now she'd have another reason to avoid the bank.

"Sorry about Lori," the teller said. "That was so terrible."

"Thanks."

As Hank settled back into his chair, Samantha took another look around. She'd never been in the bank before. The vault was next to the offices and behind the tellers. Above it there were four more offices along a balcony. They painted the inside walls of the lobby with some Greek or Roman gods.

"Samantha," Aunt Jan said. "What brings you here?"

"Payroll Report." She offered it to her aunt Jan.

"Well, look at you, first day on the job and already working on payroll. Will you be back later on?"

Samantha shrugged. "Gayle just told me to give this to you."

"Okay then. Good job."

# # # #

The mayor invited Samantha to lunch in his office. He had hamburgers, fries and milkshakes waiting for her and for Derek.

"Just like old times," he said, as they sat at his desk.

They had lunch with the mayor many times when they were little, feasting on the fried food from the takeout restaurant down the street.

It had been years, though, since the last time, and she almost had forgotten about it. "Oh God. This is hilarious."

"Don't get used to it," Derek said. "He hasn't bought me lunch since my first day last year."

"I pay you good money," her grandfather said. "You could offer to buy me lunch."

When Derek dipped his French fries in his milkshake, Samantha asked, "Are you going back to college?"

"Maybe," he said. "I haven't decided yet."

"He's going," Grampa Peter said. "We need a lawyer in the family."

"What if I want to run the bank?"

"A lawyer could do that," Grampa Peter said.

"Wouldn't Aunt Jan run the bank next? Isn't she Assistant Manager?"

Derek laughed. "Now that would be hilarious. My mom running the bank."

"Why is that funny?"

"Running the bank is a man's job," Grampa Peter said, smiling. "It's just the nature of the business."

"I could be her boss," Derek said. "That would be even funnier."

"You could tell her to clean up her room," Grampa Peter said.

"I don't think that's funny," Samantha said.

# # # #

Back at her desk, bored as she continued updating Gayle's Rolodex, a question popped into her mind. Lori mentioned that Rebecca slept with someone—someone even creepier than the business owners her father knew. Who was it?

She couldn't shut her mind up, so she went looking for Blaine and found him in a lower level hallway. "I have a question," she said. "Something that's bugging me."

Blaine was mopping the hallway floor and looked at her just long enough to shake his head. "Can't talk now."

"But this is important—"

"Is there a stopped toilet?" a man's voice boomed from behind her.

Samantha looked over her shoulder and saw Blaine's boss, Milosh Dabrowski.

"I, uh..." Samantha said.

"Your important thing: is it about a spill or burned out light bulb?"

"What? No. It's kind of personal, I guess."

Milosh nodded. "Perhaps it's best left until after work."

"Sure."

# # # #

At two o'clock, as Samantha slogged through the boredom of updating Gayle's Rolodex, Gayle summoned her. "Ready for part two of payroll?"

"Sure."

They returned to Carla's desk in Tax and Accounting and picked up the bank transaction slip. Carla took it back from Gayle's hand to double check a number.

"I need to make sure the account number is correct," she said as she handed back the slip.

On the way back to the main floor, Gayle handed Samantha the slip. "I can show you this."

It was a bank slip Village Municipal Bank printed along the top. Carla had filled in "Payroll" for the account name, filled in an account number, and then a very large amount for the deduction.

"Is that number correct?" Samantha asked. "It's over eighty-thousand dollars."

"Yes. That's the weekly payroll."

"Wow. That seems like a lot."

Gayle looked over her shoulder as they paused at the door. "I can tell you that the average salary for city employees is twenty-thousand. Your grandfather pays pretty well around here."

"I guess."

Gayle led her to the Police Department.

"Why are we going here?"

"The police always escort us to the bank."

They went to the dispatcher's desk, where Gloria was on duty.

"Money time?" Gloria asked.

Gayle nodded. "Samantha is helping today."

"Well, how about that," Gloria said.

There were three cops at desks in the office, drinking coffee. "Show time, boys," Gloria said.

Gayle and Samantha walked across the parking lot with a cop known as Big Mac.

Samantha had known Big Mac forever and remembered they called him Big Mac because he liked the McDonalds hamburgers. Now he appeared to weigh three-hundred pounds, and she couldn't help but wonder if that's why the name stuck.

Big Mac kept up with Gayle's pace, which even Samantha found challenging. When they reached the bank, Big Mac was panting but didn't complain.

"We're just finishing up," Jan said when they came in. "Only a couple more minutes."

There was was a teller at each window, but Jan seemed to be the only customer. She clutched a few transaction slips in her hand and offered them, one at a time, to each teller. The tellers would count out money, insert it in an envelope, and pass it back to Jan.

Jan gathered the envelopes and carried them back to a man in a suit who stood at the gate to the office area with a large valise. As he took each envelope, he made a check mark on a clipboard and then put the envelope in the valise.

"This is Payroll," Gayle explained. "They make withdrawals from our payroll account, one for each employee, and check it against the payroll report. Then they tally up all the withdrawals, and we verify that the amounts match the payroll report and this withdrawal transaction from Tax and Accounting."

"It blows my mind that they pay everyone in cash."

"It's always been cash."

"I took bookkeeping in high school, and they said most businesses use payroll vendors to issue the checks."

"It's all manual, here."

They placed the last envelope in the valise and then Gayle, Jan, and the man in the suit compared the numbers, smiling when it all matched.

"How about that," Aunt Jan asked Samantha. "I'll bet you've seen nothing like that before."

"Wouldn't it be better using checks?"

Jan crossed her arms. "The way we do it is better." She looked at Gayle. "When was the last time we made a mistake?"

"I don't remember a mistake," Gayle said.

"That's right. Everybody is happy this way. They don't have to go to a bank to cash their check."

"Okay, I'm sorry."

"I was going to introduce you to Mr. Jones, the bank manager, but maybe some other time."

"Aunt Jan, I'm sorry."

"It's fine."

Outside, there was a patrol car blocking the driveway, and another positioned in the parking lot. The two cops were outside of their cars, on guard, with shotguns in their hands.

"Oh my God," Samantha said.

"You thought it was dangerous in there with your Aunt Jan," Big Mac said. "But out here it gets real."

"Don't worry," Gayle said. "It's just a precaution. Nothing has ever happened."

"And nothing ever will," Big Mac said. "Not on my watch."

Then they started the walk back to the municipal building, with Big Mac carrying the valise in one hand and his service revolver in the other.

# # # #

At the office, they assigned Samantha to delivering the payroll envelopes to the police department, stopping first at the desk of Betty, who was secretary for her Uncle Tom.

"You know almost everyone," Betty said. "We'll start in the break room. I think they're all in there."

"They're all in the break room?"

"Sure. Gloria called them in when you went over for the envelopes."

The break room was over flowing. The noisy men fell quiet as she and Betty handed out the envelopes.

A few minutes later, they were back at Betty's desk. "I'll call your dad and let him know. If he wants you to bring it home, I'll get it to you before you leave, okay?"

"Yeah. What about these?" Samantha had two extra envelopes. Instead of names, they just had initials: "D.W. and E.B."

"I'll give them to your uncle. He'll handle it."

"Who are they?"

Betty smiled. "Not my job to worry about that. And none of your beeswax."

22

Francine sat on the front balcony with coffee and the newspaper and her Filofax. Upset over losing her job, she slept little and realized now that she was in shock after losing her job yesterday. Now the reality that she'd never work as a reporter in Cleveland again set in.

If she sorted this out story, it wouldn't endear her to the publisher. Maybe she could sell it to the Columbus Dispatch, or the Detroit Free Press, and get hired. Either way, she'd have to move.

Her stomach was twisted and her head ached. She was hungover. She worried she'd feel like this every day until completing the story.

Robaroni pulled up to the curb in his Firebird and honked. She laughed at how ridiculous it was, the young, tough cop now playing a civilian tough guy, driving a fast car, and picking up a former newspaper reporter dressed in jeans, T-shirt and windbreaker.

Judging from the look on his face, she disappointed him.

"Sorry," she said. "Were you expecting a sexy trophy wife for this little charade?"

"What? No. You just look stressed out."

He sped up hard and threw her against the door with the turn. "Jesus," she said. "Should I put on my seat belt?"

"It wouldn't save you," he said, laughing.

At the stoplight, he asked, "Are you worried about what

we're about to do?"

"No. I mean, I wasn't, but now I'm worried about your driving."

"Just stop worrying."

"I'm thinking about the coroner's report."

"Look at the bright side."

"Which is?"

"We may die today, like those two fishermen, and then you won't have to worry about it."

They drove past the Service Garage, confirmed Jakov's car in the parking lot, and continued along the road.

They hadn't paid attention the day before, but Jakov's house was on the stretch of road leading to Cleveland, fronting the property used as the city dump. There was a house on either side, spaced far apart and separated by tall trees and thick underbrush. And both houses looked abandoned, as far as they could tell from the road as they drove back and forth.

The house had been a farm a hundred years ago and hadn't been repaired in decades. That it looked abandoned comforted Francine, and she indulged the idea that Jakov didn't exist. The visit would not be any trouble, because Jakov had gone away. But she didn't dare mention such a silly idea.

Rob parked in the driveway in front of the house, so he could drive the car across the yard and onto the road if they needed to leave in a hurry. He grabbed a twelve pack of Busch beer from the trunk and they walked around back like they knew what they were doing. By the time they were behind the house, they each had a beer open.

Scraps of wood and flowering weeds littered the back yard.

"Looks like a dump," Rob said as he looked around.

"Where's the boat?"

"Maybe the barn?"

"You want me to look in the barn?"

"I'll post up out here to keep watch."

Before going in, she looked at the windows of the house,

watching for movement. Streaked with filth, nothing could be seen inside but the darkness. Her heart pounded with worry that she'd have to confront Jakov.

The back of the house was shabbier than the front, rotted clapboard siding turned gray, and several gaps near the stone foundation. A tree grew out of the eavestrough.

Find the boat, take the picture and get the hell out.

The barn smelled of rot: rotten hay, rotten eggs, rotten wood. Something had died here.

The clutter in the barn quickened her pulse. There would be no way to escape if cornered. Ropes dangled from the rafters like massive strands of a giant spider's silk. The haymow to the left of the door had just enough piles of hay to conceal an attacker.

The boat sat wedged into the corner and surrounded by equipment caked with mud. She could make out a riding lawn mower, a farm implement like a thrasher, an upended wagon, and a motorcycle with two flat tires.

Hearing something scurry along the edge, she screamed and jumped back, felt something sharp against her calf and jumped forward again, bumping into rough-hewn timbers propped up against a post.

A timber fell over, crashing into an old metal shelf, which tipped over, spilling the contents of its shelves onto metal sheeting leaning against the wall.

Francine watched all this happen as if it were in slow-motion, the chain reaction like a Rube Goldberg machine in a cartoon. As the contents of the shelf thundered against the sheet metal, the barn reverberated with the noise, and Francine froze in horror.

Robaroni appeared in the door. "What the hell was that?"

"I just touched it, and..."

They struggled to get the timber back where it was, but then another seemed about to topple over.

"Fuck it," Robaroni said. "Just take the picture and let's get out of here."

She took the camera out of her bag and set the dials for the lighting.

"Do you think we should move some of that stuff out of the way?"

"See how close you can get, first."

# # # #

Jakov had come to the shack to start a new pot of mash. He was at the very beginning, and he needed enough wood to cook and enough to boil later on. He liked to do all that first, find the wood, chop it up, and stack it in piles near the shack.

Once he had the fire for the cooking pot going, he could sit and watch. He enjoyed watching the fire, and he'd stay up all night doing it.

Before he could chop the wood, he had to sharpen his ax. He enjoyed sharpening the ax. He enjoyed swinging the ax to chop things and then watching the fire burn.

To sharpen the ax, you turn the wheel and press the blade into it, sending sparks. The smell of stone dust and hot steel filled your nose. With metal scraped fresh, you press it to your tongue and taste the steel, dull but satisfying, like blood.

He'd been drunk when he got home from work, so he only brought a couple of beers with him to the shack. Once the ax was good and sharp, he opened the first beer and planted his ass on the stump next to the shack to drink.

Past the trees was the creek. The creek came from around the side of the hill, emerging from the ground and snaking its way through the woods. At that end where it started, there was a hill and on top of the hill the road where he lived. The creek went underground a couple of places where they built houses, stores and roads above it.

At the other end, it flowed past the animals in the zoo and then joined with the bigger river. From there, it flowed through the city and then into the lake.

But here it was just a creek, and it felt like his creek. He thought this whole place, the valley, the trees and the creek, were his kingdom. Down here, no one could tell him what to do. If he wanted some wood, he chopped it. If he wanted a squirrel, he shot it. If he wanted a drink, he made it himself.

He tossed the bottle on the pile behind the shack as he started his search for wood. The hill rose above the shack, and that was a good place to start. Branches fell during the winter and gathered in a tangled mess near the bottom, or up the hill a little way. He grabbed at the limbs and pulled them apart, lining them up for the ax.

He dragged them closer to the shack when he thought there was enough and then grabbed his ax.

One more beer would have been better, he thought. The second one was for after chopping, but he was thirsty now from dragging limbs. If he drank it now, he could have another later when he walked back up the hill.

He opened the bottle and sat on the stump by the fire pit to drink. Leaves were sprouting on the trees. Squirrels rushed from branch to branch, and birds swept in from above.

It'd be nice if there were fish worth catching in the creek, but there wasn't enough water for those kinds of fish. Walleye sounded good about now. Once this batch of whisky cooked, he'd go fishing out on the lake for Walleye.

Up on the hill, there was a loud crash of metal and wood falling over. Like a car driving into his barn. It had to be loud to hear it down in the valley.

Jakov tossed the beer and grabbed his ax. The chopping could wait until later. He headed up the hill to see about that crash.

# # # #

Francine was going to need the flash, as the light from the cracks in the walls and roof would make the shot worse. She was adept at handling the camera, a Canon range finder, and took shots at three different light settings.

"Hey," a voice shouted.

She put the camera back in her shoulder bag and came to the door. A bald man wearing grease-stained work clothes was walking from around the barn. She recognized him as the man who had collected the wreckage of Marko's boat.

The man, who had to be Jakov, carried an ax in his right hand, holding it mid-handle. He went toward Rob, who was still at his post across the yard near the corner of the house.

Francine kicked her beer over where she left it in the doorway, drawing Jakov's attention. He turned and looked at her, his eyes narrowing with anger.

"Get out of my barn," Jakov said, and started toward her.

"Hey," Rob said, hurrying. "You want a beer?"

Rob got between them and held out a beer. "You must be Jakov."

Jakov took the beer but didn't open it. "What the hell you doing back here?"

"We heard you had a boat for sale."

Jakov cracked open the beer. "Nope. And you shouldn't be back here. You might get hurt."

"Good to know, man," Rob said, laughing. He took a swig of his own beer and threw Francine a wink.

Jakov cracked open his beer. "You mind getting the hell out of here?"

"I'm looking for a twelve- or fourteen-foot aluminum fishing boat with a good-sized outboard. Right? Is that it in there?"

"Who sent you?"

"I was drinking with these cops at The Duo, right, talking about fishing and boats, said I was in the market. One of 'em said come talk to you."

"Which one?"

"I don't know," Rob said. "I was pretty drunk, to be honest."

"Do you fish much?" Francine asked, backing further away from Jakov.

"What?"

"I asked if you fish much? Do you go on Lake Erie, or

maybe a smaller lake?"

Jakov set his beer on the ground and took hold of the ax with both hands. "Get out of my yard."

Rob set the twelve-pack down and backed away. Francine was walking, glancing over her shoulder, trying to decide whether she should scream.

"Those cops are my friends," Jakov said. "They don't care what I do."

"When I see them," Rob said, "I'll tell them your boat is not for sale."

"Fuck off."

They got to the car and Rob reversed out of the driveway and into traffic without looking first. A car honked and swerved, missing them.

"Oh my God," Francine said. "Drive. Drive faster."

23

Samantha slumped in the leather chair, stared sidelong out the window, and wondered if she'd made the right choice. It was nine o'clock in the morning and, after talking with Alicia, she'd be back at work by ten-thirty and facing a day of boredom. Had she waited until the afternoon for her appointment, she could have killed time at the mall and called it a day.

Aurelia kept quiet, waiting for Samantha to start.

It reminded Samantha of how their grandmother babysat them when they were little. Grandma sat on the sofa, listening to the big-band music on the radio, waiting for the time to be over. Samantha and Lori both knew she loved them, but she didn't know what to do with them.

Samantha and Lori played on their own, knowing that giving their grandmother any trouble would mean a spanking when they got home.

But Grandma wouldn't even talk to them. At first, Lori had asked for stories, but Grandma just wanted to watch them, and bring them snacks, while listening to her music.

Aurelia wasn't as bad as that, but she was close.

"I don't know why I'm here," Samantha said.

"Tell me what you've been feeling."

"I don't know."

"Last week you seemed sad. Are you still sad?"

Samantha realized another week had gone by. She'd gone to work all day, collapsed on the couch, and done it again in the morning. She spent the weekend on the couch, either her own or over at Blaine's. Another week gone by and that much further away from the last time she saw Lori.

"Of course I'm sad. My sister is dead."

"But is that what you feel the most?"

"No. I'm feeling a little mad."

"Okay, that's good that you told me."

"What are you mad about?"

"My sister is dead."

"I see."

"I'd like to know why it happened."

Aurelia nodded, making notes.

"That's it?" Samantha asked.

"Closure is important when losing a loved one."

Samantha nodded.

"Is that what you're feeling, perhaps? A need for closure?"

Samantha shot another look across the coffee table. These sessions were so unlike how they began. With Lori and her father there, it was a place of comfort and hope.

"Well then. Shall we talk about your mother?"

Samantha shook her head.

"Or your sister?"

Samantha shook her head again.

"Your father, then?"

Samantha lowered her head.

"Then I suppose we can talk about you."

This got Samantha to look up. Aurelia smiled, hoping to convey her sincere desire to help.

"I think I'm just going to go back to work."

"How's it going?"

Samantha shrugged. "Today is pay day, so everybody will be in a good mood."

# # # #

Gayle smiled at Samantha and handed her the payroll report to take over to the bank. "You might get a dirty look from your Aunt Jan because it's a little later than normal, but you can handle that, right?"

"I don't know that I can handle it, but I'm used to it."

Rebecca was at the desk inside the gated area, and Samantha locked eyes with her for a second before Rebecca looked away. Next to her was Samantha's classmate, Vickie, who was the new bank intern.

"Hi Samantha," Vickie said. She smiled and waved.

"Hey." Samantha walked over, waving at Hank the security guard who was chatting with a teller at the counter.

"Hey Samantha," Rebecca said.

"I have the payroll report for Jan."

Rebecca smiled and took it from her, then handed it to Vickie. "I think she's in her office, so just hand it to her."

Vickie chatted with Jan because she stayed in the office. Samantha had lingered, expecting some acknowledgment of the delivery, and now felt awkward waiting.

"How are you?" Rebecca asked.

"I miss Lori."

"Me too."

Samantha noticed a slight smile on Rebecca's face and felt better about the moment. "Can we talk some time?"

"What about?"

"Just stuff, I guess. You were Lori's best friend."

Rebecca shrugged. "Her roommate was her best friend, but yeah, we can talk."

"Should I come over some time?"

"Or we could go to lunch," Rebecca said. She brightened at this. "We're two young professional girls. We can splurge on lunch."

"Sure."

"I'll call you some time."

On the walk back to the office, that word popped back in her mind. Splurge. Her father was, like, a millionaire. What did splurge mean to her?

Back at her desk and staring across the office, Derek wrapped on the side of her desk with a clipboard.

"Where's your boy?" he asked.

"Who?"

"Blaine. I need him."

"I don't know."

"Go take a quick walk around the office and I'm sure he'll follow you back here."

"What?"

Derek laughed. "Come on, you know he's sniffing after you. I mean, he'd lick the bottom of your shoes if you told him to."

"Shut up, Derek. Blaine's my friend. You should be his friend, too."

"Yeah, right? We never talked the entirety of school, kindergarten to graduation. I'm not starting now."

"Okay, fine. Be a jerk. Just go find him yourself."

Derek tapped the clipboard with a pencil. "Yeah, I'm planning the ceremony tomorrow, so I need him to do some stuff."

"What ceremony?"

"Uncle Tom's award for two years of a crime-free city."

Derek heaved a sigh and got up from his desk.

24

Francine submitted the Freedom of Information Request, but the progress of her investigation was too slow. Six weeks had gone by, and the odds of finding a solid lead grew slimmer by the minute. Even if she found something, the police were letting the investigation die with the victims.

She parked on the street a few houses away from her place and walked to Lawson's to pick up milk for the morning. The thought of going out later was repulsive.

In fact, she'd treat herself to ice cream. She had to have something for dinner, and ice cream sounded good.

Around the corner, she glanced down the alley and a few boys were playing baseball—something they shouldn't be doing. A window would get broken. Even a near miss that hit the side of a house would piss off the owner. But they were having fun, and it lightened her step to hear their playful shouts.

She glanced back at her flat, the second story of the third house, and noticed one of her chairs out of place. The door looked ajar. Someone had drawn the window shade over the kitchen sink.

Her chest tightened as she realized that someone was in her apartment.

She ran to Lawson's to get away and out of sight from her own place. There was a pay phone outside the store and she went there and dropped a quarter into the pay phone, her hand shaking as she dialed, looking back at the way she came, ready to take off running again. If she needed to, she could run in her stockings. She looked both ways while it rang, jumping at every sound on the street.

"Hello?"

"It's me. I think Jakov's in my place."

"Are you sure?"

"No, but the door's ajar. I wouldn't leave it open. Can you come?"

"I'm on my way."

"What should I do?"

"Can you get to your car?"

"Not without going past my house."

"Is there a public place you can go?"

"I'm calling from a Lawson's."

"Wait inside. Tell the clerk to call the cops and report a suspicious character bothering you. Got it?"

The next minute seemed to take an hour. The minute after that took two more. Francine paced the aisle farthest from the door with a bottle of ketchup in each hand, not sure what she would do with them, but taking some comfort in their presence.

The clerk called the cops, but the way he looked at her made her worry he told the cops she was the suspicious character.

When Robaroni arrived, he put one arm around her and kept the other in the pocket of his sweatshirt. "Okay, you ready to go check it out?"

"Shouldn't we wait for the police?"

"Nah. That could take all night. We never respond to the suspicious character reports. Cops always have something better to do than that."

"Why d'you tell me to say that?"

"To calm you down."

They walked back, looking up at the back of her place.

"You see how it's ajar?" she asked. "I didn't imagine it, right?"

"It's ajar."

When they turned the corner, Rob stopped. "You can get in your car now and take off. Then I'll check out your house."

"Any other option?"

"You can either wait here outside or follow me up."

"I'll follow you. I have to know."

"Then I'm going in loud, and he'll run out the way he came in."

"Don't we want to catch him?"

"I don't. I might get shot, or you might get shot, or I might have to shoot him. None of those are good options."

"Fine."

They flung open the front door and waited before going up. Rob made a point of yelling and stomping his feet.

At the top of the stairs, he used the key to unlock the door. "This sucks," he said as he crouched two stairs from the top with his service revolver pulled.

"I'm coming in," Rob shouted and flung open the door. He crouched down again, his service revolver pointed through the door.

Francine realized she should have gotten in her car and driven away, to Florida, perhaps, to stay with her mother.

"Jakov?" Rob called. "Get the hell out of there."

There were footsteps inside. Rob put one hand back to keep Francine down and below him on the stairs. Then they heard the back door swing open and footsteps on the back porch.

"Jakov?" Rob called again. He crept up to the landing for a better look.

"Stay here a minute," he said. Then he stepped through the doorway and Francine watched as he checked the corners. He peered into each room, secured the back door, and then re-checked each room as he made his way back to the front door.

Francine watched Rob do this, catching glimpses of him as he moved back and forth. She realized Jakov might circle around to the front door and come up from behind, and she wanted nothing more than to be beside Robaroni and his service revolver.

"All clear," Rob said, and Francine scurried inside.

Rob showed her how Jakov pried open the back door, shattering the wood. "Now you can call the cops and report an illegal entry."

"Don't you want to go after him?"

He shook his head. "We have to do it by the books, or I might lose my job, and you might get hurt."

The police came and took the statement. Rob gave them the make, model and license of the suspicious vehicle.

"Any reason for him to be doing this?"

"We stopped by his place to inquire about a boat for sale," Rob said. "I think he might have be a little obsessed with the young lady here."

"What kind of boat?" the cop asked.

"Fourteen foot aluminum," Rob said.

"With a big Johnson," Francine offered.

The cop nodded. "Any valuables missing?"

Francine had checked and nothing was missing. Her Filofax was still in her handbag, slung over her shoulder. During her tour of the apartment, it was clear he had been sitting on her bed. How awful to have come home unsuspecting only to find a crazed man trying to kill you. "Nothing I notice."

The cop offered a card with a phone number and the case number to Francine. "Can you get that door secured tonight?"

"I'll get it," Rob said. "But I'll talk her into sleeping somewhere else."

"Good idea," the cop said.

25

Francine, sitting on the side nearest the front door, kept scanning the room, making notes in her Filofax, trying not to attract attention to herself.

Men filled all the seats in the municipal building lobby. She assumed they were members of the city council or employees of the administration, the best and brightest of the middle-class citizens the city could offer. The camera crews were in position. Lined up in the back, as if for inspection, were two dozen police officers in dress blue uniforms.

Samantha's father, David, stood in the front and center of the first row of cops, his hands clasped before him as he looked on with a somber expression on his face.

At the front, seated near the lectern, was Mayor Peter, his daughter Jan, and Robert Marko, the City Council President. Standing to one side, chatting with Gayle and Chief Sykora, was a portly man in a suit.

Rebecca Marko was in the back, near the police officers.

Samantha Sykora entered from the door marked "Municipal Administration" with Blaine Taylor, who appeared to be on-the-clock because he wore gray work clothes. Samantha seemed content to stand to one side, chatting with Blaine, when she noticed Francine and made her way across the room.

"Hey," Samantha said, taking the seat beside Francine. "It's a little bizarre, don't you think?"

"I covered a few civic events," Francine said. "They each

have their own version of bizarre."

"They may release doves."

"Inside or outside?"

"I don't want to ruin the surprise."

Francine wanted to tell Samantha about the break-in at her house, and that she was now living like a refugee at Robaroni's place, but she also didn't want to alarm the girl. There would be an appropriate time to mention it. They were both living with a cop, so maybe it would be a bonding thing.

Chief Sykora noticed her and scowled.

"Uh oh," Francine said.

When the bells at the Catholic church across the street played and the mayor stepped up to the podium, Francine had to stifle a chuckle.

"I love our city," the mayor said. "I'm proud to have been mayor for over forty years, and I think it's the greatest city in America thanks to our dedicated police force."

The cops in the back of the room smiled and nodded.

"I am pleased—very pleased—to introduce Anthony Muchado, from the National Organization of Municipal Law Enforcement..."

Aaron Key stepped through the front doors, pausing just inside. He looked lonely there, alone, the only black man in the building.

"...an organization dedicated to promoting the role of police in a civil society..."

The mayor glanced at Aaron Key. First a few heads turned. A moment later, every head turned to look.

The portly man in the suit, Anthony Muchado, stepped up to the lectern, and the mayor stepped aside. "Thank you, Mayor Sykora," he said. "It is with great pleasure that I present this award, today, because I believe that law and order are the cornerstones of our society."

Aaron took a step further inside, and one cop, a guy so fat he looked wider than he was tall, stepped out of the formation behind the seats and lumbered toward where Aaron stood.

"But without great leadership," the presenter said, "there

will only be chaos. As the riots that ruined our cities taught us, only an engaged and well-trained police force can contain that chaos."

Francine exchanged a look with Samantha, who seemed as unsure of what would happen next as she was. When she looked back at Aaron, he stared at her. He seemed distracted, concerned; and well he should be.

"Can I help you?" she asked.

"But not in this fair city," Muchado said was saying up at the lectern. "This is a place of law and order."

"Hey," the big cop said. "Let's go. Outside."

"I only want to ask a question. Do you mind if I ask a simple question?"

"Not today," the cop said. "Invited guests only."

Two more cops broke formation to join the big cop, then two more after that. David Sykora trailed after them.

Aaron's gaze fixed on the big cop. "I want to see the coroner's report of my son's death," Aaron said, his voice now loud and resolute. "All of it. May I see the coroner's report of my son's death?"

"Get him out of here," Chief Sykora said.

The policemen grabbed at Aaron, moving him through the doors, lifting him off his feet as they hustled him outside and out of sight.

"Everything's fine," Chief Sykora said, and motioned for the speaker to continue.

"Why can't he see the report?" Samantha asked. She looked at Francine and then turned to face the front of the assembly. "Why can't he see the report?" she said again, loud enough to carry over the murmur of voices.

Up front, Chief Sykora, the Mayor, and Jan Garczynski huddled in conversation.

"Why can't he see the report?" Samantha asked, even louder than before.

"Samantha," her father barked from the where he lingered near the door. "Stop it."

The Chief looked up from the huddle and smiled at her.

"That's not how the system works, sweetie."

"It seems pretty reasonable," she said, almost shouting. "His son died. He'd like to be sure of why and how it happened. Why can't he see the fucking report?"

Her father grabbed her by the arm. "What's wrong with you?"

"It's not a secret, is it? The report?"

"You don't ask about it though."

"Shouldn't the police look into this matter and let us know what happened?"

"It was an accident."

"Do you know that for sure? Did you look at the report? Did anyone?"

"It was an accident, and that's that. She's dead."

"Well then fuck it all." Her eyes welled up, and she sobbed as she left the building, followed by her father.

Francine looked around the lobby, trying to see what might happen next. For a couple of minutes the chaos spread with chatter from all corners as the people told each other what they just saw to convince themselves they hadn't imagined it. Up front, the mayor spoke to the television crew producers, and conferred with his guest.

The mayor's daughter, Jan, walked down the aisle assuring people everything was fine and by the time she circled back around to the front, everyone had calmed down.

The mayor stepped up to the lectern and smiled. "I love our city," the mayor said, starting over as if nothing happened. "I'm proud to have been mayor for over forty years..."

26

Samantha sat at the kitchen table, one hand propping up her head, and stayed just like that as she endured her father's lecture in detached silence.

"I have no idea what is going on with you," he said. "You couldn't have chosen a worse possible moment to cause a scene."

He grabbed a beer and took several drinks, shaking his head in between.

"Do you hate your family?" he asked. "That's what it seemed like. But they're family. If you hate them, it's like you're hating yourself."

He dumped his beer and looked in the refrigerator again. "I don't even know what to do for dinner. Should we try to see your counselor? Do you want to talk to her?"

He pulled some cash out of his pocket and dropped it on the counter. "If you're hungry, get yourself a burger from the corner, okay? I should lie down. I don't feel well myself."

Samantha spent the rest of the afternoon in self-imposed exile, trying to read upstairs in their bedroom until the stifling heat and reminders of Lori drove her to the cool air and poor lighting of the basement.

Her father paced around the first floor like a caged animal, then threw himself back on his bed.

Around six o'clock he shouted, "I'm going to my softball game. We'll talk later, okay?"

But he didn't wait for her to respond.

Once alone, she called Blaine, and they walked down the street to get hamburgers.

"Did you watch the six o'clock news?" Blaine asked.

"Oh God, was I on it?"

"Nope. It was like none of that stuff happened. They explained Tom's award, showed a clip of him receiving the award, and then took a quote from your grandpa. It was all smiles and good news."

As they walked through a yard to get to the municipal park, Blaine lit up. Samantha refused his offer, as she always did.

"I have no idea how you deal with reality," he said.

Samantha and Blaine sat in one of the outfield bleachers, as they had the other night. Out on the field, grown men in pajama-like costumes were back at it chasing the ball. Samantha disliked the attention paid to sports, but this was ridiculous.

Blaine, being high, giggled at the sight of the men running around in their matching pajamas. He was useless to her, now.

"I wish I'd brought a book," she said.

Blaine looked at her and giggled. "Uh oh. Trouble."

Her grandfather, the mayor, approached. He wore slacks and a sport shirt, the closest thing to casual dress he ever got. He smiled at Samantha and offered her his popcorn.

"Thanks Grampa," she said. "I'm sorry I made a scene at Uncle Tom's thing today."

He climbed onto the bleacher and sat beside her. "You know I worry about you. And your father."

"I know."

He put his arm around her and Samantha rested her head on his chest. He smelled like old, but it comforted her.

"I miss Lori, too," he said. "Not a day goes by I don't think about her. This is not how life should be, our family suffering like this."

Samantha nodded.

"I think you should talk to your Uncle Tom."

Samantha pulled away. "I'd rather not, Grampa."

"I'm thinking maybe if you saw the police report, the investigation into what happened, you'll understand."

Samantha's stomach tightened. "Are you sure? I'm not sure that would work for me."

"Maybe I'll have your father there with you, and he can help explain things."

"Okay."

"Let me arrange things. Trust me."

# # # #

In the morning, the lobby was quiet and cool. They went to the police station on the right, but Samantha paused inside the door, feeling unsure about reading the report.

In front of her was the duty officer's desk, where a cop sat reading the newspaper.

"Good morning, Foster," her father said.

Foster looked up from his paper, nodded, glanced at Samantha, and lowered his gaze back to the paper.

Her uncle's secretary, Betty, kept her eyes on the stack of papers she was sorting on her desk as they approached.

"Tom in?"

Betty nodded to her father but would not look at Samantha.

Samantha was ready to run from the building in tears, just like the day before, but somehow followed her father into the office.

Tom was at the window, looking down at the municipal park. He was in uniform, but the back of his shirt was untucked, something her father would never allow to happen.

He motioned for them to sit. "Betty," he called out the door in an impatient, exasperated tone. "Would you tidy up a bit here, please?"

He was referring to food wrappers and empty cups littering his desk, and which Betty gathered in a trash can.

It had been years since she was last in her Uncle Tom's office. They redecorated at some point, because the sofa and chair were leather, the console television was huge and the carpeting was deep pile. Nicer, even, than her grandfather's office.

On the wall opposite the television was a trophy case. On the top shelf were his high school trophies from football, basketball, and baseball. Below that were trophies he earned at college, although she didn't think he graduated from college.

Below the shelves was a credenza covered with softball and golf trophies. On either side of the credenza were massive trophies, taller than herself, with a softball player at the top, awarded when Tom's team won the city league championship.

Samantha noticed Betty give her a dirty look as she pulled the door shut on her way out.

"Okay," Tom said. "Let's do this."

He unlocked the credenza beneath his trophies and pulled out the file drawer, removing a large envelope and locking the drawer again.

He sat back at his desk and leaned back in his chair as he removed the contents of the envelope. The television was on, but he had turned the sound down. "So where're you going to school this fall?"

"I'm not."

Her father looked at her. "What's this? Of course you're going to college."

She felt the blood rise to her ears. When he glanced at her, she shook her head.

Tom nodded. "Your grandfather can let you keep your job, you know, answering phones or something."

Samantha shook her head.

"We'll talk about it later," her father said.

Tom flipped through the papers, lingering, it seemed, at a series of eight-by-ten photos in the back. He kept it all close in his lap, and Samantha saw none of the contents.

He took the top sheet of paper from the stack and slid it across the desk. Before Samantha could take it, her father placed his hand on top of it.

"This is not a good idea, Honey. We talked about it."

"You talked."

"It will not be anything like you're used to."

Nothing was like anything she was used to these days. She was tired of explaining this. It was like he just wanted to ignore the truth. "Can I just look at it?"

The page was a typed sheet from the Cleveland Police detective, Wagner. It read:

> "Regarding the matter of the deaths of Michael Key and Lori Sykora, recovered from Lake Erie on April 28, 1979 by the Coast Guard cutter Morro Bay, I conclude that they died from a boating accident of their own fault. No further investigation warranted.
>
> "The Medical Examiner concluded that no suspicious circumstances are present. Toxicology reports showed drugs and alcohol in both bodies. "Lack of witnesses and physical evidence support the conclusion that the deaths involved no other parties and were accidental."

Samantha looked up at her Uncle Tom. "If they ruled it an accident," she asked, "why did the newspaper blame Michael?"

Tom glanced away from the television. "Maybe they're trying to sell more newspapers."

Samantha turned the paper over, but there was nothing on the back. "Can I see the rest?"

"That's not a good idea." Tom slid the stack of paper in his lap back into the envelope, then held out his hand for the memo.

"Where did she get the drugs and alcohol?"

"What?" her father asked.

"Lori turns twenty-one next week. She's too young to buy alcohol, so she had to get it somewhere or from someone."

"The black kid was over twenty-one," Tom said.

"What about the drugs?"

"You know how college students are," Tom said.

"No, I don't," Samantha said. "But I've watched enough Starsky and Hutch to know more about police work than whoever wrote this. It's like a police report from Barney Fife."

"That's enough," her father said as he snatched the memo from her. "This little game is over."

He grabbed her by the arm and pulled her out of her seat. Samantha pulled away, yanking her arm free. "Keep your God damn hands off me."

She turned and left the office, breaking into a run to get out of the office.

27

Aaron luxuriated on the sofa in the front room. He could have been in a jail cell at this moment, and had to appreciate that he still enjoyed his freedom, such as it was.

Somehow the Village police had not arrested him the day before. When they carried him from the building, they put him in his car and escorted him with a police cruiser to the city limits. Mighty white of them.

At home, he told Louise that he'd gone there to ask about the coroner's report, omitting the confrontation with police from his version of events.

Of course he assumed she'd learn soon enough when the Action 5 News came on at six p.m. But there was no mention of the confrontation. The story, quoting the mayor, praised the Chief of Police.

"That's where Michael lived?"

"Yes, but..."

"But what?"

"Never mind."

It was like the confrontation didn't happen.

This morning, seeing him lounging on the sofa, Louise asked if he was sick.

"Just tired. I'll get on my route soon."

He was balancing this need to understand what happened to Michael with the pleasure of the life now enjoyed. He still had a wife, and a house, and a business that provided enough income to keep both. They had another daughter and two grand babies. If he pushed too hard with these hard-ass white cops, he might lose more than Michael.

Still, it galled him that something may have happened that needn't have happened. Someone may have gotten away with something.

The phone rang. As he answered it, he assumed it would be Louise checking on him, and that she would tell him to get his butt moving or drag it to the doctor's office.

"This is Francine," the caller said. "Can we meet somewhere? I think we need to talk again."

"I have some time right now."

"I'd rather we talked in person."

Aaron thought a moment and suggested a diner in Cleveland Heights. "The neighborhood is rough, but you'll be fine at this time of day."

"Well, I don't feel safe in my home, so this can't be any worse."

Aaron got there first and waited outside, chuckling at Francine's worried expression as they went into the restaurant. "You look like how I felt walking into city-fucking-hall yesterday."

"I hope you don't take it personally. I'm a little more out of my element than usual."

"If the newspaper covered cultural events on the east side of Cleveland the way it covered events in the suburbs, maybe you'd be a little more comfortable over here."

She nodded her head. "Point taken."

"Nothing to worry about," he said, hoping to ease any discomfort he caused. "It's not like we expect an in-flux of visitors for the blues festival on Harvard Avenue. Sometimes it's kind of nice when we have the place to ourselves."

The waitress took their orders, and Aaron noticed only a momentary glance on her part. He frequented this diner and knew the staff, and this was the first time he'd been here with a woman other than Louise.

"I admire what you did the other day," Francine said. "Few people question what happens in that little city."

"I'm afraid I didn't help."

"You inspired Samantha Sykora to demand to see the coroner's report."

"Oh yeah? The cop's daughter? Well, I assume she didn't get the same response as I did."

"No, it was the same, but it was her father who chased her out."

Aaron watched Francine as the waitress brought their coffee. Francine didn't seem anxious about being the only white woman in the diner and seemed sincere in thanking the waitress. Some people would have wiped the spoon before stirring their coffee, but Francine took it all in stride.

He gave her his full attention. "So what was it you wanted to talk about?"

"I think there's more to this story. The way the Medical Examiner has handled the investigation is odd, and you're not alone in your curiosity about it."

Francine explained how she filed a Freedom of Information Act request to see the report, but wasn't sure they would honor it. "I'm wondering if you'd be willing to sue for its release. Sort of force the issue."

"You think that would work?"

"I don't know, but it's the only idea I have right now."

Aaron shook his head. "I may have to let this one go."

"I can't say I blame you," she said. She explained how the fishermen told her about the man at the boat launch who might be Jakov. "But now they're dead, and someone broke into my apartment to ambush me. We think it was Jakov. Those acts of violence are not coincidence. There's something behind all of it."

"You're still working on the story?"

Francine shrugged. "I hate the idea of turning my back on the truth. I understand if you don't want to stay involved. Your family has suffered a great deal."

He shook his head. But it wasn't the answer to her request. He denied himself the chance to hide from this one. Michael was a good boy, and a smart young man. He wanted the world to know the truth about his son.

"If I help," he said, "what's next?"

"I'm meeting Samantha and Blaine at a diner on the west side. You could join me there."

28

Samantha and Blaine entered the diner and paused in the doorway. At this hour, two in the afternoon, there were only a few tables occupied. Near them, at the front in a booth, was a woman wearing dark sunglasses, and a large-brimmed hat.

Next to her was Aaron Key.

Samantha said led Blaine to the booth.

"Thanks for coming," Francine said.

"You're lucky I answered the phone and not my dad. One of us might be in jail right now."

"It would be me," Aaron said, getting a laugh from Blaine.

"I think this might be a mistake," Samantha said.

Francine removed her sunglasses. "No, it isn't. Trying to find the truth is never a mistake."

"That doesn't mean it may not be costly," Aaron said.

They stood another moment and Samantha realized they were waiting to see what she would do, that this was one of those moments of decision.

She sat down and scooted over to make room for Blaine. "Maybe that's what happened to Lori. Maybe she was looking for the truth, when..."

They looked at her across the table, waiting, but she didn't feel like finishing the sentence.

Blaine leaned over the table and smiled. "This is like The French Connection, right? Didn't they have a scene like this?"

"What?"

"Maybe it was Chinatown."

Samantha shook her head. "Just stop. Please."

"It's okay," Francine said. "I know I'm being dramatic."

The waitress, a heavy-set woman with dark hair, brought coffee and menus. Francine waited before speaking again.

"You ain't being dramatic," Aaron said. "Do these young people know all that has happened? You should tell them, because I'm afraid Michael and Lori didn't know what they were dealing with, either."

Samantha heard a low buzz in her ears as Francine explained her visit to Michael's neighbor, the chat with Jakov, and how he lay in wait for her on her bed.

"That's awful," Samantha said.

"We still can't figure out how he snuck up on us at his house. His car was missing, so we thought he wasn't there."

"I can explain that," Blaine said. "He sometimes gets too drunk at work to drive home, and someone drops him off."

"What was he doing behind the barn?"

"Down in the Kingdom," Samantha said.

"At the shack?"

"You know it?" Blaine asked.

Francine nodded. "Rob took me there. But I forgot to ask what he does in his shack."

"Makes whisky," Samantha said.

"Yeah, that," Blaine said, "and he traps muskrat down there, and skins 'em, or whatever it is you do with muskrat."

"Have you been there?"

"Only once," Samantha said.

"And we'll never go back."

"You've heard the rumors that, many years ago, people went missing down there."

"What's this guy like?" Aaron asked. "Is he like one of those big fat white cops?"

"He doesn't look like much," Blaine said, "but he's one of the strongest guys at the city garage. Nobody messes with him."

"I'm done messing with him," Francine said.

Aaron shook his head. "None of this would be necessary if they'd just show us the damn coroner's report."

"Samantha looked at the coroner's report," Blaine said.

Francine cupped her hands before her, as if about to receive a bowl of soup. "Well, what did it say?"

"Insufficient evidence."

"Horse shit," Aaron said.

"I only saw the detective's Investigation Report. He wouldn't show me the actual coroner's report, or the pictures, or anything else."

"Did the Investigation Report look convincing?"

"It looked like a book report by a fifth grader who didn't read the book."

"What did it say about Michael?" Aaron asked.

"The police report lumps them together as an accident not worth investigating."

"It sounds like you didn't see the report," Francine said.

"I saw it in my Uncle Tom's hands. He only showed me the top page, but then he flipped through a pile of stuff. There were pictures too, but I couldn't see them."

"That's it?"

"Then he locked it up in the file cabinet beneath his stupid trophies."

For several seconds they were silent. Samantha didn't know what to do next.

Aaron cleared his throat and folded his hands on the table. "Then we have to get it."

Samantha shook her head. "You can't. Uncle Tom has it locked in his office. You can't just go in there and take it."

"They blamed my son for this tragedy. The entire city thinks he was just another bad kid from a bad family, but y'all can rest easy because he's dead."

"Yeah, but—"

"They are hiding behind that report. We have to get it before he burns the God damn thing up."

"Why did he keep it at all?" Francine asked. "If it shows what we think it shows, he'd just get rid of it to cover his tracks."

The ringing in Samantha's ears started again. "But are you saying my family is involved?"

"I don't know, but he might cover up for someone. Maybe Jakov. If it's not someone inside the city doing this, then I think they—your family, that is—they'd want to know so they can stop it."

"It makes little sense that anyone would want to kill Lori."

Francine flipped through her Filofax. "I'm trying to connect the dots to see if they're related. I need to talk to Rebecca."

"Wait," Samantha said. "Talking to Rebecca is one thing. But now you're talking about stealing something from the chief of police?"

"Keep your voice down," Francine said.

"What about you, kid," Aaron said to Blaine. "You work there, right? You're the God damn janitor, right? You have keys to the offices. It wouldn't even be that hard."

"First," Blaine said, "my keys don't work on Tom's office. Only he has the key to his office. Then he has a different key for his desk and cabinet."

"If you can get in the office," Aaron said. "picking a desk lock ain't hard."

Blaine raised his hands in surrender. "Second, I don't think I want to get involved. I mean, I liked Lori and all, but I'm not sure I can do this. Sorry, but this is not my thing."

Francine studied a page in her notebook. "Your name is Blaine Taylor?"

"Yes."

"Your father was a police officer until he died a few years ago."

"Yes."

"He died in a car crash similar to the one that killed the two fishermen: rollover accident and a fire."

"Yeah, but that's just a coincidence. I mean, the coroner said he was drunk at the time of the crash."

Francine reached across the table and squeezed Blaine's hand. "I'm very sorry for your loss. Was your father a heavy drinker?"

"He hardly drank at all. He kind of lost interest after my mother died. So it was, uh, just..."

Blaine looked across the table, then leaned back, shaking his head, falling silent.

"Samantha," Francine went on, "your mother worked at the Municipal Bank, correct? She was the Assistant Manager before she left town. Do you remember her boss?"

"Mr. Odom?"

Francine lowered her voice almost to a whisper and said, "He died on a trip to Florida."

Blaine licked his lips and swallowed. "How did he die?"

Francine pointed with a finger to a line in her Filofax. "His car rolled over and caught fire, killing him."

"Are you making this up?" Aaron asked.

"No, I'm not."

"Where are you getting all this?" Samantha asked. "You can't know all these things."

"I researched in the newspaper clip files. It indexes all the old stories going back decades. It's how we—I mean, reporters —write stories by keeping track of the old stories. What I couldn't find at the newspaper, I tracked down at the Cleveland Library."

"It can't be all the same thing," Samantha said. "It's just co-incidence."

Francine reached across the table, but Samantha pulled away. "Listen," Francine said. "I know this has been a lot to process, but I can't connect any of these deaths without some help. So anything you can find, anything at all, might help—"

"You want me steal a report from my uncle's office and then look for additional evidence?"

"I need help. I'm not sure what I'm looking for."

"So what do you want me to do? Go snooping around my house, and my uncle's house, and the mayor's office for evidence of some crazy criminal conspiracy? Like there's someone killing people in my neighborhood for money?"

"I'm just trying to find the truth."

Samantha shook her head. "No."

Blaine scoffed. "We won't find anything."

Samantha felt pressure behind her eyes, like her head was being crushed. She took a drink of water. "All I want is for the police to do their job. That's how the world works. Cops and robbers. Good guys and bad guys. I just want the police to catch whoever did this."

Francine closed her notebook as the waitress returned to their table.

"Ready to order?"

29

Francine awoke around eight o'clock in the morning when Robaroni came home.

"You were going to call me for a ride," she said as she sat up on the couch.

"I caught one. No problem."

She got up to use the bathroom while Rob changed in his bedroom.

Since the incident, they left her car at the far end of the parking lot of Rob's apartment building so they could check on it, but it wouldn't lead someone to his front door. She'd been dropping him off for his shift and then using his car, as needed.

He fixed breakfast while she told him of the meeting with Aaron and Samantha.

When she finished, he said, "Did you encourage them to steal the report?"

"Well, no."

"Did you discourage them?"

"No. But I don't think they're going to do it."

"I've seen those reports," he said. "Even if you get to look at it, they can be a mess if you don't know what you're looking for."

"I thought about that," she said, and loaded one of the fried eggs on her toast. "I'm going to give it to an expert to review."

"What expert?"

"Another medical examiner."

"Like the next county over, or someone in the same office."

"Maybe the previous one. He was pretty sore when he lost the election."

Robaroni shook his head. "I don't think any licensed doctor will look at a stolen report."

"Fine. Maybe the Freedom of Information Act request will come through."

"Okay then."

"If not, maybe he'll look at it off the record."

"Maybe."

Francine cleared the dishes and had an idea. "I could hire someone, like an expert witness kind of person, and keep it off the record."

"It's possible, but you won't be able to prove anything in court with it."

"I just need to prove it in the court of public opinion."

Robaroni changed into pajamas and came into the living room. "You know what you will prove?"

"What?"

"That you abetted in a crime. So you can't go public with it."

Francine had been feeling the anxiety about this building.

"Shit."

"Yeah."

"What if we just look at it?"

"What if one of them gets hurt attempting it?"

"Shit."

"And what if one of them gets hurt, and it turns out there's nothing in it except fair and robust investigation that shows inconclusive evidence?"

"What am I supposed to do, then?"

Rob sat on the sofa next to her. He held his head in his hands for a moment to think.

"If this was a police investigation, we'd look for another source of information."

"Yeah, but what?"

"Maybe it's a who? Maybe we need someone who has been

screwed over by them and is ready to talk about it."

"Just give up on the coroner's report?"

"Don't give up. The Freedom of Information Act will be something."

"Not if it's denied."

"The denial is evidence of something. It tells you that they don't want to share it."

"Okay. Fine. But what do I do about finding someone to rat out the current administration?"

"Good old fashioned hard work. Look up all the connections of the player, and try to find a deal gone bad that have left scar tissue."

"Ugh. Fine."

30

On Monday morning, Samantha ignored her father's shouts about getting up and going to work. She'd avoided him all weekend and still didn't want to talk to him or even think about going to work.

He came upstairs and stood next to her bed with his arms crossed.

"Hey, you sick?"

"I think so. I'm not going to work."

"Then we'll get you to a doctor."

"I think I need to talk to the counselor."

He cocked his head to one side and looked at her. "I'll make an appointment for you."

"That isn't necessary."

"Yes, it is."

She pulled the covers over her head, exhausted by her thoughts, dreading having to see Aurelia.

Samantha looked up and held Aurelia's gaze. "I'm not even sure I can talk about this."

Aurelia wrote something in her notebook. "It's an excellent thing that you're here, though. You have faced many challenges. I want to acknowledge that you're being brave."

"Hooray for me."

"How does that make you feel?"

"Which?" Samantha asked. "My sarcasm, or that you say I'm being brave?"

Aurelia smiled. "Either."

Samantha lowered her gaze to the floor once again.

"Let's try to talk about something else, okay? And then maybe you'll feel like talking about what's bothering you."

Samantha shrugged.

"Have you thought anymore about what you'll do about college?"

Samantha shook her head. "Nope. As of right now, I'm done with school."

"That's too bad. You're clever enough. You can do anything you want with your life."

"Anything?."

"Yes."

Samantha looked at her. "You can't tell anyone about what we talk about, right? That's how it works, right?"

"Our conversations are confidential."

Samantha raised her head to speak but returned her gaze to the floor, instead.

"Do you remember why you're here?"

Samantha shrugged.

"It's helping you process the emotions and trauma you've experienced. It's difficult, what you've gone through. I'm telling you this because I want you to know it doesn't matter to me whether you go to college. Of course I think you would love it, and you are more than smart enough. But I won't judge you if you choose not to."

"Okay."

"But I do hope you will work on processing your feelings."

"No matter how I process my feelings, my sister is still dead. And my mother is God knows where."

"Correct. You can't change that. So whether you choose to do nothing, or, say, go to college, either way it will be knowing that your sister is dead and your mother has left the family."

"It's all so unfair, though."

"Yes it is."

"And doesn't it seem strange how she died, and that it bothers no one?"

Aurelia nodded.

"My dad doesn't want to talk about it. He got mad when I brought up the subject."

"You mean at City Hall the other day?"

"You heard about that?"

"I have a friend who works there."

"Please don't say it was my Aunt Jan."

"She introduced me to your father when your family first needed counseling."

Samantha shook her head. "Ugh, I should just go back to my crappy job at the city, and just work there until everybody I know is dead, and then it'll all be fine."

"That's not a very healthy way to look at the situation."

Samantha chuckled. "It doesn't matter because there's no way they'll take me back."

"I think they will," Aurelia said. "They all love you, and just want what's best for you."

"What if I want to become a botanist and work at a gardening center?"

"They would still love you and be proud of you."

"I'm not so sure."

# # # #

On Tuesday, Samantha woke up early enough to go to work, and decided to at least try to get there. If she was going to do anything to uncover the truth, she'd search for it.

But it sure was tempting to stay in bed.

She exchanged minimal greetings with her father, whose own shift didn't begin until later in the day (another reason to go into work). At least she would have the house to herself in the evening.

That made her think. For so long it seemed all she wanted

was to have her family around her, and now she was avoiding the only family she had.

On her way out the door, her father said, "Have a good day."

"Thanks. You too." It was automatic, but it didn't hurt to say.

"Hey, have you thought about going to college? There's still plenty of time to get things going."

"I don't know, okay? I'm just going to get through today."

"Alright," he said with a playful lilt. "You can study botany, for all I care. I just want you to be happy."

It bothered Samantha about her father's talk of college on the way out the door. It annoyed her that he seemed to be in a good mood, looking forward to things. She just wanted to stay busy enough to not worry about the past.

At her desk, there was nothing waiting in her in box. "What day is this?" she asked Derek, who was reading the newspaper.

"Tuesday."

"Pay day."

"Yep."

"Good. I need something to do."

When Gayle returned to her desk, Samantha presented herself.

"Sorry I was out. I wasn't feeling well."

Gayle smiled. "It's fine. You're always welcome here. And your father mentioned that you might be back, so…"

"He did?"

Gayle nodded.

"Okay, well, it's Tuesday, so should I get the Payroll Report?"

"Oh, about that. Because I wasn't sure, we had Vickie, the bank intern, come over and get it. She'll handle the envelopes, too."

Samantha returned to her desk with Gayle's Rolodex to update once again. At least she had something to do.

Her father had suggested botany. It was probably a coincidence, but what if it wasn't? If Aurelia was telling her father about their sessions, what else had Aurelia told him? What had she said?

Vickie walked through the office, bounding like a cocker spaniel, reminding Samantha of why they never became friends.

She noticed Derek watching her. "You like her?"

Derek scoffed. "She's cute. But I have a girlfriend."

"You do? Who?"

"Heidi Marquardt."

"Huh. How did I not know that?"

"Because you don't hang around the softball field. Or when you do, you're out in right field with *Plain*."

"Heidi Marquardt. Is she in your class?"

"No, she's going to be a junior this year."

"In college?"

Derek laughed. "High school. Class of eighty-one."

"Uh, robbing the cradle?"

"Shut up."

"Is she fifteen?"

"She's sixteen."

"Yeah, but how long have you been dating?"

"A year."

Derek left, unconcerned if Samantha had anything else to say.

Samantha thought about the boys in her class who dated freshman and sophomore girls. There were a half dozen at least, and she remembered shaking her head at them during prom. They hadn't even chosen mature-looking girls.

She had gone to prom with Jimmy Keats, whom she could put up with because he was at least as smart as she was and seemed frightened by the entire process. She had asked Blaine, who seemed the safest and easiest option. But even he felt awkward attending prom after having graduated.

"You'll be twenty-two when Heidi has her prom," she said when Derek returned to his desk.

"Hey, you know your father is four years older than your mother. They dated in high school."

"Yeah, but..."

"Shit, Uncle Tom was dating Rebecca."

"Rebecca who?"

"Rebecca Marko."

"Are you serious?"

"Yeah. It's no big deal."

"He's like thirty years older than she is."

Derek thought a moment, then shrugged. "Yeah. Well, it's not like he forced her. She liked him. And Heidi likes me so shut up about it."

# # # #

In the afternoon, Vickie and Gayle distributed the pay envelopes. With a glance inside, Samantha counted, surprised that her entire pay was there.

"There was a mistake," Samantha told Gayle when she caught her back at her desk.

Gayle smiled and held out her hand for the envelope. "What's wrong?"

"My entire pay is there, and I missed like four days."

Gayle gave her back the envelope. "Oh, sweetie, don't worry about it."

"I don't want special treatment just because my grandfather is the mayor."

"It's not that. That's the way it is for everybody. He treats us all like family."

"Oh."

"That's why we love him. Don't you love him?"

Towards the end of the day, Big Mac lumbered through the office.

"Hey Derek," he said. But he didn't even look at Samantha.

Big Mac went to Gayle's desk, where she handed him three pay envelopes. Big Mac slipped them into his back pocket without saying a word and lumbered back out of the office.

Samantha recalled the extra envelopes from when she delivered payroll the previous weeks. She'd been willing to mind her own business then, but now she was more than a little curious.

Samantha carried a folder into the Police Department. The folder was empty, but no one knew that.

There was a blackboard behind Dottie's desk, and they listed all the policemen with their status: In, Out or Off-Duty. It listed Big Mac as "in."

As Samantha returned from her pretend errand, Dottie erased the mark for Big Mac, changing his status to "Off-duty."

Samantha went downstairs and slipped out the back door. She had left the keys to her car in it, and the doors unlocked, as always. Not only was it convenient, but who would steal a cop's car from the police parking lot.

She knew Big Mac drove a black Lincoln Continental, the only one in the lot, and she slouched down in her car and waited.

A few minutes later, Big Mac, having changed into his street clothes, lumbered out of the building and got into his car.

Samantha followed him. She let him get out of the parking lot and caught up to him at the corner where he stopped at a red light.

She left one or two cars between them, remembering something her father said during an episode of Starsky and Hutch, that only an idiot follows behind the car they are tailing.

Big Mac drove to the apartment complex on Memphis where he turned in. The winding path from parking lot to parking lot made her feel vulnerable, and she allowed the space between them to grow.

The Continental was out of site for a while when she glimpsed it at the end of one of the side parking lots. She caught a break in pulling into a spot at the opposite end and being able to peek out the passenger-side back window.

Big Mac lumbered to the last ground-floor apartment in

the building and knocked on the door. When the door opened, he handed the man inside an envelope.

Even from that great distance, Samantha was certain it was one of the payroll envelopes.

31

That evening, Samantha refused to go to the softball fields with Blaine. "And don't get high on me, either," she said. "I'm more insightful when I'm high. Like some people are funnier when they're drunk, I can tap into other parts of my brain with a little toke."

"Drunks are never funnier. They're louder and stupider. And you never stop at a little toke. You get useless."

"Okay, fine," Blaine said. "I'll smoke a cigarette and talk to you."

They sat on the patio behind the garage. The overgrown shrubs pressed in on the yard, and some grass reached to their knees as Blaine hadn't touched the back yard in over a year. It was a bit like sitting in the woods, as the rest of the vegetation grew thicker as it approached the city park. Later, when the softball games would end, the stillness would be calming. But now, shouts and cheers came and went with each inning, as the lights of the fields shone beyond the trees.

"Why else would Big Mac go there and hand some guy an envelope?"

"Maybe it's an off-duty cop."

"The pay envelopes stay with the secretary until picked up. I could have brought my Dad's home, but that was the only exception."

"I think it's just a coincidence, like he was paying off a bet. You know, Big Mac was making good on a bet because it was payday. The cops bet even more than the guys in the Service Garage. They all play cards. You should see it during football season."

"Big Mac left with three extra envelopes. I think it's too much of a coincidence that it's the apartment opposite Michael Key's."

Blaine lit another cigarette and began rolling a joint.

"Are you going to get high?" Samantha asked.

"Aren't we done talking?"

"I still don't know what to do?"

"There's nothing you can do. You can't tell anyone. If the cops want to give some guy in an apartment an envelope stuffed with cash, so what?"

"It means something's not right."

"Yeah, but if you bring it up, you're going to be the one in trouble. People kind of hate you already."

"I don't care if people hate me," she said. "I just want to know what happened to Lori."

"Okay, but then what?"

"What do you mean?"

"You're going to make a bunch of trouble, everyone will hate you for it, then you'll take off for college and I won't have anyone to hang around with."

"So you're saying ignore all of this stuff, and just pretend Lori died of natural causes, because people may not like us?"

"I'm just saying I don't know that we can accomplish anything, even if we can find the truth."

Blaine flipped his cigarette onto the lawn and lit his joint.

Samantha stood up. "So that's it? You're just going to get high and not worry."

"What do you want me to do?"

"I don't know, but I'm going to search my parents' room to see if there's anything there. Maybe my mom wrote letters and my dad hid them."

Blaine let out his smoke. "Good luck with that."

"Don't be an ass about it. You're my only friend right now, and I don't want to hate you."

\# \# \# \#

Samantha paced through the house, looking out each window in succession. Her father had driven to the softball fields, rather than walking, which meant he was going to the bar after the game. If her father were to come home, he'd pull in the driveway and park out front, then come in the side door.

She'd likely hear the car pull in the driveway, or at least the car door closing after he got out. But if she missed both, he'd come in the side door.

If she were in his bedroom, there'd be time to get out and slip into the bathroom before he made it through the kitchen.

There was little chance she'd get caught snooping, but it scared her half to death to think of how angry he'd be.

His bedroom had always been off-limits to her and to Lori. Even when their mother was with them, she would only allow them in the bedroom for very specific reasons, then hustle them out again.

They could never just hang out in there and got spanked if caught.

She and Lori had done it, of course, but there was never anything interesting in there. Her father kept a revolver in the drawer in his night stand, but they were both convinced that touching it would cause a spanking. Or being shot.

The search wouldn't take long because the room was small. There was a dresser, a chest of drawers, one nightstand, and the closet. The greatest challenge was moving around the tiny room packed tight with furniture. How her mother got dressed each morning was a mystery.

Samantha checked the night stand first. There was a box of ammunition in the drawer, a couple of letters, and one of those tiny bibles taken from a motel.

In the chest of drawers, the top two drawers held her father's clothing, and the bottom two her mother's. She slipped her hands in and felt around the clothing, careful not to disturb anything.

The dresser had a variety of drawers, with socks and underpants for both her mother and father. A thin center drawer held scarves. The one below that held fancy gloves. She never realized her mother had so many pairs of gloves.

In the bottom of the large drawer, there was a nine-by-twelve inch envelope. She pulled it out.

Before looking inside, she checked that her father had not come home. Then she sat her butt down next to the drawer and looked inside the envelope.

They were all pictures of her mother. If Samantha had ever seen them before, she didn't remember it.

Photos of her mother so young that it must have been before she met her father.

Photos of her mother and father, dating,.

Candid photos taken at their wedding, and the years that followed.

Photos of Lori and herself with their mother, right until she left them.

Samantha felt a lump in her throat. She mustn't cry. She might not hear her father come home if she was crying.

But there were no letters in the envelope.

She looked underneath the bed where, amid the dust, was nothing she cared about: a baseball bat, dress shoes and basketball shoes, and a book about Dwight D. Eisenhower.

She checked the closet. The top shelf held her mother's hat boxes and fancy shoes. She had no memory of her mother wearing any of that fancy stuff, but she recognized some pieces from the photos she'd just reviewed.

At the bottom there was a box of papers, but flipping through them, there was nothing of interest. Just tax returns and bills.

Below that was a brown paper shopping bag. Inside the bag was Lori's white oxford sneaker, the one Samantha found at Rebecca's house.

# # # #

Samantha searched the basement, finding nothing of interest. There were boxes of her school papers, the collection halting once her mother left.

She searched in anger, having learned her father did nothing about Lori's Converse basketball sneaker. He'd said it was just a shoe, and maybe it was, but why not try?

Frustrated, she walked back to Blaine's house needing a break.

She recalled how she'd left Blaine, and worried about him. He had a point that, if she left to college, he wouldn't have a friend. The guys he hung around with in high school were off to college, and guys like Derek that stayed were not his friends.

The light of the television glowed in Blaine's front room, so Samantha entered through the front door.

Blaine sprawled across the sofa, the red glow of his roach at his lips.

"What's up?" Blaine asked.

"Are you okay?"

"I don't know. Are you?"

"No."

She closed the door and sat next to him. Blaine offered the joint, but she shook her head.

"Did you find anything?" he asked.

"No. Nothing."

"I did." Blaine held up a small envelope.

"What is it?"

"I don't know what the fuck it is. I thought getting a little fucked up might help."

"Let me see."

Blaine blew smoke at her and pressed the envelope to his chest. "I think it's from your mother."

"What do you mean?"

"It's a note from your mother to my dad."

Samantha snatched it from his grasp and looked at the writing on the outside.

"Why would she?"

"I can't quite picture it."

She opened it and pulled the note out of the envelope. As she unfolded the paper, she recognized the handwriting. It was her mother's.

# # # #

Samantha walked back from Blaine's house clutching the card in her hands, thinking about what she read. How was it possible her mother and Blaine's father had an affair? How did that even work? Did they have sex in their house or Blaine's?

Did they have sex, or just exchange greeting cards with love notes written inside?

How did she and Lori not know? Or did Lori know? Did Lori suspect it but hide it the way she hid Rebecca's affair with their Uncle Tom?

Did her father suspect?

"Hey," he said.

She looked up and there was her father, sitting on the front steps of their house, wearing his softball uniform and clutching a beer in his hands. She approached across the lawn but stopped half-way there.

"You okay?" he asked.

"I'm not sure."

"Are you sick?"

"Upset about something."

Her father took a swig of beer. "Let's hear it."

Samantha noticed his tone, realized this was a traffic stop, and she had done something wrong. But she didn't know what he was thinking. She slipped the note into her back pocket.

"You can tell me anything. We have to trust each other, sweetheart."

Samantha wasn't sure what he said. A window slammed shut behind her across the street, and she jumped a foot to the side, turning to look.

Her father stood up. "What's wrong with you?"

"Nothing," she said. Her heart was pounding. Her face was flush and sweat trickled down the back of her neck. "I just want to shower and go to bed."

"Are you on drugs?"

"No."

"Were you with Blaine? Are you high?"

"No, God damn it. Just leave me alone."

She tried to get up the steps, but he blocked her path. "I want to ask you something."

"Just leave me alone." She turned to go in the side door, but he grabbed her arm. She pulled free, but he had taken the note from her back pocket.

"What's this?"

"None of your damn business."

He opened it with the hand holding his beer, and Samantha grabbed it, knocking the bottle loose. It smashed on the front steps.

"God damn it," he shouted. "What is wrong with you?"

"Nothing that isn't wrong with this whole fucking place."

"You must be on something," he said and tried to grab her arm again.

"I'm not on anything," she said. "Just leave me the fuck alone for a little while."

She went around to the side door and went inside, rushing up to her room and hiding her mother's note under the mattress of her bed, just above Lori's shoe tucked underneath in the shopping bag.

32

Samantha lay on her bed and stared at the ceiling. Downstairs, her father showered and then left the house. The car backed out of the driveway and drove away.

She wanted to search the house but it could take days, and it would still take a stroke of luck to find something useful, assuming there was something to discover, and that her mother had hidden it.

Samantha sat up in bed, surprised by that thought: what if her mother hid something from her father, waiting to be discovered? Where wouldn't her father look?

The cookbooks in a kitchen cupboard? The boxes stuffed with greeting cards she'd received over the years. The corner in the garage where she kept gardening stuff.

Any of those places might reveal her secrets, but she didn't know how much time she had to search. It was like a math problem in algebra. If he drove to The Duo for a beer, he might be back soon. But if he drove to a strip club, he might be out past midnight. Did he even go to strip clubs?

With him it was softball or The Duo. His only friends were on his team, but he didn't spend time with them outside of softball and The Duo.

He didn't spend time with any women, as far as she knew. The secretaries at work were the only women he interacted with. There was their counselor, Aurelia, but that seemed too weird to even consider.

Still, Aurelia was a woman. They spoke a lot. And hugged.

She got out the white pages and searched for her name, but found nothing. Samantha remembered seeing the name and address once. Aurelia had sent her a graduation card.

Samantha hadn't expected to receive a card from her family counselor.

Samantha flipped through the stack of cards—set aside for when she was ready to write thank you notes—and found it.

Samantha hopped in the car and drove to The Duo tavern just in case her father was out for a beer. If so, she'd go back home and do a quick search of the house.

But her father's car was not in the parking lot.

She drove into Parma with a vague sense of where she was going. It would have been smarter to check a map, first, but she recognized the street. Besides, this exercise had nothing to do with being smart.

Fifteen minutes later, she was at the foot of the State Road hill and turned on Amrap Street. She drove along it, straining to find the house numbers. The houses here were like the houses in the Village, two-bedroom bungalows on tiny lots.

The house had white siding, a front stoop with bushes on either side. There was a light on behind the drawn shades in the window. And there was a car in the driveway pulled up alongside the house.

The car was a blue Ford Crown Victoria, just like her father's car.

She parked two houses up and walked back. It was dark beside the house but she found a Friend of Police sticker in the back window, and her father's softball hat on the back ledge.

The house belonged to her counselor, Aurelia Delacruz.

Samantha felt sick and staggered back to her car. Now that she knew, what would she do?

She didn't want to talk to him about it now.

She wasn't sure if she would talk to him ever again.

At three in the morning, there was pounding on Blaine's front door. "Samantha," her father shouted. "Are you in there?"

Samantha had been dozing on the sofa, wrapped in a blanket and still dressed in her clothes, expecting this visit. She went to the door but didn't open it.

"I'm okay Dad," she said. "I'm staying here tonight."

"What the hell are you talking about? Are you drunk?"

"Nope, just sleeping on the couch."

"Where's Blaine?"

"In his bed, asleep."

"Open this God damn door."

"Where were you?"

"Just open this door."

"Tell me where you were."

"I was out. I'm an adult."

"Who were you with?"

"Okay, what the hell is going on? Just open the door, and let's go home, and we'll talk about it in the morning."

Samantha waited a second, hoping he'd say something else. "I'm going to sleep here for a few days."

"Tell me what this is about."

"I need a few days. I'll be fine."

"Samantha. Please open the door."

"I'm an adult," she said. It sounded strange. She hadn't thought of herself that way until that moment. "I can stay here if I want to."

"Fine," he said. "Do whatever the fuck you want to do."

33

Aaron joined the reporter at her preferred cafe in Cuya-hoga Heights. Her expression confused him. She seemed morose and concerned, the same look his wife had when she bailed him out of jail.

"You okay?" he asked.

She was drinking coffee and spooned two ice cubes into it. "I'm fine. I just want to talk to all of you."

"Did you tell them you'd buy them dinner?"

"No."

"You should have," Aaron said. "They both look like they need a good meal."

That got her to laugh. "You seem so relaxed. After all this, and what we've seen..."

"I'm not relaxed. I'm pissed."

"That's okay if you are."

Aaron glanced around, concerned the other patrons might pay attention to them. "Listen, Francine. I need you to make something happen. You're looking a little worn down. If you're folding your cards, you need to let me know."

"I'm not folding."

Aaron gave her a reassuring smile. Or as reassuring of a smile as he could muster. After all, they smashed his hopes to mother-fucking smithereens. He didn't want to be on a wild goose chase.

The two kids arrived and Francine lightened up a bit,

telling them to order whatever they wanted.

"Me too?" Aaron asked.

She laughed. "Of course."

"Now tell us what's bothering you," he said.

"I don't want you to take anything that doesn't belong to you because of what I told you the other day."

"You mean like the coroner's report?" Blaine asked. "I had no intention of doing that."

"Good," Francine said. "I shouldn't have even suggested such a thing, let alone ask you. It was unprofessional of me, and I'm sorry."

"Do you have a Plan B for breaking this story?" Aaron asked.

"I'll try to find a source, either in the Medical Examiner's office, or in the Police Department, who can provide information without breaking the law."

"Sounds like it may take a while."

Francine nodded, drank her coffee, stalling. "I'm sorry about that. Often these big stories take a while to put together."

"Months?" Samantha asked.

"Yes," Francine said. "Months. Years?"

"Did you ever talk to Rebecca Marko?"

Francine shook her head. "That has turned into a tough nut to crack."

"I'm going to go to lunch with her at some point," Samantha said. "I'll call you."

"That would help."

"Also, I saw one of our police officers deliver an envelope of cash to the apartment across from where your son lived."

"She doesn't know for sure it was an envelope of cash," Blaine said.

"It was payday," she said.

Aaron exchanged a look with the reporter. As Samantha explained the city's weekly cash payroll process, they exchanged more looks.

"That's how my father got paid thirty years ago," Aaron said.

"I saw the cop with extra envelopes at the office and followed him out to the apartment building."

"It's every Tuesday?" Francine asked.

Samantha nodded.

"Well, that's something. I'll stop by there next week."

"Let's go there now," Aaron said. "I'll just ask them about Michael, right?"

"That might not be the best," Francine said. "I'll go there. I promise."

She was right. He'd only have one chance at such a move before the cops were all over him. He wasn't sure he'd walk out of the police station if those cracker cops dragged him in again.

"Make sure you get pictures, then."

Francine nodded. "If they're protecting someone, it won't be a simple thing to get enough info for a story. Even after completing the research, there's time needed to make sense of it—"

"Yeah, okay," Aaron said. "We get it."

He wasn't so sure. They could still buy this young woman off, or she might settle down with the cop, or get another job somewhere. Options Michael never had. Options he himself never had either, not that he was complaining.

"I'm curious about this cash payroll," Francine said. "I know it was normal before the 1950s."

"There are rumors that the city launders mob money," Blaine said.

"What the hell are you talking about?" Samantha said. "My grandfather is not part of the mob."

"He wouldn't have to be part of the mob," Blaine said. "Just takes cash in for a fee and uses it to pay the employees."

"That sounds illegal."

"It's just a rumor."

"You shouldn't say that."

"Okay," Blaine said. "Sorry."

Aaron waited a moment, expecting Francine to say something about this rumor, but she said nothing.

"I hope it's just a rumor," Aaron said. "That's a whole 'nother level of crazy."

"It's not true," Samantha said. "Stupid people always say dumb stuff about politicians."

"I said I was sorry," Blaine said.

After Francine paid the bill, and they walked outside, Aaron shouted to Samantha, "One second."

He hurried over to the two kids. "Thank you," he said. "You're making a few things happen and I needed that. I don't want whoever did this to get away with it."

"Me neither," Samantha said, although Aaron wasn't sure she believed her own words.

"Where can I call you? I think we should talk outside the reach of our reporter friend."

"Call me at City Hall tomorrow," Samantha said. "You can just ask for me if I'm not at my desk."

"Don't tell them it's you, though," Blaine said.

"And why is that?" Aaron asked.

"You know, because you're black. No offense."

"None taken, white boy."

# # # #

Aaron drove to a filling station with a pay phone and called Samantha Sykora at the Village municipal offices.

"Who may I ask is calling?" a woman asked.

"George Jefferson."

"Please hold."

When Samantha answered, and he was certain that she knew who he was, he wasted no time. "Is that coroner's report still in your uncle's office?"

"I suppose."

"Then will you help me get a copy of it?"

There was a few seconds' pause. "I'm just not sure how that would work."

"You can get your boy to help you. He has keys, and a reason to be poking around offices."

"He might, but I wouldn't rely on him."

"That's smart," Aaron said. He wasn't sure he'd rely on Blaine, either.

"I just don't know when I'd have a chance."

"You can't get in during the night?"

"The office never closes," she whispered. "Police station, you know?"

"All we need is a distraction."

"It will have to be a big one."

She had a point. They must have thirty cops total, with a dozen hanging around all the time. "Maybe a fire would empty the place."

"Uh, wouldn't that just attract more attention?"

"Maybe a fire next door, at the bank."

There was another pause. "Maybe."

"Okay. Now we're talking."

"Wait, no. I mean, I'm not sure..."

"We need to meet."

"Uh..."

"Can you meet at your boy's house? He lives close to you, right?"

"Yes."

"Around midnight, okay?"

"Wait, how are you going to get here?" Her voice dropped to a whisper. "What if someone sees you?"

"If I get there, you'll know no one saw me."

# # # #

Aaron didn't bother to hide his face as he walked in the park along the edge of the backyards. If anyone saw a man with a hood pulled over his head, they would call the police, just like if they saw a black man.

And with what he carried with him in a brown paper bag, the cops would throw him in a hole and never let him out.

He found the yard and walked in, hoping that most people didn't walk their dogs this late.

He paused at the garage, looking at the houses on either side to make sure no one was out for a smoke or enjoying the evening out back.

The kitchen light was on inside Blaine's house. The houses on both sides of Blaines were dark. He went to Blaine's side door and knocked. Samantha let him in.

"Draw the shades," he said. "People will look in the windows."

"Okay," Samantha said from the front room once she'd closed them all.

"Where's your boy?" Aaron asked.

"I'm not a boy," Blaine said. He'd just stepped into the kitchen.

"Good. I wanted to hear that."

He offered Samantha the brown paper bag, and she peeked inside.

"What is it?"

"Lock pick, pry bar and screwdriver. What you need to pick most locks."

"Burglar tools," Blaine said.

Aaron nodded. "You ready to learn?"

"Where d'you learn this?" Blaine asked, rocking in his recliner.

"All black people know this stuff," Aaron said and threw him a wink.

"Really?"

"No. I used to be a locksmith, before I started this business."

"Why d'you give that up?"

"The shop where I worked burned down in the riots, and I had to hustle. The vending machines paid well, so that was that."

Blaine looked worried, and Aaron would not push it. If the kid wasn't ready, they were better off without him. "Hey man, nothing is happening soon. Sammy here needs some time to practice and monitor her uncle's office to figure out when she can do this. I have to figure out how I'm going to distract an entire police force without getting myself shot."

"Good luck with that," Blaine said.

"You going to rat your girl here out if we try this?"

Blaine shook his head. "I still don't think you'll figure anything out."

"How about you?" Aaron asked Samantha. "You still interested?"

The girl nodded.

"Then let's get you started."

34

Samantha was at her desk updating another Rolodex, this one Betty's, her uncle's secretary. She worried that she'd re-type hand-corrected contact cards the rest of her summer. She also didn't care, because Lori's death consumed her thoughts.

Uncle Tom entered the City Administration Offices, accompanied by Vickie, the intern from the Municipal Bank. They were laughing about something. Tom leaned down to whisper something, and Vickie laughed even louder. Tom beamed.

It confused Samantha. Tom was at least thirty years older than Vickie. He was taller, and the bulk on his frame dwarfed the teenager.

"Why are they together?" Samantha asked in a whisper to Derek at the next desk. "Is that weird?"

"They've been hanging out."

"What do you mean?"

Tom and Vickie walked into the mayor's office. Gayle glanced at them, then met Samantha's gaze before returning to her typing.

Tom and Vickie walked out of the office a moment later, giggling anew, and left the area.

"Like are they dating?"

Derek shrugged. "You could call it that."

"She's still in high school."

Derek nodded. "She comes to his softball games, and then

they go out after."

"Like on a date?"

Derek laughed. "What is the big deal?"

"You still don't think that's weird?"

"Hey it's her choice."

"Uh, gross."

Samantha walked to the Police Department and heard Vickie's laughter inside the chief's office. As Samantha approached, Betty looked at her and she realized she had no reason for being there.

"What do you need?" Betty asked.

"Oh, uh, when did you want the Rolodex back?"

"As soon as possible."

"Sure."

"Why don't you just pull out the changed cards and give me back the Rolodex, and you can insert the updates as you go."

"Sure."

Samantha looked into Tom's office and Vickie glanced over her shoulder at her. She seemed content.

Samantha, disgusted with her father and repulsed by her uncle, fumed as she pulled contact cards out of the Rolodex.

She returned the Rolodex to Betty's desk and, having waited until Betty was away from her desk, Samantha looked in Tom's office.

He was leaning back in his chair, reading the sports section of the newspaper. There was a greeting card standing on the corner of his desk.

"Is it your birthday?" she asked and pointed at the card.

Tom lowered the paper. "What?"

She took the opening and grabbed the card. The front was a goofy cartoon character under the heading "Thinking of You..." Inside, they signed it, "Vickie."

Tom snatched it out of her hands. "No it's not my birthday."

"Are you and Vickie dating?"

Tom took a set of keys from his pocket and opened the credenza beneath his trophy case. The key was stubby, no different from the keys for the desks.

He riffed through the folders in the drawer and dropped the card into one of them. "Don't worry about it."

Samantha backed out of the office.

"Hey," Tom said. "You got a problem with something?"

Samantha shook her head.

# # # #

Lori once told Samantha how she and Rebecca rode their bikes to Jakov's house. Lori spent the day at Rebecca's, which she often did in summer, and of course Rebecca had an extra bike. The stories about Jakov were like the stories of Mary Jane or the Bogey Man, and to trespass at his old, broken-down house would make them legend.

They knocked on the front door and retreated across the yard. At first, nothing happened, so they talked themselves into knocking again, just to be sure.

As they approached the door, Jakov opened it, his mouth open and his clothes covered in filth.

They ran screaming to their bikes and pedaled back to Rebecca's house, where they locked themselves in the bedroom.

What if Jakov never forgot about that visit? He would have seen the girls growing up, playing in the park while he mowed the lawn. He would have seen them swimming in the pool when he emptied the trash or repaired the fence, or whatever the hell he did.

Samantha recalled that Lori had said that Rebecca was having some kind of problem. Maybe bringing up the bike trip would help Rebecca remember what she and Lori talked about before Lori died.

Samantha left without a word and walked across the parking lot to the municipal bank. It was quiet, as usual, and Hank nodded to her from his chair inside the door. Rebecca was at her desk, reading a magazine.

"Do you want to go to lunch tomorrow?"

Rebecca stared for a second. "I don't know. I'm kind of busy."

"I need to talk with someone who knew Lori. My dad just doesn't get how I feel."

"Sure, I guess."

"You want me to pick you up?"

"What kind of car do you drive?"

"It's a rusting Plymouth Fury."

Rebecca scowled. "We'll take my Camaro."

The next day, Samantha felt giddy as Rebecca tore out of the parking lot and chirped the tires when the stoplight turned green.

"Okay," she said. "This car is pretty cool."

"What's in the bag?" Rebecca asked, glancing at the brown paper bag in Samantha's lap.

"Just something to show you later."

"Okay, cool. It worried me it was your purse." Rebecca laughed and then sped up.

When Samantha told her where she wanted to go, it confused Rebecca. "I thought we were going to splurge."

"I like this place. Don't you like greasy spoons?"

"Gross."

"No, not actual greasy spoons. It just means it's a simple place with homey food."

"Yeah. I know. Gross."

Rebecca looked around the neighborhood after they parked. "I have never, ever, been here. Or within twenty miles of this place. Are we safe?"

"It's okay, Rebecca. We're just two miles from home."

"It's gross."

Inside, the waitress pointed to a booth by the front window and brought them water and coffee.

"Could I get a Tab?" Rebecca asked.

The waitress took their orders, frowning as Rebecca ordered the cottage cheese while questioning its fat content.

"Thanks for coming out," Samantha said. "These past weeks have been so weird without Lori, and now I'm fighting with my dad."

"Yeah, I heard you're living with Blaine. You're not sleeping with him, are you?"

"No."

"Thank God." Rebecca laughed.

"I didn't realize how many things I missed by not working at the city or hanging around the softball games. It's like this entire world is happening and I have no idea it's even there."

"You did nothing in high school, right? So you missed a lot that way."

"I was in choir, band, and a bunch of clubs."

"Okay, but you weren't a cheerleader, like Lori and me, so we knew everything that was going on through most of the school year. Then we were at the softball fields pretty much every night, starting in spring. And we both worked in the bank, and your Aunt Jan seems to know everything about everybody."

"I was also the student council president, but you're right: you and Lori did a lot."

"Yeah. So how do you like working in your grandpa's office?"

"It's fine. A little boring."

"You know he and my dad were like partners from way, way back."

Samantha nodded. Of course she knew that. "Hey, I think Vickie Fulton is dating my uncle Tom."

Rebecca sipped her Tab and stared.

"Don't you think it's a little weird, this fifty-year-old man dating a girl in high school?"

"He's forty-eight."

"What?"

"Tom is forty-eight. He was born in 1930."

"It's a thirty-year difference in age. And I'm not even sure she's ever dated anyone else."

"You think she's like you? Well, nope, not at all. I heard she's a bit of a slut. And I don't mean that as criticism. I'm just saying, she's been on her back before. And on her knees more than once."

"Oh. Wow."

"Yeah. So...let's not talk about her. She's a little bitch and her father started another family, so I think she's fucked up and a bitch about it."

The food arrived and Rebecca picked at her tuna, complaining that it was too fishy.

"Was Lori dating the guy who was with her in the boat?" Samantha asked.

Rebecca froze mid-chew. "What?"

"I thought you might know, because she never mentioned him, and no one else ever mentioned him. It just seemed weird that she would have somehow met this guy who didn't go to her college, didn't even work near her college, and didn't seem to know anyone else in the city. I mean, did you know him?"

Rebecca shook her head as she took a bite of the cottage cheese.

"It's weird she ends up on your boat with this guy."

"Yeah, I don't know."

"She never mentioned having a boyfriend?"

"No, never."

Samantha, coached by Francine on how to ask these questions, bit into her B.L.T. and chewed.

Rebecca broke the silence.

"I think it was like a secret thing of hers that she didn't want anyone to know about. I mean, he had no friends, at least in the Village, and he was a black guy."

"Micheal," Samantha offered. "That's his name."

"Right. Michael, but he had no connections, so I think he was just cute and, you know, she was having fun."

"So you think they were lovers?"

"I don't know. I guess we'll never know."

Samantha took another bite, but she broke the silence this

time. "That night, she stopped by the house around nine, and told me she was going to see you because you were having a problem with your former boyfriend, and that you were seeing someone new."

"She did?"

Samantha nodded as she took a drink.

"I don't know why she'd say that," Rebecca said. "I mean, I didn't even see her."

"Did she come over to your house?"

"When?"

"That night."

"I guess she had to, right?," Rebecca said with a shrug. "She took the keys for the boat."

"And where were you?"

Rebecca put down her fork and glared. "What is your point?"

"It just seemed like Lori thought you'd be there."

"I was at the mall."

"Oh."

Samantha lifted the paper bag from her lap and took out a shoe. It was a white canvas Converse basketball sneaker.

"What the hell?"

"It's Lori's shoe."

"Okay, that's creepy."

"I found this outside your house that day I came over. And I can't figure out what would have happened to Lori that she lost a shoe but didn't go back for it. Would you do that?"

"What?"

"Would you lose a shoe and then go somewhere, like on a boat, on a frosty night without a jacket and one bare foot?"

Rebecca stood up and grabbed her purse. "You're being so weird and rude right now, I just—"

Rebecca left the diner. A minute later, Samantha heard the Camaro tear out of the parking lot and race down the road.

The waitress asked if something was wrong.

"It's fine," Samantha said. "Thank you."

Francine, who had been sitting in the next booth, got up

and joined Samantha.

"Did you get it?"

Francine nodded as she placed the tape recorder on the table. Then she grabbed her coffee and sat back down.

"Are you going to be okay?" she asked.

"I'm not sure," Samantha said.

She ate the rest of her B.L.T. and put money on the table for their bill. "I don't know what she'll do."

"I don't think she'll ever go to lunch with you again."

"No, we can rule that out."

Francine glanced around the diner, then leaned over the table. "I want to talk to the people living across from Michael in the apartment. They must have seen something."

35

Tom sprawled on the sofa in his office when the phone rang. Lunch sat in his gut, so he let the phone roll over to Betty. He closed his eyes to nap.

The door opened. "It's Rebecca Marko for you," Betty said. "It seems urgent."

"What does she want?"

"To talk to you."

"I'll call her back."

Betty sighed. "She's upset."

"About what?"

"She didn't say. And you know she'll keep calling, so you may as well take it."

"Fuck it."

Tom heaved himself up from the sofa and settled in at his desk. He took one more breath, appreciating how good the lunch was, and picked up the phone.

"Hey."

She was crying.

"Hey. You want to talk, so talk."

"I just..."

"You just what? No, stop. Hang on." He returned to the sofa and pressed the receiver against his chest to drown out her sobbing. Once he sprawled out, he put the phone to his ear.

"Okay," he said as he arranged himself on the sofa. "Okay. Whatever it is, it's going to be okay."

There was a delay as Rebecca sobbed and tried to catch her breath. She calmed down. "Are you fucking Vickie Fulton?"

"No, and why are you asking me that?"

"Because that's what your niece, Samantha, thinks."

"She's an idiot."

"And she said some awful things to me."

"Like what?"

"Weird things about Lori and Michael."

"What'd she say?"

"She asked me if I thought they were dating. Which they couldn't have been."

"Yeah, but they must have been talking, right?"

"I still don't know how they could have been. I didn't even talk about him to Lori."

"Her father is a pretty good cop. Maybe he looked into it for her, and then, well, who knows what happened."

There was a pause on the line.

"You're not fucking Vickie?"

"We're friends, that's all."

"Oh shit. God damn it."

"What? Relax, will you?"

"But you told me to lie low for a while, that I needed some time."

"You do."

"Then what are you doing with Vickie?"

"Nothing. I swear to God. She's a good kid and she's just figuring stuff out."

"Okay, but don't help her figure out too much. And by that I mean don't fuck her."

"I promise. Jesus, why are you so upset about this?"

"It's Samantha. She asked me to lunch, and then she attacked me with these questions and Lori's shoe. It was so morbid."

"Where are you?"

"I took the afternoon off because I couldn't work. It was so weird."

"You're home?"

“Yeah.”

“Do you want me to come over?”

“No, my mom is here.”

Tom took a minute deciding if he needed to keep talking or if he could hang up.

“You know,” he said, “you’re lucky that wasn’t you on the boat. You just don’t know about some people until it’s too late.”

“That’s so weird. He seemed so nice.”

“That’s what Lori thought, too.”

“Ugh, I just can’t picture it.”

“Yeah, well, maybe we should get back together this weekend?”

“Uh, yeah, right.”

“I still care about you.”

“That’s nice.”

“You could come over my place.”

“I don’t know. Let me think about it.”

“Okay.”

“Can you do me a favor, though?” Rebecca asked.

“Sure.”

“Fire Samantha.”

36

Samantha whittled the stack of contact cards down to her last dozen when Gayle stopped by her desk.

"Are those Betty's contacts?" she asked.

"Yes, I'm almost done."

"I'll take them. Betty asked me to finish them up."

"It will just be a few more minutes. Like an hour, at most —"

Gayle smiled as she scooped them up along with the typed cards already completed. "They'd rather I do it and bring them over."

"Was I taking too long?"

"No."

"What then?"

"Do you have to question everything?"

Samantha watched as Gayle settled back into her desk and began typing. Then Samantha went to see her grandfather, not bothering to look at Gayle on the way in.

"Grampa?" she asked. "Is everything okay?"

"I suppose," he said. "Why do you ask?"

"Gayle seems angry at me. Did I do something wrong?"

He placed the papers he'd been reading into a manila folder and pushed it to one side of his desk, leaning forward and gazing at her.

"It's all about perspective and perception."

"What is?"

"You talked Rebecca Marko, right? You said a few things or asked a few things, having to do with Lori. Is that correct?"

"Yes."

"It upset her."

"A lot of things upset Rebecca."

He nodded. "That's true. From your perspective."

"From every perspective."

"Lori and Rebecca were best friends. I think Lori would want us to worry about how this tragedy has affected Rebecca, don't you agree?"

"I guess."

"So I'm sure you'll understand."

"Understand what?"

"We think you should stay out of the bank for a while, stay away from Rebecca until this blows over."

"Yeah, fine."

"Also the Police Department."

"What? Why?"

"There's been a bit of chatter and the troops are a little less than pleased with the comments you made during your uncle's award ceremony."

She shook her head. This seemed a little weird, but how do you say that to Grampa Peter? Everything he said was always the best thing.

"You're still seeing a counselor, correct?"

"Yeah."

"That's all," Grampa Peter said. "If you confine yourself to our offices here, then everything will be all right. Okay?"

She nodded. She'd seen that look on his face before. He was done talking to her.

# # # #

She sat at her desk with nothing to do, arms crossed and staring out the window. Derek offered his radio with the ear piece for listening and she accepted it, wiping away the yellow wax with a tissue before searching for a station. All she could find was an AM station, but it was something.

Her father visited before lunch. "How are you?"

"Fine."

"You okay? Maybe you should go see Aurelia?"

"Oh, because seeing her is what makes you happy these days?"

He drummed his fingers on her desk. "I'm going to get Lori's things from her apartment. I could use some help."

She glanced at him but didn't answer.

"Well? Do you want to help?"

"Can we talk about it later?"

"When's later? You don't live at home anymore, remember?"

The anger in his voice helped stall her tears.

"I guess."

"Don't worry about it. Jan will help. I'll call her."

"No. I'll do it. When?"

"Tonight."

"Fine."

"Should I pick you up at Blaine's?"

"I'll come home." Anything to keep Jan out of Lori's things and her father away from Blaine.

Lori's roommate, Julie, had moved out after the funeral, leaving the apartment in a state of abandonment. It made the apartment sadder, and Samantha stayed in the entrance. She wasn't sure about going inside. This seemed like a mistake.

Her father came in with a bundle of cardboard. He, too, paused in the entrance. At first, Samantha thought he felt the apartment's sadness. But he was just making plans.

"I think we should start in this room. Do you want to put together the boxes? I'll go get the garbage bags."

The living room furniture was still there, and Lori's things scattered about so she could almost believe it was normal. But she couldn't help but see the empty walls and shelves. In one corner, stacks of Lori's books and papers seemed lonely.

The dining room table seemed like a monument to Lori with piles of sports programs, student newspapers, and photographs stacked.

Lori's bedroom, however, was a mess. She scattered clothes across the bed and floor. Towels draped over the desk. Toiletries and tissues on the floor.

"Where are the boxes," her father called from the living room.

Samantha found a clean tissue and wiped her eyes. "Here I come."

"This is pretty good," he said as he looked through the kitchen cupboards. "Julie did a lot."

"Should we look for clues?" she asked.

"What do you mean?"

"Maybe Lori left some notes, or a diary, or something that would help us understand how she ended up on a boat on Lake Erie, rather than at her friend's house."

"Samantha, you—"

"You're a cop, Dad. Aren't you just a bit curious?"

He put down his garbage bag. "Sweetie, I'm afraid we're just going to live with the mystery of why this happened. She was doing something she shouldn't have."

"No, Dad. I don't believe it. Something happened that shouldn't have, but I can't believe it was Lori's fault."

"I can't force you to believe anything, but I can ask you to not make things harder than they have to be."

"What do you mean?"

"The incident during Tom's award ceremony. The thing with Rebecca. Now this. We need to appreciate the family we have and get on with our lives."

"You still don't think it's strange that the investigation was a joke? Don't you want to see the coroner's report?"

"Tom has looked at it, and that's good enough for me."

"You have heard no rumors about Jakov?"

"What are you talking about?"

"He might be involved somehow."

"That makes no sense."

"Right. It doesn't. But here we are with all of Lori's stuff but no interest in looking around and making sense of it."

"Take a critical eye to what you see. I think we'll both be happier once you've gotten these ideas out of your system."

Samantha felt pressure in her stomach, anger, like when she found out her mother left. "What was that thing you used to tell Lori about not quitting?"

"I don't know what you're talking about."

"You told Lori that she had to play sports like she was in a fight for her life."

"Okay, sure."

"You said, 'Keep fighting no matter what. If your hand gets cut off, you keep punching with a bloody stump.'"

He nodded. "That's right."

Samantha didn't mean to, but she cried. "Sounds like you quit fighting."

He raised his hands in surrender. "I don't see anyone to fight, just stuff to pack up and take home. If you find a smoking gun, let me know. But everything else please put in a box and tape it shut."

Samantha wanted to say something else, but she knew from the look on his face he was done talking to her.

Samantha fumed in the car as they drove home. There were no journals and no diary. Lori left no cryptic messages hidden in case something happened to her. There was no folder of evidence that she'd gathered pursuing a mystery.

Lori had been gregarious and funny. She'd been adventurous and fearless, charming and witty. Those people don't keep journals. They don't brood and worry and pour out their dark secrets in a diary. They live an amazing life and then write their autobiography once they've settled down.

Lori just didn't get the chance.

It was even possible that this Michael had met her, made

some outlandish suggestion about going out on a boat, and Lori stole the keys and went out on Lake Erie. It was possible she'd died during one of her amazing life adventures.

Samantha hated that possibility. She didn't want to go through life blaming Lori for leaving her alone.

In the back seat were half-a-dozen boxes of Lori's things that were personal mementos and they wanted to get them home. Movers would pick up the rest in a couple of days.

Was there something in one of those boxes she missed?

"Did you eat?" Her father asked.

"Not hungry."

He pulled into the hamburger shop on the corner and went inside. Samantha felt the pangs of hunger but wouldn't give him the satisfaction of feeding her.

Once she was back at Blaine's, she'd walk back to the corner and get her own hamburger.

When her father got back in the car, he handed her a sack. "I got you one, anyway."

They carried the boxes inside and stacked them at the foot of Lori's bed upstairs. It was upsetting, and Samantha couldn't help but cry.

After they carried in the last one, she sat on her own bed and sobbed.

She thought maybe her father would choose this moment to talk to her. Instead, she heard him open a beer and turn on television.

Samantha found an old gym bag and packed more of her clothes.

She stood in the living room doorway for a second. "That burger's in the kitchen if you want it later."

"Where are you going?"

"Back to Blaine's."

He twisted around in the recliner to look at her. "You hate me that much?"

"I don't want to just sit around here like Mom and Lori never existed."

"Hey. That's not fair."

Samantha left without responding. If she tried to say another word, she'd burst into tears.

As she walked, the Müllers watched from their porch across the street. They might wave or say hello, but she wasn't in the mood for them. They watched things happen in this neighborhood, said, 'Hello' and 'Nice weather, you think?'

She felt sorry for her father. That might have been all he ever wanted in life was to sit on the porch with his wife and watch the world go by.

But that didn't excuse him not doing something about what had happened instead.

37

Aaron returned home from his Saturday rounds and found Louise in tears, collapsed at the dining room table. "We have to clean out Michael's apartment," she said. "We can't put it off any longer."

"Do we need to pay his rent?"

"There's no point. I talked to that lazy-ass Detective Wagner, and the investigation is over. He will not do anything more, and we can do whatever we want with his stuff."

Aaron figured this would be the case, but he'd hoped there might be a change. The police would not deliver justice.

"I'll go over there," he said. "I can pack."

Louise glared at him. "I don't want you packing his stuff in garbage bags and tossing it all aside."

"That's not what I would do."

"We'll go over together and sort it out."

"If that's what you want."

"Of course that's what I want. We didn't see him, and this will be the closest we get ever again, until it's our time to die."

Aaron suggested renting a truck, but Louise about bit his head off.

"That's my point. This isn't a race to get the job done. We're saying goodbye, not get the hell out."

Once inside the apartment again, he understood. The first

time he'd visited, he was still in shock and looking for some-thing that would explain.

Now he had lived with this new reality enough to feel dif-ferently about it. He noticed, for instance, that Michael had put some of his plastic army men toys on the shelf next to his bed. He would play with those army men for hours as a kid. Maybe he had them on the shelf to remind himself of playing. Or maybe they were there to protect him at night.

In one of his drawers were all the T-shirts and jerseys from every baseball, basketball, and football team he'd been on. What they wouldn't give to talk with Michael about those games.

"I have to do something with those," she said.

She assigned Aaron to the kitchen. "Toss all the food."

Louise went through the mail, found the banker box Michael used as a filing cabinet, and packed all that up. Then they went through the newspapers and magazines to check that nothing else was mixed in.

Louise realized Michael's rent was overdue and made out a check. As she walked it to the office, Aaron sat in the chair and looked out over the lawn beyond the patio.

The neighbors across the lawn might have seen what hap-pened. Maybe they saw something the night before.

"Alright," Louise said when she returned. "That's about all I can stand for one day. Let's go."

"I think I'll stay awhile."

"How will you get home?"

"I'll take Michael's car."

"That it? You just going to sit here?"

"I'm just going to sit here."

"And do what?"

"Look out the window."

Louise shook her head. "Okay then. Go on and look out the window, I guess. If our boy was here, I'd plant my behind right next to you and sit there with you."

"I know Baby."

"You need anything?"

"If I think of something, I'll let you know."

"Don't make a spectacle of yourself," she said. "I need you to come home to me at some point."

"Don't worry about that."

Aaron kept the vertical blinds open at the sliding glass doors, and the shades raised in the bedroom. He also kept the lights off and minimized his movements.

If Michael's apartment seemed empty, the people across the lawn might go about their business as if they thought no one was watching.

He sorted more of Michael's things, searching the house more like a burglar, checking odd places for things that Michael might have hidden.

Along with the toys near his bed, he found baseball and basketball trading cards. He found sports magazines under the bed.

And he found a catalog of courses offered by Cleveland State University.

There were no drugs stashed in the box spring. There was no marijuana or cash stuffed in the back of the freezer.

All that Aaron found was that his son had been a normal, decent young man who liked sports and was planning to improve his life.

The pictures and baseball cap he found on his first visit were the only things of interest.

He pondered these things as he sat in the dark, gazing across the lawn at the couple in the opposing apartment.

The woman got home first. She checked the mail and then started dinner, cooking in the kitchen but crossing into the living room to change channels on the television.

After six o'clock, the husband came home from some kind of factory work, it seemed, dressed in a long sleeve shirt of light blue and pants a darker shade of blue. He kissed the woman and cleaned himself up, changing into jeans and a T-shirt.

They ate at their dinette and then sat on the sofa to watch

television together.

At some point, the man pressed his ear to his wife's belly. Maybe she was pregnant. How nice for them to be young and building a life together.

Someone robbed Michael of that opportunity.

Aaron realized watching them might not tell him anything about these people. If they saw something that happened to Michael that night, they were over it now. They were as normal as the sun rising in the morning and setting at night. They were like gold fish in a bowl who swim to the surface to eat the food sprinkled.

He ought to go knock on the door and ask them. Of course it'd draw attention, and they would summon the police. At least he'd ask the question.

Had they ever sat in the dark and watched Michael in this apartment? Did Michael seem happy as he cooked himself a meal and ate it on the sofa while watching television?

Aaron wanted to pound on the door across the lawn, but that would involve the police. He could only sit and watch.

As the eastern sky above the building turned deeper shades of blue, and the first stars poked through the dull gray slate above, the couple in the apartment took a walk around the complex. They were back around nine, and then the woman tidied up the kitchen as the man read the newspaper. Once it was dark out, they closed the vertical blinds.

Aaron kept watching until the light in the bedroom turned off.

In the dark, he heard Michael's voice. "Thanks Pop-pop." It was the nickname Michael had given him, the catch-all closure to their conversations, whether or not Aaron had done something deserving thanks.

Tears welled up, and Aaron allowed them to come, sobbing so as not to worry the neighbors.

# # # #

On Sunday morning, several trucks driving past the apartment door awakened Aaron. He rolled off the couch and crawled to the sliding glass doors and peeked out.

Four dump trucks from the city service garage rumbled along the driveway and parked at the curb between the two buildings.

Three men got out of each of the trucks and walked toward the other apartment.

There were already six men inside the opposing apartment packing things in boxes. With these extra men, there was constant movement inside.

Aaron called the number Francine had given him. "They're moving," he said. "They're packing up the apartment right now."

"How soon you think before they're gone."

"At this rate, I'd say half an hour and the place will be empty."

They packed and taped shut boxes in mere minutes, then carried them out the door. Aaron couldn't see it, but there must be a moving van on the other side of the building. Of course, he couldn't just walk over there to see what was happening.

"I'm coming over."

"You'd better hurry."

"Can you follow them?"

"I doubt it. If the city workers are doing this, I gotta' believe there's a police escort for the couple and the van. And I do not want to meet that big fat cop again."

She hung up without saying goodbye.

The men finished packing boxes and moved their attention to furniture. The sofa, chairs and bed went first. Then the dressers and a desk. Lastly, they carried the television and a few miscellaneous out.

Aaron was wrong. It was over in under twenty minutes. They drew the shades and then the men got back in their trucks and left.

Francine arrived after Aaron had settled back into the

chair. He watched as she walked around the building and peered inside the sliding glass doors, trying to see past the blinds.

After a few minutes, she drove back over to his building and knocked on the door.

"I hope I'm not blowing your cover," she said when he let her in.

"Louise is coming over anyway, now. I told her I got no point to sit here. We'll finish up today, I guess."

Francine looked around. "I'm so sorry about all this."

"You want any furniture?" he asked as they settled down in the living area.

"Do you have any idea what happened?"

"My guess is that they found a place for them to stay. Maybe even bought them a house. Some place closer to where he works, or closer to family. Something like that."

"They must have seen something to work a deal like that."

"It probably wasn't their idea, either."

"Why not?"

Aaron leaned forward in his chair. "Let's say they saw enough to blackmail the pizza man in the hat?"

"The pizza man in the hat?"

"Whoever belonged to the baseball cap I found here the day after they killed Michael. If they were blackmailing him, and he had the means, they would have disappeared without a trace."

"Okay."

"Let's say, instead, they saw the pizza man in the hat, but not him killing Michael. Whoever that man is wants them to get the hell out of here so nobody can ask them questions. So they arrange a new place to live and bring over the troops to get them out of here fast."

"How many service garage men did you see?" Francine asked.

"Seemed like eighteen. It was a blur over there, so I never got a final count."

"Milosh Dobrowski could get that many men here on a Saturday?"

"You're saying he's the pizza man in the hat?" Aaron asked.

"He's the Service Garage Director."

"Can you talk to him?" Aaron asked.

"Yeah, but I doubt it will get us much. I'd rather talk to the people who just moved out and ask them what they saw."

"I bet you can find them."

"But it'll take some time."

Francine fell back on the sofa and shook her head. "Now they are scared to death, or indebted to someone. Either way, they won't want to talk about what they saw."

"You giving up?" Aaron asked.

"No," Francine said. "I just wish I had something to go on."

"Whoever is doing this," Aaron said, "you think they know what they're doing, or just figuring it out as they go along."

"A little of both."

38

Samantha did laundry on Sunday, completing hers in two loads and then starting on Blaine's. While the washer and dryer rumbled, she continued practicing using the lock pick.

There was a filing cabinet and a desk in Blaine's basement, surplus furniture from the police department. Similar items were in her own basement and she realized, now, that every cop had at least one of each. Whenever Uncle Tom upgraded the office, he took care of his men by giving them the old furniture.

What seemed impossible four days before was now almost possible. She could insert the wrench and pick at the pins, unlocking those simple locks.

Now she was practicing with the rake, trying to get fast. It was almost easier, though, to use the pick. That made little sense. She had to be doing something wrong.

"You here?" Blaine called down the stairs.

"Yeah. Doing laundry."

Blaine paused at the bottom of the stairs, looking at her with bewilderment. "What are you doing?"

"Practicing." She showed him the tools and pointed at the lock on the filing cabinet.

"Wait, you're considering doing this?"

"Yes, and you're going to help."

"What?"

"I can't get in Tom's office by myself. I need a distraction."

"You need your head examined."

"I'm serious. This might be our last chance to figure out what happened."

Blaine sat in the desk chair and covered his face with his hands. "Don't you like things the way they are?"

"You mean with Lori dead, my mother missing, and nobody seems to care?"

"I have a job, you have a job...I know it's not perfect, but we're here, right?"

"Oh, it is far from perfect."

"But nothing you do will bring Lori back."

"No, but maybe I can put Jakov in jail if he did this."

"What about your Uncle Tom? If he's covering up for Jakov, what can you even do?"

"I don't know, Blaine, but I'm feeling like I can't live with my family if I don't know the truth."

"At least you have family."

Samantha hugged him. "I'm sorry. This has all been so crazy and sad."

"It's alright."

Blaine pulled open the bottom drawer of the desk and took out a coffee can. Inside the can was a zip-lock bag of weed, and he measured off two lids, zipping up each one in its own bag.

"What are you doing?"

"I have to make a delivery."

"Wait, you sell drugs?"

"Not a lot. Just enough to defray my costs."

"Holy shit."

"What's the big deal?"

"Nothing, I guess, except my dad, who's a cop, always called you a drug dealer, and I told him you weren't."

"That's funny."

"It's not funny. Aren't you afraid of being caught?"

"I'm not too worried."

39

Tom had been out late the night before and crashed on the sofa with the television on. He wore his softball jersey and underwear, but no pants. Where had he taken off his pants?

There was a knock on the front door.

"Come in," he called out.

Blaine Taylor entered and held up a brown paper bag.

"Is it Saturday already?" Tom asked.

Blaine closed the door and offered the bag. Tom reached out for it. "Thanks," he said, and closed his eyes.

"I, uh, need the money."

Tom lifted his head and looked around. "If you can find my pants, then I can get my wallet."

"Where should I look?"

"Fuck it," Tom said. He worried he left the pants at The Silver Fox. There was no way he would get any of his cash back if that was the case.

"I'm hoping they're in my car," he said.

"You want me to look?"

"Never mind."

Tom pushed himself up from the sofa and staggered into his bedroom where he had a small stash of money in a drawer. He returned with three twenty-dollar bills and shoved them into Blaine's hand.

Blaine handed back a twenty. "Too much."

Tom fell back on the sofa. "That reminds me," he said. "How's it going with my niece?"

"Uh, fine."

"Had you dated her before?"

Blaine turned back from the door. "We're not dating. She's just sleeping on the couch."

"So nothing else?"

"Nope."

"You hoping to get something from her?"

Blaine shook his head. Tom smiled. He felt the urge to laugh but kept it in check.

"Okay, well, I hope you don't pull any shit around the office like she has."

Blaine shrugged.

"You know what I mean. She's family, so she got away with it. But you won't."

"Okay."

"Like this little hobby of yours, selling weed, won't look good to a judge. You'll go to jail."

Blaine laughed. "Okay, I get it. Funny."

Tom sat up and stared. "I'm not kidding. You move a lot of weed. I could get the feds in here if I wanted."

"But you're buying the weed. And there are other cops—"

Tom held up his hand. "That doesn't matter. You know that doesn't matter. If I want, it's all on you."

"Are you serious?"

"Dead serious."

"Okay, fine. I'll quit selling."

"Nobody is talking about that."

"Yeah, but—"

"Just keep your mouth shut around the office. Don't make me look bad, and everything will be fine."

"Shit. Fine."

"And mention it to Samantha, too, when you get home, that she shouldn't do anything to embarrass me. Tell her to stay away from Rebecca."

"Yeah. Sure."

Tom opened the end table drawer and took out some papers and positioned himself to roll a joint. "Thanks."

40

Samantha took the folded laundry upstairs to Blaine's room. "Hey, you decent?'

She heard no response, so she figured, at worst, he'd be napping. As she carried the laundry basket towards his bed, she realized he was staring at her.

"You okay?" she asked.

Blaine shook his head.

She set down the basket and sat on the floor next to it. "What's wrong?"

"You don't like-like me, do you?"

"What?"

"You know: like me."

"Romantically?"

"Yeah. That's what I mean. Do you?"

"No," Samantha said. "Sorry, but I'm not just liking anyone right now."

"Yeah, of course."

"We've always just been friends, you know?"

"I get it."

"Wait, do you like-like me?"

"No, I mean..."

"Not like you like-liked Lori."

Blaine shook his head and looked away.

"It's fine. Guys just didn't find me attractive. Lori had something that attracted attention. She and Rebecca. And they knew it."

"Rebecca likes it."

Samantha nodded. "Is that what's bugging you? That we're just friends?"

"I don't know. I'm just worried, okay?"

"About what?"

"About you taking the coroner's report from your Uncle, who is the Chief of Police, and what might happen."

"There's a good chance he won't even know it happened."

"He'll know."

Samantha nodded. If he was covering up for someone then, yes, sure as shit, he'd know it.

"So what if you didn't take the report, and you just stayed here forever? With me."

"I do like being with you. You're my friend."

"Cool."

"But I won't stay here forever. Okay? And I have to do this."

Blaine sat up in his bed, his face stricken with fear. "I have all these crazy thoughts, though."

"About what?"

"So you take this report, and Uncle Tom figures it out. He's going to come looking for it, and he knows you're staying here, so he'll search this house. My house."

"Yeah. He might."

"I have pot, here. He'll find that and send me to jail."

"Oh. Shit. That's a problem."

"Yeah. I don't want to go to jail."

"Okay, well, can you hide it?"

"I'm going to have to."

"You have today."

"You're stealing the report tomorrow?"

Samantha nodded. Her stomach tightened at the thought of it. Until that moment, it was just a theory. But the day after to-morrow, she was going to steal something from the Chief of Po-lice.

"Great. I have zero days to find the perfect hiding place be-cause on Tuesday, the police will tear up the city looking for the report, starting with this house."

"If you say it like that, I guess it would worry you." Samantha rolled onto her hands and knees and held her head in her hands. What was she going to do? She'd thought that, once she got the report, they'd have won some battle. In fact, they would have started a battle.

She needed to think through getting the report away from city hall and keeping it safe until she could get it to Francine.

Francine, however, would be surprised. It's not like she would tell them to put the report back.

"You okay?" Blaine asked.

Samantha nodded. "I'll figure it out."

"I'll hide my weed."

Samantha lifted herself up. "We could start now. I'll help you."

"I'm just going to get high and pick out a spot."

Samantha wanted to join him. But she knew she needed to keep practicing with the lock pick. If she couldn't get the drawer open, all of this was just talk.

In the evening, Samantha realized she couldn't pick a lock. Her hands trembled, and she had no idea if a pin had tripped into place. If she tripped one, she pushed it away within a second. This would not work.

She called the phone number Aaron gave her and asked for him when a woman answered.

"Who's this?"

"Samantha Sykora."

"You're related to Lori Sykora?"

"Yes. She was my sister."

"I'm sorry for your loss. I'm Louise Key. Did you know my son Michael?"

"No, ma'am. And I'm sorry for your loss."

"Thank you. So why is it you need to speak with my husband?"

"He's helping me with something. I just need some advice."

Louise cleared her throat. "Young lady, do you know what you're doing?"

"I thought I did. Now I'm not so sure."

"Let me get him for you."

Samantha apologized multiple times that it just wouldn't work. She explained Blaine's concerns, and how they had worried her. "I'm afraid he might freak out when he sees me try this. Like he'll make things worse. I don't know."

"Tell him to stay home. Call in sick."

"Yeah. That's best. Of course, that's all academic."

"How's that?"

She explained how she seemed to lose everything she learned the past few days. "I don't think I can open a lock if I had the key."

"You're up in your head," Aaron said. "It's like taking a math test, easiest thing in the world, until you think about the fact that you're taking a math test. Then nothing adds up."

"This isn't like taking a test, though."

Aaron whistled a tune Samantha didn't recognize. "You got some other place you could practice?"

Samantha thought of her own basement, where there was the same filing cabinet as in Blaine's basement. "I could go home."

"Is your father home?"

"I'll see."

"Go break into your own house, open the file cabinet in the basement, and call me back."

"That's silly."

"It's low risk, so no pressure. Just practice."

41

Tom sat in the passenger seat of his Lincoln Continental as Vickie Fulton drove. They'd been cruising around, listening to music and talking.

This one liked to talk, so it was fun. She was a cheerleader, seemed to know everyone, and sang along with her favorite music on the radio.

She even had a pleasant voice.

They were getting low on beer and Tom remembered the weed under the seat, one of the two lids he'd gotten from Blaine earlier.

"What do you think of Blaine Taylor," he asked as he rummaged in the glove box for rolling paper.

"Who?"

Tom cupped a rolling paper and ground weed from the bag onto it. "Blaine Taylor. Graduated last year. Lives around the corner from me. Janitor at city hall."

"That guy?"

He nodded as he rolled the joint and dipped it in his mouth to seal it.

"He's kind of mopey, I guess. I didn't realize he went to school with me."

Tom started on a second joint. "Seems harmless, right?"

"Seems retarded."

He directed her down West Park Avenue. A mile later, he said, "Turn in here."

"Where?"

"That driveway."

The headlights revealed the old farmhouse, the decrepit barn out back, and the lawn gone wild with growth.

"What the fuck are we doing here?"

"Jakov lives here."

"I know who lives here," she said. "Everybody knows. We also know to stay away from him. And don't get caught in the Kingdom, either."

"You'll be fine," he said. "Ready for an adventure?"

"No."

He teased her until she agreed to go inside, promising it would be worth it.

They walked in the front door and came upon Jakov lying on the coach, the room's only light coming from the television. Tom thought he looked dead, but he knew better, having seen Jakov like this many times before.

There were empty beer cans scattered on the floor at his feet, and a cardboard box of beer on the end table.

"Hey get up," Tom said. "You ready to party?"

Vickie giggled, which was what he was hoping for.

"Come on, man, I brought you some weed."

Jakov raised his head and Tom tossed the bag onto his chest.

"Don't say I never gave you anything."

Jakov sat up and blinked. When he noticed Vickie, he stared.

"What's he doing?" she asked.

"Just looking." Tom lit joints for them.

"You want to sit?" Jakov asked.

Vickie shook her head.

"We're not staying long," Tom said. "I just wanted her to see the place. This is like the oldest house in the Village."

He motioned for her to follow and began the tour.

There was a disassembled small engine on the kitchen table and a carburetor soaking in the sink, grease and soot splattered across the floor.

"Where does he eat?" she whispered.

Tom hooked a thumb at the front room. "I don't think he cooks much."

He led her back through the house and flipped on the bathroom light. The fixtures were from the twenties or thirties. The bathtub had lion claw feet. There was a curtain rod circling it from above, but no shower curtain.

Inside the tub was a small block V-8 engine.

"Where does he wash?"

"There might be a spigot and drain in the basement."

"Oh my God."

They stepped back into the front room. Jakov was well into the joint and had opened another beer.

"How'd that engine get in the bathtub?" Tom asked.

Jakov looked at him, not understanding the question.

"Did you carry that engine block into the bathroom and put it in the bathtub?"

Jakov nodded. "Yeah. I gotta' finish that."

"The lesson here is to not mess with Jakov."

Jakov raised his beer to them.

He took Vickie around back where there were two cars in the yard, one with the hood up. They walked towards the barn.

"I'm not going in there," she said.

"You scared?"

"Yes. Let's go."

"Sure. You want to go back to my place?"

"Anywhere but here."

42

Samantha walked in the park along the edge of the backyards, moving through the shadows. Every tree shrub that separated the yards from the park was familiar, as she'd grown up with them.

Across the park was the swimming pool, tennis and basketball courts, and the softball diamond.

At the other end of the park, the police and fire departments, at opposite ends of the central building, had lights in the windows. But the mayor's office was dark.

She slipped into her own backyard and paused behind the maple tree, gazing at the back of the garage, looking for movement. It was unlikely that her father was sitting out there. When she was little, they'd sit out back as a family to enjoy the night. It had been ten years already, but who knows what he was thinking these days.

She paused again next to the garage. Her house was dark and quiet. Both neighbors had lights on, but there was no movement. None of them were likely to have a party. If they did, it would have been an afternoon picnic. A wild time on this street was sitting on the front steps to enjoy the cool air.

There were no cars in the driveway. The coast, as they say, was clear. Despite that, Samantha looked around as she took the lock pick tools in hand.

She found a familiar feel from having practiced on Blaine's door. It took two minutes, which felt like forever, but the lock opened. It surprised her.

Once inside, she locked the door and checked the ground floor to be sure she was alone. Then she went into the basement.

The desk and file cabinet were in the far corner. At first, her hands trembled as before. Maybe this wouldn't work.

She sat in the desk chair and turned around, realizing that her father rearranged things. He stacked Lori's boxed things against the cinder-block wall.

That was it for Lori's life? Boxes of things and furniture stacked in a basement. The rest of the world was getting along just fine without her, it seemed.

Samantha returned to the file cabinet and found comfort in concentrating on the lock. She found each pin and set them in order, and the wrench unlocked the drawer.

She did the same to the desk locks and then returned to the cabinet.

Confident she'd be able to do it, she put the chair back where it was and lingered a moment in front of Lori's things.

These boxes were full of school books, papers, and clothes. She poked around until she found some clothes and held a sweater to her face. The smell reminded her of Lori.

The door at the top of the stairs unlocked and opened. She heard her father talking to someone, then the basement light snapped off.

"Sam?" he called.

She said nothing. She wasn't sure why, but she didn't want to talk to her father.

"You're sure we're alone?" said a woman. It was Aurelia Delacruz.

Samantha wanted to get out. They walked around the kitchen for a few minutes, then made their way to the front room. She heard the television come on.

Samantha crept up the stairs and unlocked the door.

"Sam?" her father called out.

"Fuck you," she yelled, and ran out the door.

RUTHLESS

43

Samantha arrived at work early and brought a magazine so she'd have something to do. Derek read the newspaper at the next desk over, and Gayle didn't look at her or not look at her any more or less than she had the past week.

She defied her restrictions and went into the Police Department around quarter to nine, when the duty meeting would have ended.

Gloria shot her a look.

"I need to ask my father something," Samantha said.

"He's not at his desk," Gloria said. "I'll have him stop by."

"Thanks."

Samantha wanted to see if her Uncle Tom was in the office. She didn't even want to think about having to pick that lock only to get inside and pick another.

Samantha got herself coffee and walked around the lobby to move around. The plan was to wait until eleven o'clock, when all the night-shift police were off duty, and the day-shift were out on patrol.

They had decided that would be best because they wanted as few police in the building as possible, requiring Tom to leave his office when the diversion started.

Aaron was arranging the diversion, but he hadn't told her what. She had a pretty good idea. To pull Tom from his office, it would have to be serious.

"Don't worry about me," he told her as they completed

their plans. "You just seize the moment, open the drawer, grab the report, and get out of there. I'll do my part, then you'll do yours, and then we'll get Francine to take it the rest of the way. Nothing to worry about."

That was a day ago.

Her father waited at her desk when she returned. He eyed her carefully, his face calm and void of emotion.

"Sorry about swearing at you," she said. She was sorry, but also felt somewhat justified. However, now was not the time.

"What were you doing?"

"I was missing Lori, so I wanted to smell her clothes."

Derek looked up from his newspaper, but she ignored him.

"That was rude to yell," her father said.

"Yeah. I'm sorry."

"Are you going to come home soon?"

"I don't know."

His look betrayed the disappointment he felt, and he turned to leave.

"Did she spend the night?" Samantha asked.

He turned and faced her, this time with anger on his face. But he said nothing and left.

Samantha collapsed in her desk chair and only then noticed how Derek stared at her.

"Your dad is dating?" Derek asked.

"I don't know what to call it," she said. "I don't want to think about it, and I sure don't want to talk about it."

"Is it someone you know?"

"I don't want to talk about it."

Derek chuckled. "I guess if he brings her to the Labor Day picnic at Grandpa's, we'll have our answer."

\# \# \# \#

Aaron was driving a rental. He left his own car at the rental agency, the keys locked inside, so Louise could retrieve it with the spare set of keys if need be.

He didn't want to think about why she'd have to do it, but he had to include it in his plan or what kind of husband would he be?

Aaron worried about the timing, and whether this stunt would be enough to draw the chief of police out of his office.

He'd brought along a trump card, and if he played it right, everything was going to work.

Three minutes before eleven o'clock, Aaron parked outside the bank. The biggest problem, in his mind, was getting inside without causing a premature ruckus. It was possible he was the first black man to even approach these doors, and the security guard might lock the door before Aaron stepped inside.

Aaron left the car unlocked with the keys in the ignition, and strode towards the front door.

The security guard was at the counter chatting with a teller. Aaron had asked Samantha the night before and learned that the guard's name was Henry.

"Hey Henry," Aaron called out, smiling.

Henry looked at him like he'd just seen Big Foot.

Rebecca was at her desk, just inside the office area railing. She stared, more surprised even than Henry.

"You're Rebecca, aren't you?" Aaron asked.

She nodded.

"I recognized you from the picture." Aaron held the Polaroid up as he approached. It was one of the pictures he'd found his first visit to the apartment. "Michael was my son. I'm sure he'd want you to have this."

"You need something?" Henry asked as he crossed the lobby.

"Nah, I'm good. I'm just talking with Ms. Marko."

"Do you know him?" Henry asked Rebecca.

The tellers were all up in their windows, staring. A woman stepped out of the first office, and then a man stepped out of the second office. "Is there a problem?" the man asked.

"Who is he?" Aaron asked.

"The bank manager."

"I got it, Mr. Jones," Henry said. He came up right behind Aaron and took a stance, as if this were his house, and he was here to defend it.

Aaron smiled, walked around him and approached the first teller window, keeping it cool. Don't agitate the white guy with a gun just yet.

"Excuse me," Jones, the bank manager, said. "You must leave."

"I just need a minute," Aaron said. He stopped and smiled again at Rebecca, looking over his shoulder as if he just had an idea. "Would you mind calling Tom Sykora? I'd like to see him, here, in the bank."

"What? No."

"I'll call him," the manager said. "You bet your black ass I'm calling the chief of police."

Aaron shrugged. "Tell him Micheal Key's father wants to talk to him."

Then he walked up to the teller window and leaned in.

# # # #

Inside the administration office, phones rang and a murmur of voices arose. Samantha noticed, but refrained from mentioning it.

Derek took a phone call and said, "Holy shit," as he hung up. "The bank is being robbed."

"I bet we can see it from the window in the police department," Samantha exclaimed.

Derek bolted from his seat and hurried out.

Samantha grabbed her shoulder bag and followed.

Inside the police department, it bordered on pandemonium. The office workers from Administration, Finance, Accounting and the other departments bunched at the far window with a view of the bank. Gloria spoke into the radio and the telephone. Betty was on her phone placing a call.

Two cops in street clothes came in from the front door and grabbed their back-up revolvers locked in their desk before running down the stairs to the armory.

Her father grabbed Samantha by the arm. "Stay here. Understand? I don't want you getting hurt." Then he ran down the stairs, as well.

Samantha walked toward Tom's office, cruising past Betty without making eye contact. Tom was not in his office, and she stepped inside.

Samantha waited, listening to Betty outside the door. Betty was calling the off-duty police officers, telling them to report to duty.

Samantha left the office door open and tugged on the desk drawer where Tom stashed his keys. He locked it, so she went to work on it with the pick and wrench.

At first, her fingers trembled, and the pick felt as useful as a Popsicle stick.

She took a deep breath, thought of Lori, and tried again. There were only three pins to move, and she got them in order, front to back. The lock turned, and she pulled the drawer open.

"Hey," a man shouted. Samantha turned, but she was still alone. It was a voice outside the office.

"He's going in," the man shouted.

"Oh my God," Betty said, and Samantha heard her get up from her desk and her heels clacking across the floor.

Inside the drawer, there were twenty-or-so hanging file folders. As she flipped through them, she realized it'd be quicker to grab them all.

She pulled out the black, plastic garbage bag she'd packed in her shoulder bag and stuffed all the file folders in it. The entire bag still fit in her shoulder bag.

She slid the drawer shut, considered locking it for a split second, but decided it wasn't worth the risk.

Outside of Tom's office, only Gloria could have seen her, but she was still too distracted to look up from the radio. With fifty people looking out the window, Samantha walked out into the lobby.

She went back into the Administrative offices, past the now-empty desks, and down the back stairs towards Finance and Accounting. Just past the Service Center offices, she went out the back door.

She bumped into Milosh, the Service Center Director, on his way inside.

"Hey. You know where you're going?"

"Yeah. I'll be fine."

"Stay away from the bank."

Samantha nodded. "I just need to run home real quick."

Milosh nodded, then stepped aside to let her pass.

# # # #

"Okay," Jones announced, "I spoke to the Chief of Police. He'll be here in a minute."

"Great," Aaron said. "Now I recommend you go lock the doors."

"I will not do that."

"Look at this situation, with me in here. The police are going to storm in here any second now, right?"

"You damn right they are."

"And if they shoot, you think I'm the only one they're going to hit?"

He thought about it a moment, exchanged a glance with the woman from the next office, and nodded. "Henry, lock the front door." Then he hurried towards the back.

Satisfied that he had done everything possible, Aaron sat down on the chair next to Rebecca's desk.

"Did you like Michael?" he asked.

Rebecca stared at him.

"It's okay. I just want you to know I think he liked you."

Rebecca nodded.

"Was he good to you?"

She nodded again.

"Wonderful," Aaron said. "That's all his mother's doing. I want you to know that."

"He liked his mother," she said. "I'm sorry I didn't meet her."

"She's smart. You know how I know that? She married me." Rebecca smiled.

"And she did a wonderful job with our son."

"I'm sorry for your loss."

"Thank you."

Through the front window, he saw half a dozen police officers take up positions. Cruisers blocked the parking lot with their lights flashing, and half a dozen more police officers blocked foot traffic from the city park at one end of the parking lot, and blocked the driveway from the other end.

"Excuse me," the manager called out. "I let the Chief of Police inside," he said. "I hope that's what you want."

Aaron looked out the front window again and noticed a lone figure walking across the parking lot towards the row of houses that backed up to the city park. It was a young woman. She had a bag slung over her shoulder. She seemed to be in a hurry.

"That's cool," Aaron called over his shoulder. "It's your bank. You can let whoever you want in."

Aaron winked at Rebecca. She smiled, but he was pretty sure she was scared to death.

# # # #

Samantha glanced back at the bank. Police cruisers with flashing lights blocked both ends of the parking lot. Cops lined up outside the bank, many of them with shotguns, vests, and riot helmets.

Kids in the park gathered to watch. There was no splashing in the pool because all the swimmers stood at the chain-link fence watching the situation unfold.

Samantha didn't dare look back at the municipal building. She kept her eyes fixed on Blaine's back yard.

"Hey what's going on?" Mrs. Peleshi asked from her back fence.

Samantha gasped, but caught herself. "I'm not sure. Something at the bank."

"Oh my," Mrs. Peleshi said. "I hope everyone is all right."

As she passed her own yard, she looked inside, half-expecting to see her Uncle Tom waiting with his service revolver drawn. Instead, she saw Blaine, and he waved for her to come in.

Samantha concealed herself from the park behind the large maple. "What are you doing?" she asked.

"You can't stay at my house," Blaine said.

"Don't worry. I wasn't going to."

"What are you going to do?"

"Can I take your car?"

"Are you serious?"

"Yes. They'll be looking for my car."

They went to his back yard where Samantha had stowed an escape bag. Her working assumption was that she wouldn't have time to get in the house and change. Once Uncle Tom realized what had happened, he'd hunt for her everywhere.

If Francine had been part of this plan, maybe they could have handed it off within the hour, but now Samantha still had a lot of work to do.

44

Aaron remained seated in the middle of the lobby, but what he wanted was to be in his rental car and driving fast away from this place.

When he first thought of this as a diversion, he knew it would work because hitting these people in the pocketbook would summon all of their attention.

But now, watching the three cops walk into the bank with guns drawn, he would trade all the money in the vault for a gun. Given the number of cops out front, he was going to be shot.

It'd be nice to take one or two of them with him. He needed two six-shooters, like those dudes in the spaghetti westerns that faced down a gang of desperadoes and dropped them in a hail of bullets.

That would not be how his story ended.

"You wanted to talk to me?" Chief Sykora asked.

"Just wanted to say hello. I don't want no trouble."

The chief's brother flanked him on one side and the fatso cop on the other.

"You going to go?"

Aaron nodded. "Yeah. Thanks."

"Cuff him."

Officer Sykora holstered his revolver and grabbed his handcuffs.

Aaron kept his hands in full view. "Hey, I did nothing."

The chief didn't even glance at him. "You scared some

friends of mine today. You caused a public disturbance, and you are under arrest."

Aaron made eye contact with Officer Sykora as he approached. "I'm sorry for your loss."

The cop didn't blink.

"My son wouldn't do such a thing as y'all say he did. Not like the newspaper said he did."

"Let's just get these cuffs on, okay?"

"Okay, man," he said as the cop helped him stand up. "I know you're a wonderful dad. My son was a good man, too. He couldn't have done anything to hurt your daughter."

They walked him out the back door and around the building. The 40-officer-strong Village police force, arranged into an informal gauntlet, stared with a mixture of contempt and hate.

At the end of the gauntlet, Aaron saw the greatest thing in the world: Francine, the former newspaper reporter, interviewing the mayor, and the mayor's daughter. There were two television crews pointing cameras at them.

"I'd like to make a statement," Aaron said.

"Shut the fuck up and keep walking," Big Mac said.

The cops in riot gear, their shotguns at the ready, accompanied them all the way to the rear entrance.

Aaron paused at the door as Francine pointed her camera at him.

Once inside and away from the cameras and reporters, Big Mac and one of the other cops escorted Aaron to a jail cell, handcuffing him to the bars so that all he could do was lower himself to the cement floor and sit.

Maybe the newspaper and television news crews bearing witness might keep him alive. If not, he hoped it was worth it. But he was pretty sure Louise would not forgive him for this stunt.

# # # #

Samantha liked that she had Blaine's car to drive. It was a Dodge Dart, as plain as the day was long, and blended in with traffic as just another crappy car cruising the streets of metropolitan Cleveland.

As she neared the border with Parma, two police cruisers with sirens blaring and lights flashing came up from behind. She pulled over and gripped the wheel, ready to floor it.

They roared past, and Samantha exhaled. Cars stopped behind her, pulled around her. She hoped she'd get where she was going without vomiting all over herself.

As she rolled forward with traffic, she dreaded even a simple fender bender, which would require a call to the police. She drove extra slow, but that seemed to worsen the situation as cars honked and sped up around her.

Only when she made to the driveway of her destination did she think it would be okay.

There were plenty of cars at the Parma branch of the Cuyahoga County Library. She parked in a row with other cars, hoping to just blend in.

Once inside, she chose a thick book from the shelves and sat at a table in the reference section. She flipped through the book long enough to feel as if no one cared what she was doing.

Then she opened up her knapsack and flipped through the files, looking for the coroner's reports.

Most of the folders contained nothing like what she expected the chief of police to have filed away. There were photos, notes and greeting cards. There were a few clippings from the newspaper. There was a pair of girls underwear.

Then there were a series of four folders with typewritten sheets of paper of twenty pages each. Two of them were on letterhead of the Medical Examiner's office—the coroner's report. The other two were from the Cleveland Police Department.

Another folder contained a large envelope. She glanced inside and gasped. They were photos of Lori. Not just Lori, but Lori's corpse.

Samantha pressed down on the folders to hold what was in them down and breathed. She wanted to cry, but there wasn't time for that now. She had to get this done.

# # # #

Tom wanted to put the office back in order. The bank would remain closed for the day, but he'd asked his brother, David, to take a detail and stand guard even after it was empty and locked up for the night, escorting their sister home, if she wanted.

He broke up the gab sessions in the armory and the locker room, telling the cops to get into the duty room. He did the same upstairs and told them that anyone who wanted the extra hours could patrol.

"I want as many officers in the community as possible. Pick a spot and just walk around. I don't care if it's back and forth in front of your house, just get out there."

The overtime would set a record, but he didn't care. He didn't want anyone calling his father to complain that they didn't feel safe.

On his way back into his office, Betty held up a hand.

"My father?" he asked.

Betty nodded. "He brought a friend."

Tom took a breath. He had nothing to worry about. The old guys just needed to vent.

He expected them to be on the sofa. Instead, his father and Milosh had pulled chairs up to the desk. Tom closed the door.

"Boy, what a day," he said as he came around the desk. "I think that's the first incident at the bank, ever."

"There was a robbery in 1932," his father said.

"1932, huh?" Tom asked. "You don't say."

His father nodded, his face grave with worry. "We had just set up the bank, although it was nothing more than a Savings and Loan."

"Okay, well, the first incident in forty-seven years."

"They got little back then," Milosh said. "But it was everything we had."

"No, not much," his father said. "But we worried because the reason we started it was the failing banks in Cleveland."

Milosh chuckled. "We ran the asshole's car off the road and shot him in a ditch."

"The photo made the front page of both newspapers."

"Okay, well, we got the guy," Tom said. "I'll go shoot him and then we can have a parade."

Milosh smiled.

"What did he want?" his father asked.

"Nothing," Tom said. "He was just sitting there, waiting."

"Did he have a gun?"

"Nope."

"Did he ask for money?"

"Nope."

"Then why did he do it?"

Tom shrugged. "He's bent out of shape over his son's death. I think he wanted attention, like a publicity stunt. You saw that bitch reporter."

"I heard he asked to speak to you," Milosh said. "What did he say?"

"He fucking said more to David than he did to me."

"Then he wanted you out of the office."

Tom walked around the desk and opened the door. "Betty, did anyone come in my office while I was at the bank?"

"What, today?"

"Yes, today."

"No."

"You sure?"

"I was sitting right here."

Tom closed the door. Why the hell would they want him out of his office. Nothing here but his trophies and the—

He fished his keys from his pocket to unlock his desk, but it was open. Tom walked to the credenza beneath his trophies. The drawer, also unlocked, was empty.

"Fuck."

"What was in there?" his father asked.

"The fucking coroner's report for Lori." Tom looked out the window, half expecting to see someone. "And some other things."

"Who could have taken it?" his father asked.

"Whoever it was, I'm going to kill him."

"Not him," Milosh said. "Her."

"Who?" his father asked.

"Your granddaughter," Milosh said. "Samantha."

45

Tom asked Gloria to summon a select list of cops to his office, starting with his little brother, David. "Send them in one by one."

Tom craved a little energy boost, just a tiny snort to get him into this moment. It would be a way to channel his anger, but his stash was back at the house.

He remembered the prisoner in the lower level, and all but kicked himself. He was better than this, better than all these assholes doing their best to screw him over.

"On second thought," he said to Gloria as he charged out of his office. "I'll be in the chicken coop downstairs. Send them to me down there."

"You got it, boss."

Aaron Key sat on the floor and glanced up as Tom approached.

"I have a question," Tom said. "If the answer helps me, this will go easier on you."

"You can ask," Aaron said.

"Who's getting the report."

Aaron shrugged.

"That doesn't help. I will not give you a lot of chances. I got three guys that will make you wish you were never born."

Aaron smiled. "I already wish that."

Tom kicked him in the back. "Go on, lean forward so I can snap your wrist."

"Go fuck yourself."

Tom kicked him again, and a third time.

"Hey!" David shouted. "Back off."

The foot stayed ready to kick again. He wanted to kick this guy in the kidney until he pissed blood. Then he'd make him drink the bloody piss.

"You're the Chief of Police," David said. "Come on."

"Okay, little brother," Tom said. "I'm fine."

"There's no call for that."

"We'll see."

His little brother was a right and wrong kind of cop. Black and white. Usually, that made him a pretty good cop, but sometimes the gray areas troubled him.

This was a gray area.

"Let's talk," Tom said, and they stepped into the hallway.

"You better tell him something helpful," Aaron said. "Or he might kick you, too."

Tom closed the door without looking back.

"What the fuck are you doing in there?" David asked.

"Here's what you don't know," Tom said. "While that worthless piece of shit in there was fucking around in the bank, someone broke into my office and stole reports from my locked file cabinet."

"Why would someone do that?"

"I don't fucking know. To embarrass me. Or try to."

"But who?"

"Samantha."

"What? No."

"Do you know where Samantha is right now?"

"Isn't she back at her desk?"

Tom shook his head.

"She wouldn't do something like that."

"No?"

David shook his head, but he was quiet.

"Do me a favor and help us find her," Tom said. "Would you do that?"

"She just went home because of the incident. Or to get

something to eat."

"Maybe. We searched the building. No sign of her. I hope it's something simple."

"Did you ask Blaine?"

"He called in sick today."

David nodded. "I still don't think…"

"I hope I'm wrong, okay? But we need to settle this matter."

"Fine."

"So go to your house and see if she's there, then let us know."

"Okay. You know she's been staying at Blaine's house."

"I'm sending a car there."

David thought a moment and looked him in the eye. "If you find her, you bring her to me, understand?"

"Sure, little brother. But I need you to stay at your place in case she shows up."

"Anybody hurts her and there will be hell to pay."

"Nobody is going to get hurt."

David looked at the door to the holding cells. "That includes him?"

"He's nobody."

"You're the chief," David said. "You know better. Do your duty, and I'll do mine."

Tom smiled. "Sure, little brother. No problem."

David nodded. "Promise me you'll tell all the assholes to keep her safe."

"Son of a bitch, Davey, we're family. All the cops are family."

46

Francine received two phone calls that morning, both from Aaron. The first call told her to be by the phone at ten-thirty, because he might have something to tell her then.

"Do nothing rash or stupid," she said. "We are going to find the truth the right way."

"Of course," he said. "But I've spent my entire life making sure nothing I did seemed rash or stupid to all the white people around me. I raised Michael to be the same way and look what it got us."

When Aaron called the second time, he suggested she get to the Village Municipal Bank as soon as possible.

"Are you out of your mind?" was all that she asked.

"Not as far as I can tell."

It was her own idea to call the three news stations. That two of them showed up with video crews meant it was a slow news day. She just hoped it would help Aaron.

The sight of police in riot gear outside the bank shocked her.

As things quieted down, Francine drove to Samantha's house around the corner. There was no answer, so she continued up the street to Blaine's house and knocked on his door.

"I'm guessing she'll call you at some point," Blaine said from the front door. "But I don't know where she is."

"Come on, you two are best friends. Do you mind if use your phone? I need to call in what I have."

"I think you should go."

"Are you serious?"

"Yes."

"Are the police coming here?"

"Yes."

Francine noticed he was shaking. "Do you want to come with me?"

He shook his head. "There's only one thing I could do to help today, and that's look nervous and distract them because they'll assume I know something. But I don't. At least nothing they don't know already."

"Okay, but I'm going to want to—"

"Please go, okay? If Samantha did what we think she did, she's going to want to talk to you soon, so you can't wait around."

He was right. Also, his fear was infectious. She had to get away and protect herself until she knew more.

As she walked back to her car, a blue truck from the Village Service Garage turned onto the street.

She started her car and took off, and the truck followed.

At the next intersection, it pulled close and bumped her car. In the rear-view mirror all she saw was the face of the driver: Jakov.

He stared back with a darkness in his eyes that worried her more than anything else she'd seen in her life.

47

Tom left the asshole in the chicken coop alone for the time being and returned to his office.

"You have a visitor," Betty said. The look on her face worried him.

"What, again?"

"Not them," Betty said. "She."

Rebecca, dour and crying, waited in his office on the couch.

Tom closed the door and leaned on his desk, hands in his pockets and biting his lip. This was the last God damn thing he needed.

"I'm confused," she said.

"What about?"

"Michael."

"Michael Key. The boy I was dating, who died."

"Okay. What about Michael?"

"What do you think? I still don't get why he would kill Lori and himself."

Tom stood up and grabbed her by the arm. "I'm not having this conversation here. Not now."

"But it makes little sense."

"Too bad."

"I need to talk to you."

"Okay." He pulled her up from the couch. "Go get in my car and I'll be out there in three minutes."

"What?"

Tom pulled her toward the door. "I have an enormous pile of shit I'm dealing with. You're now the cherry on top. So give me just three minutes, and I'll talk to you in the car. And don't let anyone see you."

After she left, he paced back and forth. He wasn't the pacing type of guy, but he couldn't sit down. He needed just a bit of blow, and then he could think. Trying to think like this, with problems everywhere, was pointless.

He was the God damn Chief of Police. He could make anything happen.

"Betty," he said as he stepped out of his office. "I need to run home. I'll be back in fifteen minutes. Call me there if I'm needed."

"Okay, Chief."

In the car, Rebecca was crying.

"For Christ's sake," he said. "What is the matter?"

"I'm sad," she said with stilted breath. "I miss Michael."

"We all wish that."

The car was in the covered garage beneath the building, reserved only for himself, the mayor, the fire chief, and Milosh, the Service Garage director. Everybody else parked out in the open behind the building.

"Did anyone see you get in the car?"

"What?"

"Did anyone see you?"

"No."

"Good."

"Are you ashamed of me?"

"No. Of course not. But this is a very sensitive time. People are losing their fucking minds over nothing."

"Okay, well thanks for that."

Tom looked out the back window. Parked in the shade, someone would have to walk right up to the car to see through the tinted glass.

"I'm sorry Michael died, but you saw how fucking crazy his father is. I can't help that."

Rebecca fished around in her purse and pulled something

out, waving it in his face. "He wasn't troubled. He liked me."

It was a picture of the two of them, Michael and Rebecca, smiling at the camera.

Tom knocked it out of her hand. "I don't want to look at the piece of shit. He killed Lori."

"That reminds me. Why was Lori's shoe out in my front yard?"

"What?"

"Lori's shoe. Just one shoe, out in my yard."

"How the fuck should I know?"

"You said she must have gone in my house, taken the boat keys, and then met Michael. But then why would she leave a shoe and not pick it up?"

"She was tripping on something. The coroner found drugs in them. It's a wonder they didn't crash the car. Either way, they were going to end up dead."

Rebecca retrieved the picture from the floor. "He was a good guy. His father seemed nice."

"The kid would have ended up in jail, eventually. They're all fucking animals."

"I think you're just jealous."

"Shut up."

Rebecca flashed an angry look at him. He didn't like that shit from her.

"You're jealous," she said.

"Just shut up."

"His cock was enormous, by the way, and he could fuck all night. Not like you with your little—"

He shoved her face into the dashboard, smashing her nose.

Rebecca sucked in air, holding her hands to her face, her shoulders twitching. Then a howl of pain emerged from her throat.

Tom would not listen to that shit. He grabbed her hair and slammed her face down into the dashboard again, gripping the steering wheel with one hand for leverage, twisting his hips to get more power, grunting from the exertion with each blow.

He slammed her face down three, four, five times, adjusting his aim to bring her forehead down on the edge of the glove box, shattering it as it fell open.

That shut her up.

He realized his grip was the only thing holding her up. He relaxed his hand, and she slumped down onto the floor in front of the seat.

As he caught his breath, he looked around. There was never any foot traffic here in the middle of the day. All the cops were out on patrol. No one saw a thing.

Blood dripped from the dashboard. Tom grabbed a T-shirt from the back seat and wiped it off, then tossed it over her head.

He grabbed his softball jersey and threw that over Rebecca. Then he backed up and drove out of the parking lot, ignoring the cops still standing guard outside the bank.

48

Aaron caught himself flinching when the door opened. Don't do that, he thought. Do not let these motherfuckers get to you.

Two cops escorted Blaine into the detention area and put him in the cell opposite Aaron's. From where they'd handcuffed him to the bars, he had to twist himself around to even glimpse a corner of Blaine's cell, but the pain in his arms and back would not allow it.

He wanted a drink of water, but didn't dare ask. Now that he wasn't alone, maybe they wouldn't be so quick to kick.

Aaron braced himself for another kick—cops had visited every few minutes and booted him with all their might—but they left without bothering him.

"Holy shit," Blaine said. "What are they doing?"

"Fucking with me," Aaron said.

"But that's not right."

Aaron shook his head. He wanted to laugh, but knew it would be too painful.

"Can they just do that to you?"

"Do your eyes deceive you?"

"Holy shit," Blaine muttered and sat on the steel bed frame.

"So who did you piss off?" Aaron asked.

"Everybody, I guess. They're looking for Samantha, and they don't want to lose track of me, I guess."

"Let's watch what we say. Got it? They're listening, assuming we know each other, which we don't, and that you or I had something to do with whatever your girlfriend did, which we didn't. Got it?"

"Yeah, sure. But she's not my girlfriend."

"You gotta' rectify that."

Blaine got up from the bed frame and paced back and forth. "I liked her sister."

"Okay, well, I can see how that would confuse the both of you. I'm not saying ask her out tonight. Just, you know, keep it in mind."

"Sure."

"I'm serious, man. The best thing I ever did was get Louise pregnant with our daughter, Alina." He chuckled, wincing at the shot of pain in his back.

"Shit," Blaine said. "We have to get out of here."

"I'm open to ideas."

"I want to do something."

"See if you can get me a drink of water. That'd be something."

Blaine shouted and rattled the cage door.

A cop came in. "Hey!" he snapped. "Shut the hell up."

"We need water."

The cop walked over to Blaine's cell. "Use the God damn sink. That's why it's there."

"He needs it too. Bring him a glass of water. Please."

"Your father was a cop, right?"

"Yes, he was. Todd Taylor."

The cop walked out. A couple of minutes later he returned with a paper cup of water.

The cop dumped the water on the back of Aaron's head.

"What the fuck, man?" Blaine asked.

"You know what I'd like to do?" the cop asked. "I'd like to beat the shit out of you, then throw you into his cell, and then we put a bullet in his head, and blame him for starting the fight. The only reason I'm not doing that is because your father was a cop. You should know better than to be here with this piece of shit."

When they were alone again, Aaron said, "Hey man. Thanks for asking."

"Sorry I couldn't do it."

"Well, this doesn't look good, but let's not make things worse, right?"

"Sure."

"Just in case, though, you tell my wife I'm sorry, and that I thought this was the right thing to do."

"Hey, you're going to tell her yourself."

"I hope so."

"Son of a bitch."

"Yeah, man. That sums it up. Son of a bitch."

49

Tom pulled up to his garage behind the house. A six-foot tall privacy fence surrounded the yard, shielding him from the neighbor's prying eyes.

His father chastised him when he built the fence. "Don't set yourself apart. Be like your neighbors."

But he wasn't like everyone else. He needed space to do his thing. He needed freedom. Problems like this mess he had in the car happen when you're too close to fools and fuck-ups around the city.

Rebecca had been squirming around on the floor of the car, and now she'd almost turned herself around.

"It hurts," she moaned. "What the fuck is wrong with you?"

He shoved her with the heel of his shoe, jamming her head back under the dashboard. *That's what's wrong with me.*

He searched his garage for rope. You'd think there'd be rope, but he couldn't find it.

Next to his boat was his fishing gear, and he grabbed a spool of ten-pound test line and a knife.

"Okay," he said as he lifted her up by the arms. "One second."

He got a wrist in each hand and then shoved her back down and pressed his knee down on her back. When she screamed, he put his weight on her, cutting off her breath—shutting her up—which wasn't all bad.

He tied her wrists together with the fishing line, then looped more at the elbow, pulling them as close together as they would go.

When he released his weight, she gasped for air and moaned.

He opened the trunk and took all the crap in there—the softball gear, the cooler, the dirty clothes—and dumped it in the garage.

After one more glance at the neighbors, to be sure no one was out watering their stupid tomatoes, or whatever the fuck it was they did in their backyards, he shoved an old sock in Rebecca's mouth and then dragged her to the back of the car and tossed her in, closing the lid.

He went back to the garage looking for an old blanket, and found it on his weight-lifting bench in the second bay which gave him an idea.

He carried a forty-five pound plate to the trunk and planted it under Rebecca's arms on her back, pinning her face down.

Rebecca groaned and wept. He tossed the blanket over her and closed the trunk.

There were various drugs in the cupboard above the stove. He grabbed a bottle of Valium and another of speed, a hers-and-his sampler, but what he really wanted was in the bedroom.

It was all there on the night stand, the little mirror, the razor blade and a vial of coke. That was no good. Keep this shit under wraps. It'd be too easy for the wrong asshole to see it and give him a serious fucking headache.

He pocketed the vial and then rooted through the drawer until he found the larger bag with enough for the weekend.

The weed was in there, too, but this was not a weekend for weed. Maybe Sunday night, after this mess was behind him, he'd relax.

There would be no relaxing the rest of this day.

As he headed back through the kitchen, the phone rang.

"Milosh is looking for you," Betty informed him. "Sounded pretty urgent."

"Fine. I'll talk to him."

He pulled the phone along with him as he grabbed a beer from his fridge. By the time he had it opened and tipped up to his mouth, Milosh picked up.

"You remember the lady reporter, Francine what's-her-fucking-face?"

"Tennyson. Sure."

"My guy Jakov is following her."

"What? Why the fuck—"

"I sent all my guys out to look for your niece, and Jakov fucking sees the reporter coming out of Blaine Taylor's house."

"The little fucker. Did we bring him in?"

"One of your uniforms grabbed him. He's cooling his heels in the chicken coop."

"Good."

"And Jakov fixated on her for some weird-ass reason which I don't want to know."

"Okay, thanks. Can he stay with her, or should we get another car on it?"

"Jakov's in a city-fucking-dump truck so we need to get another car on her."

"Jesus Christ."

"She headed into Cleveland, so his ass is hanging way out on this one."

"Fuck me."

"Yeah."

"I'll get a black and white after him. We can't let him do anything stupid in a city truck. Can you get his location?"

"I took the liberty and had Gloria send the wop out to get him."

"Good. Thanks."

"No problem. I'd go out after him, but I know your father wouldn't be happy about that."

"Do me a favor and have the kraut go along in plain clothes and follow her once Jakov gets pulled off."

"Alright. That's good. Hey, we gonna' see you back in the office? Your old man's a little concerned."

"Soon. I shit myself and I'm cleaning up the mess."

"Yeah, I fucking hate when that happens."

Back in the car, he could hear Rebecca's whimpering from the trunk. So he turned on the radio.

50

Once she was in Cleveland, Francine didn't bother stopping at red lights or stop signs. She didn't want to cause an accident or hit a pedestrian, but if she stopped, Jakov bumped her with his truck, each time a little harder than the last.

She swerved through traffic like a maniac, putting as many cars between herself and the blue truck as possible, but it kept after her, taking even greater risks to come up behind.

The highway was a possibility, but going faster would only increase the risk. She'd have to go over a hundred to get away, it seemed, and she would kill herself trying to save herself.

She tried to breathe, watch out for other cars, and take every chance to create space.

The four miles seemed like forty, but she made it to the District Two police station and pulled into the parking lot. She drove toward a line of parked police cruisers and caught a break when a policeman stepped out of the building.

Francine pulled up behind the parked cruisers and shouted to the cop, "Please help me."

The cop looked at her. "What's the problem—"

The blue truck pulled into the parking lot and inched toward them.

"That's my problem," she shouted.

The cop walked toward the truck. When it sped up, the cop drew his service revolver. "Don't fucking do it!"

The truck braked hard, the bed rattling behind the cabin like a freight train, and came to a stop just inches from the cop's gun.

Francine scrambled out of her car. "He's been following me and slammed into me."

Jakov turned the wheel, but a Village black and white pulled up behind it and honked its horn.

Francine considered getting back in her car, but she wasn't sure where she should go.

The two cops had a private conversation, then Jakov got into the Village black and white, leaving the truck where it was.

The Cleveland cop parked the truck and approached Francine.

"You'll be fine now, miss."

"Why the fuck did you let him go?"

"Excuse me, miss, but I don't appreciate—"

"That guy is a fucking maniac, and he tried to kill me."

"I handled it ma'am. Like I said, he won't bother you again. Perhaps your own driving contributed to the situation, so in the future—"

"Oh, for fuck's sake."

"Ma'am?"

"I'd like to swear out a warrant for his arrest."

51

When Tom returned to the office, things were worse than when he'd left. Betty stood up and handed him three notes.

"Your father wants to see you right away, in his office. Milosh also wants to see you. And Sergeant Hudak has to talk to you, as well."

"Fucking great."

"Your brother called three times, asking about Samantha. I told him you'd call as soon as you could."

"Got it. Also great."

Tom closed his door and put his back against it so they'd have to use a battering ram to open it up. He took the vial from his pocket and gave himself a little toot, rubbing the residue from his nostrils on his gums.

That felt good, so he took another. Things seemed okay. He knew he'd figure this out.

With renewed vigor, he visited his father's office.

"You wanted to see me, Mr. Mayor?"

His father waved him inside. "Close the door."

Tom leaned against a chair, feeling in control, meeting his father's gaze. If there was one thing he'd learned early in life, it was to meet his father's gaze.

"Marko called. Rebecca hasn't come home yet. He assumed she'd be home early, after the incident at the bank. Her car is here, and no one has seen her."

"I'll look into it."

"Betty told me she visited your office, then left. She seemed upset."

"Of course it upset her. She didn't know what that crazy bastard was going to do."

"Was she upset with you?"

"No. I calmed her down. That's why she visited."

"I see. I thought maybe you were the crazy bastard."

Tom pulled the picture from his pocket. "Look, she told me something and gave me this."

His father took the picture and then looked up with surprise. "The boy who killed Lori?"

"I didn't know this, but she had been dating the black kid. Then when the kid's father showed up at the bank, he gave Rebecca the photo, and it upset her. She was afraid he was going to hurt her."

His father set the picture on his desk and kept his fingers on it, pressing it down. "I don't understand."

"The guy was unstable. She felt threatened by him coming there. It was too much for her."

"That doesn't explain what happened to her."

"No, and I'm worried. I don't know if she had some other secret affair. Maybe with our guy downstairs, or maybe someone else. She could have walked through the park and met someone on Parkside Drive, for all we know."

His father nodded. "What do you suggest we tell Marko?"

"We got everybody out looking right now. I'll spread the word. I'll call over to Cleveland, maybe have Wagner follow up on some leads."

"Thank you," his father said.

Tom pointed at the picture and his father lifted his hand, allowing Tom to pick it up.

# # # #

On his way back into the police department, the wop had returned with Jakov.

"What the hell are you two doing?" he asked.

"Nothing," the wop said.

"Jakov, in my office."

"Anything else?" the wop asked.

"Nope. I owe you one."

Tom leaned on Gloria's desk. "Will you please find the kraut and get him on the phone?"

"Got it, Chief."

"You're a good girl."

Tom returned to his office and closed the door. Jakov stood waiting. His face betrayed nothing more than the menacing anger he always shared. One eyelid drooped, his mouth open, and one ear swollen like cauliflower from his days as a wrestler, before they had kicked him out of school.

Tom took another quick hit from the vial and offered it to Jakov, who refused. He liked that about Jakov.

"You still want to get that bitch you were following?"

Jakov nodded and his droopy eyelid raised up.

"Good. The kraut is going to call and tell us where to find her, and then I want you to take care of her."

"My car is at the garage."

"That Cleveland cop is with her. You said they were at your house. So they saw your car?"

Jakov nodded.

"Okay, I want you to take my car. You can do whatever you want to it. I need to dump it, anyway."

Jakov shrugged.

"You can do whatever you want to the reporter."

Jakov smiled. That worried Tom a little, but he pushed it out of his mind.

"You know David's daughter, Samantha? She stole some things from me. The reporter might go to meet her, so follow them for a while. Samantha took files and I want them back. Got it?"

"You want me to leave David's daughter alone."

"If you can, grab her and bring her back. I want to find out what she did with the file."

"Okay."

"I need to talk to her, understand?"

Jakov nodded.

Tom held out his car keys. "But first I need you to take care of a minor problem I left in your barn."

52

Rebecca awoke in pain. The pain was everywhere and everything. Never had she felt such total, all-consuming pain.

Her arms, shoulders, hips and legs ached. Her brain throbbed in agony with every beat of her heart.

Opening her eyes took several minutes. The tiniest glimmer of light refocused pain to the front of her head, and she shut them again.

The worst pain was her nose. It burned with every breath. Something jammed in her mouth blocked the air and tasted terrible. Swallowing was like forcing sandpaper down her throat.

At last she opened both eyes, confirming her worst fear: she was in an old barn, her face pressed down into hard-packed dirt. The orange light of sunset glowed at the cracks in the wall.

Her face pressed into the hay on the dirt floor. Rusting tools with gray wooden handles hung from a wooden post. A rotted rope fell in a spool, its other end lost in the dusty shadows of the beams criss-crossing above.

The cloth in her mouth, tied in place, prevented her from calling for help. She only managed a moan and pitiful whimpers.

No, that brought more pain as her body convulsed. She'd go mad if it didn't stop, if she hadn't gone mad already.

It felt like she was being crushed by a weight, and she remembered the steel plate dropped on her back, how it forced her face into the dirt, and she was certain she would suffocate.

Desperate now to live, she twisted her hips and brought her knees in front of her. With her bound legs, she pushed herself over.

The plate slid across her back and she pushed again, screaming into the gag until the plate fell with a dull thud. Yet another rope dug into her throat, choking off her breath. Panicked, she kicked with her legs, pushing her face onto the plate, but loosening the tension enough to allow herself to breathe.

She rested there with the cool steel, offering a tiny relief to her throbbing head. A glance at her legs revealed that fishing line had been used to bind her, wrapped several times around. There was no way she could break them.

With more squirming, she thought she might twist her head through the looped line. She had to press her face through the agony of her nose, but she could get the pressure of the fishing line off of the back of her neck. Then she pulled her knees up and rocked backwards, freeing her head.

She fell to her side and groaned in agony, but relieved she had done it. When the pain subsided, she worm-crawled into the hay, seeking a spot that would ease the pain.

In the mess of hay and dirt, something sharp poked her, and she shrunk away. Squirming again at a different angle, she got a look at what had stabbed her. She'd expected some long-forgotten farm tool. Instead, it was a white stick a few inches long.

There were other white sticks, some with sharp, jagged tips. Others worn and rounded on the ends.

She realized they weren't sticks, but bones.

She screamed through the gag and rolled away, suffering intense pain but desperate to get away.

Rebecca came to rest against a pile of rotted wood planking, nails and sharp splinters threatening like claws. She saw a spider and squirmed back toward the bones.

She stopped in the middle and cried at the pain thudding in her head as she choked on the burlap in her mouth.

A car door slammed shut outside the barn and she stopped

crying. Her heart beat so fast she was sure it would explode.

53

Francine was almost as angry with the Cleveland cop as she was with Jakov. When the cop suggested she get a restraining order, she laughed herself into tears.

"I don't see why that's funny," the cop said.

"You think a lunatic cares about a restraining order?"

She waited in the lobby, watching through the window until Robaroni came in from patrol.

"Hey, it's okay," he said, trying to comfort her.

She wasn't in the mood. "This is insane."

"Give me a few minutes and we'll head back to my place."

"No. Do you mind if we go to my place first? I have to go write this down and I want my typewriter."

"Write it down? For who?"

"I don't know. Maybe United Press or The Times. I just have to get it all down."

"Okay, let's go to your place."

"Thank you."

Her flat was undisturbed. Maybe a bit stale from lack of circulation. Rob waited, reading the sports section from a month-old newspaper, while she banged out her story.

She wanted to think this had all been a bad dream, but she realized there was a real and terrible story. She just didn't know how to figure it out before she became part of the story, rather than its teller.

The phone rang, and Samantha Sykora was on the line.

"Blaine thought you might call me," Francine said, "but I didn't think Jakov would try to kill me first."

"Oh my God, I'm sorry. What happened?"

"Later. First, are you safe?"

"I think so. I'm at—"

"Don't tell me. I might be crazy, but I don't want you to say it over this line."

"Okay, well, I have something for you."

"Yeah, I was afraid of that."

"Don't you want it?"

Francine took a breath. The adrenaline from being chased and attacked had long worn off, but writing a summary had stirred many worries. "Yes, I want it. I don't want you to get hurt though."

"There's more to it than we thought."

"Oh?"

"It's worse. This has to come out. Find a way to publish it."

"Okay. Do you remember that place we first met?"

"Yes."

"Meet me there in half an hour."

54

Rebecca couldn't catch her breath as Jakov dragged her behind the barn. She was light-headed and unsure if she was walking or falling.

She hit the ground, pain exploding in her knee and shoulder. Jakov nudged her with his foot.

"You want me to kick you the rest of the way?"

Panting through her nose, she shook her head. He had kicked her out of the barn, and she didn't want him to do it again. She took three more breaths, tried to swallow, but couldn't because her throat was dry.

"I'll untie you soon, and give you water, okay?" He nudged her again.

Rebecca sat back and raised her head. The brush was thicker; she couldn't see beyond a few feet. She remembered a hike she once took with her mother, the smells of dirt and leaves. "Mommy," she moaned in despair. She would not see her parents again.

Jakov grabbed her arms and lifted her up, pushing her forward into the brush. Branches and thorns scraped across her face. They caught her and pushed her back.

"Damn it," Jakov said.

He shoved her hard, and she fell through the brush, tumbling and skidding down the slope, before catching hard at the base of a tree.

Jakov stepped close behind her and rolled her out from behind the tree. He dragged her by the ankles down the hill over the tree roots and stones.

At the bottom, every part of her body screamed in pain. But as he reached to lift her up, she kicked and twisted to get away.

He was taking her into the kingdom, and she would do everything she could to get away.

For a moment she was free of him, rolling through the tall grass. She found her legs and pushed to right herself.

Jakov pulled her down and pinned her to the ground with one foot on her chest.

He raised the tree limb in his hands high over his head, then brought it down on her head.

It was dark inside the shack. She lay on her side on the planked floor. The gray wood was rotting. Jakov lit a kerosene lantern, and she saw a table, a chair and a cot. Next to the cot was a stack of Playboy magazines and several mason jars, some empty, some filled with a yellow liquid.

There were no windows. He had nailed squirrel, raccoon, and skunk pelts to the wall.

There were a few buckets, tubes, and cannisters lined up on the floor.

Jakov stood between her and the door. He grabbed an ax from the corner, and a hatchet from the table.

"You scream or try to run, and I'll kill you. Understand?" He held the ax aloft for effect.

She nodded.

"Give me any guff, or trouble of any kind, I'll take a finger or two. Maybe some toes or your ear. Understand?" He made a chop-chop motion with the hatchet.

She nodded.

"I'll take off your gag and give you water. Okay?"

She nodded.

Jakov put the ax back in the corner but slipped the hatchet into his belt. Then he removed the gag and offered her a canteen, tilting it up to her mouth to drink.

Rebecca drank, gulping water and air until she choked and spilled on herself.

There was fresh blood on her blouse, trickling past the dried blood from her smashed nose.

"I don't know what your boyfriend wants to do with you."

"He's not my boyfriend."

"Maybe that's the problem. You cheated."

"No, I didn't."

Jakov took a drink from the canteen, emptying it and tossing it on the table. He pulled the hatchet out of his belt. "That colored kid wasn't your boyfriend. Tom was. So that's cheating."

Rebecca shook her head.

"He'll be here soon, then you'll know what he wants to do."

His tone had softened. "Please let me go," she said. "I won't tell anyone. I'll go away. He won't ever have to see me again."

Jakov looked at her, unmoved, uncaring.

"If you shut the hell up, I won't gag you. Okay?"

She nodded.

He stepped past her into the dark corner of the shack and pried up floor boards with the hatchet. Then he reached down and lifted a large rock from below the floor and placed it on top of the loose boards.

He leaned down below the floor again, working at something. She could try to run for it. The water helped a little, but every part of her was sore. She might get out the door, but she wouldn't get up the hill before Jakov tracked her down. He'd chop her up for sure. She was better off waiting. Maybe.

Jakov pulled a wooden ladder from underneath the floor, lifting it straight up toward the roof and then lowering it again, like a disappearing act.

"Okay," Jakov said.

"Okay what?"

He stepped over her and grabbed her arms, lifting her to her knees, and pulling her across the floor toward the hole in the floor.

The hole in the floor was over a hole in the ground. The ladder descended into the hole, down into the pitch black void below.

"I'll untie your hands so you can climb down."

"No, please," she said. "Please don't."

He grabbed the hatchet and held it before her face. "You climb down or I crack you on the skull again and toss you down."

He tightened his grip on her hair. She nodded.

As she took hold of the ladder and stepped down, she looked for a place to crawl out under the shack. The walls extended down to the ground. There was no soil, only solid rock underneath. Even if she could climb out of the hole, she couldn't burrow under the walls to escape.

Jakov tapped the hatchet on the top of the ladder. "Keep going. All the way."

"I can't see anything."

"Just sit there."

"In the dark?"

Jakov left for a moment and returned with a candle and a box of matches in his hand. "Here." He dropped the candle and matches past her into the darkness.

She continued her descent, her feet finding the soft dirt below. Before she could consider what she would do next, Jakov pulled out the ladder of her grasp. She sobbed as Jakov worked to slide the ladder back under the shack.

When he pulled a wooden cover over the top of the hole, plunging her into total darkness, she screamed. She hadn't thought he'd do that. "No please don't."

She screamed again when he slammed the large rock down onto the cover. Then he replaced the floorboards in the shack, the sounds of his methodical work as clear to her as if she was watching someone nailing her coffin shut.

It fell silent in the hole, and she sobbed to herself, knowing for the first time in her life that she was alone in the universe.

55

The shadows of evening filled the street as they left the house. Down the street, children played in a yard. A father and son played catch along the sidewalk.

Rob paused on the front steps, holding Francine back with one hand. "I don't see it."

"The blue dump truck?"

"No. The yellow Ford LTD that followed us here."

"You didn't mention that."

"You were pretty upset as it was. No need to aggravate you."

"Ah crap," Francine said. "I may need to go puke."

"I think we're fine."

"Do we know what car Jakov drives?"

"He drives a black Ford LTD. I don't see one of those, either."

She still couldn't quite relax as they drove away, using the mix of highway access roads and thoroughfares that both divided and connected the neighborhoods of Cleveland.

It was a little easier once they were on Broadview and surrounded by traffic, although Rob seemed tenser.

"Are we being followed?"

"No, but there're too many cars to know."

"Just keep looking for that black Ford LTD."

Rob turned the wrong way on Brookpark and nodded when Francine pointed it out.

"I'll turn around. Don't worry."

He dropped a U-turn in a gap in traffic, and it reminded Francine of a scene in a movie. "Was that from The Godfather?"

"Yeah," Rob said. "But we learn it in cop school, too."

"Cop school?"

"You know what I mean."

He drove past the shopping plaza where they were going to meet Samantha and went around the block. Francine twisted around in her seat to look. "There has to be an easier way."

"In a few weeks, it'll all be easier, right?"

Once inside the parking lot, they took a lap as they looked for Samantha's car.

"I don't like this," Francine said.

Rob pointed. "She's right inside the restaurant."

"Good. I don't want to wait."

"I think we're safer in the car."

"Have you forgotten what happened to Fred and Lou in their car?"

"Oh shit."

"So in we go?"

"In we go," Rob said.

# # # #

Samantha had gotten to the diner quicker than she expected and ordered food. She hadn't eaten since morning, and was famished, adding to her exhaustion. She couldn't wait until all of this was over.

Seeing Rob with Francine was a relief. She might not up-chuck the sandwich she just devoured.

She met them at the door, turning her back to the waitress waiting to seat them. "I am so glad to see you guys," she said.

"You didn't do what I asked you not to do, did you?"

"I'm afraid I did."

"Okay," Rob said. "Do not talk about it."

"I have to show something to you."

Francine turned to Rob. "Should we look here?"

"Uh, no," Rob said. "Back to the cars."

Rob peeked outside while Samantha paid her bill. When there were no moving cars in sight, we waved them along.

They proceeded with caution. Shoppers laden with bags exited stores and walked into the parking lot. Cars entered the lot, driving as they searched for empty spots. It seemed as normal as any other evening.

"I can't believe you found something in the report already," Francine said.

"It's not the report. I grabbed a dozen files, maybe more. There are pictures."

"Pictures of what?"

"All the girls my Uncle Tom has dated."

"Like school pictures?" Rob asked.

Samantha took a breath. She hadn't spoken of this yet, and her throat tightened at the thought. "They're naked. He has pictures of the girls naked, in bed, on floors, in a car."

"Oh my God."

"Some of them are with a man's penis. It's so disgusting."

"How many?"

"Ten different girls. I only recognize two of them, Rebecca and Vickie."

"Who is Vickie?"

"High school junior who is interning at the bank."

"Oh my God. He's a monster."

"I'm so freaked out."

Samantha handed Francine the large envelope. "Here's the report." Then she reached into her shoulder bag and removed one of the other folders.

They stood in front of Rob's car, shoulder to shoulder, looking at the photos, gasping at the tragedy of what Tom had done to so many girls.

Rob growled with anger. "What are they, fourteen? Fifteen?"

Pubescent girls looked up at the camera, their cheeks full,

skin blemished, and shame in their eyes.

"There was like half a dozen of each girl."

"How awful."

The sound of the engine invaded her thoughts, and she looked up. A white car came at them, its grill snarling like bared teeth. Her skin tingled and her head felt as if it might fly off her body as her legs moved. The asphalt rushed up at her face as she fell.

The car slammed into Rob's car with a crunch of metal, pinning Francine and Rob, who cried out in pain.

They looked down at the white car pressed up against their legs and hips, pressed their hands against the hood as it rose against them, and then they leaned forward as it backed away.

Then the howl of pain and the dull thud of their bodies hitting the pavement next to her.

She looked at herself and realized she was okay. Rob or Francine must have shoved her out of harm's way. They had saved her.

Rob and Francine, however, gasped and moaned on the ground, flailing their arms. Francine coughed and spat blood. Rob's eyes were open, but he seemed unconscious, his head bleeding where it had slammed onto the asphalt.

Then the door of the white car opened and steel-toed work boots approached. It was Jakov. "What the fuck is wrong with you!" Samantha screamed in anger.

Jakov looked at her before he picked up the report where it had fallen beside Francine's body. He noticed the photos and grabbed a few of them.

"You son of a bitch—"

Jakov kicked her backwards as she was getting up. Pain exploded across her face and she rolled away, bracing for another blow.

He grabbed her by her hair and dragged her between the cars. The blood spouting from her nose splattered on the pavement, but that was not her biggest problem.

She grabbed his arm and got her feet under her to pull

away, but he kicked her in the stomach and she collapsed. Then he lifted her up and dropped her into the trunk.

She heard shouts nearby and called for help. Then Jakov tossed her shoulder bag into the trunk and closed the lid, plunging her into darkness.

56

Rebecca wasn't sure how long she'd been in the hole. It seemed like hours, but that couldn't be. The pain across her body made every minute seem like an hour. She focused on each breath, trying to move as little as possible. Movement made pain.

There was no noise from above. She prayed for someone, somehow, to save her, unlikely as that seemed.

Jakov said that Tom wanted her down there. When he attacked her earlier, she thought he needed to vent his anger, and then he'd apologize.

What a fool. She deserved to die if she let this happen to herself, to end up in a hole in pitch darkness.

She felt around her on the ground for the candle and matches. Just reaching a few inches was excruciating, but she was cold and frightened, and couldn't stand not seeing anything.

She found them, getting a match in one hand and holding the box in the other. But she wasn't sure how to do it. She'd never struck a match. Both her parents smoked, but they used lighters. That's what she did too.

When her mother lit candles on the dinner table, she used her cigarette lighter, and had a smoke to go along with it.

Maybe it would be okay here, in the hole. Her father would realize she wasn't home, and he'd come looking for her.

She scraped the match along the side of the box, but nothing happened.

The tears came, then a sob, and then a howl of anguish from deep in her stomach. With it came the pain, but she couldn't help herself. She was just going to suffer.

57

Samantha tried not to panic in the car's trunk, but every bump, sharp turn and hard stop tossed her around, and she could only think of the worst. Blood continued to ooze into her mouth. With one hand she lifted the collar of her shirt to her nostrils for the blood; with the other, she pinched the bridge of her nose.

The next time the car stopped, as the glow of the brakes offered a modicum of light, she assessed what was available. She had her shoulder bag, which had a few of the pictures inside. She felt around for the tire iron, but she couldn't even find the spare tire.

There was a canvas bag with a flashlight and two road flares. She was hoping for a screwdriver. A gun would have been nice. Not that she ever fired a gun, but maybe she could learn if given the chance. Maybe she could do something with the road flares.

She hadn't ever lit a road flare, either, but she saw her father do it.

She'd hit him with her shoulder bag if she thought it would help. Keep fighting, she told herself. Even if your hand gets chopped off, you keep punching with the bloody stump.

58

Tom closed his office door and had a little toot from the vial. He needed the phone to ring and for Jakov to tell him he'd gotten everything done. The stupid coroner's report. The pain in the ass newspaper reporter. And his little bitch of a niece.

This was the shit Jakov did well. Tom needed it to happen the right way or it would screw him.

Sitting still was not an option, so he paced back and forth and took another little toot from the vial. Then he did it again.

He wanted a joint, but he couldn't do that in the office. There was something he could do, however, and grabbed the vodka from his desk drawer and poured himself a glass.

The phone rang. A moment later, Betty knocked on the door as she opened it a crack.

"It's for you."

Tom picked up. "This is Chief Sykora."

"Okay," Jakov said. "I got it all."

"What about the girl?"

"Yep. I'm going to put her with the other."

"Great. Hold tight. I'll be over later tonight."

He hung up.

He wanted to go now, that moment, and get it all over with. Take care of the problems, get rid of his car, and get on with his life.

But he had to wait until things calmed down. His brother

would lose his mind any minute now. The cops on extra patrol would get bored and want to go home, even with the overtime pay.

Until that time, he needed to relax. So he poured another glass of vodka and sat on the sofa, staring at the night just outside his window.

59

When the trunk lid opened, a bright light blinded Samantha. She felt his touch and lashed out, kicking and scratching, knocking the flashlight out of his hand.

Samantha paused for a second as her eyes adjusted to the darkness, looking for a target, preparing to kick. She felt his grip on her wrist tighten and then he pulled her from the trunk and lifted her into the air.

With her sight restored, she realized he had slipped a rope around her wrist and hoisted her above the barn floor by a pulley in the rafters. Below her was the Lincoln Town Car, a tractor, and piles of hay scattered across the barn.

She clawed at the rope, but there was no way to loosen it.

The pain in her arm socket matched the pain in her wrist, and she gasped.

Jakov lowered her to just a foot above the floor and tied off the rope. He picked up a shorter length—he had prepared before opening the trunk—and approached.

Samantha kicked at him, ignoring the pain in her arm, hoping to strike him, to keep him away at all costs.

Jakov dodged her kicks and circled. He grabbed a pitchfork and approached. "Kick at me again and I'll gut you."

"You killed Lori."

She kicked at his face and he plunged the pitchfork into her left thigh. As she howled in pain, he grabbed her legs and pulled, adding his weight to the strain on her wrist. The rope dug into her skin, and a trickle of blood ran down her arm. *Oh God, I'm going to lose my hand. I'm going to have a bloody stump.*

Jakov had gotten a rope around her ankles and pulled the slipknot tight, looping it around. He grabbed another length of rope and tied her knees together.

Jakov released the end of the rope lifting her up and she slumped to the ground. He pounced on her, using his weight to pin her down as he secured her hands behind her back.

She couldn't breathe. There was a ringing in her ears, the darkness turned to pitch black, and she was certain she was going to die.

When she regained consciousness, she was being lowered down a hill, sliding past trees and brush. She could only twist around a bit, but she was certain it was Jakov behind her.

He had tied her to a wooden toboggan, the curved front end pushing past the tall grass, rising over the stones. Her hands and feet were still bound. Burlap tied in place with rope filled her mouth, forcing her to breathe through her nose.

At the bottom of the hill, Jakov walked to the front of the toboggan and dragged her out of the trees. There was a quarter moon, and she could see a shack in the clearing at the bottom of the hill.

She was in the Kingdom.

Jakov dragged her, toboggan and all, into the shack. When he closed the door, it was pitch black for a minute until he lit a kerosene lamp.

He lifted the floor boards, reached below the shack and lifted a large rock up out of the hole, placing it beside the toboggan. He leaned back into the hole and worked at something else for a few seconds.

"Help me please," Rebecca said. Her voice came from the hole.

"Shut up," Jakov said.

Samantha couldn't imagine what Rebecca was doing down

there, and she strained at her bindings, desperate and panicked.

Jakov hung the kerosene lamp from a hook in the rafters
over the hole in the floor. Then he lifted the toboggan and lowered it down into the hole.

Samantha, descending upside down, panicked again as the
blood rushed to her head. When all was dark around her, the
toboggan bumped into something solid, and a body moved near
her.

"Untie her."

"I can't. I can't see the knots."

"Untie her or I'll burn you alive."

Rebecca worked at the knots, struggling. Samantha felt Rebecca's body trembling, and shoved her bound hands against
Rebecca, who understood and untied those knots first.

"Hurry."

With her hand and arms free, and her eyes adjusted to the
scant light from the lamp far above, Samantha loosened the
ropes around her waist and ankles, and fell from the toboggan.

He pulled the toboggan up out of the hole. Samantha's
shoulder dropped beside her as she released her gag. She
looked up just as Jakov pulled the lid over the hole.

When he dropped the rock onto the lid, she screamed and
rolled against the wall.

"Hey," Rebecca said, her voice just a whisper. "I'm sorry
you're in here, but I'm glad I'm not alone."

Samantha coughed before she could speak, her mouth dry
from the burlap.

Rebecca placed her hands on her and Samantha shrunk
away without thinking. "Are you okay?"

Samantha sat up and leaned against Rebecca. They held
hands. "Where the fuck are we?"

"In a hole under Jakov's shack in the Kingdom."

"I guess the crazy stories about this place were true."

"Do you think we'll get out of here?"

Samantha thought a moment before answering. "Have you
explored at all?"

"No," Rebecca said, her voice burdened with sadness. "I couldn't light the candle and then I lost it so I gave up."

Samantha felt around the floor. She found her shoulder bag. Inside was the flashlight and road flare from the trunk of Tom's car. Jakov must not have looked inside. At least her fight with him did that.

She shined the light on Rebecca: swollen face, one eye closed, her nose caked in blood, and both lips red like sausages.

"Oh God."

"Is it bad? It hurts like hell."

"Did Jakov kick you?"

"Your Uncle fucking Tom did it. I thought he was going to kill me."

Samantha turned the flashlight on herself.

"Christ, you look like I feel. What happened?"

"Jakov kicked me in the face."

"Oh, right. Yeah, your nose looks broken."

Samantha shined the light on her wrist. The damage appeared minor, despite how it hurt. She could move her hand and make a fist.

The wound in her leg appeared to still be bleeding. She gave the flashlight to Rebecca and tore the lining out the shoulder bag, doing her best to bandage the wounds by stuffing the fabric into the hole in her jeans. She found the rope that had gagged her and tied off the bandages.

"Where d'you learn to do that?" Rebecca whispered.

"I saw it on an episode of M.A.S.H."

They found the candle and matches, and the extra light revealed a little more about their hole in the ground.

The hole was a vertical shaft, like a well, a little more than Samantha's arm reach across, about six feet wide. The lid was ten feet above them. If she stood on Rebecca's shoulders, maybe she could reach it, but neither one of them was able to pull that off.

The floor of the hole sloped to one side and a crevice in the wall widened near the bottom. It was a darker pit beyond.

Samantha held the candle near the hole, and a slight breeze

blew out the flame.

"We're not in a hole," she said. "We're in the mouth of a cave."

"I'm not sure I like that."

With her good hand, she dug the dirt around the hole, widening it with relative ease.

"Maybe this dirt just washed down from the hill above over the years."

Samantha pulled more of the dirt aside, pushed still more down into the hole, until it was big enough to fit.

"What does it matter if it's a cave?" Rebecca asked. "We're still trapped."

"The air was moving. That meant there's an opening somewhere through that hole."

"How do you even know that?"

"I saw it on a television show."

"So what if you did?"

"I'm going to find that opening."

Samantha grabbed the road flare out of the shoulder bag. "Come on."

Rebecca inched away. "I'm not going down there."

"You're just going to wait here? For what?"

"Someone will rescue us. My father has to be looking for me."

Samantha shook her head. "They won't know to look here."

"I don't care."

"I'll go through and look, okay? Then I'll let you know if it's worth a shot."

Rebecca shook her head. "Don't do it. We have to just wait."

"I don't want to go in there," Samantha said, "but I'm not waiting to find out who opens the lid next."

60

Tom stretched on the sofa in his office, considering his next move. His coke vial was empty. The vodka wasn't cutting it anymore. On an ordinary night, he'd look to beer to solve this problem, a beer at the Silver Fox, served by a topless girl.

It was going on eleven o'clock. Over the past hour, he'd sent all the extra patrols home with the promise of additional overtime the rest of the week. The station was down to its bare crew. The overnight dispatcher, a fat woman known for sleeping through phone calls, was at the desk reading a magazine.

Tom got up and called his brother on the phone. "It's me," he said. "I'm coming to get you."

"What is it?"

"I'll explain in the car."

Out in the office area, he snapped his fingers to get the dispatcher's attention, remembering that he didn't know her name. "I'm going home. Anybody needs me, call me there."

She nodded, then returned to her magazine.

61

Blaine lost track of how many times a cop had walked in just to kick Aaron in the back.

He didn't bother trying to talk to Aaron because the poor bastard seemed to need rest more than stupid chatter. Also, Blaine didn't know what else to talk about. Watching the abuse made him want to scream. He felt like crying. Neither one of those would help. Somehow, Aaron suffered the abuse with minimal complaints, adjusting his position as best he could, but saying nothing in response.

It seemed like the cops grew bored with it, as if they were being forced to do it like a chore. Even the kicking seemed less intense, but, of course, it had to be agonizing for Aaron to have the same spot pummeled.

Big Mac lumbered in and opened Blaine's cell door. "Let's go," he said and walked toward the door.

"What's going on?" Blaine asked.

"You can go home, or do whatever the fuck you want to do," Big Mac said. "Just get the hell out of here."

Blaine lingered outside of his cell and pointed at Aaron. "What about him?"

"The fuck you care about him?"

"Let him go."

Big Mac shook his head.

"You guys need to stop."

Big Mac walked up to Blaine and then kicked Aaron in the

back.

"Just stop."

He kicked Aaron again, this time eliciting a groan from Aaron, deep and mournful, as he breathed through his nose.

"Alright, I'll go," Blaine said. "You need to fucking stop."

Big Mac raised his leg to kick again and Blaine scurried towards the door.

Blaine walked through the park and into Samantha's yard. As he came around the garage, the side door opened. Samantha's father was leaving.

"Mr. Sykora," he said and hurried along the driveway.

"Blaine?"

"I need your help back at the jail—"

"No time, Blaine. I can't talk." He got in the car and started it.

"But it's Aaron. I'm afraid they're going to kill him."

"Who?"

"Aaron Key, the man from the bank, whose son was—"

"I can't worry about him. I have to help Samantha."

"But—"

Samantha's father backed out of the driveway and drove away.

Blaine looked up and down the street. It was evening. The sun had set and the street lights flickered on. Around the corner, little kids played in a front yard. The Kleegans were out for a walk.

No one cared about the man in the jail. No one even knew about him but, if they did, they still wouldn't care.

His father might have cared. Blaine wasn't sure, but he'd like to think that his father wouldn't have been the type of cop to abuse an innocent man left vulnerable in a jail cell.

He needed to go find help, but there was no one left.

He ran home and went into his father's bedroom. On the dresser was a jewelry box, and in the jewelry box was a set of keys.

One of those keys opened the metal box inside the top dresser drawer.

And inside the metal box was his father's service revolver.

Blaine ran through the park towards the police station. Within seconds, he was out of breath, and walked the rest of the way. How was he going to help anyone if he couldn't even run across the park?

"Where do you think you're going?" a woman's voice called out to him. It was Samantha's Aunt Jan, who lived four houses down from them.

"Sorry," Blaine said. "I have to—"

"I hope you had nothing to do with what Samantha did to-day."

"What are you talking about?" Blaine tried to walk away, but Jan stepped out of the yard toward him.

"Mrs. Peleshi says she saw Samantha talking with you," Jan said. "I don't know why they let you out of that cell."

"I did nothing."

"Well, that bitch reporter is in the hospital, and it's all Samantha's fault."

Blaine walked away, not bothering to respond.

"If you know where Samantha is," she called after him, "you'd better tell me now."

There were police cruisers in every spot of the parking lot, and the rest of it was empty, meaning someone sent the police force home for the night. As he neared the building, Blaine froze as the mechanic walked out of the garage door and drove one of the cop cars into the garage.

Blaine took one more deep breath. He very much wanted to not have to do this.

He used his father's key to unlock the back door, and Blaine entered the lower-level of the police station.

There was the armory to his right, the locker room next to that, and the conference room through the hall. The chicken coop was on his right, past Big Mac, the cop at the duty desk.

Big Mac looked up from his newspaper. "You forget something?"

As Big Mac folded the newspaper, Blaine drew the revolver and pointed it at Big Mac's chest. "I need you to open the chicken coop."

"The fuck you doing with that thing? You don't deserve to even touch your old man's piece. And you sure don't have the balls to pull the trigger."

"Open it, Mick. Please. I will kill you."

"Did you bring clean underwear? Because you're gonna' shit your pants when you try to squeeze the trigger."

Blaine noticed his hand shaking. "You can pick on me. I'm an easy target. But so are you, Big Mac. Once I shit myself, I'll keep pulling the trigger."

The cop seemed to consider his options. "You're ruining your life for that worthless piece of shit in there?"

"Unbuckle the belt and let the gun down easy," Blaine said. "Then open the goddam chicken coop."

Blaine followed him into the chicken coop and had him release Aaron.

"Are you out of your mind?" Aaron asked.

"That's what I was wondering," Big Mac said.

"Get in," Blaine said, pointing with the gun at the cop. He locked Big Mac in the cell.

"Next time I see you," Big Mac said, "you better be dead."

Outside the station, Blaine was confused. He wanted to go home, but didn't want to risk walking past Jan again. But should he take Aaron home?

"I don't see my car," Aaron said. "I left it at the bank."

Blaine looked. There were police cruisers nearby, but then the lot behind city hall was empty, as was the lot at the bank.

"You okay, man?" Aaron asked.

"What should we do?"

"I should go see a doctor. Can you call my wife? Or get a car?"

Samantha had taken his car. But just outside one of the garage doors behind the station was a police cruiser. "Uh, yeah," Blaine said, and helped Aaron into the passenger seat.

"I'd ask if you know what you're doing," Aaron said, "but I'm pretty sure I know the answer."

The keys were in the ignition, and Blaine eased his way out of the parking lot. He glanced at the radio to see if it was on, expecting to hear the car's call number shouted by the dispatcher.

Once they were on the road, he sped up.

At the hospital, they decided Aaron would go in alone and have them call his wife. He'd left his wallet at home that day, and she would have called every hospital in Cleveland by now.

Blaine went to the information desk. "Is Francine Tennyson here?"

The woman behind the desk placed a call and made a note as she listened. "She's in Room 301," she said. "But visiting hours are over. You can see her tomorrow morning at eight."

"Thank you."

Blaine found Aaron as he was being wheeled into the examination area. "You going to be alright?"

"Maybe," Aaron said. "What about you?"

"I know what I'm doing next."

Blaine found a men's restroom. As he washed his hands, he noticed his father's service revolver was rather obvious under his jacket, and arranged things. Then he slipped past the woman at the information desk and went into the hospital.

He continued the gambit on the third floor, walking past the nurse's station like he was in a hurry, and slipped into Room 301.

Francine's right leg was in a cast, and an I.V. dripped into her arm. Blaine pulled the chair close to her bed. The sound woke her up, but she was far from alert.

"Hey," Blaine said.

Her eyes opened a little more. "Hey," she said. "Where's Samantha?"

"I don't know."

She closed her eyes and rocked her head for a moment. "It

was Jakov. We were with Samantha, and he drove into us. Then he grabbed Samantha and drove off with her."

"Aw geez."

"It was bad."

"I told the police and the paramedics and the nurses, but I don't know if they told anyone else."

"Okay."

"Can you find her?"

Blaine nodded. "I'll find her."

"Wait," she said. "It's not just Jakov. The files Samantha found..."

"Yeah?"

"It's her Uncle Tom, too. It's the Chief of Police."

Blaine nodded. "Oh boy."

62

Samantha slid through the opening and immediately regretted the decision. The walls of the passage squeezed down and the dirt on her backside turned to mud. Water seeped from all around and dripped from above like rain.

What appeared to be an opening from the upper level in the dim light was an illusion of the rock. Her feet could fit into the cupped formation at the bottom, but there was nowhere else to go. The mud gripped her backside. She might get stuck down here.

Wanting to scream in frustration, she considered giving up. Why fight to get back to Rebecca when there were no options? Maybe she should just stay here.

She turned off the flashlight and let her head fall back into the mud. Cold water soaked through her shirt, and she shivered.

Had Lori had a moment like this that night? Had she fought and had to give up at some point?

Samantha turned on the flashlight. She scanned the walls and noticed a steady flow of water, then moved herself near it and put her mouth against the rock. She had had nothing to drink in hours.

With her head twisted back, she noticed a gap in the rock formation. She duck-walked closer, only to realize that the space constricted even further. The flashlight revealed another opening at the other end of the gap, so she squirmed on her back through the mud.

The opening increased, and Samantha caught her breath. Twisting her head around, she saw that the space would allow her to get off her back if she just squirmed a bit more.

Once there, the space increased further, allowing her to stand up. She swept the walls with her flashlight.

"Oh God," she blurted out and smacked her head against a rock when she jumped back. A corpse, rotted and intact, lay face up along the base of a wall. A second corpse lay a few feet away from the first. Beside that one, a collection of bones.

Samantha sobbed, moaning with despair. She looked all along the other walls, but there was no opening. It seemed there was no where else to go, as these poor souls had learned.

She swept the light up. There was an opening about ten feet above where she stood. It might be big enough to slip through, but there was no way to get up there. Glistening in the light, water seeped out of the opening and slid down the rock.

That opening led to a shaft allowing air and ground water to flow into the cavern. But it would not help Samantha any- more than it helped the people who died and rotted away just a few feet from where she stood.

Feeling defeated, Samantha shone the light on the corpse again, risking a step closer. The shirt was a short-sleeve plaid, and the trousers were denim. The hair suggested it was a man.

He lay with his hands folded over his chest, as if placed that way. More likely, he'd known death was coming, and laid himself down to prepare for his eternal rest.

She ventured one step closer, thinking she might notice something to help identify this man. Beneath the rotting flesh of his hands was something white.

It was a bone. But it didn't look like a complete bone. There was something different.

Samantha took a deep breath and got close enough to reach for it, her hand shaking, her heart beating with the dread.

She grabbed the bone and backed away from the corpse. She shined her light on it but didn't realize at first what had happened.

Then it made sense: this poor, doomed soul laid himself down to die, but until that moment, he was preparing to live.

She took another look around the cavern to convince herself it offered no more options. Then she crawled back towards the opening, trying to get back to where Rebecca waited.

And she brought the bone with her.

63

In the car, Tom told his brother the situation. "Two kids playing stink-finger at the Metro park told one of our patrols that they saw a guy dragging a girl through the park."

"Down in the Kingdom?"

"That's where they seemed to be going."

"But why would Jakov grab her? All she did was take your files."

"There was nothing in those files," Tom said. "That reporter was nosing around, bothering Jakov, and maybe it's been him all along."

"Jakov?"

"He seems like a dolt, but maybe he fixated on Lori, and now Samantha. Maybe he grabbed Rebecca, too."

David pulled his pistol and checked it. "Samantha better be okay. Then we'll get some answers."

"Do you have your backup piece?"

"Ankle holster."

"Good."

Once they were in Jakov's yard, Tom suggested they head straight for the Kingdom. "He probably has her in that shack."

David snapped on his flashlight and took his pistol in hand. "Where's the backup?" he asked over his shoulder as he jogged past the barn.

Tom, struggling to keep up, said, "I have them surrounding the Kingdom. We have guys coming from the landfill, another along the creek into the valley, and a third from the north, com-ing in across the creek. They're all converging on the shack."

David pushed through the brush and paused a moment at the crest of the hill. By the time Tom caught up to him, David had chosen his path down and started the descent.

When Tom was down the hill, David had already taken a position behind a tree twenty feet from the shack's front door.

"Where the hell is the backup?" David whispered.

"On their way."

"I don't want to wait. Cover me."

"Roger that."

Tom watched as David crept up to the shack and pressed his ear to the wall. He grabbed the door and pulled it open, then fell back at an angle with his weapon raised and shined the flashlight inside.

"Jakov, I want to see your hands."

"What?"

"Come to the door and show me your hands. You won't get hurt."

Jakov appeared at the door, the glow of the kerosene lamp behind his head, his eyes squinting in the flashlight's glare, his hands up in surrender.

"Okay, now step out. Hands on your head and kneel."

Jakov did as he was told.

David glanced at Tom. "Cuff him!"

# # # #

Down in the hole, Samantha sat with her arms around Rebecca, sharing body heat. Rebecca had been slipping in and out of con-sciousness, and was incoherent when awake, worrying Saman-tha that Rebecca's concussion was worse than her own. Or maybe she herself was the incoherent one and was too far gone to notice.

She laughed then, aware of the uselessness of it all. She

should settle herself in and prepare to die, like the poor soul in the cavern. Samantha stared at the candle's flame, trying to ignore the pain and the chill and her thirst, then closed her eyes and hoped she would fall asleep.

A noise from above disturbed her. Something was going on up in the shack.

"Samantha," her father called, his voice muffled but still recognizable. "Samantha?"

"I'm here," she said, surprised at how difficult it was to raise her voice. She took a few deep breaths and shouted, "I'm here."

They both started as someone struggled to move the rock and open the lid. Looking up with dread, she saw her father's face in shadow.

"Dad?"

He shined his flashlight down the hole, blinding her, but she wouldn't avert her eyes. "Oh my God, Samantha."

"There's a ladder under the shack."

The minute he spent getting the ladder lowered into the hole seemed an eternity. She felt every muscle ache as she pulled herself up, but no amount of pain would stop her from climbing up that ladder.

When she neared the top, her father grabbed her and helped her with the final few steps. He hugged her as they kneeled together. "It's okay," he said. "You're okay."

"What happened to Jakov?" she asked.

"We got him. He's right outside."

She sighed with relief. "We have to get Rebecca out. She can't climb up herself."

"What? Who?"

"Rebecca Marko. Tom beat her senseless and Jakov threw her in the hole."

"What?"

"Tom did it."

Samantha felt her father's body tense and turn.

"Nope," Tom said, shining the flashlight on them. "Don't move, brother."

"You fucking bastard—"

"Nope. We're going to talk about it, but first show me your hands and amble out here. Both of you."

Outside the shack, Jakov was kneeling to one side of the door, his hands behind his back.

"I don't like what this became," Tom said, "but it wasn't my fault."

# # # #

Blaine pulled into the gravel path that served as Jakov's driveway, and the headlights revealed a police cruiser behind the house.

His hands shook as he grabbed a flashlight and radio and jammed them in a kit bag in the trunk. He glanced up, half-expecting Jakov or Tom to emerge from the brush surrounding the yard and attack him.

He pulled his father's service revolver from his belt and checked the cylinder. It was empty. He'd been waving around an empty gun.

There was a box of .38 shells in the glove box, and he dropped several bullets loading the gun.

The car's headlights revealed the side of the house. Once he turned the corner, he swept the backyard with the flashlight. There was tall grass along the side, the old barn, a shed and the police cruiser. He cut the light and backed up closer to the house.

Over the pounding of his heart, there were no other sounds. No shuffling or talking inside the house, and nothing from the outbuildings.

He inspected the empty police cruiser. The radio lights were on and the keys in the ignition. Then he swept the ground and the outbuildings again with his flashlight.

Blaine approached the barn. There were gaps in the walls where boards had fallen away. The doors were open and tilted at an angle that suggested they'd never shut again without a lot of work.

Inside, the flashlight revealed a white Lincoln Continental, and rusting farm equipment in chaotic abandon, and two vehicles stripped to the frame.

He didn't like the idea, but he had to go down into the Kingdom. His heart beat faster as he pushed through the brush and ducked beneath branches.

When he reached the crest of the hill, the cover of trees blocked the moonlight, and the path down seemed no better than jumping into a bottomless pit.

Then he began his descent.

# # # #

"Nice and easy," Tom said. "Nobody gets hurt."

"I don't know what you're thinking," David said, "but we can figure everything out."

His brother was two steps out of the shack, and little Samantha, the big pain in the ass, was still in the doorway. Keeping the gun on David, he hit her with the light to get her attention. "Plant your ass right there, sweetie."

"Tom, tell me what's going on."

"He killed Lori," Samantha said.

"Nope," Tom said, and felt himself smile. He moved himself closer to Jakov. But he was over-thinking it. He knew what he was doing, he just needed to do it.

"What's she talking about Tom?"

"She doesn't know shit about anything, little brother. You know that."

David drew his revolver and Tom fired, knocking David down.

Samantha screamed. Tom wanted to scream as well. This was different. He just put a bullet in his brother. This was like nothing else he'd done before.

When she moved he snapped out of it, and as she went towards her father, Tom fired at her. She stumbled and fell in the dirt, but he was sure he missed. She might have shit herself, but she hadn't made a sound.

Tom remembered David's gun and swept the ground with the light. It was in his brother's hand, so Tom moved left and approached David from above, not worried because David was looking at his daughter, muttering something, reaching with his other hand toward her. The idiot should have returned fire. It's his own fault then...

Tom stepped on David's wrist and kicked the gun away. There was no fight left, anyway. Tom scooped up the revolver, studied him for a moment—David stared past him, blood oozing from shoulder—and then got David's backup piece out of the ankle holster. Now he had four guns. He had to make sure he used David's next, then planted the one that shot David on Jakov.

"You were right, brother," Tom said. "I never learned to shoot straight. I goddam almost missed you. Wouldn't that have been something?"

Samantha had crawled to her father by then. He could give her that. First things first. He kind of wanted to choke her out, so she'd die the same as her sister, in case anyone figured that out, at least it would match—

"Get these cuffs off me," Jakov said as he stood up.

"Hang on."

Tom jammed the flashlight under his chin so he could look at the guns, holstering the one he used on David, and looking for a spot to hold David's backup piece. He jammed it in his belt, but his stomach pressed down so hard on it he worried he might shoot his own balls off.

Jakov took a step. "What the fuck—"

Tom turned and fired David's revolver, hitting Jakov and throwing him backward to the ground.

Samantha screamed, turning where she lay, trembling in the dust.

"This is on you," he said to her. "Everything would have

been fine."

He stepped closer to Jakov to take another shot. The angle had to be straight in, so it would appear to have been a simple shootout with two losers. The record would show that David fired two shots but was also shot in the exchange and bled out, never realizing Jakov strangled and buried Samantha in the hole beneath the shack.

Blood oozed out of Jakov's mouth. So he'd hit a lung, which is not a bad shot, all things considered. Under the glare of the flashlight, there was no life left in the poor fool.

He squeezed off another round. It startled him, sounding louder than the others, the report echoing in the cool air off of the surrounding trees and hill.

As he uncuffed Jakov and planted David's revolver in the lifeless hand, he realized the gun in his belt had slipped out somewhere. And he still had to make sure Rebecca was dead, and he ought to just use the gun in Jakov's hand...

Of course, he still had to take care of Samantha. He'd do it with his own hands. He was going to enjoy this one.

# # # #

Samantha's brain raced with a thousand thoughts, caught up in her head, clutching to her father's hand for comfort. He squeezed her hand. His breathing reassured her.

He moved his lips, turning his face toward her, trying to say something. Samantha inched closer, crawling through the dust at a snail's pace.

She'd almost understood what her father was saying when a shot rang out and her body convulsed, her legs pulling up close to her chest. Tom was doing something to Jakov's body.

All she heard for the next several seconds was the pounding of her heart. She placed her cheek on her father's cheek, and this calmed her heart.

"Run," he whispered.

She raised her head and looked in his eyes. She let go of his hand and pushed herself up to her knees.

But before she took a step, her uncle's thick forearm wrapped around her throat and her feet lifted off the ground, spinning her around.

There was a sharp poke in her left ass cheek, and she remembered the bone.

Releasing her grip on his arms, she reached behind her back and pulled the bone out of the waistband of her jeans. She couldn't breathe, but she got the best grip she could on the bone and brought the pointy end down towards Tom, hoping to find his groin.

"Ah God damn it," he cried and released her, fumbling at his pants pocket where she'd stabbed him.

The bone had been sharpened to a point by the doomed man in the cave, rubbing it against the cave wall, hoping to use it as a weapon of escape—or revenge.

As Tom grabbed at his wound, Samantha adjusted her grip of the weapon. With one hand on the shaft, and the other on the end, she charged him, aiming at his throat.

He deflected her attack, but she planted the tip into his shoulder and drove it into his flesh. He knocked her to the ground, but the bone had impaled him, and he stumbled backwards as he pulled it free.

Samantha planted her hands to push herself up, ready to run, and felt a hard object in the dust. It was a gun.

A calm settled over her as she gripped the revolver and raised it. Tom's looming, dark bulk came at her and she squeezed the trigger. She squeezed again and again, the reports of the gun happening in slow motion, the dark figure of her uncle revealed in the flash of light, his body falling away and hitting the ground, then twitching with each successive shot.

She squeezed the trigger four more times before realizing the chambers were empty.

# # # #

In the stillness that settled on the Kingdom, Blaine called out to Samantha and she screamed in anger.

"It's me," he shouted. "It's okay."

"Blaine?"

He staggered through the dark, the prone figures taking shape only when he wrapped his arms around Samantha.

"My dad," Samantha muttered, and dragged herself to where her father lay. "Help me."

Blaine shone the flashlight on him. The blood oozing from his shoulder had darkened his shirt. His eyes blinked in the light.

Blaine kneeled beside her, digging in the bag, and found a first aid kit. As Samantha pressed gauze into her father's wound, Blaine grabbed the radio.

"Officer down," he said. "Gloria, you there?"

"It's Dottie," she replied over the radio. "Gloria is off tonight. What did you say?"

"Officer down. David Sykora needs an ambulance."

"Copy that."

As Samantha took up her father's hand, he turned her head towards her.

64

With her face and leg bandaged, and resting her head on Blaine's shoulder while waiting for news about her father's surgery, Samantha tried to sleep. The first dose of painkillers was wearing off and as she considered taking another, her grandfather and Aunt Jan arrived.

"It has been a terrible day," her grandfather said, his voice clear, as if beginning a speech. He opened his arms to hug Samantha, but she shied away, avoiding him.

"Is something else wrong?" Aunt Jan asked.

"It's okay," her grandfather said. "She's been through a lot."

The four of them sat without speaking. Samantha closed her eyes, her heart pounding in her chest, stopping herself from screaming as she waited for someone to talk.

An hour later, the surgeon came and spoke to her grandfather, whispering a few feet away from them.

"I'm his daughter," she said, intervening. "Please tell me what's going on."

The surgeon smiled. "I was just saying that it was a success, and we expect a full recovery. Your father is in the Intensive Care Unit, and can't have any visitors just yet."

"Tomorrow, perhaps?" her grandfather asked.

"Yes," the surgeon said.

Aunt Jan picked up her purse. "Come on then," she said. "I'll take you home."

"I'm staying here," Samantha said.

"Don't be silly."

Samantha shook her head. "I'm not leaving without my father."

Her grandfather crossed his arms. "You should come with us," he said. "Once your father recovers, we'll talk about what happened."

She'd heard this tone from him before. He seemed doting and gentle, worried about everyone in the city; but there was an edge in his voice revealing anger in his heart. "I told you what happened," she said.

"Of course, you did. I just meant you don't need to worry about anything right now."

"Worry about what?"

Jan stepped closer to her. "You shot and killed my brother. That's what he's talking about."

Samantha wasn't sure if she was imagining things. She took several breaths to think about it. "Your brother tried to kill me and my dad. He killed Jakov."

Jan shook her head as Grampa Pete touched her shoulder.

Samantha said, "Your brother raped and assaulted Rebecca and a dozen other girls while they were still school children."

"What are you talking about," Jan said. "That's nonsense."

"There are pictures. I saw them."

"Do you have these pictures?" her grandfather asked.

"I saw them," she said. "Isn't that enough for you?"

Jan crossed her arms, looking around the waiting room to see who was listening.

Her grandfather stepped closer. "Without proof..."

"There were a lot of girls."

"No one has ever complained," Jan said.

"They will," Samantha said.

"You have copies?" Grampa asked.

Samantha stepped back and sat on the chair next to Blaine.

Jan glanced around the waiting room once more. "When your mother left, she took a suitcase full of cash from the bank. Over two-hundred thousand. That's why you haven't seen her in four years. I guess it's pretty obvious who you take after."

Blood rushed to Samantha's face and her broken nose throbbed with pain. "What?"

Jan waved in dismissal at Blaine. "And your father would have gone with her if the drunken idiot hadn't killed himself first."

Jan turned and left the waiting room without looking back.

"What is she talking about?" Samantha said, her voice quivering with anger.

"We've waited," her grandfather said, "hoping she'll come to her senses. We would have welcomed her back into the family, but it's clear now she was only thinking of herself."

Samantha pulled her legs up onto the chair and hugged herself.

"As for you, young man," Grampa Pete said, wagging a finger in Blaine's direction. "Officer Machowski would like a word with you. I've told him to give you some time. Your father was a good, dutiful police officer, and served honorably until your mother died, so you can take a week to move out. But I don't recommend you stay in my city a day more than that."

# # # #

A nurse at the hospital took pity on them after midnight and showed them to a lounge area. "It's more for receptions and meetings," she said, "but no one will bother you tonight."

Samantha told Blaine to stretch out on the sofa, knowing she didn't want to sleep. Before he fell asleep, he told her how he'd helped Aaron escape, and that what her grandfather meant was that Big Mac wanted to kill him for pointing a gun at him.

"I'd tell him it was unloaded, but I think it'll just make him madder."

"Is Rebecca here?"

"I think her parents took her to the Cleveland Clinic."

"Figures."

"If Aaron had checked in, we could have gotten our own

wing with Francine and Robaroni."

She dozed off but woke up every couple of hours with a stiff neck, worried about her father.

She found a nurse each time to ask if his status had changed. Each time they assured her he was still stable.

In the morning, before visiting hours were to begin, Samantha freshened up in the restroom. When she emerged, there were two men in police uniform waiting outside. "Samantha Sykora?" one of them asked. "I'm Deputy Robert McKenzie with the Cuyahoga County Sheriff's Department, and I have a warrant for your arrest."

The other deputy handcuffed her. As they led her away, she called for Blaine. He emerged from the lounge and saw them just as they dragged her out the door.

# # # #

Samantha said nothing and tried to show even less. If growing up with a cop for a father taught her one thing, it was to answer the question asked and offer nothing else. Angling for sympathy was not just a waste of time, but annoyed the cop. Follow orders and things got done.

But her heart pounded and her hands and legs twitched with every sound. Every male cop with a gun reminded her of her Uncle Tom standing over her, the smell of gunpowder fresh in her mind, the report of the gun ringing in her ear. Footsteps sounded like Jakov twitching on the ground. Doors closing sounded like the second gunshot that put Jakov to rest.

Samantha wanted to scream and cry and lash out at these assholes, but she knew it would only bring her restraints and abuse.

The cop completed her processing and handed her off to a female corrections officer. That officer strip-searched her, issued her an orange jumpsuit, and took her to a holding cell. It was six feet by eight with a bunk, a toilet and a sink. The walls were cement, and the door was steel, with a slot and an obser-vation window.

"What about my medicines?"

"What medicine?" the officer asked.

"My painkiller and antibiotics. I was assaulted."

"I'll look into it."

The cell door slammed shut, and Samantha was grateful she would be alone. Then she sat on the bunk and cried.

# # # #

The guard awakened Samantha. "You have a visitor."

Blaine waited for her at a booth with a phone. Reinforced glass separated the prisoners from the visitors, and she sat on the chair and picked up the phone.

"Hey," he said. "How are you holding up?"

"I've been sleeping a lot. What day is it?"

"Wednesday."

"Okay, I guess I only slept eighteen hours."

"How's your head?"

"How does it look?" she asked.

Blaine shook his head. "Better, but not great. I asked about bailing you out, but it hasn't been set yet."

"The judge denied it at my arraignment, so that's that."

"But it was self-defense."

Samantha shrugged. "How's my dad?"

"I haven't been able to get him on the phone. Do you want me to get you a lawyer?"

"It's fine. Don't worry."

"Don't you want to get out of here?" Blaine asked.

"I don't know. I don't know who to trust."

"You can trust me."

She nodded, but she wasn't sure. "How are you?"

"Fine, but cops are following me everywhere."

"Where are you staying?"

"Francine's place. I used her car to shake the kraut long enough to get her notebook out of Rob's impounded car. I thought that would be when they arrested me, but he had called ahead and it was cool."

"Holy shit."

"They gutted my car looking for whatever you took from your Uncle Tom, I guess."

"One minute," the guard announced.

"I guess I have to go," Samantha said.

"Hey, Francine said there was pretty damning stuff in the files."

Samantha nodded.

"Did you make a copy?"

"Why are you asking?"

"I think it'll help you get out of here. It will kind of solve a lot of things. You know, you were right. They were wrong."

"Thanks for coming," Samantha said, and hung up the phone.

65

On Wednesday, two days after being shot, they moved David Sykora into a private room on the third floor. The bullet damaged the joint and bleeding had been a problem, but a second procedure stabilized him.

When Jan visited, she assured him that Samantha was fine and safe. Nothing to worry about. "You realize your brother is dead, right?"

"Good," he said. "He shot me. I was there."

Jan nodded, her eyes fixed on the wall above David's head. "You lost a lot of blood," she said. "I'm glad you made it."

It seemed Jan didn't want to talk anymore. "Thanks for visiting," he said.

David called the house every hour and worried that he couldn't reach Samantha. He tried Blaine's house, but no answer. Then he watched the news at noon and saw the story about the Sheriff arresting Samantha.

After he called Jan and yelled at her over the phone, his nurse threatened to sedate him. He promised to calm down if she brought him the newspaper for the past two days.

When he read that the reporter was still a patient there, he disconnected his I.V. and walked over to her room.

"I'm sorry this happened to you," he said. "This whole thing is fucked up beyond recognition."

"Thank you, I guess," she said.

"Samantha said that Tom killed Lori. Do you know anything about that?"

"There were pictures," Francine said. "The girls your brother had been dating were underage. It was rape, and he kept pictures of them naked, like trophies."

"So Rebecca, too?"

"Yes."

"God damn it." He found a chair and sat down, feeling weak. "Lori wanted to talk to me about something the day before she died. The day before he killed her, I mean. I was busy with something. Lori and I argued."

"I'm sorry."

"Now Samantha is in jail."

"I saw the news," Francine said. "She needs a superb lawyer."

"The pictures," he said. "Where are they?"

"Jakov put them in the trunk of the car when he grabbed Samantha."

"God damn it."

"I saw them. They were sickening."

David took a cab to the municipal building and headed for his father's office. Gayle stared at him, gape-mouthed. David wore a hospital gown as a shirt tucked into his pants. A sling over his shoulder supported his right arm.

"Gayle?" he said, feeling short of breath, "Ask my sister to join us here, if you don't mind."

David barged into his father's office and sat on the sofa.

His father rose from the desk and sat across from him. "Can I get you anything?"

"I'm curious," David said, loud enough for Gayle to hear at her desk outside the door, "whose idea it was to have Samantha arrested. If I had to bet, it would be Jan."

"Take it easy,"

"Jan always seemed to have the devious ideas growing up. Or was it you, Dad? Either way, this takes the cake."

"Calm down," his father said. "Let's talk."

"Fuck talking. Do whatever you have to do to get her out."

His father stepped out of the office. Gayle brought David a glass of water and asked if he needed anything. Then his father and Jan came in and closed the door.

"Get Samantha out now," David said. "She did nothing wrong."

"That's not how it works," Jan said. "Samantha wanted justice and the truth. So no, we'll see what the truth is."

"Our older brother was a lunatic. He shot me, he shot Jakov, and he strangled Samantha. And then there was everything he did to Rebecca."

Jan folded her arms and leaned back in her chair.

David spilled the water while adjusting his seat. "He dumped those girls in a hole in the ground. They were going to be killed."

"If it's proven in a court of law, I'll believe it."

"Fuck you, Jan."

"Please, David," his father said, hands open, his eyes beckoning. "We just want it all by the book, according to the law, so everyone understands. There can't be any shortcuts. The District Attorney made this decision. He's convening a Grand Jury —"

"Oh horse shit," David said. "The last thing you want is a Grand Jury, unless you helped get that District Attorney elected, as well."

"David," his father said, "I need you to calm down—"

"I know you can place a phone call and pull in some favors."

"That's absurd," Jan said.

"No. What's absurd is that my brother had been assaulting girls and killed my daughter. And your idea of justice is to bring charges against Samantha. You make me sick."

Jan stood up. "Jakov is the monster. I refuse to believe Tom did any of that."

David looked at his father. "Well?"

"I just want everything in the open, in the courts. You can understand that, can't you?"

David left without answering him.

66

Francine stayed at Rob's house to manage his rehab, although she couldn't do it without Blaine, who was purchasing a house on Rob's street and staying with them, as well, to avoid his own house.

She rented a ramp for the front steps, a hospital bed, and Rob's cop buddy rearranged the furniture with Blaine.

Francine's mother wanted to fly up from Florida, but Francine convinced her to stay put, and that she'd visit as soon as she could travel. Of course, she wanted the story settled first. If she didn't figure it out soon, she was going to ask Rob to move with her to another part of the country, anyway, because they would both need a fresh start.

Francine worked on the story at a standing desk they'd assembled from an old door and two book shelves bought from Uncle Bill's Discount.

When she first began her investigation, it had been to uncover and document something sensational enough to reflect well on her reporting. Now she craved finding and revealing the truth. Francine also understood that how the story was told mattered as much as the truth.

The newspaper article published two days after the event, for instance, focused on the rescue of Rebecca Marko from abduction, assault, and a likely fatal ending. The article described Jakov's decrepit farmhouse and barn, and the filth and drugs found inside, but omitted the shack in The Kingdom or the pit beneath it, or that the property was owned by a shell corporation, likely controlled by the mayor.

They placed special emphasis on the bones—both human and animal—found inside the barn, and how the State Police took control of the forensic investigation and the evidence on the scene. The article speculated that there was more to discover on the isolated and over-grown location near the city landfill.

The story claimed that Chief Sykora died in an exchange of gunfire that left his brother, Officer David Sykora, in critical condition. The way it was told left open the possibility that Tom had given his life saving Rebecca and David.

It mentioned Samantha as an after-thought, saying that her presence at the scene was under investigation. It said nothing about the attack with the Lincoln Continental Town Car owned by the late Chief Sykora.

Francine reached out to Samantha, starting on that Friday, when her father found a lawyer and got her out of jail. But Samantha wouldn't come to the phone.

"She doesn't even come out of her room," David told her.

"Is there something I can do to help?"

"She says she doesn't know who to trust anymore. Me included."

Francine was aching to ask Samantha why she hadn't made a copy of the report, or the photos, but she didn't want to burden her with more guilt.

# # # #

On Monday, Blaine drove Francine to the near-east side, to a small house in Cleveland just over the border from Cuyahoga Heights.

"Who lives here?" he asked.

"Do you remember the couple who lived in the apartment across from Michael Key?"

"Holy shit. You found them?"

"It took two days of digging and asking favors, but yeah. I found them."

The man who answered the door looked to be in his late twenties, dark complexion, the bridge of his Roman nose flat with his brow. With his prominent cheekbones, he was attractive. He wore work clothes. "Nathan Dombrozio?"

He nodded, his expression guarded.

"I'm Francine Tennyson. I'm a reporter, and I'd like to ask you about your former neighbors back in the Village."

"What?"

"Maybe you saw something in the news last week..."

"Sorry," he said. "We got nothing to say."

He closed the door, but Blaine stopped it with his foot.

"You want to lose that foot, or your teeth, or both?" Nathan asked.

"Tom and Jakov are dead," Blaine said. "They can't hurt you."

"I don't know nothing," he said.

"Did they arrange the loan for you?" Blaine asked. "Of course not. Milosh arranges things like that."

"Excuse me?" Nate said.

"My guess is that Milosh got a bank to approve your mortgage, and the apartment manager canceled your lease without penalty."

The way Nathan cocked his head, Francine thought he was going to lose it. "It's our house," Nate said. "And it's time for you to go."

"But if you don't tell the story, you won't be safe," Blaine said.

Nate folded his hands. "What the hell is that supposed to mean? Are you threatening us?"

"They have charged Samantha with murder," Blaine said. "She's the dead girl's sister. She shot Tom Sykora, saving her father and another girl. Tom, the chief of police, had beaten a young woman that night, killed one man, shot Samantha's father, and was strangling her when she got a gun and shot him.

She did nothing wrong. She did everything right."

"Good for her."

"The truth is the only thing that can protect you now," Blaine said. That's why we're trying to find it."

"We did nothing," Nate said.

Blaine said, "Once all this quiets down, like five, six, months from now, when it's winter and dark before five, and you're over here where no one knows your story... what's stopping them from showing up in the middle of the night? I assume they know where you live. Even if you move again, Francine found you. They can too."

Nate closed his eyes and took a breath. Then he opened the door and waved them inside.

# # # #

Samantha stayed in her upstairs bedroom, minimizing her movement to deal with the heat, and slept as much as her brain would allow.

After a sweaty, sticky afternoon nap, a memory returned from years before. It was Lori's thirteenth birthday party. The family had gathered in the backyard for barbecue, beer and cake. The Markos were there, as well, courtesy of Rebecca being Lori's best friend.

Uncle Tom and Uncle Wally, Jan's husband, drank beer all afternoon. Tom grew louder and more boisterous, telling stories about his exploits in high school in football, basketball, and baseball.

Rebecca and Lori wandered past Tom, who grabbed Rebecca and held onto her. Rebecca seemed too afraid to move but Lori punched and kicked Tom, as the other men laughed, even their father. Tom released Rebecca and grabbed Lori, instead, wrapping his thick arm around her throat and pulling her into his chest.

"Say you're sorry," he said, but she couldn't talk. She

couldn't breathe.

Their father and Uncle Wally grabbed Tom and he let her go.

"I was only kidding around," he said.

Lori and Rebecca stayed inside the rest of the party. Samantha had always avoided Tom, anyway, feeling afraid in his presence, but then she'd been mad, as well, for his ruining the fun.

Was that memory real?

She washed her face to cool off, and the memory seemed more vivid than when she first woke up.

Samantha dialed Rebecca's phone number.

Mrs. Marko answered.

"May I speak with Rebecca, please?"

"Who is this?"

"It's Samantha."

"Who?"

"Samantha Sykora. Lori's sister."

"Oh God."

"Please, I just want to see how Rebecca's doing."

"She's still recovering."

"Would you ask her if she'd like to speak with me?"

The line was silent for a minute, but then Rebecca picked up.

"How's the pain?" Samantha asked.

"Physical or emotional?"

"Both."

"Terrible. How about yours?"

"Pretty bad."

After a pause, Samantha said, "Do you remember Lori's thirteenth birthday party."

"What?"

"Lori's thirteenth. It was in our back yard?"

"I don't know. Why?"

"You remember what Tom did?"

The line was quiet for a second. "I guess not."

"He grabbed you."

"What do you mean?"

"He took you in his arms from behind and pulled you close. Then he said, 'You're under arrest.'"

"I don't remember."

"Yeah. Then he grabbed Lori. You don't remember it?"

"Maybe, I guess. I mean, it sounds like something he would have done. Sorry. I not sure."

"Okay."

"Was that it?"

"Yeah. Just popped in my head, you know?"

"Sorry, I don't remember. I hope you feel better."

"I hope you feel better too."

# # # #

They gathered around the kitchen table at Samantha's house. Francine sat in the corner with her leg stretched out. Blaine leaned back in his chair. Samantha's father leaned against the counter, a grim expression on his face. Samantha was subdued, and Francine worried that she was worse than the day before, that this threat of jail had a deep impact on her.

Saul Jacob, the lawyer, had covered the table with his pad of paper, the case file and his briefcase. His face was round and his receding hair line made his head look like a tan ball on top of an expensive suit. He looked at Francine with all of his attention, his face relaxed and his dark eyes unwavering.

"Tell me again what they said?" Saul Jacob asked, referring to the couple who had witnessed the assault of Michael in his apartment.

"On the night Michael died," Francine said, "they saw that he was home, and that he had a young woman over, as he often had the previous few months, to watch television."

"That was this Rebecca?" Saul asked.

"They're not sure. They'd have to look at her picture."

Saul made a note on his pad of paper.

"Later," Francine said, "they were sitting outside with their lights off, watching the stars as they enjoyed a drink. Michael watched television by himself. He had the lights off, too, but they could see him from the light of the television.

"There was a commotion in Michael's apartment. Two men struggling with Michael."

"What time was this?"

"Late. Almost midnight, but they weren't sure."

"Then what?"

"Then Michael's television turned off and they couldn't see anything inside. But they didn't hear shouting, either, so they weren't sure what it was."

"What did they do?"

"They went inside and called the police."

"Why didn't this guy help?" David asked. "It didn't occur to him to at least knock on the fucking door?"

"I asked that," Francine said. "They were celebrating the news that they were pregnant. He was afraid of leaving his wife alone, so he stayed with her and called the police."

"That's what people are supposed to do," Samantha said without raising her head to look at them.

"And did the police investigate?" Saul asked.

"Almost three hours later, a police officer knocked on their door, pounding on it until they woke up. It was Chief Sykora himself, following up on the call. He told them that if they wanted to talk about what they saw, they should call him, and only him, or they would be in trouble.

"They recognized him as one of the men in Michael's apartment. They were even more frightened. So, of course, they said nothing."

"Nobody else ever came by?"

"Just me," Francine said.

"Did they mention the cash payments?"

"No, and I didn't ask."

Saul looked around the kitchen. "Will someone explain those payments to me?"

Before anyone could answer, there was a knock on the

door.

67

Rebecca knocked again, feeling exposed on the front steps with bandages and bruises on her face. She'd done the best she could with a scarf and sunglasses.

"Hey," Lori's father said when he opened the door. "Would you like to come in?"

He stepped back, and she entered, keeping a few feet between herself and Lori's father.

"I have something I need to tell you."

"Me?"

"Everyone, I guess."

He explained the situation. Her throat tightened when she saw the group around the kitchen table. She'd hoped to find Samantha and her father and tell them what was on her mind. This might be the best time to tell her story. Or the worst. At least with so many people there, her mother would be less likely to deny she'd said it.

"I'm sorry," she said. "I should have called first."

"Not at all," Lori's father said. "We're all friends here."

"Okay, but..."

They looked at her and waited. She needed a minute to begin.

When her parents arrived at the hospital, her mother cried and her father raged at whoever had done this to her. "I'll kill him," he said. She heard him say it.

After the examination and the X-rays, Officer Petronek

came into her room to take a statement. Her father interrupted when she said that Tom Sykora attacked her.

"You mean Chief Sykora?" he asked.

Rebecca nodded.

After that, he didn't get enraged about her assault again, and didn't say a harsh word about Tom. Her father kept asking how she was doing, and seemed concerned, but no more outrage.

Her mother was the same way, shaking her head a lot, but not too worked up that a family friend had done this to her daughter.

At first, Rebecca told herself she should have known better than to betray Tom. Like it was her own fault.

But the past few days she wasn't so sure it was her fault. At least she thought that she didn't deserve to be beaten, kidnapped, and left to die in a hole in the ground.

When Samantha called the other night, she didn't have any memory of what she described happening at Lori's thirteenth birthday. In fact, Lori's thirteenth birthday had been at the city pool, reserved by the mayor, and almost all the girls they knew had been there, along with a few select boys.

She woke up this morning and recalled Lori's fourteenth birthday. That was the one in the Sykora's backyard. Samantha had gotten the year wrong. The family picnic was the precursor, only for the family. The actual party was back at her own house with a few more girls and boys.

In Lori's backyard, they'd grabbed cans of beer from the ice bucket in the garage, and went around back to drink them.

And she remembered how Tom surprised them, grabbing her arm, and told her she was under arrest for underage drinking. He pulled her in close, and she felt his erect penis pressed against her ass.

"That night..." Rebecca said, but trailed off.

"The night that Michael and Lori died?" Francine asked.

She nodded. "Lori was supposed to be at my house. We made that plan. I should have been there too, but I stayed with Michael." Ashamed, Rebecca lowered her head. Keeping this to herself was making her sick, making her think she deserved to be beaten and left to die, and that had to be wrong.

Rebecca took a breath and began again. "I had been seeing Tom on and off for a while. I thought it was over, and I began seeing Michael. Tom knew I was seeing someone, so I kept it a secret. Also, once I realized he was black, I thought it would be best for everyone if we kept that a secret, too.

"Tom kept getting more agitated, and insisted on seeing me, and I didn't like that. It felt like I was cheating on Michael, so I wanted to stop seeing Tom. But he didn't want to stop.

"That night, Lori was going to wait for him at my house and tell him to stop bothering me. She was going to threaten to tell people about how he preferred to date school girls. She thought that would get him to leave me alone. I swear I didn't know about any other girls he'd dated.

"I stayed with Michael at his apartment that night. Around eleven, I headed back to my house. When I got there, nobody else was there, so I thought it worked, that Lori chased Tom away for good, and I went to bed."

Rebecca heaved a sigh and leaned against the counter. She looked at Lori's father, as if his look would tell her whether he forgave her, and if he excused her to leave. But he seemed to expect more.

"I didn't know she was dead," she said. "I swear to God. When I woke up the next day, and you guys called me asking about her and the boat, I had no clue. I mean, I was living a lie, but the lie was dating Michael. I had no idea what happened to Lori."

"Did you talk to Tom about it?" Francine asked.

Rebecca nodded. "When my best friend and boyfriend died in my father's boat, I was so fucking confused and heart broken. I turned to Tom because I thought he still cared for me."

"What did he say?" Francine asked.

"He said they must have been seeing each other behind my back. He said that Lori must have gotten the idea to steal the boat, that she and Michael were jealous of our money or something, and that Michael was just a gold-digger. I don't know why

I believed it, but it was so bizarre, I guess I just wanted to be-lieve it."

No one said anything for a while. She felt uneasy when David pursed his lips, and Samantha covered her face with her hands.

"I know it was stupid," she said, "but what was I supposed to do? I mean, he was the Chief of Police."

"It's okay, Rebecca," Lori's father said. "This isn't your fault."

Rebecca took a deep breath, then another, trying hard not to burst into tears.

"What do you think happened?" Francine asked.

Rebecca shrugged. "I think Lori confronted Tom and he killed her. Then he went over to Michael's and waited until I left and then killed him. He must have found out about Michael. I was pretty stupid for believing Tom. I'm so sorry."

When she left, it relieved her that no one had yelled at her for not telling them sooner.

In the afternoon's sunshine, there were birds singing in a nearby tree, and kids playing around the corner. The world seemed normal, except that her best friend and her boyfriend were not there to enjoy it.

She decided to visit Michael's grave.

68

Once Rebecca left, and her father and the lawyer returned to the kitchen, Samantha felt crushed, like the walls and ceiling of the tiny room were closing in. She ran out the side door and sat against the garage door, looking back at the house.

Now with all of her Uncle Tom's crimes laid bare, she felt desperate, as if she was on a boat lost at sea in darkness. Revealing the truth should have been a relief. But now she realized all those years of loving her family were gone and wouldn't return.

Her grandparents would blame her, if only because she would remind them of everything their son had done. Aunt Jan was a bitch, anyway, so the truth wouldn't change that.

Francine and Blaine made their way from the house to the garage. "The lawyer has an idea," Francine said. "Can you listen to it?"

Samantha looked at Francine and Blaine. She thought she could trust them. She trusted them at one time. They had suffered in all this, as well.

"Okay."

"Saul suggests filing a wrongful death suit against Tom's estate."

"For what?" Samantha asked. "Money?"

"It brings pressure to get your grandfather to have the charges dropped. It would be a chance to tell the story in court and present the evidence."

Samantha thought that would be okay. She nodded.

"Of course, if we had the report or those photos, it'd force his hand."

Samantha took a breath. "I made a copy of everything."

"What?"

Samantha nodded.

"Can you find them?" Francine asked.

"I mailed them to Lori, for general delivery, to the Parma post office."

"Why did you do that?"

"I didn't know who to trust. You worried about me stealing it in the first place, Dad and I were fighting and Grampa didn't want to do anything about Uncle Tom."

"Do we know how to pick it up?" Francine asked.

Samantha nodded. "I read about it at the library and called the post office to confirm. We take Lori's Death Certificate and get some form notarized."

# # # #

They took two cars: David and Saul in the lead, followed by Blaine, Samantha and Francine. The postal clerk had never made a general delivery before but, once convinced, she found the envelope, and Samantha carried it outside.

Samantha had seen everything inside the envelope and had no desire to see them again. But she held onto the envelope like her life depended on it.

She tore it open, though, and offered the contents to her father, who pulled some copied photos out, cringing at the sight of the naked girls, so helpless in the flash of light.

The lawyer flipped through the report.

"Cause of death for Michael Key," he said, "was asphyxiation." He tracked down the photo of Michael's throat and pointed to the bruising around the neck. "There's evidence of trauma right there."

"Not drowning?"

"No."

He flipped several pages further into the report and studied it. "Same for Lori. Asphyxiation. Bruising on the neck. No drugs or alcohol in her system."

Samantha and her father hugged each other and cried.

# # # #

The next day, Samantha realized she needed to leave. Like for good.

It wasn't ever going to be the same, there.

At first she stuffed things into a bag, like when she'd run off to stay at Blaine's house, but it didn't feel right leaving her things behind for her father to deal with. He had to deal with the belongings of two loved-ones already; adding a third would be just cruel.

Rather than run off, she prepared to leave and would break the news to him later.

She scrutinized her things, sorting them into what she could take with her, and what she would cast off. This took longer than she realized as her childhood things, laden with memories, demanded attention, like the child who once treasured those things. That attention was long overdue.

Also, her mother stuffed boxes of school papers and clothing into the attic eaves. After ten days of opening boxes, donating things, and filling the tree lawn with trash, she had winnowed her belongings down to essentials of both function and nostalgia. It all fit into a couple of bags.

Her father had recovered enough during this time to feel like himself again, and they'd returned to the awkward pattern of taking turns cooking. He made sandwiches and soup. Samantha made casseroles or macaroni and cheese.

One afternoon, about a week later, when Samantha had no

other boxes to open, David made B.L.T. sandwiches and warmed up a can of green beans.

"You've been busy," he said. "Up and down the stairs, in and out. You going somewhere?"

"I'm thinking about it."

"That's good. We need to put this stuff behind us."

"I think so too."

"Hey, you know I think you did the right thing."

"Yes, I know, Dad."

He nodded, focusing on his sandwich for a few seconds.

"Well? I trust you're going to college. Where did you decide to go?"

"I don't know where I want to go."

"You could just go to Cleveland State. You don't have to pick out a degree or anything. Live here, drive downtown, and start a new thing, you know?"

"No, it's not that."

"It's not what?"

"I'm not leaving to go to college. I just want to get away."

"But this is your home."

"I don't think so."

"How can you say that?"

"Because I feel like everybody hates me for what happened, like none of the bad things Uncle Tom did matter. Only that I pulled the trigger."

"They'll come around."

"No, they won't. I heard about what Grandpa and Aunt Jan said about him, like he was a fucking hero. I can't live here like that, being the hero-killer."

Her father picked up the plates with his good arm, stacking them next to the sink. "How soon are you going?"

"I guess not right away. I should make some kind of plan."

Her father grabbed a beer and offered one to Samantha.

Samantha sat on the front steps with her beer.

The Müllers across the street were sitting on their porch in the shade. Samantha noticed they were staring and raised her can to them. They waved.

Her father joined her, bringing extra beers. He offered her an envelope.

"What's this?"

"The mail. You got a letter."

It was a letter from Aaron Key. It read:

Dear Samantha:

Thank you for what you did to discover the truth. I am horrified at the risk you took, and that I encouraged you. I should have known better. There was too much death already, and I would have never forgiven myself had you been lost to this world.

It was a bittersweet delight to read the report about Michael and Lori, and to relive their tragic loss. We will each carry the memory of our lost loved ones with us until our last breath. May your memory bring you joy for the time you had with your sister. Of course I know it's not enough, but it's all that we have.

My wife and I have decided to move to Columbus to be near our daughter and grandbabies. Louise has a lead on a job already, so we are going as soon as we sell our house.

I'll start a new vending supply route down there as soon as possible.

Once your wounds have all healed, I hope you can find an interesting life for yourself. I also hope you never have to deal with such evil again in your life, but I know that there are plenty more assholes in this world, and we'll just have to do what we can with them.

God bless you.

Sincerely,

Aaron Key

Samantha was crying. She wasn't sure why, but she didn't

worry about why anymore. Crying came easily these days.

She offered her father the letter to read while she wiped her eyes.

"What day is it?" she asked.

"June 29th, I think. You can still go to college."

Samantha laughed.

"What's so funny?"

"Nothing. Everything. I don't know."

"Okay," he said. "It's nice to hear you laugh."

"I think I'm going to go," she said. "For real this time, even if they reinstate the charges against me."

"Now hang on—"

"I'm not kidding, Dad. I can't stay here."

"Aren't you making a plan?"

She nodded. "I'll see if Blaine wants to go with me."

"That's not a plan."

"Maybe I'll find some place I can go to college."

That seemed to mollify him. "Okay."

She might come back. Or she might go to college. First she'd track down her mother. Then she'd see what she felt like doing after that.

RUTHLESS

ABOUT THE AUTHOR

Mickey Hadick lives near Lansing, Michigan where he has worked on short stories, novels, screenplays, and books for the past couple of decades.

Whenever possible, he's telling stories, telling jokes, or messing around with computers.

He lives with his wife, two cats, and as many dogs as possible. He also chases after his adult children as needed.

If you enjoyed this story and would like to know when the sequel is available, join him at:

MickeyHadick.com

ACKNOWLEDGMENTS

This story was a shapeless thought that lived for many years in my head like a squirrel, trapped in the attic, not paying rent, and scratching to escape.

I first dared to transform the squirrel into a story during a series of workshops I took with Corey Mandell. He couldn't help about the squirrel, but he suggested a way to tame it and the story began to take shape. I thank him for his patience and insight.

Next, I developed the story with Andrew Kersey. He appreciated some of the story I was telling, but he challenged me to figure out the lingering squirrelly parts and tell it again. I thank him for his enthusiasm and encouragement.

I'm indebted to my friend John Hutson for his knowledge about story and his support as a fellow writer.

Thanks and gratitude to Shelly Willoughby who provided feedback and helped shape the story.

My great friend, Brian Wallace, has patiently endured my stories since we met in a creative writing class in 1986. Thanks, as always.

Finally, many thanks to my wife, Mary, and my now-adult children who have lived with my writing efforts for many years now.

PARKSIDE BOOKS

Be sure to check out the other titles available at:

ParksideBooks.net

Make sure you get in on deals and keep up with Mickey by signing up to receive the Mickey Picayune at:

MickeyHadick.com/joinus/

ERRORS

Although Parkside Books goes to great lengths to fix all errors before we go to print, we're not perfect. If you see a problem, please notify us via email at:

support@parksidebooks.net